PENGUIN B

MY IDEA O

Will Self's short-story collection, *The Quantity Theory of Insanity*, was one of the most highly acclaimed debuts of 1992. It won the 1993 Geoffrey Faber Memorial Prize and was shortlisted for the 1992 John Lllewellyn Rhys Prize. Both *The Quantity Theory of Insanity* and his highly original novellas, *Cock and Bull*, are published by Penguin.

WILL SELF

MY IDEA OF FUN

A CAUTIONARY TALE

PENGUIN BOOKS

PENGUIN BOOKS

Published by the Penguin Group
Penguin Books Ltd, 27 Wrights Lane, London W8 5TZ, England
Penguin Books USA Inc., 375 Hudson Street, New York, New York 10014, USA
Penguin Books Australia Ltd, Ringwood, Victoria, Australia
Penguin Books Canada Ltd, 10 Alcorn Avenue, Toronto, Ontario, Canada M4V 3B2
Penguin Books (NZ) Ltd, 182–190 Wairau Road, Auckland 10, New Zealand

Penguin Books Ltd, Registered Offices: Harmondsworth, Middlesex, England

First published by Bloomsbury 1993
Published in Penguin Books 1994
1 3 5 7 9 10 8 6 4 2

Printed in England by Clays Ltd, St Ives plc

FOR ALEXIS

CONTENTS

BOOK ONE

THE FIRST PERSON

I have told myself a thousand times not to be shocked, but every time I am shocked again by what people will do to have fun, for reasons they cannot explain.

Isaac Bashevis Singer

Prologue

'So what's your idea of fun then, Ian?' It was the woman diagonally opposite me, the one with the Agadir tan. For a half-second or more I thought I hadn't heard the question right but then she repeated it. 'So what's your idea of fun then, Ian?' It's often things like that that really claim my attention, the things that happen twice. The first time she said it, it sounded to me like, 'So wus yernidee f'n, 'n?' Only the rise in pitch at the end indicated the interrogative. The second time, however, I took it in fully, I sopped up sound and import like intentional Kleenex. And then it pulped me – my idea of fun – took all my layers, my multi-ply selves, and wadded them into a damp mass. I sat there clutching the edge of the table, feeling the linen twist excruciatingly over the polished wood, with everything pushing together, melding inside of me.

Then Jane looked at me from across the table. Looked at me with her special look, the little moue that means total intimacy, total us-apart-from-the-world, and said, 'Oh I don't think Ian has much of an idea of fun at the moment, the poor old sod's too bound up in his work.' But by then the group conversation had passed on; someone further around the table – he'd been introduced to me when we arrived but it hadn't taken – was giving us the benefit of his idea of fun. As I remember it was crass in the extreme, utterly befitting his Silkience hair and onyx spectacle frames. You can imagine, all centred on nude teens, cocaine and a hotel suite in Acapulco. It was adman crap, slick-surface kicks for a magic-screen mentality. But I wasn't paying any, I was lost inside myself, caught up in my own horror show, my private view. I was thinking:

My idea of fun? This woman – who I don't even know –

she wants to know what it is? Hey, if only she did know . . . ur-her-her . . . If only she could see . . . but then, that could never be. See me tearing the time-buffeted head off the old dosser on the Tube. See me ripping it clear away and then addressing myself to his corpse. See me letting my big body flop over his concertinaed torso, and then see me arching like a boy whose hard little belly muscles provide him with a fulcrum when he leaps on to a metal post.

That's what I was thinking and at the same time I was wondering, idly speculating, how I could convey this particular sensation to her, this idea of fun. She'd probably never even seen a neck without a head on it, let alone felt one. I could have told her, though – using an analogy she'd readily grasp – It's a bit like a mackerel, a bit like a mackerel in that all the tissue, the sinew and the muscle, is packed into the dermis quite tightly. Putting my hand around that neck was just like grasping the silvery skin of a fish and feeling the compact rigidity of its body. That's why I had to hoist myself right up on top, I needed all my weight to penetrate the still-seeping stem. And the dosser's head, that fitted into the analogy as well; as I worked myself up and around, as I sucked in and out of his ribbed ulcerated gullet, I stared down into his face – nose wedged in the rubber runnel that ran along the carriage floor – and watched his personality, his soul, his identity? What you will. I watched it retreating, going away. It was a mackerel's pointed countenance, freshly caught but already dulling, losing its lustre and fading into a potentially battered finger – away from being a life form at all.

Even so, even given my painfully acquired powers of description, such as they are, I don't think I could have done justice to the experience. All that would have struck this woman, this nameless woman, an acquaintance of an acquaintance, adrift with me for a few hours on the sociable sea, would have been – what? The horror of it all, the ghastly anti-human horror? The studied contempt involved in such an action? But could she have seen it, as I do, as the moral equivalent of a cosmological singularity, the Holocaust writ small? Could she appreciate the almost celestial cloud of despair that gusts out from my insides?

A cloud bearing catatonic spore, seeds for a new but even more fatal speciation.

I doubt it – she was passing me by. This encounter was so slight it might never have been; the very moment we met we were speeding away from one another – goodbyeeeee – screaming children on time's train. A more likely outcome, were I to have vouchsafed to her my idea of fun, would have been for her to say to someone else a week or so hence, 'I met a man at a dinner party the other night, it was very strange. We were all talking about having fun. You know, "having fun", really kicking back your heels and letting go, and he said to me that his idea of fun – stressing that this was just one example he could summon up – was fucking the severed neck of a tramp on the Tube. Well I mean black or what! I mean that-is-black, it just is. The things that people will say nowadays, simply because they think that they can get some kind of a rise out of you.'

No, when this happened, when I took this chance cue and let it usher in the deluge, I didn't think of her because I don't know her. Instead I thought of the person who would really be affected by the truth about my idea of fun, I thought of Jane.

Because I love Jane, I really do, I love her the way people are meant to love each other, sacrificing themselves over the little things, the inconsequential things, as well as the big ones, the life decisions. And I've also been letting down my personal barriers, you know – the drawbridge to my ego. She's been coming inside me at the same time that I enter her. I've allowed her that, allowed her to see the shyness, the vulnerability in my face as we make love. It sounds corny, doesn't it? Soppy, wouldn't you say? But that's the truth, love is going for that corny burn, running that corny marathon together and keeping right on to the tape. People who are in love with one another look into each other's eyes for a full minute after they've orgasmed without hesitation, without repetition, without deviation. They are like the confluence of two rivers, two processes rather than two objects. Yeah – and that as well – like two verbs rather than two nouns.

Of course, even in those moments, those very special

moments we share, I've kept something back. This tramp-fucking stuff, to be specific, this evil stuff. I've kept it back because I really don't want to hurt her, I don't want to hurt her especially now that she's due and we're about to complete on the house. That's two big uncertainties – or rather two big insecurities – that she has to deal with already. Why give her a third of the form, 'Oh and by-the-by I'm the devil's disciple – thought you ought to know, old girl, what with bearing my child and all of that stuff.'

But then I wasn't counting on these odd fish, these throw-away lines that like verbal can openers have prised the lids off all my rotten selves. Mine is after all a worm's-cast identity, a vermiculation of the very soul.

All the rest of the evening – it blurred by – I had eyes only for Jane. I knew that at long last I would have to give her a fuller account of myself, that I would have to go some way towards telling the truth.

Coffee succeeded crème brulée. We moved from the dinner table to the sitting room. The talk was of people, mutual friends who were conveniently not present. Their stock rose and fell on the conversational Nikkei with incredible speed. Someone would say of X, 'Oh I think he's idiotic, there's no point to him at all – ' and then someone else would chime in with an anecdote confirming this. Before long almost everyone present would be vying with one another to come up with examples of X's awfulness. Within five minutes it became clear that absolutely nothing could redeem X short of the Second Coming. He was venal, he was dishonest, he was gauche, he was pretentious, he was snobbish and yet . . . and yet . . . Just when X was hammered flat and ready for disposal, the tide turned. Someone said, 'The thing about X is that he'll always help you out if you're in a real jam, he's loyal in that way.' The emotional traders swung around to face their dealing screens once more. With X so low he had become worth investing in again. Before long his stock was being snapped up by all and sundry. X was now witty, unassuming, possessed of a transcendent sensibility . . .

It went around and around. I brought my wine glass lazily

to my lips, spotting the stripes on my suit trousers. Jane was opposite me again, situated in a Scandinavian concavity that made up part of the G-plan. She sat knees akimbo, her pregnant belly cupped by body and chair, as if she were proffering it to the gathering. She gave me 'our look' again and spoke betwixt the strands of general talk, spoke to me alone, 'You look all in, love, do you want to get home?' I affirmed this, because it was the easiest thing to do. No point in saying that I couldn't care less, that I might as well be anywhere. Here or there. Lying on a desert floor under the cold glare of the stars, or slumped against weeping bricks in some shooting alley off the Charing Cross Road – it made no odds.

We said goodbye to our host and hostess and to our fellow guests. I nodded at the woman with the Agadir tan, my never-to-be confessor. She nodded back. Out in the street the lamps were orange-aureoled, damp leaf smell banked the sopping pavements. 'Did you drink a lot?' Jane asked. 'Do you want me to drive?' I gave her the keys and she pointed the pulsing fob at our car, our steel pod. The central locking chonked, I got in on the passenger side and let my head droop against the headrest.

When Jane got in on her side I was struck once more by the way that things seemed to accommodate her belly. Here the primary function of the car was to support her tumescence. The moulding of the plastic fascia swept around to bracket it, the foam of the seat welled up to support it. When she struggled down and yanked the lever to hunker the seat forward, it was as if she were bringing her unborn child into the very centre of the car's shell, so that cosseted by impact-resistant materials it could be transported safely home. She started the engine and we pulled away from the kerb.

'They were nice, weren't they?' She sounded unconvinced. 'At any rate they put on a good spread. Mind you, I can't stand that friend of hers, what's his name – the one who's into microlights?' She ran on. We drove. In the artificial light the street furniture had lost its scale, it might just as well have been model bus stop signs and model Belisha beacons that studded our route. How was I going to tell her – that was what preoccupied me – how was I going to broach the subject? I pondered our relationship, plotted its conventional course with my heat-sensitive aerial camera. Our assimilation into one another had been beautifully timed, with each little revelation of unpleasantness acting as a modest baffler, a groyne to our mutual inundation. Now all of this was going to be flooded, drenched in poisonous ichor.

At home I snapped on the lights in the kitchen. While I descended to the eating area, Jane stayed up on the dais which was bounded by our file of white goods. She moved about, propping her belly on clean kitchen surface after clean kitchen surface. In her stretchy black hose she was like some feminine Marcel Marceau, mimicking mime. 'I'll make you some camomile,' she said. 'That'll rehydrate you.' I grunted and she flicked on the electric jug.

And then it came to me – the way forward, that is. I was sitting at the round kitchen table, my elbows on blond wood, caught in the spectral webs of the natural beiges and greys that consulted together in our living space. I felt foetal, amniotically lulled. I felt as I imagined my son-to-be to be feeling. But that was it, though, he wasn't my son, not remotely. I knew that it couldn't be so, not when I considered the overall shape of things. I couldn't have said how he had done it – The Fat Controller, that is – his powers are so indiscriminate. He might have intervened at any stage. He could have miniaturised himself and crawled down my urethra just prior to the relevant ejaculation and there replaced some of my spermatozoa with his own. Or he could have gone smaller still, small enough to infiltrate the genospace itself. Here he might have uncoupled and relinked the long strings of deoxyribonucleic acid as casually as a farmer mends a fence. But however it was that he had done it I was certain that he had. Usurped my paternity, that is.

Jane's now talking about the new house. 'I've phoned Radley.' (That's the solicitor who's handling the conveyancing.) 'He says he's had the deeds through, so it's only a matter of a few days now.' I grunt noncommittally. 'You don't sound very interested.' She's piqued, fluffed up by it as she pours the boiled water on to the bags.

'No, I am, really I am, it's just – '

'You're tired, I know. Don't worry, drink this and come to bed.' She plonks mine down in front of me and taking hers goes on up the angled stair. I can hear her moving about up there. She's stripping off her damp clothes, pausing by the mirror to observe the darkening swell of her abdomen, the fecund brown stripe from button to mons. She's a stolid young woman, built for bearing children just as a clay vessel is meant to be drunk from. The way the veins on her breasts strike blue lightning, the way her ankles swell with healthy oedema, it all speaks of success, jingle bells maternity and chocolate box consanguinity.

Ah, but if I dive into her, plunge through the drum-tight skin and swim on, I know what I'll find. No unformed Jane-sprog or me-sprog, sucking a vestigial thumb and taking on nutriment by hose, like a baby tanker inside a mummy tender. Instead he will be there, or at any rate his new homunculus. I instantly recognise his smooth impassive face, hairless and football round, his hard-boned eyebrow ridges, his flat-bridged and flaring nose, his vulpine mouth – thick-lipped and sneering – and then that voice:

'Come inside for a decco, have we, boy?' He isn't fazed, he never is. His solid body is conservatively clothed, as ever, suited despite the blood heat. And, as if to cock a preemptive snook at the health-and-safety lobby, one of his vile stogies is clamped between his fingers and defying the elements by merrily combusting in fluid. 'I love it in here, don't you? It's so warm and smoochy. A vat of malmsey would suit me fine but failing that I'm happy to settle for total immersion in liquor.' To emphasise how at home he is he cuts a weightless caper, like an astronaut clowning it up for the camera, and bats against the soft walls of his capsule.

Sick irony abounds as Jane leans against the doorjamb, poised to enter the bathroom and feeling The Fat Controller's kicks inside her. He harkens to her, sensing her reaction; with a flip of his city shoes he propels himself up to where the placental macaroni ruckles against the wall of her womb. His hand reaches out, shooting a snowy cuff, and grasps at the stuff, plunging into the elastic membrane and clutching a handful. Jane gasps and so do I.

'It's up to you, boy,' he's chortling, loving it, revelling in it. 'You signed on for this. You can have your fun now, or you can wait another month or so, in which case I will take the greatest of pleasure in informing her myself. Which do you prefer?'

It isn't a question worth answering. I'll tell her myself. Because, after all, the telling is a big part of the fun, perhaps even more fun than the fun itself. This, I realise, is what my life has been leading up to, the quiet suburban house, the loving trusting woman and me, sitting down here in the semi-dark knowing that I am about to tear it all apart – tear her apart.

I've courted this moment assiduously, longed for it even. It's all very well getting your kicks from hurting people, defiling them, causing them untold suffering, but it doesn't really amount to anything when they don't even know you. Ignorance is, relatively speaking, bliss, when even as they give up the ghost they can still comfort themselves with the thought that you are some kind of daemon, not human, not like them.

With Jane it's going to be different. She knows me, she trusts me, she says she loves me, she thinks she is bearing our child. When I tell her that things are not at all as they seem, she will be utterly incredulous; and then, as she comes to believe, what exquisite pain there will be, what complete betrayal. The man she cherishes, the man she butterfly-kisses, the man she sleeps curved around like two spoons in a drawer. It is he who is evil, he who is sworn to destroy her, an emotional quisling of the first water.

I can bide time now, polish up my adamantine treachery, since I've decided now what I want to do. It's pointless for me to dwell on The Fat Controller's unsportsmanlike tactics. Wasn't evil always thus, banal, pinching its plots from elsewhere and shamelessly bastardising them? This business of cropping up in Jane's womb, it's only the latest in a long procession of shoddy gimmicks. I don't want to react, to show myself to be any weaker than I am, because that's quite weak enough.

Jane will be asleep soon, she's not a big sitter-upper. She'll probably take a couple of sips of her camomile, read a few lines of a novel and then start sliding down into the dark burrow of sleep. Usually, when I come upstairs, I tuck her in and turn off the lamp on her side of the bed.

So that leaves me here, I'll be undisturbed whilst I'm being disturbing. Here in the dun kitchen, listening to the fridge, with the whole night ahead of me, I want to try and explain, if I can, how all of this came to be. How it could have been that my idea of fun diverged, so far and so fast, from what might have been expected of someone like me. But I also want it understood by you that this explanation isn't intended as justification of any kind. I don't need to justify myself, I only want to be understood. That's always the cry of the weak man, isn't it? He cries out for understanding when he has none of his own. But I ask you, do you understand, do you really comprehend what has happened to you? If you look at the entire course of your life does it resolve itself into a series of clear-cut decisions, places where the route divided and you took the right way rather than the left? Couldn't it just as easily have been the Hand of Fate, blind or otherwise, that nudged you? Either scenario would make as much sense for anyone. At least it isn't like that for me, I can actually point to my determinants, I can name them even: The Fat Controller for one, Dr Gyggle for two, and if I were pressed for a third it would have to be Mummy.

Here's the hook. When I'm done we'll decide on it together, you and I. I'll give you the opportunity to participate in the denouement. I'm all for audience participation. After all, what's your fleeting embarrassment set beside my life's work? Don't worry, I intend to give full weight to our deliberations. When we're done I'll either go on upstairs, wake Jane, tell her the truth and have my fun as she expires, or I'll give up on the whole thing, pop my clogs and shuffle off into some other dimension altogether.

I don't think I'm being overly dramatic about this and nor do I feel I'm shanghaiing you. After all, you're like all the rest, you like the world on your plate ready to be forked into two chunks, don't you? There's nothing more comforting for you than saying, 'This is either this, or it's that.' You do it all the time, it's as primary as breathing for you. I'm merely providing you with another opportunity to exercise your fine discrimination.

Oh, and another thing before I go, before I sink into my own narrative. About that woman, the one at the dinner party this evening, the one with the Agadir tan. Why was it that what she said got to me so, prompted this gush, this breaking down of the safety bulwarks in my unsinkable Titanic psyche? Well, you see the thing is, I may have killed, I may have tortured, I may even have committed the very worst of outrages, but it hurt me too. Not as much as it hurt my victims, I'll grant you that, but it hurt me. I felt for them, you see, each and every one. From the woman The Fat Controller dispatched with his poisoned cane at the Theatre Royal to Fucker Finch's pit bull, all inclusive. I felt for them as they whimpered, as their bowels loosened – I felt for them as only someone who is precluded from feeling with them could ever feel.

You catch my drift? Look, I'll make it clearer for you. Indulge me in a little exercise, if you will. What do you think the definition of 'empathy' is? Got that? Good. Now, what do you think the definition of 'sympathy' is? Jot it down on a scrap of paper if it helps you to fix it in your mind. Now go and look these two definitions up in the dictionary. I think you'll find that you've got them the wrong way round, that what you thought was empathy is really sympathy and vice versa. You see, that's been my problem – all the time I thought I was sympathising I was really empathising. I'm not going to make big claims about this semantic quirk but I do think it's worth remarking on, for when two key terms tumble over one another in this fashion you can be sure that something is afoot.

CHAPTER ONE

WHAT YOU SEE IS WHAT YOU GET

'Why do you call yourself the Beast?' I asked him on the first occasion of our meeting.

'My mother called me the Beast,' he replied to my surprise.

Julian Symonds, Introduction to
The Confessions of Aleister Crowley

A word first about a tricky concept that you need to be able to understand if you are to accompany me through what follows without flagging, and without getting lost. Woe betide you if you do, because where we are about to go is virgin territory. It's a wild primeval place, a realm of the id, where the very manifold of your identity can easily be gashed open, sundered, so that all the little reflex actions that you call your 'self' will spill out, just so many polystyrene personality pellets, tumbling from a slashed sag-bag. I will not be able to help you in this place and nor, may I say, do I wish to.

This concept is eidetic memory and I am an eidetiker. Perhaps I was always meant to be one – whatever that means – or maybe it was part of the set-up, something to do with the way my destiny has been queered by you-know-who. But no matter, that is not the issue here.

Eidetic images are pictures in the head. They are internal images that have the full force of conventional vision, but which are realised solely in the mind of the eidetiker. For me, it is almost impossible to imagine how it could be otherwise than that when I conceive of, say, a philosopher, I can see that philosopher as surely as if he were lying on this table in front of me. He's on his side, the deep notch between his sagging belly and his hard hip for all the world like a pass through mountains to a happier valley.

Furthermore, if I look closely at this image of a philosopher that I have; I can see all his details, the stitching in his pullover, the 'druff on his cuff, the very particular gleam of his spectacle frames. I can even rotate my philosopher, spin him with great rapidity through three hundred and sixty degrees in all three dimensions; and yet stay him stock still again, if I so choose, without disturbing so much as one hair of his beard. It matters not what I do with my philosopher; in my mind's eye he will retain his pictorial integrity, his notable variegation, his subtle interplay of parts and whole.

I know it's not like that for you. I know that when you imagine a philosopher, any philosopher, for instance the one you saw asleep in the park yesterday, his scalp-scurf merging seamlessly with a mossy wall, your mental image is sharp only when it is hazy and hazy as soon as you attempt to bring it into sharper focus. Isn't that so? The more you concentrate on your visual memory, the more you attempt to fix it securely, the more it slides away, like a quicksilver bead.

If this example seems contrived to you, why not try it with something a little less abstract than a philosopher, for example, the visage of the one you love most. Come now, there must be someone to whom you can ascribe such status? Why don't you summon them up, enjoy the charming singularity of their countenance. Now, what can you see? That their eyes are such-and-such colour, that they style their hair just so, that their skin has this very fine grain, quite like microscopic hide? I'll grant you all of that – but not all at once. What you've done with Little Love is to describe an outline for them and then fill it in, piecemeal, as required. As it is to the sympathy, so it is to the photography. You cannot tell me that, when you appreciated the hue of those sympatico eyes, you also managed to take in the raw triangle of the Loved One's tear ducts? And if you did, did you perchance notice if they had any rheum on them, any at all?

That's what's so achingly sad about your love – that's why it bulges in your heart like an incipient aneurism. For the harder you try to cement it to its object, the more that object eludes you.

Let me reiterate: it's not like that for me. I can summon up faces from my yesteryears and hold a technician's blowtorch to their cheeks. And then, once the skin has started to pullulate, I can yank it away again and count the blisters, one by one, large and small. I can even dig into them and savour the precise whisper of their several crepitations.

Now that's how eidetiking differs from yer' average visualising.

Usually eidetikers are idiots-savants. Many are autistic. It's almost as if this talent were a compensation for being unable to communicate with others. So it's hardly surprising that they don't find much use for their exceptional gifts. From time to time one will crop up on television, giving the donators at home an opportunity to adopt the moral high ground of someone else's suffering. Or else her résumé will appear, boxed in by four-point rules, well stuck in to a fourth-rate chat mag. These prodigies can take one glance at Chartres and then render it in pencil, right down to the grimace of the uppermost gargoyle on the topmost pinnacle. Big deal. That gargoyle might as well be the eidetikers themselves, for all the jollies they'll get out of their unusual abilities.

I can tell you, it wasn't like that for me. I didn't have to spend my childhood in an institution, slavering on the collar of my anorak, and waiting for parental visits that never happened. I was an exception – an eidetiker who could communicate normally, who didn't have to resort to calculating fifteen digit roots in my head, in order to get some kind of attention.

That being said, my eidetiking was something that I was virtually unaware of as a child. Indeed, had I not come under the influence of an exceptional man it's doubtful that anything would have come of it at all. After all, who cares whether someone's visual imagery is particularly vivid or not? Furthermore, how can this vividness be accurately described? I've done my best, but I know that I've begged as many questions as I've answered. Suffice to say that as long as I can remember I've been able to call up visual memories with startling accuracy and then manipulate them at will.

Most of the time I didn't choose to, and for a longish period, in early adulthood, I temporarily lost the ability. But now I've got it back again. Casting behind me, looking over my shoulder, down the crazy mirror-lined passage that constitutes my past, the skill comes in handy. For I find that I only need to summon up one picture, one fuzzy snapshot – serrated of edge, Kodachrome of colour – to be able to access the entire album.

A place that is not a place and a time that is not a time, that's where I spent my childhood. In a place that was chopped off and adumbrated by the heaving green of the sea and at a time that was never some time but always Now.

When I stand in this place, a high chalk bluff that curls down in a collapsing syncline to the bleached bone of a rocky foreshore, what do I see? Not what I saw as a child, for then I had only the raw sense of imminence to project on to that horizon. Time was child's time, the time that is like water, bulging, contained by the meniscus of the present. Now I have become aware – as have we all – of the true Trinity. God the Father, God the Son and God the Cinematographer. And so it is that I await the word rather than the flesh. For only humungus titles, zipping up from the seam between the sea and the sky, will convince me that I have really begun. Without them it is clear to me that my life has been nothing but a lengthy pre-credit sequence, and that the flimsiness of characterisation was all that was required by the Director, for a bit-player such as me.

My father was a tenebrous, as well as a taciturn man. When I was a small child, say up until the age of seven, he was little more than a shadowy presence in my life. And soon after my seventh birthday he improved upon this status by beginning to absent himself from the family home. He would go off, initially for days but soon for weeks, along the South Coast, from ville to ville, reading in public libraries. And by the time I was ten he was little more than a ghost in the domestic machine. By the time I was eleven I hadn't seen him for a full year and a half. I don't know precisely when it happened, so attenuated had my relationship with him become, but one day I realised he wasn't coming back. I haven't seen him since.

As if to underscore his peculiar irrelevance, unlike most of my recollections, my only memories of my father are not of his appearance, his manner, his wit or his wisdom, but solely of his smell. It's true that I only have to look in a mirror to see what he looked like. For as my mother has never tired of telling me, I am his spit, his *doppelgänger*. But stranger still is that his smell is my smell. Imagine that! When I lift my arm I get a whiff of him in the urine tang of my hardened coils. And if I smooth down the gingerish hairs on my freckled arm, the attic odour of dead skin is his as well. I think I could make out a case for this being sufficient – this nasal inheritance – to explain everything that follows. But as if it weren't enough to have someone else's bodily odour, added to this there is the Mummy smell. For the world has always smelt of Mummy as far as I am concerned. By this I mean that if bacon isn't frying, tobacco burning or perfume scintillating, I am instantly aware of the background taint. It's something milky, yeasty and yet sour, like a pellet of dough that's been rolled around in a sweaty belly button. It is the Mummy smell, the olfactory substratum.

I'm searching, searching through my portable photo-library for shots of Daddy, evidence of him to support whatever claims his genes may have made to shape and direct me. Ah, here's the bungalow – starker, leaner, than it later became. The trellis-work around the door supports a spindly climber, Mummy holds little Ian – who's one and a half, maybe two? – like a misshapen rugby ball that someone has passed her; and which she wishes she could immediately pass-kick forward, beyond the touchline of maturity. But in place of Daddy, there's just this painted-in glob, this fuzzy outline. Somebody has got at my eidetic memory and retouched it. They've removed Daddy the way that the Stalinist propagandists painted out Trotsky. When Lenin arrived at the Finland Station and mounted the crude, hastily erected rostrum, Lev Davidovich was there. But as Vladimir ranted, Lev, like some Cheshire Cat, began to fade, the planks started to show through his brow; eventually all that was left was a stain.

It's the same for the rest of my childhood. At all the Party Congresses that we know Daddy to have attended, he has been negated, erased, excised from the picture. Whether propped against the bonnet of the family Mark 1 Cortina (same birthdate as my own), or sprawled on the sheep-cropped and sheep-bedizened grass around the Chantry, it's the same. Only Mummy and Ian, or Mummy, Ian and maternal relatives – plus this Daddy-absence; this Daddy-vacuity; this Daddy-erasure.

I am a big man, like my father. I have his mousy hair and low forehead. I couldn't possibly be said to be ugly, for my features, in themselves, are shapely enough. The cratered dimple in my chin lines up precisely with the scoop out of my top lip and the narrow bridge of my long nose. No, my problem is the same as Daddy's – my features are marooned, set too far in to the middle of my wide face. Furthermore, the way everything falls away at the edges of my face is rather unpleasant. It gives a sodden, lippy impression, like the margin of a peat bog.

I have my father's figure as well. Sometimes, when I inadvertently catch sight of myself getting out of the bath, I freeze, startled, and think: Who let that Russian peasant woman in here? But it's only me, because – you see – my hips are wider than my shoulders and my solid legs look as if babies could be squeezed out from their confluence as easily as grapefruit pips. I'm built like a babushka.

And another thing, another point of resemblance. When I was a child I was reasonably well co-ordinated, but as I have grown up my sense of body has become both cloudy and diffuse. My fingers and toes are now distant provinces, Datias and Hibernias, cut off for years at a time from the Imperial nervous system. Without The Fat Controller's instruction in the blacker arts of physicality I would undoubtedly have become as hamfisted as Dad was. I certainly look as if I ought to be.

If I mention my father at the outset, it is because I want to get his having been out of the way, out of the way. After all nurture has trumped nature a thousandfold as far as my being is concerned. And if I were to see Dad now (I have no idea if he is alive or dead), I should feel compelled to dispose of him. I have no doubt about that. His presence would be an affront to my body; so, for it, there would be the rare delight of extinguishing an imperfect and distressed version of itself, a prototype, a maquette. I should enjoy the bludgeoning of my own features, the pulverising of my own thick bones and the slashing to ribbons of the nauseating congruence of our flesh – more, perhaps, than I've enjoyed any of my other little outrages.

Why, oh why, oh whyeeee! Why did Daddy abandon me like that? That's the $64,000 question, that's the Golden Shot. Why didn't he care for me, love me? He must – I am forced to conclude – have been a weakling, an emotional eunuch. That much is certain. He stepped aside and indifferently flicked a wet blanket at the raging bull of paternity. For that I can never forgive him.

When I was at university, The Fat Controller saw fit to supplement that version of my father's history that my mother had retailed when I was a child. It is characteristic of The Fat Controller that he should have extemporised in this fashion, dropping bombshells of feeling as casually as crumbs. We were sitting in a café and I recall that he was dunking a doughnut as he spoke, paying no mind to the tea slopping on his cuff, or the granular snowfall on his jacket lapels.

'Your father – Harrumph! A contemptible Essene and no mistakin' – I knew him well, of course.'

'You've never said so before.'

'Well, why should I? I've had no cause to. But now you are about to embark on a career it is only fair that you should know a little more about him. I dare say that your mother always spoke of him as a "brilliant man".'

'She did.'

'Quite so, quite so. Did ye believe her?'

'Well, not entirely, I never saw any evidence of it. While he was at home he never left the sun porch. He sat there all day reading the newspapers. Not even the nationals – he didn't seem to have the gumption to deal with anything much but the local advertiser.'

'And then he went on his pilgrimage, by bus, I believe. He did at least understand this much, that the timetable expresses a set of mutable, quasi-astrological relations, the coming and going of ferrous bodies –'

'Aren't you getting off the point?'

'What point!' he exploded – he could never abide interruption. 'Don't be a booby, sir, you know I will not have a booby for an interlocutor!'

'I'm sorry.'

'Sorry isn't good enough – never is.'

We sat in silence for a while. The Fat Controller dunked. I looked on as the customers in an adjacent emporium crammed themselves into unsuitable denims. Eventually The Fat Controller spoke. 'You knew that he was a businessman, of course?'

'Yes, Mum told me that. I assumed that it was something insignificant, perhaps wholesale dry goods.'

'Oh no, you've got it wrong there, boy. You probably can't remember but the furniture your mother had in the bungalow when you were a child came from the old St John's Wood house. It was really quite good, perfectly substantial. It dated from the time when you were very small and your father ran Wharton Marketing.'

'He had his own company then?'

'Absolutely. Your father was one of the most successful marketeers in sixties' London. He had a real flair for it. Knew just how to launch a product, what activities were required, sales promotion or advertising. He had a nice line in statistical interpretation as well.'

'What happened, why did the business fail?'

'Well, people at the time said that it was mismanagement. They pointed to several large accounts that your father had either lost or failed to win, but that was a facile explanation. The truth was that he got bored.'

'Bored?'

'Oh yes – yes indeed. I knew him, as I say. Naturally, for I knew everyone of consequence. I had even done business with him on a number of occasions. I actually went to see him not long before the final collapse. The receivers were champing at the bit, I passed a man with a writ in the vestibule. Your father told me himself: "I just can't be buggered, Samuel," that's what he said, "I can't even summon up the energy to sign a cheque. I can't engage any more." That was the whole explanation, he was subject to a kind of fatal ennui. There was no other reason why the business should have gone down at all.'

So my father had retreated into his apathy and my mother moved the family to Saltdean. That much I had known already, and it was because of this that my conscious life began on a cliff. I say a cliff but really the site was more like a monstrous divot, kicked out from some golf course of the gods. On the divot sat the interleaved environs of the twin resorts of Saltdean and Peacehaven. Behind them was the ridge of the South Downs. Their rounded summits had a humanoid aspect, as if they were the grassed-over skulls of long-buried giants. In the lee of the Downs, between Saltdean and Rottingdean, were two contradictory edifices. One was a sprawling red-brick manse, the girls' public school, Roedean. The other was a hideous Modernist joke, the prefiguration of ten thousand bypass-bound corporate compounds, the blind people's home, St Dunstan's. Both establishments were to play a part in my upbringing, a pivotal part.

Saltdean and Peacehaven, taken together what did they imply? Well – for the property speculators that built them – that the less well-heeled could, like their posher counterparts in Regency Brighton, be pickled into health. Fish in a fabricated barrel. But their heyday had been short-lived; a fifty-year season, during which the dregs of the English middle classes had been washed against the guttering of the Channel, before finally being sluiced down it, out into the Bay of Biscay and the Med.

Even by the time I was a child, the green-and-white picket fences, the pink-and-pebbledashed bungalows, the tea shops and other colourful amenities, all of them were in distempered decline. Psychic tumbleweeds blew down the cul-de-sacs and skittered around the crescents. It had become a landscape where everything that looked temporary was in fact permanent, and where everything that looked permanent was already scheduled for demolition.

My mother's caravan park capped it all. Besides the bungalow cum B & B there were twenty or so fibreglass sheds for holidaymakers. But their wheels were bound to the turf by weeds and nettles, and their quaint fifties' aerodynamicism only served to underscore the hard truth that they – and by implication we as well – were going nowhere.

On this not-quite-Beachy head my mother made her stand. My father was grey enough but he had no eminence and my upbringing was left in my mother's more than competent hands.

It's difficult to talk about the woman with any objectivity, especially as she's still alive. Perhaps when she's dead the Mummy smell will disperse, like mustard gas from a trench-scarred battlefield, and I will be able to see her, and smell her, for what she really was. But not now. Now I can only think of her as an assisting adept, a distaff manipulator. It was she who set it up between me and The Fat Controller. I have long suspected that they may have been lovers at some time or other. I admit, it does sound preposterous. The technical problems would be well nigh insurmountable, for a start. The Fat Controller is just too fat to have penetrative sex in the normal way. Either his penis would have to be fantastically long and flexible, or he would need a series of finely calibrated, servo-mechanised clamps. These to be positioned in the deep furrows between his belly and his pubis, so as to lever the flab interfaces apart when the crucial moment came. I digress – but not entirely. This matter of the potential relationship between The Fat Controller and my mother is of some importance in what follows, and were I intent on constructing a defence for myself its actuality might well be at the core.

But I am blocked from further investigations, for The Fat Controller has thrown up some kind of numinous barrier or force field around his nether regions, and I cannot – with the best will in the world – get inside his trousers. So the above is only speculation.

Mother hailed from a Yorkshire family, the Hepplewhites. But although their name sounds authentically white rose, the truth is that they were fringe people. There was more than a dash of Romany blood in the Hepplewhites, Irish too. When my mother was a child the family lived in an extended, clannish sort of ménage which my grandfather, Old Sidney Hepplewhite, had established in a gaggle of dilapidated farm buildings outside Leeds.

The Hepplewhites lived by costermongering, car and caravan trading, scrap-metal dealing and worse. They were reluctant to go to law, preferring to settle their disputes themselves. They were the sort of family who nowadays would have their children placed automatically on the 'at risk' register. Their lifestyle might have been affected on purpose, to inflame the suspicions of social workers. According to my mother, Old Sidney always carried a double-barrelled shot-gun, dangling from the poacher's hook inside his jacket, just in case a dispute should arise.

She wasn't embroidering. When I finally met Old Sidney, some five years ago, he still carried a gun. He threatened me with it when, wandering around Erith Marsh, I came upon his raggle-taggle encampment. I like to think that he had no idea that I was his kin when he drew the bead, but I cannot be sure.

At any rate, the shot-gun wasn't required when Mum married Dad. They met when my father was doing national service, mustering mattocks or somesuch in a depot outside Halifax. My mother must have seen something in Wharton senior, some potential. Clearly he was from a better class and perhaps that was sufficient. Mum is an expert, like so many English people, not only at detecting class origins in others, but also at obscuring her own. The Fat Controller has told me that she took to shopping at Worth and Harrods with a vengeance once my father was earning, and that her natural sense of style was a big contributor to their social success as a young couple on the make. She could mix a gin and 'it' or a dry Martini with consummate ease. But by the time I was conscious of such things, she had relapsed into a petit-bourgeois backwater. Her accent swung haphazardly between the broad vowels of the Dales and the clipped intervals of received pronunciation. Her once cultivated taste had collapsed back into itself, becoming notably deadened and bland.

Now, of course, she's gone the other way again. She sits sipping her 'lap' while chows and spaniels chew the laces of her Church's walking shoes and waxed rainwear steams on the leathern settle. I wonder if there will be any end to my mother's rollercoaster ride at the English social funfair.

She didn't wean me until I was three. So, what with my capacity for eidetic images, it's no wonder that her breast still has such significance for me. Indeed, I can see it clearly, right down to the precise accumulation of nodes on the surface of her oval brown aureoles. Oh Mummy, Mummy! That was real sex – everything else, everything that has followed, has just been afterplay. I can see you now, still young, with your S-bend figure and dirigible breasts, blood seeping into your complexion like runny jam into rice pudding. You must have been perpetually in a lather; the way you toyed with me, raised me up, so that my first intimations of the fleshly have remained for ever fused to your nylon armature.

At night I would be found by you, crying softly, slumped in the laundry basket, having walked in my sleep the length of the bungalow to find the cottony warmth of the airing cupboard. One of the slick cones of your brassière would be clutched in my chubby paw. It was as if by chafing it – I could somehow chafe you.

I can remember that and I can also remember you giving me my first words, teasing them in to me. It was at a time in childhood when the fictive world was still interleaved with the real world, and like an opium dreamer I moved between them. Mummy took me on her knee. She licked a looped fold of handkerchief and smeared away the chocolate stains from my mouth with an adamant digit. Then, with the same pointer, she thrust me on to the Island of Sodor. I wandered over the green page and marvelled at the way the blue steel slashed it cleanly apart. The engine people zipped this way and that, buffeting the coaches. They were apple-cheeked, their pink-fleshed humanoid faces tore out of the metal of their boilers as if they were some early form of bio-engineering.

'Now, who's that then?' said Mummy. 'You know that engine's name, now don't you?'

'Gor-on,' said I, all gum and lip, palate as yet unfused.

'And the little green engine, what's his name?'

'Perthy.'

'And what about that man? The big, fat man, who tells all the engines what to do. What's his name, Ian?'

'Fa' Co-ro-ro! Fa' Co-ro-ro! Fa' Co-ro-ro!' I exulted in the syllables. I trilled and screamed them.

Mummy had bought the bungalow along with the caravan park. It was an L-shaped structure that had grown up over the years in a series of extensions. Mummy added the fourth and last. The long length of the bungalow was bounded by the forty-foot sun porch, roofed with green corrugated iron. While Father picked at his provincial free-sheets, Mummy squelched up and down the linoleum drumming up business on the telephone. She had one with an especially long flex. Or else she would stalk between the caravans, hunting the tradesmen who were meant to be toshing the place up, making it lickety-spick for the next load of work-pummelled urbanites who came to Cliff Top for their week or two of ozone and salted air.

Like all children whose parents are employed in the tourist industry, my life was divided into the 'on' and the 'off' season. The off season belonged to school and rain hammering on the corrugated roof of the sun porch, while the on season to belonged to the holidaymakers and their children. My mother had many regulars who came back year after year, and I was always accepted by them. It was a friendly atmosphere for a young child, with little to disturb it. As an only child I had my mother's undivided attention, the full force of her complacent love. And then there were also the aunts.

Old Sidney had had four daughters, all of whom had married wispy and ineffectual men. The whole bunch, aunts, their men-folk and assorted cousins, descended on Cliff Top every year for their two weeks of holiday. Indeed, in the early seventies during the worst of the slump, when even ordinary working-class families were all bound for the Med, I think it may have been my aunts' custom that really kept my mother's business afloat. I can remember muttered discussions at night in serious, adult tones:

'What would you do without us then, Dawn?'

'Aye, what would y'do? You'd be on your uppers, lass, with Derek all gone to pieces, like – and that tubby brat of yours gobbling owt in sight.'

The aunts were like caricatures of my mother, such was the family resemblance. While Avril may have been thicker in the waist than Dawn, and Yvonne was perhaps prettier than May, all four of them had the same broad, sincere faces, chestnut eyes and mousy hair. They also painted their faces up in the same naive manner, adding cupid bows of lipstick to the powdered flesh above their lips.

It was like having one big four-headed Mummy when the aunts were in residence. They gathered us up in a giggling ball of blood-relatedness. During the off season my mother's smothering affection was often cold-tempered by financial chills – she would snap at me, deny me love and withdraw the physical affection I craved. During the winter I sometimes became the failed husband she had, rather than the demon lover she had always desired.

But each summer it all came right again. She would lie around with her sisters drinking beer, eating scallops, whelks, mussels and cockles. They would all smack their lips – sometimes in unison. Whenever a child got near enough to this recumbent maternal gaggle it would be grabbed and kissed, or raspberries would be blown on kid flesh, sticky with ice-cream and gritty with sand.

When the aunts and cousins were in residence I ran free. Together with my cousins I would plunge down the steep steps to the rocky beach. Then we would make our way along the undercliff walk to Brighton where we would ride on Volks Electric Railway, or play crazy golf, or thud along the warm boards of the West Pier. In the pier arcades, antiquated mechanical Victorian tableaux were still in place. These were cabinets, in which six-inch-high painted figures, animated by a heavy penny, would jerkily reenact the execution of Mary, Queen of Scots, or the hanging of Doctor Crippen. The shingled beaches along the front at Brighton rattled and crunched with the exertions of many thousands of rubber souls. There were motor launches, rentable for a shilling's cruising on the oblong lagoons beneath the esplanade at Hove. Further along still, towards the *ultima Thule* of Shoreham, there were the salt-water baths of the King Alfred Centre. My favourite, situated as if in open defiance of the laws of nature, up a steep, magnolia-tiled stairway.

We would often stay out until way past dark.

The scents of piss and soap, blown around the concrete floor of the shower block. A thin man – possibly an uncle – braces down his back, shaving in the chipped mirror. The moles on his shoulders are bright pink in the wash of morning sunlight and he accompanies himself with a rhythmic little ditty, 'Cha, cha, *cha*! Cha, cha, *cha*!' the emphasis always on the last '*cha*'. Gulls are squawking overhead. While along the horizon a freighter weeping rust proceeds jerkily, as if it were just a larger version of the plaster ducks in the shooting gallery on the Palace Pier. In this sharpened past I'm always sinking my mouth in my mother's hair, which is frazzled by her accumulated sexual charge. It's sweet, undulant, as sticky as candyfloss. You get the picture. Mine was a childhood that was sufficiently problematic to make me interesting, but not enough to disturb. The on season, that is.

I was about eleven when Mr Broadhurst came to live at Cliff Top. I had passed the eleven-plus and was shortly to become indentured to Varndean Grammar. This would mean an eight-mile round-trip every day to the outskirts of Brighton. To celebrate the result, Mum had bought me a new briefcase of blue canvas and black vinyl, and stocked it with a tin-boxed Oxford Geometry Kit and plastic-backed exercise books. I was carrying this self-importantly around the caravan park, very conscious of the interplay of my feelings: the adoption of the correct professional stance when holding the briefcase and the sense of foreboding I always had, standing on the verge of the off season.

Under quickstepping clouds, a chorus line of nimbus, the Downs, the cliffs and the sea form a frame within which to direct fresh action. In the clear air the resort towns are strewn over the land, each pocket-sized manse perfectly visible. I watch, playing with my sense of scale, as toy cars, each one a different colour, process along the coastal road.

Then a schoolfriend's dad, Mr Gardiner, pulled off the coast road and drove his bulbous black truck down the thirty yards of track leading to the caravan park and into actual size. I stood against the wall of the bungalow, my plump palms wedged between buttock and pebbledash, while Mr Gardiner talked to my mum. Then I accompanied him as he backed his truck between the caravans, down to the cliff edge.

'You did all right in the exam then?' he said, shouting over the banging engine.

'Yes, I did,' I replied brightly, anticipating more praise to add to my aunts' and cousins'.

'Well then, you'll be off to Varndean with the other smartarses.' Too late I remembered just how thick Dick Gardiner was. But I swallowed my humiliation and helped his father position the big metal hooks under the base of one of the caravans.

'I'm having this one,' he said. He was poking around inside it. He sat down on the boxed-in bed, squashing the foam mattress pancake flat, and fiddled aggressively with the dwarfish kitchenette appliances. 'Not that it's worth eff-all, mind. I'm just gonna put it on blocks in the garden. I'll use it to store tools.' He stood and the caravan rocked on its defunct wheels. Mr Gardiner was larded with avoirdupois. His breasts bulged out on either side of the bib of his overall, as if it were a garment specially devised to enhance his womanliness. He poked his finger along the top seam of the caravan. 'Mind you, I'll have to put a deal of work into it. I reckon I'm doing your mother a favour just by takin' the thing away. Look – look here.' He had been addressing me via the mini-dormer, but now I stepped inside the fibreglass cabin.

'See that?' His digit had dislodged a wet gobbet from the ceiling. 'I'll have to get busy with me mastic. Frankly it's a wonder your mother gets anyone to rent these things – they're probably infested.'

After that he wouldn't talk, he just hitched the caravan up and made ready to drive off. He was already in gear when I chimed up, 'But what's going to happen, Mr Gardiner, with the van gone?' It would be like a gap in a full set of dentures.

'Well . . .' He rounded on me. His face was mottled with prejudice, smeared with bigotry. 'Your mum's got a new lodger coming. That's what she says. An off-season lodger, and guess what – he's got his own caravan!'

His own caravan. The very idea sent me into a lather of expectation. I tottered on the turf, the gulls screamed at each other over my head. Mr Gardiner was grinding his way back to the road, but he took time out to shout back at me, 'Fucking gyppo!' I couldn't work out whether he was still angry with me, or whether he was referring to the new lodger, the mysterious man who had his own caravan.

CHAPTER TWO

CROSSING THE ABYSS

There is nothing so agreeable as to put oneself out for a person who is worth one's while. For the best of us, the study of the arts, a taste for old things, collections, gardens, are all mere ersatz surrogates, alibis. From the depths of our tub, like Diogenes, we cry out for a man. We cultivate begonias, we trim yews, as a last resort, because yews and begonias submit to treatment. But we should prefer to give our time to a plant of human growth, if we were sure that he was worth the trouble. That is the whole question. You must know yourself a little. Are you worth my trouble or not?

M. de Charlus in *The Guermantes Way*
Proust

Mr Broadhurst arrived the next weekend. In one way his arrival was a reassurance – he certainly didn't look like a gyppo. But on the other hand it was confusing, because the men who accompanied him most definitely were.

To begin with it was like a rerun of Mr Gardiner's visit. The truck was as big and if anything blacker – an ex-army three-tonner. The mysterious new lodger's mobile home was hitched on behind. And what a caravan it was! Nothing like the cream-and-blue hutches dotted around the site. This one was twice as big and made of mirror-shiny aluminium. It was so long that it had a double set of wheels at the back.

Up on tiptoes while the adults stood chatting in the garden, I peered in on an expanse of fluffy white carpeting, a wide bed covered with a white-lace counterpane, glass shelves lined with newspaper-wrapped ornaments and in the corner a colour television. With its windscreen windows, fore and aft, the caravan was like a storefront display of American opulence.

Mr Broadhurst was a big fat man. He was over six feet tall and bald save for a moustache of fine grey hair shadowing the crease between the third and fourth folds at the back of his thick neck. He was dressed like a part-time undertaker in a down-at-heel black suit. His tie was black as well and his shirt had clearly dripped dry.

Fat was too simple a description of Mr Broadhurst, I knew that as soon as I clapped eyes on him. For he wasn't plump in the way that I was aged eleven. I couldn't imagine poking my finger into him and then drawing it back, having created a pale dimple that sopped up red. His was a fat that implied resistance rather that yielding. If his chest resembled a barrel and his head and limbs five smaller barrels, it was a formal resemblance only. I could tell just by looking that these vessels didn't contain dropsical fluid, or scrungy sponginess. Instead Mr Broadhurst's solidity was clearly founded on enlarged organs that filled him right up; a double heart like a compressed air pump, a liver the size and weight of a medicine ball and hundreds of feet of firehose-thick intestine.

He was sucking at the edge of his blue Tupperware tea cup, as I drew closer to hear what was being said. Supping greedily, as if he were about to take a bite out of the cup's rim. The two gyppo men stood apart, regarding him with expressions that I could not read at the time, but which – with the benefit of hindsight – I would say were full of awe.

Then I caught an earful of what he was saying and it was a revelation. In that moment I knew I was hearing one of the great talkers, the consummate rhetoricians, of all time. For Mr Broadhurst's discourse was as unlike any ordinary conversation as an atomic bomb is unlike a conventional weapon. It was an explosion, a lexical flash, irradiating everything in the immediate area with toxic prolixity. I caught a lethal dose of this, that has been decaying throughout my half-life, ever since.

It was clear, even to a child, that the most mundane tropes, the purely factual statements and flippant asides, that fell from his lips, were more akin to the run-offs and overflow pools of some mighty river than the babbling brooks and cresslined streams of sociable chatter. I could sense that this stream of speechifying was always there – in Mr Broadhurst's mind – and that what we were hearing was simply the muted roar of a currently submerged cataract. When he paused, it seemed to me only as if this great torrent of verbiage had been momentarily blocked by some snag or clotted spindrift of cogitation, and I felt the power of his thought building up behind the dam, waiting to sunder it, so that the sinuous green back of this communicative Amazon or Orinoco might stretch out once more, towards the transcendent sea. No hyperbole, no matter how extreme, could do justice to the strength of the impression that that first encounter with Mr Broadhurst's speech made on my pubescent sensibility.

'It's a remarkable enterprise that you have here, Dawn,' he was saying. 'The hills rearing up behind and' – he swept his telegraph pole of an arm round in a wide arc – 'the sea below. Nothing could be finer for a man such as myself, no Epidaurus could provide a more suitable arena within which to lay my tired body. No proscenium could be more delightfully elevated, so as to present the remaining days of my reclusion and retirement.' He paused, adopting a pensive mien which befitted this fatiloquent observation, and I was transfixed by the thick, almost Neanderthal ridges of bone that took the place of eyebrows on his mondial head. These ran together like the arched wings of a gull and became the high bridge of Mr Broadhurst's prominent nose. But, saving this, his head was peculiarly lacking in other features, such as cheekbones, or the extra chins that might have been expected. Also, there was a depilated, creaseless look to his flesh. His lips were wide, thick and saturnine. His steady basalt eyes were protuberant, amphibian under lashless lids.

'Muvvat' 'van nerr?' asked one of the gyppos. To me they were stuff of nightmares, clearly beyond the fringe of Saltdean – and perhaps any other society.

'Do that, do that. Do it now.' His voice at first merely emphatic, gathered emotional force. 'Position the machine in the wings, so that the god may be ready to descend on a golden wire.' The gyppos set down their mugs on the edge of the rockery and, addressing one another with glottal stops and palate-clickings, leapt back up into their truck. Their black bushes of hair, their raven faces, the way they dressed in dark coats fastened at the waist with lengths of rope, the way they spoke and drank and moved, in short, everything underscored their moral insouciance. 'Do what we will,' the gyppos seemed to say, 'that is the whole of our law.'

But Mr Broadhurst, despite his advanced age, dared to order these Calibans about. When he barked, they snapped to. 'Mind out for my things,' he shouted after them. 'My impedimenta, my chattels, my tokens of mortal desire – you'll pay for any breakages!'

That winter Mr Broadhurst became a fixture at Cliff Top.

I was puzzled by the ambiguity of my mother's relationship with him. She had few friends apart from her sisters, and I had seldom heard her called by her first name by anyone who wasn't a family member. But the more I pressed her over it, the more she demurred.

'Tush now, luv. Mr Broadhurst is like part of the furniture for me. He's always been around. I can't remember whose friend he is, to be honest.'

'But, Mummy, you must remember, you must.' The society of my new school, like that of provincial England as a whole, was so alarmingly codified and stratified that I couldn't conceive of anyone whose provenance and emotional valency weren't absolutely fixed. My mother, with her working-class airs and upper-middle-class graces, only served to point this up still further.

'You're a great questioner, aren't you? Always questioning and querying.' She leant down and kissed me. The Mummy smell was overwhelming. I felt the corner of her mouth against mine. 'You don't get it from me – that's for sure – but I can't imagine it comes from yer father either.' I was aware that all that she felt was there, bound up in the way she said 'father'. She pronounced it as another might have said 'old rope'. Without emphasis, as if this paternity were of no account.

She always got around me in this way, by placing her body against mine whenever she felt herself challenged, mentally assaulted. In doing this, I realised, she was re-presenting the fact of her maternity, her original power, to me. Each time contextualising me with her increasingly ample flesh. Despite myself I was seduced and became a toddler once more. Being chased to be tickled, I subsided into the mummyness.

Mr Broadhurst had quickly settled into a routine at Cliff Top. Which is, of course, the way to become a fixture. He had signed up to do voluntary work at St Dunstan's, the blind home, on Tuesday and Thursday afternoons. First thing in the morning, he walked to the shops in Saltdean to get his shopping and his newspaper. I would often meet him there, as I came out of the sweet shop fondling a paper bag full of gonad bonbons with the fingers of an aspirant sensualist.

'Ah! The young Rosicrucian.' Although his voice was pitched normally I was always aware of the distant booming of riverine surf. 'With a sack of sweetmeats – may I?' He would take one with fingers rendered all the more queerly huge for their precision and dexterity.

On Sunday afternoons he would come to tea, and he and my mother would talk of people they had known back in Yorkshire. From this much at least I gathered that Mr Broadhurst had been a friend of the Hepplewhites for many years. He also condescended to help me with my homework. On the arts and humanities subjects he was vague and often out of sorts with my textbooks. But in maths and the sciences he was an adept if overbearing didact. Maths in particular he excelled at; he called it his 'favourite subject'. And it was by tutoring me in maths that he first gained a toehold on my mind.

One Sunday a month Mr Broadhurst would take my mother and I to the Sally Lunn, an old-fashioned tea shoppe in Rottingdean where they served an eponymous tea-cake of which the three of us were especially fond. Mr Broadhurst could eat as many as thirty of these 'Sally Lunns' at a sitting. He mounded so much honey on top of the buns that they looked like miniature stupas. Truly he was a big pale Sambo.

I can see the Sally Lunn now. In a small whitewashed room with a dark beeswaxed floor, lobster pots, nets, glass floats and other marine decorations are hanging about the walls. Mr Broadhurst and my mother are chatting about this and that, nothing of consequence, prospects for the on season, a fourteen-year-old Saltdean girl who was having an abortion (they are euphemising but I get the drift). On this particular Sunday Mr Broadhurst looked up from his piled plate and scrutinised the tea shoppe. Examined it critically as if seeing it clearly for the first time.

'D'ye know, Dawn,' he said, 'I don't think this place has changed much since I used to come here regularly, and that must have been before the Great War.'

My mother didn't seem to register the significance of this statement, but it stuck with me. Later, when we were heading home through the rain-dashed streets, my mother and

Mr Broadhurst walking ahead of me, their contrasting figures like a Grimm illustration framed by the tip-tilted housefronts of the old village, I figured out the arithmetic. If Mr Broadhurst had been grown up enough to visit a tea shop regularly before 1914, he would have to be at least eighty by now, easily. Yet despite his declared retirement there was nothing obviously decrepit about him. Had there been I would certainly have spotted it.

I knew about old people the way a boy who lives next to an airport knows about planes. Our slice of Sussex coastline was already beginning to fill up with the moribund – or, as they prefer to put it nowadays: was becoming a growth area for the grey market. Saltdean even boasted specialist shops for the old, retailing surgical supports, Zimmer frames and herbal remedies. But Mr Broadhurst just didn't have the shuffling gait that I expected of the old, only a certain calculated languor to his movements. This was a comprehensive slow-motion, affecting his gestures and orotund tones as well as his locomotion.

'What's a gyppo, Mum?' It was the following week. I was eating high tea after school. Beans on toast, Ribena.

'We don't say gyppo, Ian, it's common.' She was wiping the kitchen surfaces with a J-Cloth, rubbing them vigorously, her features distorted with distaste, as if they were the limbs of a Formica corpse.

'Mr Gardiner said that Mr Broadhurst was a gyppo, and he had gyppos with him when he came, didn't he, Mum?' This jarred her and she grew terse.

'Look, Ian, I know this much, that Mr Broadhurst worked for many years in the salvage industry and I believe that he counts a number of travelling people among his acquaintances. That's all, now eat your tea.'

The undercliff walk, which ran from Rottingdean along to Brighton, was my special haunt. This was where I consummated my boyhood. It was a peculiar place, especially during the off season, when detergent waves span against the dirty parapet. The two-hundred-feet-high cliffs rose above it and the shoreline below it was a torn shattered prospect, strewn with huge lumps of chalk and discarded trash from the Second World War; pillboxes and dragons' teeth, which were in the process of being reduced to rubble by the tides.

Some mothers said the undercliff was dangerous and wouldn't let their children play there. They spoke of high tides washing little ones clean away (there was no access to the top of the cliff for over three miles). My mother wasn't amongst their number. I was allowed to go down there all I wanted. I transformed the pillboxes into Arthurian redoubts and tenanted them with my fellow knights. It was only child's play but highly charged and for me more emotive than the real world. My eidesis allowed me to paint the storybook characters on to the rocks around me; and often, so enmeshed had I become in make-believe that a solitary dog-walker coming along the concrete causeway would terrify me, as much as if they had been the Black Knight.

The winter after Mr Broadhurst came to Cliff Top, on two or more occasions, I thought I saw him down on the undercliff. This was strange enough, for how could such a big man be at all elusive, especially to one as sharp-sighted as I? And yet I couldn't be sure if it was he, backed into one of the chalky gulches at the base of the cliff and chatting conspiratorially with one of his hawk-faced gypsy friends, or just some ordinary be-mackintoshed pensioner, a sad stroller on the far shore of life.

Increasingly the off season at Cliff Top belonged to Mr Broadhurst. It became associated with him in my mind, in just the same way that the on season belonged to my aunts and cousins. Like many only children of single parents I was emotionally precocious. I sensed that my mother was pleased and even relieved by the interest that he took in us. I knew that he helped Mother with her accounts and made suggestions as to how she could drum up more custom for the caravan park. For some reason these stratagems seemed to pay off. Come summer there were more guests. More than half of the static caravans would be filled. The older people – middle-aged or elderly couples – Mother would put up in what she grandly termed the 'PGs' Wing'. In the mornings I would catch sight of them, their unfamiliar nightwear rendering the sun porch sanatorial, as they processed to and from their allocated bathroom.

Mr Broadhurst wasn't there to see the fruit of his business acumen, for come Easter he would be off, winging away like some portly and confused migratory bird, to different climes. Or at any rate that's what I imagined for him – he wouldn't tell me where he went. He wouldn't even hint at it.

'Where d'you go in the summer, Mr Broadhurst?'

'That, my lad, I am afraid I am not at liberty to disclose. My perennial peregrinations are perforce secret. All in good time – should you appear worthy of my confidence – I will divulge elements of my itinerary.'

However, far more affecting than Mr Broadhurst's seasonal leave was the impact on my home culture of the improved management of Cliff Top that he had bequeathed. This amounted to a paradigm shift in the social status of my mother's household. As Mr Broadhurst became more familiar to us, more heavily entrenched in the winter seaside, so my mother upped herself. It was as if, with the failed father gone, she was once again free to resume an aspirational trajectory. Dinner became lunch and tea became supper.

'There'll be more guests again this summer,' I remember my mother saying, setting the femurous receiver back on its pelvic cradle and closing her bookings ledger. 'That extra advertising Mr Broadhurst suggested we do has certainly paid off.'

More guests meant that there was more money; and more money meant better clothes, new caravans for the site and new interior decoration for the bungalow.

Kitchen and carpet were fitted. A central-heating system replaced the gas fires' bleating and the controlled explosion of the geyser. The winter mornings, when in darkness I would bolt from the warm confinement of my bed to dress in the kitchen, became instant memories. Nostalgia for a simpler, more technically primitive age.

Once the bungalow was vitalised people started to come by for drinks, rather than simply having drinks when they came by. There was also an alteration in the ambit of my mother's socialising, for the drinks people tended to be the parents of my schoolfriends at Varndean Grammar. They were a cut above the shopkeepers and tourism-purveyors that I was used to. Their business was more elevated, further removed from the raw stuff of exchange. Their conversations with my mother referred to a world where the ambiguity of the relationship between value and money was greatly appreciated.

The people who had had drinks when they came by, well, they were a distinctly odder crowd, including Madam Esmerelda, the thyroid case who had the palmist's concession on the Palace Pier. Her boyish friend was an old circus midget called Little Joey, who still wore his stage clothes ('It's all I have, you see, Sonny Jim, unless I want to wear kids' gear'), Norfolk jackets in screaming plaid, topped off with a Derby hat. Joey and Esmerelda's talk was colourful, peppered with the showbusiness expressions of an earlier age. It was set against types such as these that Mr Broadhurst was able to insinuate himself into my life, without appearing quite as aberrant as he might otherwise.

I will say one thing for my mother. I will grant her one, severely back-handed compliment. And that is: that as we ascended the greasy pole of English class mobility together, she seldom embarrassed me. For, if her great fault was the almost-sexual intimacy with which she blanketed me in private, her great asset was the preternatural sensitivity she showed towards me in public. She never patronised me or made me jump through the hoops of propriety the way that I saw other children forced to by their parents. Indeed, she treated me with an easy egalitarianism that was far more effective – in terms of my succesful acculturation, that is.

Of course the person we were both really taking instruction from was Mr Broadhurst. It was his long-winded locutions that we both began to ape – never using one word where five would do. And it was his heavy-handed delicacy to which we aspired when our everyday Tupperware was replaced with bone china.

At school things were better for me as well. During my time at Saltdean Primary I had always been subject to the tiny-mindedness of a tiny community. My father's desertion of us was well known and often commented on. No matter that this was without malice, it meant that I felt excluded, cut off, beyond the pale. But at Varndean Grammar no one knew about my father. When I started there I simply lied about him and said that he was dead, which gained me sympathy as well as cloaking me in something like mystery. This, I now know, was a mistake. Perhaps I even realised it as a child, because the lie was supported by my mother; and such complicity was worrying, bizarre even, to a twelve-year-old boy.

Nonetheless it gave me a brief lull, a fall in the feverish temperature of my life which I made full use of. Puberty and individualism don't mix. Running with the pack was something new. Mutually masturbating with skinny-hipped boys and mentally torturing sensitive student teachers, this became my idea of fun, but not for long.

There was one final summer before Mr Broadhurst began to take a more advanced interest in me. A summer when I ran as free with my cousins and the children of my mother's guests as ever before. That was the summer when I first became fully conscious of the arbitrariness of the division between the 'on' and the 'off'; the last summer when I saw the sun twitch away the net curtain of mizzle that hid the mounded Downs and transform the world, so that the sky and the sea defined the land, giving curvature to the earth. The last summer that was acted out in the round.

I showed the guests' children where to shop for sweets, where to go crabbing, how to get into the Dolphinarium for free. We ranged along the coast from Saltdean to as far as Shoreham. I felt engaged – masterful. Unlike the holidaymakers, this was my burgh, my manor. The tatty holiday glitz was my finery. I knew all the people who ran the amusements and all the roustabouts who worked on them. I could spring on to a dodgem at one side of the rink and proceed to the other by leaping from one rubber-flanged buggy to the next. My little crew would look on amazed.

The one bum note, the one hint that something was changing for me – and mind you, I cannot be sure that this isn't an intimation that belonged to that ultimate off season, the first autumn of my apprenticeship – was my heightened awareness of the very peculiar marginalisation of the Hepplewhite men. These wraithlike uncles of mine, who only came down for the weekend and never stopped for the week, were always 'stepping outside for a pipe', or even 'just stepping outside' with no explanation. Neither my mother nor my aunts ever enjoined them to 'take an interest in Ian'. I cannot recall any of them saying, as might have been expected, that I needed a man's influence. Instead it started to dawn on me that this collective silence-about-men, this domination of the Cliff Top sodality, was in some way calculated, a willed silence between the emasculated overture and the powerful first act. The Hepplewhite sisters were preparing me for the stentorian bulky basso of Mr Broadhurst.

Towards the end of that summer the full weight of sexual maturity fell on me, and with it came the hormonal reclamation of the sea. The two formerly separate continents of the 'on' and the 'off' were reunited into one landmass of vertical concerns: term times and bus times; holiday times and homework times. I became sharply aware of the differences between my boy cousins and my girl cousins. Little furled genitals had long since been buried away under compost clothing, the better to mature there in the dark. I feared they might be gone for the duration.

I cannot explain why that from the off, my sexual feelings were so circumscribed by such awful shame. It made no sense – but it was true. Perhaps it was my chronic lack of male role models. To define myself as a man in relation to my mother and my aunts was an impossibility. Theirs was an unknowable sex, even to look at it was a kind of astronomy, so vast and remote were their bodies. The idea that they could possibly have been banged up by the uncles was flatly preposterous. With the girl cousins and the beach girls it was a different story. There were stirrings and presentiments. I longed, more than anything, to be a pebble or some shingle, pressed beneath those squash buttocks.

If the holidays were sexually perplexing, when term time came I also recoiled from schoolboy smuttiness. I couldn't handle ejaculation as a form of micturation. The ways of looking at the business were stark. Either gonorrhoea, syphilis and non-specific urethritis, explained by Mr Robinson with the new visual aids, or else German porn, bought by the older boys and displayed under desk tops. These pictures, which showed moustached men sinking their pork swords into the wounded abdomens of grimacing uglies, bore no relation to my fantasies, which were chivalrous in the extreme. It may sound pathetic to you, but at that time to be a man was for me to be a Roland or a Blondin. Lute-strumming on a forty-four-date castle tour, content to die for the sake of a radiant eye – let alone a thigh.

Why elaborate? The stuff of adolescent sexuality is known to us all, a wondrousness that increases in memory bulkily to match the rusting hulk of subsequent disillusion. How much harder it is to admit that the disillusion was there all along.

More to the point I was tubby, pink and unappealing. My body was awash with glandular gunk and my face dusted over with pustules. No matter the burgeoning advice-column culture, no matter the democracy of pornography – I felt disenfranchised by my lust. Was it Oedipal? Having dispatched Daddy on the A22 to Southampton was I desperate to get home, answer the riddle that complemented the brewery advertising on the coaster, then cover Mummy where she lay, panting on her electric blanket? Nothing so simple. No it was eidesis. Up until puberty I had taken this for granted, seen it as little more than a clever skill, but now it began to preoccupy me. I started to see it as intrinsic to my nature.

Returning home from school, on the first day of that autumn term, I got off the bus as usual, at the stop midway between St Dunstan's and Roedean, and turned to look towards the Downs. The whole raised tier of the bank the blind home sat on was networked with concrete pathways. These were ruled into existence by guide rails, all painted white, as befitted the giant canes that they were. I thought of Mr Broadhurst and how he had once told me that the blind should never lead the blind. Their halting progress along these paths already struck me as laden with symbolism. Wasn't this the human predicament, fumbling along and then falling off? Waiting on the grass for the attendants to swoop down and reclaim you, reconnect you to the vivifying rail?

I wondered if Mr Broadhurst was among them – he was due back from his summer sojourn any day now – but I couldn't make out his pepper-pot shape amongst the attendants and the vision-crips, the spazzy sightless who fumbled their way beneath the cruel-joke edifice. (Can't you just imagine the architect pissing himself with laughter as he shaded in the hideous eaves, ruled the brutal perpendiculars and traced the shaved pubis of the concrete façade! Confident that here at last was a clientele that would be in no position to object to his conception of the modern.)

Maybe Mr Broadhurst was inside. As he was a voluntary worker he could be up to anything, from assisting in the complex foreplay of braille instruction, his hand hovering delicately over another's, to participating in the free-form, consensual ritual of tea time, imagining himself – as he had told me he often did – as blind as his charges, so that the urn became a dragon, capable of shooting out a boiling wet tongue to scald him.

I too became eyeless in Sussex, toiling along the tangled verge. How many steps could I take before I had to open my eyes? Or would I waver and have my shoulder clipped, sliced off by a whooping bus side? A commonplace enough child's game, but on this ordinary afternoon eidesis reared its ugly head.

I was looking into the red darkness of my own retinal after-image, the plush of my inner lids. I summoned up an eidetic facsimile of the road ahead, its diminishing perspective, the pimpling of the tarmac, the toothpaste extrusion of the white line dividing the carriageway. In this there was nothing remarkable. My head-borne pictures, as I have said before, were always exceptionally vivid. But on this occasion I became aware of a new Point of View. That's the only way I can describe it, as an awareness of being-able-to-see but with nothing lying behind it, no intricate basketry of muscle and coaxial nerve.

In that moment – there was no moment. Time was child's time again, the always-now, caught up and cradled like water by the surface tension of the present. I was inside my own representation and that representation had become the world.

If there's any one way that I could express this sensation to you it would be this. Imagine yourself to be a free-floating Steadicam that can move wherever it wishes at will. For in the very instant that I packed myself into this new perspective, I became aware of flexible ocular prostheses like joysticks and rudders.

Effortlessly I shot high up into the air, pirouetted through a three-hundred-and-sixty-degree pan and then zoomed down again, to hover a foot above the Rottingdean bus as it batted along. I zipped by the pasty faces of my schoolmates, sitting still in transit, and their beady eyes stared straight through me. I was – I realised, powering up into another heady sky-scraping loop – free.

Immediately I started to consider, where should I go? What use should I make of my new and apparently astral body. The two great buildings set on the flanks of the Downs were an obvious objective. I didn't hesitate, I swooped down and entered the red-brick precincts of Roedean. Here, I roamed the dormitories pushing my invisible, yet inviolable, lens into the shower block, the changing rooms. I stopped off in the sanatorium, I doodled beneath the desks. And everywhere I went I immersed myself in the spectacle of many many hundreds of well-turned little misses, unaware and unsuspecting but all perfumed, deliciously scented, by affluence.

When I was a primary school pupil, my eidesis had been noted by the arts and crafts teacher. During her lessons, anything she gave me – an empty yoghurt pot, or a dying daffodil – I would replicate with near-photoreal accuracy, even on thick paper with a soft pencil. She took an interest in me and at parents' evening approached my mother saying, 'Mrs Wharton, your son really does have the most unusual ability.' The higher-ups at the local education authority, prodded into action by Mrs Hodgkins, sent me to see a clinical psychologist.

Mr Bateson, who worked, handily enough, at St Dunstan's, was a little ball of a man with one of those heads, capped and cupped by hair, that would look just as probable upside down. He was a barefaced grinner who seemed impervious to embarrassment, a stranger to even the simplest concept of a gaffe.

'Ho, ho!' he chortled at me from behind his desk. 'What have we here, an eidetiker. Funny that, here I am researching the concept of visualisation amongst the congenitally blind' – he indicated with a tiny hand the three blind people who sat with us in his office – 'and they send me you! Tee-hee, tee-hee-hee-huh!'

The blind swung their antennae heads in the general direction of this prodigy, training on me three pairs of clear-lensed glasses, behind which puffs of cotton wool were imprisoned, like some awful kind of oxidisation.

Despite the fact that Mr Bateson found me intriguing and even wrote a paper on my singular gift for a professional journal, neither I, nor – more to the point – my mother, had seen any benefit in his mind games. His experimental method, which I was to meet again later in life, entailed setting me tasks. I had either to draw objects that were presented to me for a split-second, or else draw pictures from the further recesses of my memory. He then went further, getting me mentally to image complex forms and rotate them in my mind, much in the manner that I requested of you earlier. About the time I left primary school for Varndean, the sessions petered out altogether.

I gave up on eidetiking, except as a party turn. At Varndean some boys could set light to their farts, others could stub cigarettes out on their tongues, I could take a glance at a page of text and then recite it from memory. Unfortunately this didn't in any way aid my comprehension. I was not a successful student.

Sex galvanised my eidesis, sending it straight to the top of my agenda. I can understand why. After all, sex is a language of sorts and insofar as eidesis goes hand-in-hand with autism, why, here was a form of communication I couldn't make use of. In the realm of the senses there was no real identity available to me, only a series of impostures bound in to the repetitive action, like jerking hands to jiving cocks.

Now I found that I could also introduce myself into these formerly static visions, as a purposive if disembodied agent, I couldn't stop. The Roedean incident was only the start of eidetic voyaging – soon it was my principal form of travel.

It became a compulsion and a very scary one. Because the discoveries I made were not to my taste at all. While it was true that the human anatomy – as I had suspected – did not conform to either the lurid colours of pornography or the desiccated line drawings of textbooks, I was not prepared for all these revelations of viscous complexity. I wanted human flesh to remain as obvious and undifferentiated as that of fruit. Worse still, I soon found myself eidetiking involuntarily, acting out aggression.

At school Holland, an arrogant and self-satisfied boy, moved to cut me off from the clique in which I had gained some slender acceptance. For two or three days I stalked the woodblock corridors choked with self-pity. Then, caught unawares, I found myself eidetically slamming his gullet against the sharp jam of the classroom door. The vacuum-nozzle ridging of his slashed oesophagus was far more revolting than anything I could have invented. In some lawless and incomprehensible way, although the material, the embodied, Holland was walking free, whistling and swearing, what I had seen had to be real.

Because of these outrages I found myself, once again, feeling marginalised, cut out from the herd. I sought frantically for methods of controlling my gift, ways of staving off chaos. I became certain that if I didn't do something I might be sucked out of the fuselage of reality altogether and sent rolling and tumbling into the void.

I found salvation in the development of personal rituals. And I would guess that, even had he not rumbled in another way, Mr Broadhurst would have soon spotted what I was up to merely because of my total self-absorption that autumn and winter.

I had no guidelines for these rituals, so they were a creative act on my part – possibly my most creative ever.

I devised a galaxy of interleaved physical and mental acts that it was necessary for me to perform throughout the day.

They went all the way from the sublime to the mundane, from the profound to the ridiculous. It became vital for me to piss, belch, wank and shit in a certain manner, while exercising my way through mental scales.

The feelings that people had for me I now saw as ductile things, influenced not just by daisy petals (love and love not in a circle of deceit), but by the number on a bus: if it's a 14 everything will be all right between us, and if it's a 74 the terminus is here.

All of these rituals were important. In perfecting them I glimpsed the many versions that were packed into my one thin reality. I toyed with travel to distant worlds, I even thought of sliding down the spiral banister of time itself.

The purely bodily rituals were the most important. They were crucial if I was to avoid eidetiking myself, with all that that would imply. I was terrified that I might inadvertently compose a view of my own body and then unpack my sense of it from within. Can you imagine a worse torment? No, somehow I doubt it. These rituals were also designed to keep off prying eyes. There might be others like me, similarly endowed. Like any self-conscious boy I had a horror of being seen naked in the changing room, or someone catching an up-and-under view of my snub-snot nose. I was not going to be used as another's plaything.

While it's true that some of the rituals I devised were aimed at empowering me in ways that were not natural, I hardly ever used them. I developed them in response to normal adolescent hungers, for peer-group acceptance, parental approval and the like. When things did go wrong – as with Holland – I resorted to wish-fulfilling pictorial violence, but left the will to power of truly dark ritual right out of it.

My more fantastical rituals need not bother us here, concerned as they were with things that we know to be impossible, or at any rate beyond the reach of a Sussex boy in the early seventies. Although the time-travel rituals are of some interest, for my eidetic skill was at least a form of temporal manipulation. This I realised when I found that it didn't matter how long I roamed in my visual fugues, I always returned directly to the appropriate now. Of course this was not time-travel *per se*, more like time-tailoring, the insertion of a pleat or a flare into the apparently straight leg of time, but it was a beginning.

We come now to the thought-rituals, and if I have had difficulty retaining your credulity so far I may hope now to regain it. By thought-rituals I mean simply those systemised patterns of thought that go with wishing, hoping and desiring. Surely it is these little mental ticks that keep us all functioning, growing, adding rings to our trunks? They are formulae of the kind: Think X and Y will occur – or indeed vice versa: Think Y and X will not occur. Magic formulae. We all have the queasy sense that an all-seeing eye is poised in the best of all possible vantages, whilst we inhabit the worst of all possible worlds; and although we may admit that rationally these mental habits cannot work, nevertheless we cannot abandon them, nor our faith in them.

So much for the rituals. I developed them – as I say – to ward off the intimations of chaos that came along with my revived eidetiking, and I developed them very quickly. Within a month of the Roedean incident most of this schema was in place. That is why my encounter with Mr Broadhurst, the first of his new dispensation, happened as it did.

It was a leaden, autumnal Sunday afternoon; I was standing on the beach beneath Cliff Top. I had come down the concrete stairs with great care, pacing myself according to an arithmetic progression of my own devising. I was silently incanting, running through the chants that I felt certain would exorcise my humiliating spirits. Seaweed and empty detergent bottles garnished my hush-puppied feet. Suddenly I was conscious of having someone with me, standing right next to me. I started and turned to see Mr Broadhurst, but he was only just descending to the beach and at least four hundred yards away.

'Ah! There you are, Ian,' he bellowed. 'I've been looking at you, so I thought I would come and find you.' The words issued directly from his chest, as if a loud hailer had been set into his ample bosom. I was struck immediately by two things. Firstly, the fluidity of his movements as he came rolling across the shingle towards me. It revived the suspicion I had had that, as I was growing older, Mr Broadhurst had acquired a second wind, or at any rate ascended to a physiological plateau where the ageing process was stilled. When he first came to live at Cliff Top he had complained constantly about the walk to the shops, how the wind and rain seemed to drive right through him, how the winter chill played havoc with his rheumatism. I had only ever observed him making longer forays on his Tuesday and Thursday trips to St Dunstan's and these, he claimed, took it out of him grievously. So much so that he had to spend most of the rest of the time 'recuperatin''. I had often seen him, deep in recuperation, lying across the great white bed in his caravan. A Cumberland sausage of a man, the lurid colours of the television reflected on his wide screen of a face.

The second thing was his suit, which was a rather snappy hound's-tooth-check item cut fiendishly tight. As I have remarked, Mr Broadhurst's habitual clothing was that of an unsuccessful undertaker. To see him dressed smartly, if archaically, was shocking.

'Mmm-mm!' he exclaimed, drawing in a big gout of air and then noisily expelling it through his nose. 'That does me good. I always miss the seaside when I'm hidden away from it during the summer.' I was shocked. Why was he doing this, alluding so shamelessly to the on season? Did he want me to ask him where he had been? Since his earlier embargo on the subject I had often tried to imagine where it was that Mr Broadhurst might go, but all the likely alternatives seemed inconceivable. Mr Broadhurst naked on some foreign beach? Mr Broadhurst photographing the Taj Mahal? Mr Broadhurst's relatives? Even I couldn't form the flimsiest mental pictures of the on-season Mr Broadhurst. He was such a conspicuously self-contained person, so poised in the moment. I found it easier to think of him as temporarily entombed in some salty cavern under Cliff Top itself, in a state of suspended animation from Easter through to late September.

Before I could take the unfamiliar mental steps necessary for framing such a probing question he had run on. 'I was up St Dunstan's yesterday, lad, and the Director asked me to clear out some of the old files, you know, defunct paperwork and such. While I was so engaged I came across these.' He pulled a buff file from the inside of his tightly buttoned jacket. 'They're yours, aren't they? I wager that you are an eidetiker, like me, aren't you, boy?'

I took the folder gingerly from his banana-bunch hand and opened it. The drawings were the ones I had done for Mr Bateson. They looked familiarly unfamiliar, like some solid form of *déjà vu*. The personal histories of children have that quality, don't they? They seem only slenderly moored to their possessor, on the verge of drifting away and tethering themselves to another.

'Y-y-yes . . . I s'pose so. I . . . I haven't thought about it for so long. It isn't important.'

'Isn't important!' he roared. 'Come, boy, don't cheek me, we both know just how important it is.' To emphasise this point Mr Broadhurst ground one of the plastic bottles with a foot-long foot inside a two-ton shoe. It rackled against the pebbles.

'What I mean, Mr Broadhurst, is that I don't use it, I don't do drawings any more. I'm not even going to do art for O level, it's not one of my options.'

'O level? Oh, I see what you mean, school certificate. No, no, that's not what I meant at all. What these drawings represent is nothing but the merest of gimmickery, freakish carny stuff. Any of us who has real potential soon leaves off turning tricks for psychologists. After all, it is not we who are the performing dogs, but they. No, no, I mean pictures in here.' Mr Broadhurst tapped the side of his head, forcefully, with his index finger, as if he were requesting admission to his own consciousness.

I was chilled. How much could he know? Did he suspect the uses to which I had put my over-vivid pictorial imagination? Could he perhaps have seen my projected form, hovering through the portals of Roedean? How humiliating.

But Mr Broadhurst said nothing to indicate that he knew. Instead he took the folder of eidetic drawings away from me, tucked them back inside his jacket and invited me to tea in his caravan.

'Come, lad,' he said. 'We will take tea together and speak

of the noumenon, the psi and other more heterogeneous phenomena. Behave yourself, comport yourself any more than adequately, and I may be prepared partially to unpack the portfolio of my skill for your edification. Naturally this will be nothing compared with the full compass of my activities, but it will suffice to be, as it were, an introductory offer.'

So began my apprenticeship to Mr Broadhurst. So began, in a manner of speaking, my real life. I had crossed the abyss and henceforth nothing would be the same again. In between *The Big Match* and *Songs of Praise*, time turned itself inside out, the loop became a Möbius strip and I was condemned for ever to a life of living on the two sides that were one. Suitable really that this extreme occurrence should be meted out thus: measurable by televisual time.

Many years later, grown up and employed in the marketing industry – like my father before me – I wonder whether or not this could be construed as some kind of Faustian pact? How else can I explain my utter enslavement to the man? But this could not have been. No thirteen year old, untouched by religion – Monist or Manichean – and merely browsing in the secular snack bar, could have known enough even to frame such a possibility.

No, the truth was more disturbing. Mr Broadhurst got me, got me at just the right time. Got me when I was still prey to aimless washes of transcendence, when my consciousness still played tricks with me, when I was a voodoo child who could stand up against the Downs and chop them down with the edge of my hand. Then he played me carefully like a fish, reeling me in slowly to the truth about himself. Slowly and jokily. Rewarding me with commonplace tricks, displays of prestidigitation and telekinesis, against small tasks, errands that I could do for him.

Remember, gentle reader (I say 'gentle' but what I really mean is pusillanimous reader, guarded reader, reader walled off against darker suasion), that this boy was like a roll of sausage meat enfolded in fluffy pastry. I had no access to the world of male empowerment. I had no role model. Mr Broadhurst was the solution to this deficiency. Remember also that he was a fixture of the off season, for me naturally conjoined with the worlds of school, formalised friendship, wanty-wanty and getty-getty.

However, that particular afternoon we just had tea together and played eidetic games. It didn't take very long for Mr Broadhurst to prise my secret out of me.

'You do what you say? You do that? Oh how very clever, how terribly droll!' The interior of his caravan was capacious enough, but even so Mr Broadhurst turned it into a doll's house. When he moved the whole chassis whoozed on its sprung suspension. 'And you say that you discover things, boy – things that you could not have known otherwise. Why, you are a bonny little scryer and no mistakin'. Now see here.' He unbuttoned his lurid check jacket to reveal a lurid check waistcoat. 'Shut your peepers and give me a demo'. Tell me what I've got in the top pocket of my weskit.'

I shut my eyes. I stared at the frozen image of Mr Broadhurst. I projected myself forward, my eidetic body detached from my physical body, its outline dotted to aid the registration of this figurative tear. I floated thus, across the four feet of intervening space. My invisible fingers, devoid of sensation, plucked at the furred lip of his waistcoat pocket. Mr Broadhurst sat, impassive, his eyes unblinking, his countenance was Rameses stern. I peeked inside the pocket, there was a gold watch coddled there. I had started to withdraw, to pack myself back into the correct perspective, when something happened. Mr Broadhurst – or rather my petrified vision of him – moved. This had never happened before; it was the utter stillness of my eidetic images that gave them their purely mental character. I snapped my eyes open, numbed by surprise, and heard Mr Broadhurst, the real Mr Broadhurst, the thick flesh and cold blood Mr Broadhurst, roaring with delight.

'By Jove, boy, you are a card and no mistakin' that! A genuine card. I should not have credited it had I not seen it with my own eyes. Now then, are you sitting comfortably?' I found that I was – back on the padded banquette, the cool glass of the caravan window feeling less vitrified than my shattered head pressed against it – and nodded my assent. 'Well then, what's that you have in your hand?' I felt it at once, how could I have not done so before? It was Mr Broadhurst's full hunter, flat, cold and gold. I goggled at it, uncomprehending. He roared again. 'Ha-ha! Well, well, there you are, an artful little dodger. Had me watch and me sitting here oblivious. Well I never, now that is a thing, isn't it?' And I had to concur, although I had no idea how it had happened.

I knew that this was something I shouldn't talk to my mother about. I knew without having to ask that Mr Broadhurst would wish me to remain silent. I wasn't mistaken, for the following day, batting a tennis ball with my hand against the side of the shower block, I was confronted by my mage.

'I popped in on your mother just now, Ian.' The big man was back in his undertaking get-up; a brown-paper parcel fastened with string was wedged under his torso-sized arm. 'We chatted of this and that, of mice – as it were – and their close relations, men. Your mama was as amiable as ever.'

'Good.'

'More to the point, however, she had nothing to say to me concerning the events that transpired between us yesterday afternoon.'

'I didn't mention them to her.'

'That's good, my lad, very good. You see, I like to talk to a man who likes to talk but I also like that man to be close-mouthed. I can see that you and I understand one another, and that's as it should be. For if I am going to teach you anything it must be on the basis of such an understanding: firm and resolute.'

'That's what I want to be, Mr Broadhurst, firm and resolute.'

'Good . . . good. Well then, I will see you anon.' And he was gone. His back, as broad as a standing stone, diminished through the twilight as he trudged back to his caravan.

CHAPTER THREE

THE FAT CONTROLLER

If one had to worry about one's actions in respect of other people's ideas, one might as well be buried alive in an ant heap or married to an ambitious violinist. Whether that man is the prime minister, modifying his opinions to catch votes, or a bourgeois in terror lest some harmless act should be misunderstood and outrage some petty convention, that man is an inferior man and I do not want to have anything to do with him, any more than I want to eat canned salmon.

Aleister Crowley, *Autohagiography*

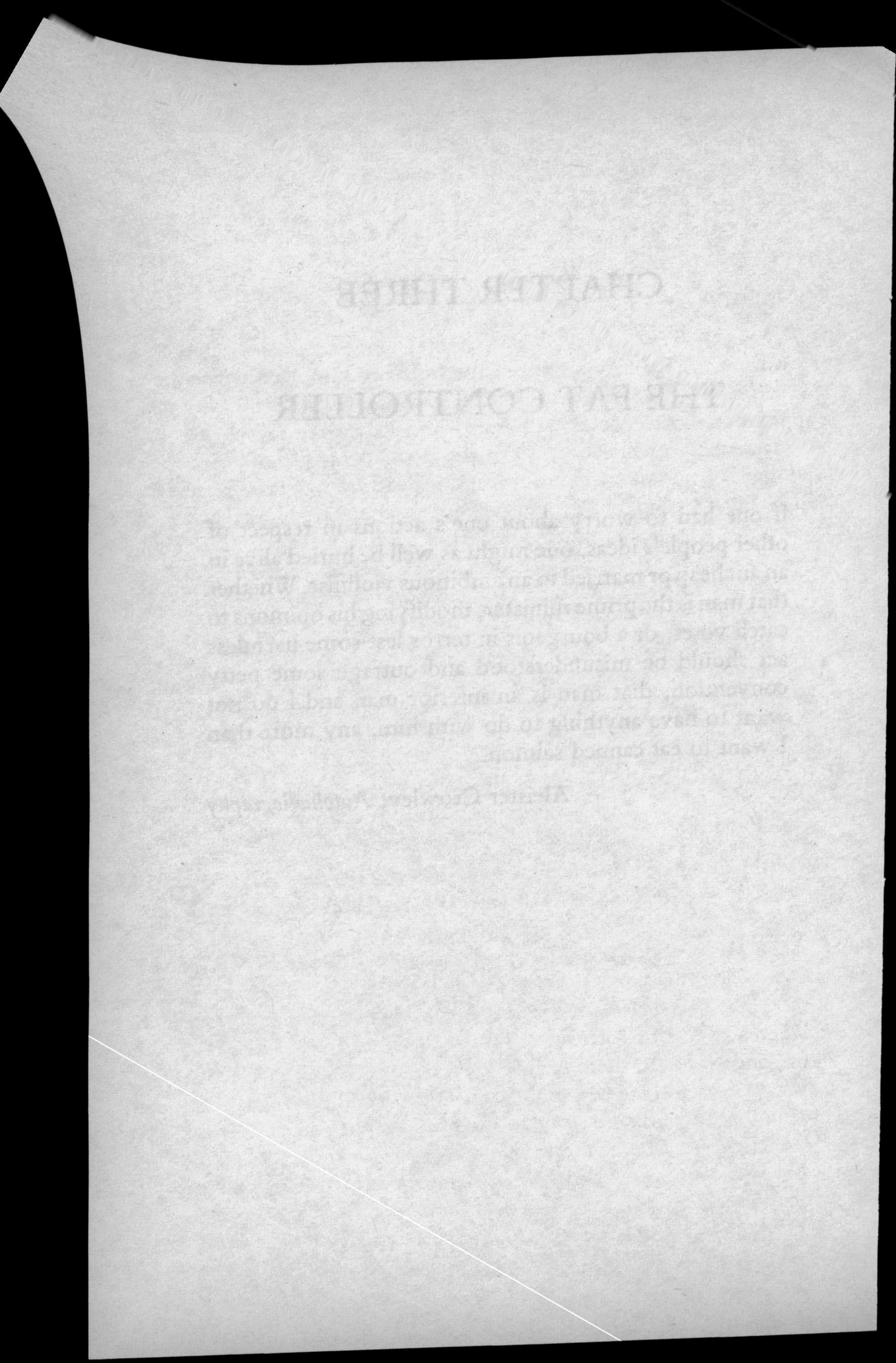

In the next week or so until I met up with him again I was suffused with wild imaginings. I braced myself for my apprenticeship to Mr Broadhurst. I anticipated the calling up of daemons, conversations with the dead, Anubis and Osiris joining the two of us for a ride on the ghost train at the Palace Pier. But Mr Broadhurst's instruction in the magical arts was not at all what I had expected.

Instead, having conducted a further searching examination, he set me to the cataloguing of the little rituals, those magical forms of thought that I myself had developed in order to cope with the stress of eidesis. Mr Broadhurst was very particular about nis and he took it extremely seriously. He met me after school and accompanied me to the newly opened branch of Smith's in Churchill Square. Here we purchased a large-format cash book, the kind with ruled columns. Back at Cliff Top over tea in his caravan, he set out the column headings for me thus:

Practice   Content   Frequency   Intent

and then explained what they meant. 'Now see here, boy.' He tapped the page. 'This first heading refers to the nature of what you do. Some rituals – the majority, indeed – are concerned with bodily functions. For example, the way you urinate. Do you aim at the commode, or at the water contained therein? How do you roll back your foreskin? What formulae do you recite to yourself when at stool? In what order do you cut your toenails? And so on, and so forth, there is no need for me to elaborate further, you understand me well enough . . .' Mr Broadhurst paused for a moment and then resumed. 'Incidentally, do you masturbate yet, boy?' I blushed. 'You do. Good, good. Had you not I would have lent you some instructional literature – onanism is, you see, terribly important, a most efficacious ritual.

'Naturally there are other kinds of practices that perforce can be described as ritualised. There are those concerned with the way we eat, the way we sleep and the way we open the door. There is even a ritual component to the way we walk down a street. Furthermore, there are rituals concertinaed within ourselves. I refer, of course, to manners of thought that have become formalised, certain convolutions, the consistent combination of apprehensions with little twistles of kinaesthetic intimation, d'ye follow me?'

No, I didn't follow him at all. Not only was the vocabulary well beyond me, but I couldn't even tell what my instructor was driving at.

'What I'm driving at, boy, is that, even when you become reacquainted with a part of your body, that meeting has its characteristic mental agenda. You think: My thighs, and attendant on that very "thighy" feeling is the acknowledgement: They are too plump and suck at surfaces sweatily – d'ye see?'

This time I did see because he had uncannily identified one of my private sources of shame and voiced my own concomitant mantra. Nevertheless I was confused. I still couldn't grasp that he understood the particular use I made of such 'consistent convolutions'. 'But, Mr Broadhurst, sir, all these things that I do and think, they're just habits, aren't they? I mean everyone does these things, don't they?'

He exploded. 'Don't be a booby, boy! I cannot abide a booby, not under any circs' 'soever. Of course these are habits, of course everyone does these things, that is not the point!'

His anger was unlike any other that I had known. It carried with it, implicitly, the threat of extreme retribution. Lines scoured on flesh in the penal settlement, or detention beyond the Styx. Ever afterwards when Mr Broadhurst barked – I jumped.

The point was – as he explained to me throughout that autumn and the winter that followed – to understand that habit was ritual, and ritual was habit.

'I am the Magus of the Quotidian!' bellowed Mr Broadhurst. We were promenading past the Metropole Hotel on the front at Brighton. I was amazed that nobody stared at us, or even shouted back. 'I am powerful precisely because I understand how habit trammels the mind's energy, d'ye see? All these people – ' he gestured wildly with a carpet roll of arm – 'they imagine that they perceive what is really there but they don't. Instead their minds are constricted by a million million common little assumptions, assumptions choking them like bindweed – and these they take for granted!

'But there is a way to break this down, to dissolve it – oh yes indeed – to unlock the Motive Force. Every time you indulge in an habitual act you bind yourself in with the others. These habitual acts are the rituals of sanity. More than that, they are sanity, d'ye see? And sanity is nothing but an emasculation, a dread deadening; and I won't have it! Oh no I won't!'

So it was that I set out laboriously to catalogue the very schema of my own sanity, to list exhaustively the full range of my personal habits. I did it, in fact, habitually, for forty-five minutes each day after I had done my homework. A typical listing would read as follows:

Practice	Content	Frequency	Intent
Bodily: nose-picking with semi-dried snot	Prise the hardened flakes away from the wall of the nostril	Variable, when bored every five minutes	To avoid nasal blockage

This was the kind of prosaic patterning of self-absorption that I knew would entrance Mr Broadhurst. But there were also other kinds of listing that had a more obviously magical significance, thus:

Practice	Content	Frequency	Intent
Mental: thinking that it will rain tomorrow	Carefully visualising the rainfall and imagining the drumming noise it makes on the bungalow roof	Most evenings	To try and prevent it raining

After about three months I had managed to fill the entire cash book with this sort of mundane rubbish. I say that now but at the time I took my task extremely seriously and I swelled with pride when Mr Broadhurst took me back to Churchill Square to buy my second book.

It was whilst working my way through this, often writing in the column headings for several pages in advance to give myself the illusion that I had completed more than I actually had, that two important suspicions that had lain dormant for some time rose up and took on the aspect of horribly credible hypotheses. I cannot say whether or not they impinged as much then as they seem to with retrospect. No matter how disturbingly accurate my visual memory may be, all-seeing is nowise all-hearing but suffice to say they were further indicators that the bridge over which I had crossed the abyss had been mined behind me.

Firstly there was the maternal complicity I have already spoken of. Mr Broadhurst was by now in the habit of picking me up from Varndean Grammar on Wednesday afternoons, accompanying me to Pool Valley, and then on home by bus. This was his midweek check-up, anticipating the full review of my homework on Sunday afternoons. (*The Big Match* to *Songs of Praise* slot had become institutionalised.) This routine became the focus for a certain amount of gossip. Gossip retailed by those selfsame people, the scions of higher platforms on the social scaffolding, who came for drinks at Cliff Top.

Without mentioning it to me Mother effectively torpedoed this submarine of rumour by putting it about that Mr Broadhurst was my guardian. The first I knew of this was when, seeing his bollard shape through the wrought-iron railings, my old humiliator Holland turned to me and said, placing predictably his malicious emphasis, 'There's your "guardian", Wharton, come to take you off for some wanky-wanky, as usual.'

A 'guardian' was a distinctly posh kind of relationship for me to have with anyone. Possibly my mother viewed the subterfuge as merely part and parcel of her continuing social climb. Could it be that, or was it more likely that she and Mr Broadhurst had agreed it between them? If so, what was in it for her?

My second hypothesis concerned Mr Broadhurst himself. I couldn't be certain, not having observed him closely before, but either Mr Broadhurst was not like other old people, or else he wasn't really old at all. In my new proximity to him I was able to see that his hands were neither wrinkled, nor dotted with liverish spots. When we walked together up the steep streets of Brighton Mr Broadhurst never wheezed. And, on looking into the lambency of his hooded eyes, I could detect no whiting-out, no glaucoma or cataract.

He still granted himself the licences of old age – even if he wasn't entitled. He had given up his voluntary work at St Dunstan's in November claiming that it was 'too fatiguin'' for him to carry on with. But be that as it may, he no longer moved with the calculated languor that I remembered. Instead he fairly hustled his big body along, as if it were a laggardly prisoner he was escorting down death row. He was growing feistier and spryer by the month – I wondered where it would all end.

Wondered as one Sunday in February at our appointed hour, I bearded him in his caravan. My ritual cataloguing had come to a halt. So feeble had my efforts become that my last entry was concerned with nothing less than my manner of dribbling.

'Good, good, very good!' exclaimed Mr Broadhurst – he was flicking through the second book. 'This is excellent, lad, and I do believe that this exercise is having a beneficial side-effect, namely an improvement in both your grammar and the general ordering of your still-immature intellect. This is all as it should be.'

'But I'm finding it harder and harder.'

'Harder? Harder to what?'

'To think up habits – I mean rituals.' I hung my head, glad to have a pretext to hide it from my mentor. For recently the random eruptions and scattered pustules that had decked my chin and brows for the past year had begun to mass, forming formidably ugly scarps and weeping lesions.

'Well, that's as may be, lad, although you haven't tackled masturbation yet, not properly at any rate.'

I blushed hard, Mr Broadhurst ignored me. I thought of my mother, she would probably be baking scones, her apron dusted with flour. Women in ugly hats would soon be Hosanna-ing on the telly. 'Erm . . . Mr Broadhurst . . . P'raps I should be – '

'Nonsense, lad. I can see that you're sensitive about this. Don't be. Masturbation is critical to our enterprise, for it connects the most repetitive and mindless of actions to the inducement of ecstasy. Now, I observe that you are shamed and discomfited by your acne – am I right?' I nodded. 'Of course I am. Now, you are too young to be aware of this but in the past there was held to be a linkage between so-called "self-abuse" and the sebaceous rigours of your time of life. I propose an advance on your future status that will assist you at this point and hold you fast to our mutual course. If I tell you that I can rid you of the damned spots will ye do what I say?'

I tried to think what I might be prepared to do to achieve this and concluded almost anything. I wasn't a brave boy, not physically, that is, but then it was unlikely Mr Broadhurst had anything physical in mind.

'OK, Mr Broadhurst, what should I do?'

'Excellent. You are amply fulfilling the weight of expectation I have placed on you. Now then, when you masturbate do you ejaculate semen?'

'Y-yes. I s'pose so.'

'Capital! I had feared that you might not be sufficiently developed. Pay attention. When you next indulge in self-stimulation, instead of summoning up the prone and panting form of some nymph of your fervid fancy, at the moment of climax I want you to contemplate your own dappled visage. Form a tight eidetic image of it, d'ye see? Then freeze it for as long as it takes. Can you do that? Of course, I know that you can. Collect your emission in a handy receptacle and then bring it here to me, yes? Got the photo? Capital! Capital!'

I returned to his caravan the following afternoon after school bearing my load, which was by then little more than a dusty stain on the inside of a beaker. Blushing, I handed it over.

'Is this all?' said Mr Broadhurst. 'Not much there but as long as you followed my instructions it will do.'

The big man arose from the bed and took a turn around the caravan, humming to himself. Then he opened one of the doors of the fitted cupboards. This was wholly unexpected. The interior of Mr Broadhurst's caravan had remained unchanged during the four years it had been sited at Cliff Top. The cut and blown glass ornaments were still set on their mirrored shelves in exactly the same positions as when he had unwrapped them. The miniature stainless-steel kitchenette looked as if it had never been cooked in. Mr Broadhurst's caravan was as unlived-in as an imaginary room constructed to display furniture in a department store.

Although I knew I probably shouldn't, I couldn't help looking as he rummaged through the marvellous things in the cupboard. Dusty robes hung from hooks. They were made out of silk and embroidered with dragons, butterflies, monkeys, each one an entire chinoiserie. On the various shelves were set items of laboratory equipment: retorts, beakers, distilling tubes and burners. These were jumbled together with what looked like pieces of electrical – or electronic – equipment, circuit boards, plasticised grips, LCD read-outs. There was also a stuffed fox and a human skull. Much more stuff was in there but Mr Broadhurst's buttocks, each the size of a chronic beer drinker's gut, obscured the rest.

When he turned to face me he held in his hand a small spherical flask with a tube coming out of it at an angle. He unscrewed the glass stopper to this receptacle, and, having filled my beaker with water, poured the solution into it.

He approached me across the marbled swirl of shag carpet, looking like a prelate pumped up with helium, and solemnly intoned, 'Now, lad, cup your hands, here comes the anti-chocolate.' I cupped my hands and Mr Broadhurst poured the fluid into my finger bowl. 'Repeat after me,' said the Magus of the Quotidian, 'I washed half my face – '

'I washed half my face – '

'In new semen soap – '

'In new semen soap – '

'For half a week – '

'For half a week – '

'The effects were shattering!'

'The effects were shattering!'

'Do it – wash your face!' I did as I was told. The watery fluid plashed against my cheeks; as it did so I felt a novel sensation, a sloughing, pulling and slipping of the skin. 'That's it, that's it,' he chided me. 'Rub it in well. Now . . . stop!' I left off having but didn't dare look at my hands.

'Look at your hands!' commanded Mr Broadhurst. I looked at them, they were smeared with blood and worse. I felt faint. He pulled a small mirror from his pocket and held it up to me. At first I simply couldn't comprehend what had happened, for all my spots were gone, dissolved, had vanished. Not only that but my face was unscarred, unpitted. It was as if the acne had never been.

Mr Broadhurst gave me to understand that this was merely another advance, another introductory offer, and that I shouldn't take it, or myself, too seriously. Nevertheless the ridding of my skin complaint by necromancy coincided with a shift in emphasis as far as my instruction was concerned. It was as if, having seen the contents of Mr Broadhurst's fitted cupboard, he were now prepared to allow me some knowledge of the rituals connected with this apparatus. Henceforth my studies diversified into tarot reading, numerology, Feng-shiu, alchemy, astrology and kabbalah, or at any rate into Mr Broadhurst's somewhat modified versions of these arts.

'It's all nonsense, you understand – utter bollocks. A pathetic attempt to use proto-scientific methods to ascertain and then apprehend the transcendent. What the Jung-lette called "a massive projection".' So said Mr Broadhurst. 'No matter, it will serve as a useful antidote to what they will try and inculcate you with at school, that's its chief virtue. And added to that, in the future – should you progress in your apprenticeship – it will provide you with a repertory of useful explanations. To use an analogy garnered from the world of espionage, it will give you "cover".'

He had a set of photocopied notes, which implied that I wasn't his first apprentice. These he would produce with a flourish during our Wednesday- and Sunday-evening sessions. There had always been something of the fairground barker about Mr Broadhurst and during this period he enhanced it. He waved his arms about a lot, wore suits that my mother's old friend Little Jimmy wouldn't have been ashamed to be seen in – barring the size problem – and generally did his best to appear flamboyant.

Each set of notes came with an attached exercise and at his behest I set to, to analyse squares of numbers, using keys to turn them into the letters that described either thaumaturgical entities, or else even the tetragrammaton itself. This had a beneficial side-effect, namely an improvement in my arithmetic. The tarot reading and astrology were presented by my mage at a fairly down-market level. To me, the disciplines involved in relating these random sequences of fixed symbols to potential destinies and character traits were an amusing game. The skill, once learnt, helped make me a little more popular and outgoing at school, where there was a craze on for such things.

As for kabbalah, I found it utterly incomprehensible. I might not have known exactly what rationalism was but it was nevertheless deeply engrained in my picture of the world. Mr Broadhurst browbeat me over it: 'I will have you know the ancient Hebrew art, its derivation and derogation, its eventual suppuration into the Rosicrucian, even if I have to badger you unmercifully – eurgh! Yuck! Ping!' This last noise occasioned by a solid pellet of his spittle hitting a brass spittoon.) For nowadays Mr Broadhurst toyed with either 'chawin'' (his own term) tobacco, or 'takin'' snuff. I didn't know which was worse – his snot or his flob.

I was forced to pay more attention to lessons in science and history at Varndean, purely so that I might better understand my other, shadowier tutelage.

As for Feng-shiu, although Mr Broadhurst declared it to be the most ridiculous of all these esoteric studies, it did help my geography. After all, how else can alignments of physical objects be calculated so as to lie along propitious meridians, save by reference to more fixed and less mutable properties of the earth?

Mr Broadhurst himself was something of an alchemist. 'Just an enthusiastic amateur, you understand, boy.' Some of what I had glimpsed on the afternoon when he excised my acne was his own miniature collection of alchemical equipment. He responded to my curiosity concerning the transmutation of metals by allowing me to assist him as he experimented with his alembic and his aludel. Many were the afternoons when I found myself priming the athenor with a set of little bellows, while Mr Broadhurst waved a caduceus about. It was one of his own devising, constructed from an old-fashioned television aerial wreathed with flexes. We looked on together as the various hypostatical principles were distillated and redistillated. We were equally disappointed when cohabitation was not effected.

But although he toyed with it, Mr Broadhurst had no patience with the search for the sophic hydrolith. 'I would wager, boy, that these types never managed to transmute anything, save for their stupidity, into vanity. And anyway, any form of currency is a mutable thing, capable of being magically imbued by the thoughts of those who utilise it. Although, that being said, I do myself possess one of Paykhull's medals.' He showed this to me and told me to note especially the inscription on the coin's obverse side: 'O.A. Paykhull cast this gold by chemical art at Stockholm, 1706.' 'You know, boy,' he mused as I hefted the heavy thing, 'these coins are excessively rare. I have no idea how I might have come by it. No doubt it will transpire that I must have known this Paykhull.'

It was from little hints such as this, undoubtedly consciously dropped, that I began to build a fuller appreciation of what Mr Broadhurst really was.

This was the way I passed through the remainder of my childhood. The zoetrope span smoothly, time's Chief Designer narrowed the legs of trousers and decreed that the cars should be more aerodynamic. If there were changes in the political leadership of the country, they made little impact on me. I was more preoccupied by my O levels. I gained seven and then, with Mr Broadhurst's none too gentle prodding, I opted for economics, maths and business studies as A level courses. At school I remained a solitary. What little human warmth I required I garnered from the aunts and cousins, who still came to Cliff Top for their annual holiday.

They still came but there was a new uneasiness in this

department of my life as well. My mother's business success had continued and the bungalow was in the throes of an ongoing transformation that would only end some five years later, when the Cliff Top Country House Hotel opened its register for bookings.

In the meantime, the aunts and cousins were put up in their usual caravans. My mother and I moved between the enterprise zone of the bungalow and the camp where the caravans squatted, adopting a different manner and diction as we did so. We were veritable chameleons of class mobility.

As for girlfriends, it was here that my eidetiking came in particularly useful. Trammelled by my exhaustive cataloguing of habit, which I had continued to practise at Mr Broadhurst's insistence, my visual escapades had become fully manageable. I didn't think I had an option – I was no teenage Lothario – but anyway I knew instinctively, without even having to ask him, that Mr Broadhurst would view the loss of my virginity as incompatible with my apprenticeship. So instead, I refined my masturbation in combination with my hawk-eyed recollection to produce a variety of sexual experience which – (I now realise) – more than compensated for the absence of the real thing.

My fellow schoolboys vied with one another for admission to the cinema, so that they could witness X-rated films. They went to see what they were unable to experience. I went to the cinema not for entertainment, but for cinematography. For it was only by studying the precise rake of extra-long pans, the trajectory of tracking shots and the jejune emotional appeal of the jump-cut, that I could add to the repertoire of my own internal shoots.

One day in the early autumn of my lower-sixth-form year, when the damp leaves were already furring the grassy median strips that cleaved the dual carriageways surrounding Varndean Grammar, I saw a familiar figure from where I sat reading in the school library. Mr Broadhurst had returned from his summer break.

I rammed my books and my binders into my briefcase. I took the steps in big bounds and pelted across the asphalt to the school gates. I knew better than to attempt to hug Mr Broadhurst, although that was what I felt like doing, for not only did everything in his manner discourage physical relations, he had also given me a strict injunction. Soon after he had taken me under his ample wing he had remarked, 'Think of me as the Brahmin of the Banal! Only the dull earth can purify me, contact with all else is a defilement so far as I am concerned. Therefore, boy, never attempt to touch me, save for when I specifically enjoin it.'

During the six months since I had last seen him, Mr Broadhurst had undergone a further metamorphosis and this time the change was more radical, more entire, than ever before. To start with there was his costume. As I have said, after the abandonment of his undertaking uniform he had gone through a dodgy bookie/snake-oil purveyor period. Now he was dressed very well indeed, even elegantly. He had on a three-quarter-length crombie with a velvet collar, a dark-blue suit with the faintest of pin-stripes and a snowy linen shirt. The knot of his foulard tie was held in place by a pearl stick pin. Up top, a bowler hat as firmly rounded as a Wehrmacht helmet served to emphasise the suitability of his head for Mount Rushmore, or any other monumentalism. In one of his hands chamois gloves were loosely bouqueted with the silver head of a cane; in the other a thick slab-sided cheroot, topped by an inch and a half of whitened ash, protruded from his knuckles.

As I ran towards him, Mr Broadhurst smiled. His smooth face was slashed open by his predatory mouth, as if an invisible hatchet were biting into fruit. The bony protuberances that he had in lieu of brows arched until they were Gothic; and he laughed – bellowed laughter and smoke.

'Ah, there you are!' he ejaculated, the implication being that he had looked everywhere. 'Come now, boy, we have much to talk of and little time.' I was now both tall enough and bulky enough to link arms comfortably with Mr Broadhurst. To my great surprise this was exactly what he did. And that is how we set off, arm-in-arm, down Sunningdale Drive past Sussex Gardens where the bowls players were dying slowly in well-pressed whites, towards the London Road. Mr Broadhurst held forth magniloquently.

'Consider the similarities between Brighton and Rome,' he

declared. 'Both are built on seven hills, both have been the pleasure centres of mighty empires. Observe the hilltops, lad what d'ye see?'

I pondered. 'Well, I can just about see the cemetery up there.'

'Quite so – and over there?' He gestured vaguely behind us.

'The racecourse?'

'Good lad, good. In fact, capital! The racecourse. The games of life and the games of death. Mortality for once defined by geography. What a relief!' He laughed again, carried away by his pun. I had never seen Mr Broadhurst in such a good mood before. He positively bowled down the pavement, puffing furiously on his stogie, for all the world like some bipedal locomotive.

'You're wondering something, boy, cough it up, spit it out, expel it, vomit it forth. In short, tell me.'

'Well . . . I don't . . . I don't know how to put it, but you seem somehow changed – '

'And you are wondering what has happened to cause this – am I correct? Of course I am, there is no need for you to elaborate. Well, sir, it's true, I have changed. I have eaten myself up and through some unprecedented act of gastromancy farted out my new incarnation – thus.

'You are also wondering something else – aren't you? You are curious as to whether there is some connection between this metamorphosis and my summer sojourn. Where do I go? That is the question. In due course I will answer it for you, that and many other things that I know have quizzed you these past years.'

So, as the two of us progressed, ascending, cresting and then descending three of the seven hills, Mr Broadhurst talked. And what talk it was! Rich and protean, his word-seam seemed to me to be the very fount of knowledge itself, a mulchy conceptual bed which might be sown merely by the fact of being listened to, thus engendering all ideas for all time.

'Reality,' said Mr Broadhurst, 'love it, hate it, you cannot do without it. Wouldn't you agree? Of course you would, for you cannot but do otherwise. And yet you, lad, are a perfect candidate for the role of skipper, suborner, seducer and traducer of that reality. Reality is a virgin whose virtue we all want to believe in, and, at one and the same time, an old whore who we've all had and had and had again, until our eyes and ears are like genitals that have been rubbed raw. We observe its regularities, its comings and goings through and in ourselves, yet we are unable to stand apart. At any rate you cannot stand apart, I cannot but do otherwise and that is why we belong together, d'ye see? Of course you don't, I will perforce have to demonstrate.'

As he declaimed we were weaving our way through the late-afternoon shoppers who thronged the centre of the town. Or rather, so magisterial was our progress that these less-solid citizens were being forced to weave in order to avoid our combined bulk. Suddenly Mr Broadhurst pulled up short, causing me to wheel around so that we were both facing the window of a toy shop.

The display in the shop window was an extravagant scenario designed to showcase a monster train set. A papier mâché scarp formed the backdrop and in the foreground engines pulling carriages and engines pulling trucks passed over hummocks, through tiny tunnels, and clattered into and out of plastic stations, never stopping, electronically hooting.

I stared at it, conscious of the big man's arm encircling mine with the coiled hunger of an anaconda about to ingest. Of all the eidetic images that remain from my childhood, frozen with crude representational accuracy, this is the most vivid. The trains moving with fluid inertia; the tiny plastic trees and buildings – their implausible neatness all too accurately complementing that *trompe-l'oeil* reality of which he had spoken; beyond the papier mâché horizon, the workings of a pocket deity were clearly visible in the brushstrokes of the painted sky. As I stared at the display, the reflections of myself and Mr Broadhurst in the plate-glass window came into focus as well, imposed over the vista. Eidesis came upon me trapping both layers into a third internal one. Then Mr Broadhurst seemed to start towards me and I could no longer be sure where he was, in my head, on the shop window or the pavement? In all three locations at once?

He spoke inside of me. 'Where am I, boy? Is that what you

want to know? Why, I am in all three places at once, that is the point, the whole of the point. Now look, look at the counterpane world, project yourself into it, look beside that bijou signal box. What can you see?'

Trying to ignore this assault on my fundamental antinomies I peered at the train set. A tiny, rotund figure was stamping up and down on the daubed green of the false ground, like a drunken redneck at a hoedown, or an aboriginal at a corroboree. It was Mr Broadhurst – and he was Hornby-size.

'I am The Fat Controller,' said the Mr Broadhurst in my eidetic vision. 'I control all the automata on the island of Britain, all those machines that bask in the dream that they have a soul. I am also the Great White Spirit that resides in the fifth dimension, everything is connected to my fingertips – by wires.'

We were walking once more. We crossed the traffic that divided around the Clock Tower and entered the Lanes. Soon we were alone, moving through a narrow defile between two teetering antique shops. Here, Mr Broadhurst broke step again, this time wheeling me around to face him.

'What is my name, lad?'

I was nonplussed, I stared at my teacher, never before had his swollen face seemed so replete with indifference, stone ataraxy. 'Ah . . . erm . . . Mr Broadhurst, sir?'

'Wrong!' An open palm, as big and fattily solid as a Bradenham ham, smote the side of my head with horrific force. I fell to my knees, immediately aware of the sticky saltiness of blood in my saliva. 'Come on, Ian – don't disappoint me – answer the question.'

'Y-you . . . you are . . . you are The Fat Controller?' I whimpered. I was certain, although I could not have said why, that if I did not answer correctly this might well be the end.

'Good, good. Well done . . . Capital!' The Fat Controller was helping me to my feet. 'I'm glad we cleared up that little problem. Some might say, "What's in a name?" but then I doubt an arsehole would smell so sweet. Now, lad, you were curious earlier as to my movements and my changed countenance. The fact of it is that my five years are now up and hence my retirement is over. Before Christ's mass I will be gone, back into the world.

'And how have I been spending this summer? Why, in refamiliarising myself with what-goes-on. These past five years my pernicious enfeeblement has meant that six months of the year I have had to hibernate, to entomb myself in the disused redoubt beneath Cliff Top, but at last I am free. Free to smell again the sweat on the brow of the bourse; free to bask in the slipstream of wide-bodied jets; free to sit in on the counsels of the alleged good and the alleged great.

'I have cantered among the hyenas of the Serengeti as they brought down *wildebeeste*; I have danced the Wellington Boot Dance with the Zulu in the township hostels; I have tiptoed through the Bibliothèque Nationale, listening to the gummy gumming of mundane scholars; I have shelled prawns with slant-eyed androgynes in the polyglot souks of the uttermost East; I have reached the nadir of a nonsensical number of psycho-sexual trances, both in the Amazonian hinterland and the plastic cultures of the Pacific rim; I have subsumed myself to the circuitry of artificial cerebella in the silicone wadis; I have crawled down the barrels of guns on all five continents, only to spring forth again – triumphant; I have tittered in the stalls and tottered by the walls festooned with epicene opera-lovers; I have sallied forth into the salons of the old world and the new; I have hefted steins in the beerhalls and pinched flutes in the Shires; I have raced laggardly protons around the cyclotron, revelling in the sempiternal sciamachy; and – let us not forget – I have also hidden under couches whilst the moneyed pulers petted their kittenish neuroses, imagining themselves trusted, secluded.

'To cut these many stories short, to tie a knot of reminder in this multifarious narrative: I have reacquainted myself with my domain. And now – let's eat.'

We ate at Al Forno, an Italian restaurant at the bottom of the Lanes. I was subdued after the preprandial violence. Subdued and also cowed by The Fat Controller's manner of consummate self-assurance. This was no longer a slightly eccentric seaside retiree with a portfolio of amusing tricks. He had become something other, or worse still, perhaps he had always been.

As soon as we entered the restaurant the proprietor came out to us from the kitchen, rubbing his hands oilier on a tea towel.

'Ah! Meester Northcliffe,' he trilled – and it was a measure of my disorientation that I took this further name-change in my faltering stride. 'We no see you for an age. Why you no come to Al Forno? Youse find someone who makes a better pizza?'

'Tommaso, how could that be so?' The Fat Controller was emollient, masterful. 'You make the finest pizzas on the Sussex coast – haven't I always said that? No, no, I have been away on business for these past few months.'

'And who is this, your son?' Tommaso gave me three-quarters of an ingratiating smile and The Fat Controller's good humour increased by a factor of nine. His trunk swelled up to resemble that of a baobab tree, matching for bulk the whitewashed curvature of the charcoal oven that dominated the restaurant. His voice boomed, 'Haha, ahahaha, no, no, more like a grandson, I should say, but it's good of you to be so shamelessly flattering – to him.' Then his good mood evaporated so entirely that it might never have been. 'Jump to it, boy! Bring us two litres of that vile Chianti and four of your large specials – we'll be upstairs.'

We climbed up a twisting staircase past two floors of tables and then took our place in the bay window on the top floor. In due course Tommaso himself brought the wine. The Fat Controller poured me a glass.

'Stick that in your laugh-hole,' he said. 'You're past the age when you can be forgiven for not holding your liquor. So pour it down your neck.' I did as I was told.

The 'special' turned out to be a cartwheel-sized pizza like a slice of the earth's crust, its five feet of rim volcanically erupting. On top of it there were all the fruits of the forest, the animals of the plain, and a few of the beasts of the sea for good measure. Everything was enmired in thick globs of mozzarella cheese. The Fat Controller ate three of these and I did my best to tackle the fourth. I was stunned by this prodigious feat of consumption. I remembered Mr Broadhurst-that-was mopping up the Sally Lunns but that was a mere warm-up exercise compared to this.

When as a child I had alluded to Mr Broadhurst's corpulence, my mother had snapped at me. 'It's a disability, Ian, like any other. Mr Broadhurst has glandular problems, that's why he's overweight. He doesn't eat any more than ordinary people.' As she spoke I had eidetiked the glands in question, embedded in the back of Mr Broadhurst's neck like obese sweetmeats.

'You're thinking about my glands, aren't you, boy?' The Fat Controller's voice sluiced me out of my wine haze. He was dissecting a gland-like mushroom as he spoke, clearly in order to illustrate his telepathy. 'The only reason people are fat,' he went on, 'is because they eat too much. After all,' he continued, deftly manipulating half a loaf of garlic bread to sop up the tomato juice on his last platter, 'you never saw anybody fat come out of Auschwitz.'

It was two beats before I realised that this was meant to be a very funny joke and then I struggled to match his guffaws, adding my own rather reedy piping to his basso mirth.

He went on to discourse at length on the nature of fat. He reviewed a gallery of the great fatties of all time, from Nero through Falstaff to Arbuckle. He dwelt especially on the insulating and prophylactic properties of excessive flesh, remarking at one point, 'Without the upholstery of embonpoint the body is a mere skeletal spring, ready to uncoil its very mortality.' He brushed up my biochemistry, informing me that the long chain fences of fat molecules are antipodean in scale set beside the dry stone walls of mere proteins, and that he himself had it as an ambition to contrive that his entire body should be sheathed in one enormous fat molecule. He concluded by reviewing the sexual properties of portliness, noting that, if you are fat enough, you can develop love-handles specially adapted for oral sex, as well as coitus.

During our meal the restaurant had begun to fill up with the pre-theatre crowd, Brighton burghers and their wives. I saw them through The Fat Controller's eyes – they were gauche and dowdy, crammed into suitings so ill-fitting that they looked like bolsters stuffed into pillow cases. They spoke quietly, deliberated over the menu and drank their wine in sips, like dipping birds. One of these types now rose from her chair and came over to where we were sitting. Our coffee had just arrived.

'Excuse me,' she said hesitantly.

'No,' snapped The Fat Controller. He didn't even look up, he was doing something with the cafetière. I gawped at the woman.

The rebuttal had done her no good whatsoever, her face was going blotchy, but she mustered all the sang-froid she could and continued, 'Since you refuse to be civil I shall not moderate my criticism. I didn't want to embarrass you in front of your grandson – '

'He's not my grandson, he's the son of the woman I lodge with – '

'Be that as it may, perhaps he would like to know that you have completely disrupted our meal. Your voice is as loud as it is insistent and, as if that weren't bad enough, what you speak of is as boring as it is unseemly. You are without exception the rudest man it has ever been my misfortune to share a restaurant with; and I think I can speak for all the others present when I say that.'

Without waiting for The Fat Controller's reaction to all this, she turned and went back to her own table, where she was greeted with little 'Well done's and furtive shoulder pats from her fellow diners.

The Fat Controller sat stock still while this woman had her say, like someone engaged in a sporting activity that has been temporarily frozen, prior to a replay on behalf of inattentive home viewers. I observed him warily, waiting for the outburst I felt certain was infusing along with the coffee, but he remained impassive and finished the meal by stoically downing a litre or so of the espresso blend, a large tin box of Amaretti di Saronno and eight grappa. He added the bill with a single saccade of his pulsing eyes. It was the first display of his own eidetic abilities I had ever witnessed; before that all his efforts in this respect had been directed at infiltrating my internal visual world. Foolishly, I took it as a good sign.

We walked out into the doldrums of early evening. The Chianti had gone to my head a little but I was a big lad and had done my share of experimenting with alcohol before, so the intoxication wasn't too hard for me to handle. His gargantuan repast seemed to have put The Fat Controller in a better mood and avuncularity seeped back into his tones the further we got away from the pizzeria.

'There are two reasons why I wanted to be sure that I met up with you after school today.' He paused to light the green-brown dirigible of a Partagas perfecto with a flickering windproof lighter. 'You will have guessed the first,' he resumed, masticating the thick coils of smoke, 'namely that I wished to inculcate you a little further in the understanding of my true nature, a little further but not too far – keep 'em guessing is my motto. My other reason was that I wanted to have an opportunity for a more leisurely chat with you about your future.'

'My future?'

'Quite so. In the absence of your having a father who is disposed to take any interest in you – if indeed he is still alive – I find that I am, as it were, in *locus pater*. Not a prospect that I relish. My values, my methods, indeed my very understanding of the world, is not, as you know, conventional. Nevertheless, I have as much of a need to hand my legacy on to someone as any biological parent. Your unusual ability for mental imaging marks you out in this context. I have decided – at least pro tem – to enhance your relationship with respect to me, from the purely formal one of "apprentice", to the potentially more intimate designation "licentiate". Do you know what that means?'

'No.'

'So much the better, be sure to look it up when you get home.'

We entered the public gardens that surround the Royal Pavilion. In the autumn twilight the great building appeared simultaneously shoddy and grandiose. The Fat Controller looked more at home in this context than I could ever imagine him to have been at Cliff Top, or anywhere else for that matter. There was something of the Regency dandy in the way he trailed his cane and rotated his globular head, as if looking out for fellow beaux to salute. Moreover the fluted columns, caryatid gateways and golden domes of the Pavilion suggested to my adolescent self a world of ambiguous pleasures involving him, which I had to suppress my tipsy mind from visualising.

Why 'The Fat Controller'? I thought to myself. Why not 'the Fat Controller'?

'It's important that you capitalise the definite article – even in thought – you understand me?'

'Y'y'yes,' I spluttered, amazed once again by the accuracy of his telepathic probing. We banked to the left, following the precisely plotted curve of a bed of flowers, which had been arranged to form a living mosaic of the municipal crest.

'Fancy a trip to the theatre?' The question was close to being a statement.

'I'd – I'd love to,' I said. And then, quite suddenly, I recognised the people who were walking in front of us through the gardens. It was the complaining woman from Al Forno together with her party. I started talking hurriedly, hoping to distract my companion. I was desperate to prevent the angry outburst that I had expected in the restaurant happening here, in this even more public place.

I said, 'I want to go to university,' although, in truth, up until that moment the desire had been incubating, only half-formed in my mind. 'I'm interested in . . . Well, I'm interested in sorts of things – '

'Sorts of things? What d'ye mean, boy?'

'Well, like products. All the different kinds of products. How you persuade people to buy this sort of thing rather than that sort of thing.' This much was true, that I often found myself in my mother's kitchen staring at the array of condiments, spices, herbs and tinned foods, wondering why she should have bought this particular kind of split peas, rather than another. It was all incomprehensible to me; and since I had begun to study economics the Marginal Theory of Preference only served to deepen my confusion. For, in a world of such demonstrable irrationality, how could there be a predictable quantification of choice? Since the resumption of my mother's upwardbound course in social orienteering, her purchasing patterns had undergone a profound change. She now cooked with garlic, took an interest in wine and spoke of fricassees rather than fry-ups.

Things had always attracted me, far more so than people. As a small child I had known all the words of Masefield's poem, 'Quinquireme of Nineveh from distant Ophir/Rowing home to haven in sunny Palestine . . .' Then the cargo was described in loving detail, the sandalwoods and spices, the ivory, the oil, the wine. I was entranced.

'Haha. Ahahaha . . . indeed, that is very interesting. Entirely germaine. Well, you shall go to the university if you wish it.' The Fat Controller sounded uncharacteristically mummyish. 'My plans for you are more in the manner of an agency. I do not intend to intrude on your life, or impinge in any direct manner. It is merely my desire that you complete your studies and take up a form of employ that may be useful for my purposes at some time in the future. Other than that I wish to make no claims upon you.' He paused, the butt of his cigar held against his brow, so that a cataract of white spume dribbled down into his eye socket. The eye behind it remained unblinking. 'And come to think of it, this isn't so dissimilar to the kind of influence your genetic father might wish to have on you, were it not for the fact that he is such a contemptible Essene, a cloistral nonentity capable of only the meanest interaction with his fellow men. You know, of course, how he spends his time?'

'No, not really. I haven't seen him for three years or so. Mum told me that he travels up and down the coast by bus, reading in public libraries.'

'Quite so. And how does that make you feel?'

'Oh, I don't know – '

'Correction: you do know. It makes you feel ashamed and embarrassed. It is as much due to his neglect as my intervention that you find yourself thus, cut off from normal society. Were I inclined to a sense of responsibility, this factor alone would go no small way towards vitiating it. Still, no mind, here we are at the theatre. And there, if I am not mistaken, is the ignoramus who was so agressively rude to us at Al Forno.'

'I'm, I'm not quite sure, is it?' I was hoping that my indecision might somehow communicate itself to The Fat Controller. No such luck.

'Oh yes, it is,' he said with heavy emphasis. 'I should imagine that you are worried – worried that I might cause some sort of scene, humiliate you in front of this jetsam.' He gestured, encompassing with his shovel-sized hand the precincts of the Theatre Royal which bustled with people, and the roadway where backing and filling vehicles jockeyed for temporary respite. 'That's not my style, Ian – you should realise that I set great store by not creating "scenes"; by not making those that I esteem suffer any unnecessary discomfort, whether it be social, physical, or otherwise.'

With that we swept past the woman and her friends and entered the theatre. The Fat Controller had reserved good seats at the front of the stalls. I refused the offer of an ice-cream but he bought an extra-large cone for himself and then, once we were seated, inserted the whole thing, wafer and all, into his mouth.

'Nyum-nyum,' he said. 'I love the cold ache, the frozen hammering on the . . . nyum-nyum . . . insides of my temples. Little Peter Quince thought this a symptom of facial neuralgia, or worse, a precursor of the hydrocephalus that carried off his sister . . . nyum-nyum . . . Puling neurasthenic, used it to justify his laudanum binges. Still, I warrant I must be hydrocephalic anyway, or at any rate inoculated against swollen-headedness, eh?'

I nodded, although I had absolutely no idea what he was talking about.

We sat in silence while the rest of the audience trickled in. His ice-cream finished, The Fat Controller began to shift around uncomfortably in his seat, puffing and blowing. Eventually he said, 'This is no good. I can't get comfortable. We shall have to try and swap seats with someone so that I can put my feet in the aisle.'

The couple at the end of the row happily switched with us and we settled down once more. However, as soon as we reached our new vantage I understood the real reason why he had wanted to move. The seats we now occupied were directly behind those of the complaining woman and her companions.

'Serendipitous, eh?' he said, and leered at me through the artificial gloom, his rubber lips curling up. 'We shall have an opportunity now to balance things up a little – would you like that?'

'I'm not sure,' I dissimulated.

'Come, lad, now is the time for you to make up your mind. I have spent a deal of time these past few years on cultivating you, submitting you to a species of metaphysical topiary, clipping, pruning, stunting. I have made no secret of the fact that I consider you to be a boy with potential, a boy I might introduce to some of the wonderful things of this world. Be that as it may, I shall be philosophic if you prove unworthy of this not inconsiderable investment – I can always write it off as a little deficit financing – but if you wish to continue with our relationship you must be prepared to place some real trust in me. Without it I cannot proceed.' As he was talking I noticed something peculiar. Although his tones were conversational – and in his case this naturally meant loud – none of the people in the adjacent seats seemed to be able to hear him. Once again he was addressing my consciousness directly, speaking straight into my inner ear without any sound escaping into the atmosphere.

'People are not all alike – would you grant me that?' His tone was now pedagogic.

'S'pose so.'

'S'pose so is not quite good enough. The point is, my young friend, that we have certain duties, not in respect of others, but ourselves. We cannot permit the foisting of indignities upon our person without some form of retribution.' He held the tip of his cane an inch away from the complaining woman's head. 'This woman here is not a moral agent in the same sense that I am, or that you will become. Her moral responsibilities are not ours and therefore nor are her rights commensurate. I, on the other hand, am in possession of powers which to the man in the street would appear awesome, inhuman, perhaps even godlike. Naturally along with these powers comes an enhanced moral capability.'

While he spoke the auditorium fell silent. At first a few individuals left off talking, then this engendered a positive feedback, more people heard the gathering soundlessness and responded to it so that whole tiers shut up. Eventually there was complete quiet. The house lights went down and the small posse of hack musicians who slouched in the orchestra pit began to saw indifferently at their instruments.

The curtain rose disclosing a set which for strident artificiality compared favourably with the train display in the toy shop. The layering of the paint on the backdrop was clearly visible; the rambling roses were plastic and immobile; the front of the stage was spread with a swathe of fruiterer's mock grass. There was a hiss over the PA, followed by the chirruping of recorded birdsong. I consulted the programme and discovered that what I was regarding was the rose garden of an English country house, *circa* 1922. A woman entered stage left. She was young and wore a dress that flared out around her calves. Her head was shrunken under a tight-fitting felt hat. She commenced to promenade up and down the stage, punctuating her remarks with hammy gestures of her *lorgnette* and preposterously long cigarette holder.

The play was a farce. Not that this mattered a great deal to me. I was aware that the threshold of the audience's suspension of disbelief lay far below mine; and that the aching gap between the supposed humour of the script and their exaggerated response was minuscule when set beside that which already separated my reality from theirs. I could also appreciate that the bulk of this supposed humour was meant to derive from the anachronism of the play's sexual mores. But these were only peripheral apprehensions, for the bulk of my attention was occupied by The Fat Controller's mesmerising amoral discourse.

'When I wish to kill – I kill.' The voice was lubricious, polite but insistent. 'And nothing that people say or do can detract from this. Fortunately I am not driven to this expedient that often, because I have many other stratagems that I have devised for attaining the same object. But every so often, such as now, killing does seem the best possible option. Observe the ferrule of my cane.' I felt something prod my leg and looked down. He was manipulating a kind of toggle or switch on the head of his cane. The woman in front – the woman who was to die – guffawed loudly at an on-stage incident, distracting me. When I looked down once more I saw, gleaming in the darkness, a long pin or needle that projected from the cane's tip. As suddenly as it was there it was gone again, retracted back into the body of the stick.

What happened next was hazy. There was a scene in a panelled drawing room. The pin-headed young woman was being surprised by her husband in the throes of simulated adultery. A Jeeves type, a servile machiavel, providentially hit the lights and the whole auditorium was plunged into darkness. I couldn't be certain but in the hubbub that followed (shrieked squeaks and 'hahas' from the audience) I thought I heard a definite mechanical 'click', but when the stage lights came up again, nothing had happened. The Fat Controller was sitting Ciceronian amongst the mob, and his intended victim was squeaking with the rest. Squeaking and even gasping with the great good humour of it all.

Immediately afterwards there was an interval. Instead of joining the press of bodies that jammed up the aisle towards the crush bar, he took my arm once again and drew me in the opposite direction. We exited into a back alley via the fire door.

It was dark outside and The Fat Controller pulled up the velvet collar of his overcoat. 'Did you enjoy the piece?' he asked, and before I could answer he went on, 'I myself did not. I found the script tedious and the performances inconsequential. How risible it is that art cannot provide a better imitation of life, when we know that life itself is so illusory. Would you not agree? Furthermore,' he went on, drawing me in the direction of Pool Valley, 'one is insistently aware that all of these actors are the meanest of impostors. That that woman who would be a flapper is in fact a naturally be-jeaned fag hag, who will soon be uttering even worse inanities in some adjacent lounge bar. Is this not so?'

I responded to his rhetoric with a question, anticipating rebuttal. 'The woman who insulted you, the woman sitting in front of us – '

'The one who I said I was going to kill?'

'Yes.'

'Well, I have done so.' He fell silent as if this was of little or no account.

'But . . . but, I didn't see anything. How did you do it?'

'Curare. No magic to it at all, except insofar as it was a direct transferral of intention to effect with very little attenuation of the causal chain. You observed the hypodermic needle in the ferrule of my cane?' He tapped the pavement with the stick for emphasis. 'A method of poisoning which I learnt of during a sojourn in Bulgaria. It struck me at the time that there was something rather apt about such a pedestrian people developing such a pedestrian means of covert assassination – ' He broke off to laugh at his own pun. 'The curare will paralyse the woman. Rude bitch. I injected her above the hairline. I cannot conceive that the pathologist will trouble to look there for a puncture mark and indeed, prior to that eventuality, it doesn't seem likely that the emergency team of paramedics they'll send out from Brighton General will be well enough acquainted with the action of this drug to hit upon the right antidote in time to prevent her from expiring.'

Perhaps I was in shock but instead of simply feeling horrified by this intelligence I was curious. 'But when they do the whatsit . . .'

'The post-mortem?'

'Yeah, when they do the post-mortem, what will they decide was the cause of death?'

'Suffocation, I should imagine. I admit they will find that something of a puzzle, but given the low critical standards of provincial audiences, they might hit upon the felicitous conclusion that she choked while in the midst of an exaggeratedly hilarious response to that pathetic farce. And now' – The Fat Controller consulted his watch; an endomorphic gold Rolex had replaced the full hunter – 'it's getting on for nine-thirty. I warrant that your mama may be wondering where we have got to, we had better enbus for Saltdean. Forward to the terminus.'

That night, as I sat on the edge of my bed, contemplating the tatter of pop posters sellotaped to the flower-patterned wallpaper of my bedroom, I found myself shaking. It couldn't be true, could it? The Fat Controller hadn't really killed the woman, had he? There was no denying that his penetration of my mind, using my eidetic memory to distort the relation between representation and that which was represented, was strident, agressive even. But there was still a world of difference between this and the vicious and arbitrary manner in which he had committed femicide. And he had done it to a woman who had done nothing to him, simply been a little rude and overbearing, not unlike The Fat Controller himself.

My head span. I felt the nausea of awakening to a brand new day of suffering, a dawn of utter exclusion from my fellow mortals. What had I got myself into? I imagined my mentor, beached on his snow-white counterpane, consciouslessly watching *Night Thoughts* and perhaps improvising his own televisual homily. I wanted to confess everything to somebody, but who? Now my intimations of the complicity between The Fat Controller and my mother grew into the utter certainty that it extended even into these murky areas. I realised that the 'trust' which he sought was silence. A comprehensive silence covering all those aspects of our relationship that might appear to an outsider to be improper, or even bizarre. I hated to imagine what the consequences of breaching this trust might be. If a woman who was rude got killed, I would surely be strung up, tortured, cut down and my heart excised.

My cursed eidetic memory summoned up a vision of the medieval rood screen in the Victoria and Albert Museum in London, the one depicting the martyrdom of St Anthony. St Anthony being boiled in oil with a companionable gaggle of fellow martyrs; St Anthony pierced by crossbow bolts fired by The Fat Controller in chain mail; and in the central, triumphant panel – his white body as flexibly two-dimensional as bacon rind – St Anthony being sawn in half, lengthwise. Instead of the almond eyes of the soon-to-be-beatified, the gaping mouth of welcomed suffering superimposed on the Saint's visage was my own. My own dead-straight mousy fringe and dimpled chin framed my face as it distorted in agony.

Without noticing its onset I found that I was crying and I went on crying until I slept.

The following day was a Saturday. Walking down to the newsagent's in the village I ran through the events of the preceding evening again. I conjured up a vivid representation of the plushy murk in the Theatre Royal, I saw the shiny tip of the hypodermic gleaming against the dark fabric of The Fat

Controller's trouser leg. I still wanted to believe that he had been fooling me, or testing my credulousness in a more than averagely cruel manner.

The day was high and bright, the salt tang seasoning the after-pulse of summer heat which still hung in the air, but nothing could shift my sense of despondency, nagging depression. I couldn't even be bothered to look where I was going. I ran straight into the hard bulk of The Fat Controller and was winded by the impact. I had always suspected him of being rather more solid than the average person and this collision provided complete confirmation. He was as rigid and unyielding as the rugby-tackling machine at school.

'Well, if it isn't my little companion, my theatre-going pal. Where are we off to this morning then, so sunk in our own fantasies and imaginings that we cannot be troubled to look out for vulnerable senior citizens, eh?' As ever he answered his own question. 'To the paper shop, I'll be bound, but there's no need to trouble yourself for I have the early edition right here.'

He pulled the local daily paper from under his arm and brandished it in the blue air as if it were a short sword. 'We made the front page!' he exulted, holding the rag up so that I could see the headline: 'WOMAN DIES AT THEATRE ROYAL'. I began to tremble violently and would have fainted, had he not grabbed me by the elbow and guided me to a low wall, where I slumped down.

'I can see that you're a trifle overcome,' he said after a few moments. 'Let me read you the copy: "A woman died last night during the interval at the Theatre Royal." What appalling style, even twenty years ago one could expect a better standard of English. Anyway, no matter, it's a digression, where was I . . . yes: "The woman, who has yet to be named, was among a party of four attending *Tea at Five for Six*. Her companions alerted theatre staff when it became clear that she was having difficulty breathing. An ambulance was called but efforts made to revive her proved unsuccessful. She was pronounced dead on arrival at Brighton General."

'Well, there you have it. Not a pretty death, but as peaceful as she could have hoped for, given the circumstances. Let me see, let me see, what's this: "A spokesman for the police said that, although certain aspects of the woman's death were unusual, they did not suspect foul play." Oh yes, oh yes indeed! Ahaha, ha ha. Of course not! Why should they? It was fair play, wasn't it, my lad, absolutely fair play. Wouldn't ye agree, lad, wouldn't ye?'

CHAPTER FOUR

MY UNIVERSITIES

Frigidity has only been better exemplified to me by the first psychotic woman I ever saw, who complained that her vagina contained a block of ice.

Anthony Storr

He was as good as his word. For the five years after the murder of the woman at the Theatre Royal his interventions in my life remained purely educative. He did not, as I had feared, ask me to perform covert assassinations on his behalf and nor did he insist on my using my eidetic capabilities to project myself into the noumenal world that he inhabited with such terrifying ease. Naturally he couldn't forbear from upsetting me, nor ruining what slim remaining chance I had of being like anyone – let alone everyone – else. He messed around with me emotionally, through dropping those bombshells of feeling – concerning my father, amongst other things – that I have alluded to before. Nevertheless this was small beer for him.

In due course I left Varndean and went to do business studies at Sussex University. For the first year I had a room on campus but I wasn't happy there so I returned to Cliff Top, where my mother put one of the caravans at my disposal.

By now there were only a few of them left, grouped like maintenance vehicles around The Fat Controller's wide-bodied jet of a home. The bungalow had been more or less cancelled out by mother's renovations. And arisen, phoenix-like, from its dusty and corrugated remains, was the tastefully false façade of Cliff Top, the hotel.

My time at university was, for a while at least, a happy one. I enjoyed my course of study and felt that the practicalities of business were a perfect antidote to the magic that had dominated my adolescence. Although we were sneered at by the arts and humanities students, those of us who were doing business studies felt, quite reasonably, that we were closer to the spirit of the age than the old hippies of the faculty.

People had begun to feel less ashamed about being greedy and of wanting more than their share of fairness. I wasn't partisan politically but I did think that choice was important, whether it was which brand you chose or which person you decided to deride. Here at least my disparate educations converged.

That first term I was very shy and awkward. I found it almost impossible to mix with my fellow students. I barely understood any of the cultural references that they took for granted. Also I couldn't shake off the imprint of The Fat Controller's locutions. His tendency towards pleonasm had infected me. Often when attempting to explain some aspect of my studies to fellow students who were having difficulties, I would look up from the textbook we were sharing to see an expression of sheer disbelief pass across their faces. I knew why, they had the queer sensation that they were being addressed by someone from a bygone age.

I was the repository for arcana of an exacting kind. The Fat Controller forced upon me the conclusion that things were not at all as they seemed. As yet my understanding of this was inchoate, but I never for a moment doubted that, while I might work hard and comprehend these studies quite thoroughly, the true meaning of my life lay somewhere else.

The laggardly limb of this awareness was tied firmly to the dominant emotion in my life, fear. Together, with fear yanking the way forward, speculation and sentiment ran the three-legged race into the future.

It may surprise the reader (who after all is charged with the task of making an important decision), that I should talk of my time at university as a happy one and yet still speak of my dominant emotion as fear, but then the worst is yet to come.

The self-styled Brahmin of the Banal kept my fear-levels up to scratch by manifesting himself unexpectedly. As I have said, even as a teenager I knew without having to ask that sexual intercourse would sap whatever magical powers I might have. Yet I craved physical affection – the raw stuff of touch – perhaps even more than emotional. I felt preternaturally over-sexed, and despite being removed from The Fat Controller's proximate influence I still stuck to this rule. I lubricated my eidetic memory, priming it to summon up still more lurid fantasies, carnal changelings compensating for the real thing.

It got so bad I wasn't able to concentrate on my studies. I couldn't open a book, attend a seminar, lecture or tutorial, even go to the library, without getting an erection. I would have to slip away to toilets, down basement stairs, off into the closed stacks of the library and there strike the flint. The friction burnt me, my imagination incandesced in the limelight of this magic lantern show.

At least these skits had grown in sophistication since my adolescence. I became catholic in my lusts. No longer did I desire conventions of little nymphets, each one wearing Playboy's plastic name badge. Instead I screwed around the crowd, all kinds of people, fat and thin, young and old, male and female. I performed cunnilingus, sodomy, intercrural sex and even safe sex – long before it became fashionable. I had become so eidetically adept that I could make these phantom partners mutate in mid-thrust, so that while I might penetrate a swivel-hipped virgin, clean and childishly scented, I would come in the flabby, dentureless, food-flecked mouth of an octogenarian.

This addiction to self-abuse began to tell on me. I was crazed with wanking. It was the lack of touch that really did me in. Without the feeling of another touching me, I was starting to lose the sense of my own body. I was becoming numb all over. If only real hands could shape my contours, then at least I would know that they were still there.

In my second year matters came to a head. Since moving back to Cliff Top my mother had boosted my grant. I was able to buy a small car in which to make the fifteen-minute drive to the campus each day. I would get up in the morning, step out of my caravan, face the ocean and do my exercises, followed by my ritual routine. I had grown to be a large, lumpy sort of man. My resemblance to my father – which had always been remarked upon when I was a child – was now startling. I knew I wasn't attractive and I didn't help myself by dressing like a young fogey in tweed sports jackets, flannel trousers and open-necked check shirts.

I was stuck in a time warp in every sense, one that encompassed my part of Cliff Top as well. My mother's hotel may have elevated her from the raw stuff of commerce – so much so that she now subscribed to *Country Living* and other unspecialist periodicals – but the caravan enclosure was decaying anew. They were flaking paint and hadn't been refurbished since I was fourteen. The brake-pad bindweed had returned and everything was seized up in the early-seventies.

The Sussex campus was stuck in the past as well. Built during a period of architectural optimism, when it was assumed that technology would triumph, it had been laid out in a series of oblong paved courtyards, surrounded by long, low, concrete-faced buildings, remarkable solely for their brutalism. It always struck me as ironic that these buildings, which had been designed to make that present appear futuristic, now served so well to make this present look exactly like the recent past.

The funding was running down, clumps of weed had pushed up between the paving slabs, and whole layers of rendering were falling off the façades of the buildings, giving them a seedy, leprous aspect. To cap it all most of the student body dressed to complement the period when the university was built. They weren't following fashion – they were trailing far behind it.

Back at Cliff Top The Fat Controller was no longer in permanent residence. The winter after the incident at the Theatre Royal he had started to absent himself. Initially for a few days at a time, then for weeks, and eventually whole months. It was like a rerun of the reel in which my father was edited out. His explanation was 'business interests' and indeed, I did start to see discrete references to him, under his working name 'Samuel Northcliffe', in the financial and economic sections of the newspaper. It appeared that his alter ego was an international financier of some kind. The name Northcliffe was linked with raising equity on all five continents but not in such a conspicuous way that he himself garnered personal publicity. I never saw a photograph of him published.

You might have thought these further disclosures would have had a powerful effect on me but, of course, I was inured to surprise where this man was concerned. I also knew better than to seek him out. On the contrary, given the formidible powers he had shown to me, I rather suspected that even during his absence he was keeping me under observation. I was right.

The autumn of my second university year then. Another autumn and another life-change. Everything of importance has always happened to me in the autumn, every new departure has always presented itself within a dying context.

I saw a girl who I really fancied, I mean really. Well, this was nothing new. I knew what to do, incorporate her into the mass grave of my fantasy world; there her real charms would soon decay and get jumbled up with my rather more rotten visions. Once she had been tarnished by my imagination, she would cease to have any power over me.

But I was slow to get started on this project and before I could something unforeseen happened. She took a liking to me. We were taking the same course module, 'marketing and statistics'. She was another young conservative, I guessed from a rather sheltered background. Her sensible shoes, neat skirts and pressed blouses spoke of home-baked shortbread and Sunday school but she wasn't as naive as I imagined. She was fine-boned and delicate, with auburn hair tied back in a leather clasp. Her neck was perhaps a trifle long and her head rather small but her features were symmetrical and her brown eyes large. Her name was June Richards.

She sat at the front during seminars and posed questions to our tutor that were more like statements. She would raise her hand to gain his attention and then use a biro to punctuate what she said with a series of invisible bullet points. The other students were all Cro-Magnons, Heavy Metal fans who scrawled graffiti on their course binders. She was different, well informed and, still more attractive, she had a real enthusiasm for the idea of marketing. She could illustrate her arguments with clever examples drawn from the real world of commerce. After only three such seminars I was smitten.

June must have noticed me staring at her. It was true, I couldn't keep my eyes from sprinting up her slim ankles, and fell-walking the contour lines of her sharp shoulders and her breasts, breasts that were improbably close to her scenic collar bone. But when she came up to me after that third seminar I was so shocked and embarrassed that I could barely speak. I started shaking and my shoes squeaked with apprehension as I shuffled on the lino.

'You're Ian, aren't you?' There was something clipped and ex-colonial in her accent.

'Y'yes.'

'My name's June. I'm doing the marketing module as well.'

'I – I know.'

'I'm sorry to bother you. It's just that Mr Hargreaves says you keep excellent notes and I missed the tutorials last year for the econometrics module. He thought you might be able to help out.'

'Why weren't you here last year?' I regretted the question immediately but there was no pulling back. It sounded so intrusive, like the beginning of an interrogation, but she didn't seem to mind.

'Well, my parents live in Kenya and I was going to study in Nairobi, but Moi has suspended the classes at the university for this year, so I applied to come here.'

'Oh, I see.' Kenya, Nairobi, Moi. How exotic, how improbable.

'These notes then?'

'Yes, yes, of course. I'm afraid I don't have them on me, but I can bring them tomorrow.'

The next day we companionably photocopied the notes together. I had got up early that morning and done my best to make myself look presentable. I still had no thought – for obvious reasons – of making any move on her but I felt it would be enough if she wasn't repelled by me.

She wasn't. Perhaps the toner fluid intoxicated her – there were over a hundred sheets to copy – or maybe it was the lack of air in the photocopying room, but after we had done and she had commented favourably on the comprehensive and detailed nature of the notes, she asked me to go out with her. Like a fool I accepted.

We went to some art-house cinema in Brighton. I couldn't

concentrate on the film at all, I was so aware of her presence beside me in the flickering darkness. I had to repeat whole sections of my 'ritual register', to stop myself from eidetiking, to stop myself from spoiling her image. I sat tight in my seat, my big knees grating against the row in front, trying to ignore the agonising cramps that tore up my thighs.

Afterwards we went for a pizza at – of all places – Al Forno. I hadn't set foot inside the place since my visit with The Fat Controller. Despite this I was recognised. Tommaso appeared as we came in from the street, hamming it up just the way I remembered.

'Ah! Meester Northcliffe's friend, you no come to see us for an age. Whassamatter, you no like our pizza?'

'Oh no, no, Tommaso . . .' I slipped into character as well.

'And with heem a pretty lady. Welcome, welcome. You shall have the best table. Meester Northcliffe's special table.'

I could tell June was impressed. Tommaso made me look like a mature man, an important man. I wasn't taken in. There was more complicity in his winks than was warranted. As I had grown some six inches since he had last seen me, I didn't for a moment believe that his recognition was unprompted.

Over food and wine I drifted into intimacy with June. Initially we talked of our course and our fellow students, but soon the conversation veered off into more personal matters. June alluded to an unhappy affair with a boy back in Kenya, plainly giving me a message. I found myself acting the part of a wooer only too well. No matter that I had no experience, I had rehearsed this role for years, blocking everything out – right down to the way I would sit, ministering to the words of the desired object – yet never believing that I might actually perform.

'He was a shit really. I think he just wanted to use me.' Her fingers drummed the table top. She wore red nail varnish. 'So I told him it was over. I guess that was just another reason why I wanted to get away.' Her cuticles were frayed, perhaps the nails were false? I resisted the urge to take an eidetic peek by recollecting the pincered click of my own manicuring habits. 'My aunt lives in Hastings, so my bloody overprotective parents thought it would be OK for me to come to Sussex. I live with Auntie, she keeps an eye on me.'

'Oh I see.'

'You're a local, aren't you, Ian?'

'Yeah, I live near Saltdean, always have.'

I told her some Cliff Top stuff, about my sort of over-protective mother and my absent father. I knew I shouldn't but I couldn't help it. It seemed so right, the low burr of two voices in the pool of candlelight.

The waiter brought coffee and some amaretti. June unwrapped the flimsy tissue paper from one of the almond biscuits and rolled it carefully into a tube. She was tanned and her hair was fairer at the roots. I could make out the tracery of blonde down on the edge of her cheek.

'Look, see this?' She took the paper tube and lit one end with the candle. Then she set it in the middle of a saucer. 'Now watch, this is magic.' The tube burnt blue and orange transforming the paper into a black filigree. But before it was consumed entirely, it lifted off and shot up towards the painstyled plaster of the ceiling. It fell back towards us and I caught the filmy ash on another plate. I felt elegant, masterful, catching that ash. She looked at me with a smile that implied fusion.

I insisted on paying the bill and on opening the door for her as if I were an ordinary gallant. We were walking along the front towards the Palace Pier when she took my arm. Outside the Metropole she turned to face me and we kissed.

That kiss, my first, sang my mouth into existence. Her conduit arms around my shoulders – as I had suspected – threw the switch for a sensation of total embodiment, which surged up to encompass me. I felt vivified by that kiss. Before I had been lifeless jumble of miscellaneous body parts but now I was Frankenstein's monster, shocked by lust into coherence and action.

'Do you really live in a caravan?' Her breath was on my neck.

'Yeah, but it's not a gypsy caravan. The caravanning life isn't all it's painted up to be. This one's a grotty little fibreglass thing, there's nothing romantic about it.'

'Still, I'd like to see it. Can we go there?'

'Yeah, all right. It's on our way back to Hastings.'

I fully intended to show her the caravan and then take her home. I felt safe – she seemed like a demure young woman. Even if I tried it on I thought she would stop me. But back at Cliff Top in the crisp violet night, we stood watching the lights of the ships in the Channel and we kissed again. Although I couldn't see her face properly, her tongue was painting my image by numbers. Her cool hands slid up under my jacket, plucking at my shirt, pulling it out at the waist.

And my hands, my heavy hands, they glided over her with careful diffidence, not so much touching or feeling but defining her anatomy. They located her shoulder blades, her spine, the small of her back, and then slid between our compressing bodies and travelled up to the tiny soft immensities of her bosom.

For the first time since my balls had dropped I felt wholly in the moment, unafflicted by my meddlesome internal projectionist. All my wank footage lay in dusty spirals on the cutting-room floor. I was free.

Then, somehow, we were in my caravan. The fold-away bed was let down. Without shyness, without hiding ourselves from each other, we undressed. She pulled the leather clasp from her hair and shook it free in a whirl of golden brown. She unbuttoned her blouse. I dropped my trousers. As I stood on one foot to remove them, the little cabin shifted on its suspension but there was no embarrassment, not even in the disparity between the utility of our underwear and the transcendence of our desire. We were alone together in some prelapsarian grotto. Her body was ochre against the light-blue side of the caravan. I held her to me as we fell across the bed, feeling her lithe life-force twitching against me as beautiful as a rainbow trout, leaping from a mill race into my outstretched arms.

She touched me with confidence. I couldn't believe it. Both her hands around my penis, cosseting it, restraining it. I licked her neck, the backs of my fingers prinked her pink nipples. We sighed. The heel of my hand was firm on her mons, my fingertips strummed gently at her lips, parted them. We rippled on the yellow sheet, the counterpane – and us – long gone.

She led me on, instructing me, indicating her desires with soft tweaks and softer pats. In due course, it was time. She moved back against the pillow and drew me on top of her. Her legs fell open and oh! The kid softness of her thighs, the honey of her breath, the sweet intensity of it. My urge to enter her, to be inside her, was stronger than anything I had ever felt.

'Yes!' she sighed. 'Now!' she gasped.

I felt the beginnings of a slithering enfoldment. I looked out of the tiny window over her shoulder, willing myself to make it slow, to make it last. A hard square of orange light sprang on in the darkness. Someone – I realised with a start – was in The Fat Controller's caravan.

Beneath me June's body froze, becoming utterly immobile, lifeless. Sex time stood still. The little door of my caravan squealed open. He stood there in full evening dress, the shiny black rim of his topper slicing across the bulge of his massive brow. His Partagas perfecto was champed between his inner tube lips, a diamond as big as a buttercup sparkled on the starched front of his dress shirt, a long white silk scarf was casually looped around his lack of a neck.

'Good evening,' he said, as I scuttled like a giant shaved rodent into the furthest corner of the caravan. 'Trying to have a little fuck-for-real, are we?' I looked back at the bed, at June rigid in *ecstasis*, her eyes blank and upturned. 'No need to worry about her.' The Fat Controller entered the caravan casually, his eyes darting about taking in my few effects, our scattered clothes, the pile of economics books on the little table. 'Got an ashtray? No? No matter.' He flicked two inches of ash on the floor and sat down on the edge of the bed I had just vacated. June's body rocked longitudinally on its curved spine, then fell sideways. It was as stiff and brittle as a lifesize plaster maquette.

'Cat got yer' tongue?' I was gibbering quietly, I felt the head of my penis stickily retreat back inside its hood of skin. 'You needn't worry about her,' he repeated, gesturing at the naked girl. 'She'll get her climax – which is more than you could have managed. I'll engineer it myself after we've had a little chat. You shan't be shamed for she'll think you a great lover, a real Lothario, a dandy Don Juan. And the very fact that the experience will never ever be repeated will make the remembrance burn for her a hundred times as bright.

'D'ye see that? When she's married ten years hence, she'll compare her husband's performance with yours and he'll come off worse – every time. Memories are cruel to the present in that way and, as far as sexual intercourse is concerned, it is axiomatic that familiarity breeds contempt.' Predictably, he chortled at his own execrable pun.

I was still gibbering. Muffled bleats and strangled gurgles leaked from my lips. 'Oh do can it! Come here, put a pair of trousers on or something. We need to talk and I'm tired. I've just been driven back from Covent Garden and I want to get to bed. You are a very lucky young man indeed. If Tommaso hadn't troubled to have me paged at the opera, you would certainly have performed coitus with this young woman and d'ye know what would have happened then?'

'N-no.' Somehow I had managed to squirm back into my trousers. I crouched on the tiny oblong floor, clutching the only breasts that were left for me to clutch – my own.

'Your penis would have broken right off inside her and I mean that quite literally. I thought you understood about coitus, I thought you appreciated what being my licentiate entailed?'

'Y-yes, but –'

'My dear boy.' He was conciliatory. 'I know this must be difficult for you, perhaps even a little traumatic, but don't take it to heart. All in good time you will have a bed partner and let me tell you, you will care for her far more than you ever could for this one. It's a function of your relationship to me, d'ye see? I have, how shall I put it, organised an elective affinity for you already. Everything in that department is in train, so don't spoil it.'

He was resting his huge hand on June's angled knee as casually as if it were the arm of a chair. He twisted his Redwood trunk on the bed and looked down at her from under his lashless lids. He scrutinised the rictus of her pleasure, which was rendered grotesque by its immobility. We both stared at her vagina. Its slick lips 'o'ed back at us. The Fat Controller blew a plume of cigar smoke at it from out of the corner of his mouth; the blue strands interleaved with her browner ones.

'Right, that's all, I'm off to bed now. I'm absolutely fagged out, grand opera is too, too fatiguin'. I had to sit next to a monstrously fat man. It was bloody hot in the stalls and his sweat stank. It was as if he were shitting out of every pore.' He spoke casually and with no sense of irony. Then he stood and gathered his hat, cigar and white gloves together in one hand. Pausing at the door he turned once more and extended the middle finger of his right hand towards the bed. I noticed for the first time that it was dreadfully long. The very tip of the finger began to oscillate. It seemed to be locked on to some invisible beam that was projecting from out of June's vagina. The colour rushed back into her face, her back arched still further, she whimpered and thrashed, her outstretched hands clutching at the edge of the mattress. The Fat Controller addressed me over the sounds of her orgasm, paying no attention to them at all. We might have been in a shopping concourse and her cries some strange species of muzak:

'Ah! Ahh! Ahhhherrr! O – O . . .'

'. . . I have business at the university tomorrow, so I'll come and find you afterwards. It occurs to me'

'H-h-a hnh . . . ha, ha, Ha! . . .'

'. . . that I have been neglecting your education. I can be of more service *vis-à-vis* your ambitions than I have heretofore. Consider it'

'Yes, oh yes, oh-yesss . . .' She was subsiding.

'. . . something by way of a compensation for this.' He indicated the young woman he was dehumanising on the bed. 'Now, pop your trews off and give her a cuddle; and make sure she's out of here soon, I don't want her mooning about in the morning.' He turned to leave but then swivelled back once more. 'Remember, put your pecker in her or any other doxy and' – he held up his stogie braced between three fingers – 'this is what will happen.' He snapped it in two – gave me a leer – and was gone, as suddenly as he had arrived.

I did as I was told. While I cuddled June I cried, wept hot tears. She was terribly moved. She cleaved to me, slipping her legs between mine. I explained, as gently as possible, that my mother was very old-fashioned and always checked up on me in the morning. About 3 a.m. I managed to get her into the car and drove her back to her aunt's in Hastings.

Powering the skateboard of a car back along the coast road, home to Cliff Top, I felt its wheels skittering on the damp surface and my arms yearned to yank the steering wheel hard round, ending this nightmare. Only The Fat Controller's talk of 'elective affinity' prevented me. Now, of course, I wish I had.

The following day June sought me out, after a seminar on management technique. We stood on the concrete set of the main concourse while extras thronged about. 'How about tonight?' she said and the pathos in her ignorant unknowing enquiry almost made me gag. My mind flew back to the sight of The Fat Controller's cigar. I had trodden on its shattered corpse that morning on my way out of the caravan.

'I – I can't, really, not tonight. Sorry.'

'What's up? Have you got to go visiting with Mummy? I thought we might do some studying together. You know I don't want "us" to get in the way of work.'

'Haha. No, I'd love to. It's just there's something else I must do. I can't really talk about it now. I'll tell you tomorrow.' I couldn't bear her look of hurt expectancy any more, so I tore myself away from her face and walked off. I realised that, if I was going to have to break with her, the process of rejection might as well get started right away. As I reached the end of the student union building I looked back and gave a little finger-wiggle. Even from fifty yards away I could see her pained expression.

Turning the sharp corner of toughened glass with its graph-paper patterning of buried wire, I ran into someone – or some thing. Although I was walking at a normal pace the impact stunned me. My head rang with that particular vibration of accidental pain, a tintinnabulating effect that always feels as if it should have preceded its cause – by way of a warning.

'You're rather good at walking into me, aren't you?' He was in a Prince of Wales check this morning. The sight of such an expanse of tiny squares, flowing up and around his massive elevation, produced more of an architectural than a sartorial impression. 'I trust your inattention is a function of scholarly absorption, rather than adolescent spooning.'

'What difference can it possibly make?' It was a measure of my despair that I dared to be so disdainful.

'Don't get chippy, boy, I cannot abide it.' But although he was terse, he didn't rage at me the way I expected him to. I suppose I half-hoped that he would zap me with extinction the way he had zapped June with orgasm the night before but his horrible middle finger was folded around a reeking cheroot and showed no sign of flexing.

He put my felonious body in the stocks of his arm and led me off in the direction of what passed for a garden at Sussex, a series of brick-edged parallelograms that couldn't have looked more artificial if they had been planted with cathode-ray tubes, instead of hardy perennials. To anyone who was watching we must have looked the very picture of youthful preoccupation and parental concern.

'What have you been studying this morning then, eh?'

'Management techniques.'

'Oh yes, and what are they?'

'Well' – I hated myself for responding to his interest – 'we were looking at different kinds of organisational hierarchy and how to construct optimal decision-making procedures in corporate contexts.'

'I see. Can you really give any credence to this ordure?'

'I'm sorry?'

'This crap.'

'Well, it's essential, isn't it? I mean somebody has to have an idea of what's to be done and how it should be communicated to the employees.' I was earnest, like any aspiring young person trying to draw out approval. He seemed to ignore the substance of what I had said.

'What Is To Be Done?' he mused. 'That's what I said to Vladimir Ilyich. Naturally he cribbed it for the title of a pamphlet, when what I actually meant by it was some advice. I urged him to have a few of the young daughters of the gentlefolk before he established the provisional government at the Smolny Institute. He was headstrong enough, although not as cold and passionless as they later made out.'

We went on walking for a while, in silence. Eventually The Fat Controller pulled me up in front of a viciously scalped hedge of box. He took the cheroot from his mouth and peered at its slobbered-on green end, as if it were a reptilian rump about to grow a new tail. 'I thought you were interested in products,' he said, a wheedling tone entering his voice. 'I can help you in that area.'

'We've done merchandising, purchasing, sourcing and inventory auditing.'

'That's not what I'm talking about. What I can help you with is an understanding of the nature of a product that goes far beyond these crudities; these academic categories masquerading as truths.'

'I'm interested in the marketing side of things. How to evolve a strategy to actually sell a product. You know, advertising, sales promotion, that sort of thing.'

'Of course, chip off the old block, aren't you?'

'Yeah, I know "contemptible Essene, cloistral nonentity", that's what you said to me.'

'You have a fair recollection, boy, I'll grant you that. Tell me, how much of that recollection is visual and how much verbal?'

'What do you mean?'

'Well, do you first need to form a picture of the two of us sitting in that café discussing your father – an eidetic image – before the words come to you, or not?'

'I suppose I do need to – '

'. . . So you were being disingenuous. You know exactly what I mean.' His thumb and forefinger pinched the sides of my neck, one big pad pressing into my carotid artery. My head roared with neon pins and needles, at once visual and sensual. He went on with the conversation, in my mind, 'Do you remember your underpants then?' I was slumped against him, almost fainting, conscious only that he had led me behind a red-brick loggia, obviously so that we would be out of sight of the people in the main concourse while he dispatched me. 'Well, do you?'

'W-what about my underpants?' I stuttered, coughed. Why wouldn't he get it over with?

'I want you to recall the label of said underpants, summon it up as fully as you possibly can. I want to know whether the legend thereon was printed, or machine-embroidered; whether the label itself was stitched into the pants, or appliquéd in some fashion; whether the label indicates an element of design, or whether the information it retails relates purely to the material constitution of the aforementioned pants. Can you do that?' He knew I could, he was toying with me. 'Now when you have the image, let me see it.'

'W-whaddya mean?'

'You know what I mean.' He relaxed his death-hold on me and made me sit down with him on a convenient bench. I idly noted that a brass plate declared that this bit of garden furniture was sacred to someone's memory. I wished it was mine.

I did as he said. The label was sewn on to the crinkled, elasticated hem of the pants, which were boxer shorts, blue-and-white-striped like mattress ticking. The legend on the label read 'Barries' Menswear, 212 King's Road, London, 100% Egyptian Cotton.' It was easy for me to summon up this everyday vision, because whenever I sat on the toilet the hem was stretched between my calves, and if I leant forward it was always the salient object in my view.

'Good. Now, what I am about to teach you is an extension of your eidetic capability which you will find of great use in your intended career. There is no word, at least in current usage, that does justice to this advanced technique, so I have had to coin a term of my own. I call it "retroscendence".' He paused and looked at me, as if trying to gauge what kind of impression this hokum was making. 'Before we retroscend allow me a few prefatory remarks on your pants. Firstly, let us refer to them simply as "shorts". You are too callow to be aware of this but the term "boxer shorts" is merely a marketing neologism, coined in order to revamp a demand for what in England was perceived as an outmoded type of underwear. In America where the loose, cotton, mid-thigh-length male undergarment has consistently maintained its market share, there has never been any need to call these things anything but shorts.

'A second point, you are not conspicuously dandyish, indeed, I would say that you have grown to adult size with but little appreciation of the value of effective turn-out. Be that as it may, I perceive in your decision to purchase these shorts – you did purchase these shorts, didn't you?'

'Yes.'

'An attempt, albeit muted, to get to grips with a world beyond Saltdean. I picture you on a trip up to London, perhaps for a day's work experience at the offices of some conglomerate. Am I right?'

'You're right.'

'In your lunch hour you head down the King's Road from Sloane Square. You walk and walk, staring at the chic emporia. Here's one that sells just belt buckles, here's another exclusively devoted to pointed boots, or country and westernalia, or whatever. It hardly matters. You do not intend to enter. You would feel yourself embarrassed, shy, in front of the shop assistant, who would be so much more metropolitan, more sophisticated, than you. Instead you peer inside and try to calculate the merchandising policy: what value of stock is required, per metre of shelf space, to meet overheads and instil profit? Am I right?'

'Yes.' His voice was hypnotic, dreamy.

'Of course I am. Nonetheless, you do still have some vanity, don't you? You still have the shame of the short-trousered recent past. You still – God knows why – wish to imagine that someone will inadvertently examine your underwear after the car crash of sexual congress. So after toddling about for a while you go into Barries' and point out the shorts where they lie in the window, interleaved with their fellows. But I'm getting ahead of myself, when all I really want to teach you is the full history of such a product. That's the title of this lecture:

"The History of the Product", and like all good modern lectures – intended simply to garnish knowledge rather than impart it – this one uses visual aids.'

The big hand was on my neck again, twisting it like the focus grip of some humanoid camera. The autumnal trees, spindly, moulting, were cast into darkness as if the wan sun had been eclipsed. I felt myself being pulled backwards, upwards, so that my visual field did indeed resemble that of a camera, a camera in some computer-graphics title sequence. The Sussex campus was shrinking below me into a collection of children's play houses, then models, then crumbs, then fly droppings. Until the cars moving along the university's peripheral roads were silverfish and the whole scene was dappled with low-lying cloud. Then we were higher still and the earth curved away from us, showing a nimbus of atmosphere at its edge.

The Fat Controller spoke inside of me again. 'Look up above you, look at the bare-faced cheek of the infinite.' I did as he bade me. Up there, set among the unblinking stars like some branding of the cosmos, was that selfsame label, the label in my boxer shorts. 'You see,' he said, 'retroscendence enables us to take any element in our visual field and, as it were, unpack its history. We have chosen your shorts, I now propose to instruct you in their origin and past life. Please do not be confused by the apparent dissolution of the integrity of your visual field. Remember that the purest of solipsism is indeed realism. For, if I am the world' – we were heading down again, his nails digging into my flesh, I could make out the Eastern Mediterranean – 'then the world must be real. Isn't that so?'

In the flat land of the Delta the babies cry themselves to sleep in the airless shade, while everyone else labours in the scintillating sun. When the dun evening comes the kids go down to the irrigation channels for some bilharzia bathing. They have little to look forward to, save for fat legs, flopping in the silt of some riverine beach.

My shorts were distributed over a half-acre of plants in the sharp silvery light of this place, in the form of white balls, fibrous globs. So fluffy to see but so hard to the touch.

'Regard those buds,' said The Fat Controller, 'for throughout the long day of pluck and twist they turn into barbs and after years of this constant abrading, a deadened rind is added to the pluckers' hands. This is the cotton workers' equivalent of Repetitive Stress Syndrome. In due course we will witness similar, half a world away on the Mile End Road.'

I next found myself lying at the bottom of a crude hopper of duck boards which was set on top of an irrigation dyke. The fruit of these people's labour ('Their name is El Azain,' he said, and his voracious lips seemed to suck on my lobes, his sharp tongue to probe my synapses) fell about my face. Then we were off, emptied along with the cotton into the truck that transported the El Azains' harvest, together with that of the five other families that made up this producers' co-operative, to the local town to meet the buyer.

The town was an organic place. A compost heap of soft walls that gently crumbled, flowing down to join the mud at their feet. Eventually the earth would be dug out, remoulded and cast once more in the form of bricks, which would take their place in fresh walls that in due course would crumble again.

Our dyad looked on as Mohammed Sherif, the co-operative head, aged and bloated by dietary tedium, went through the formalities with the buyer. They drank *thé à menthe* from dirty glasses, while a charcoal lump fizzed in the clay bowl of the hookah. From time to time Sherif's woolly old head, loosely wrapped in a dirty headdress, would fall back against the fly-speckled surface of the remaining quarter of a red sign. This dolorous thing proclaimed 'oca-Cola' in Arabic.

As this went on, the point of view without extension that was myself and The Fat Controller accompanied the product-of-the future as it was unloaded from the truck and heaped in a stall of warped boards. A man with one nostril pulled a stiff tarpaulin over us.

'There is no other buyer, d'ye see?' said The Fat Controller. 'The bargaining isn't even a formality, it's just an empty ritual. Sherif must accept the price he is offered if the five families are to have any hope of paying off their lengthening tab at the provisioner's and if – haha, a'haha – they want their thin children to live to grow thinner! Look here' – we peeked out – 'he's thinking to himself: This may be my last harvest. No such luck, I'm afraid.'

The Fat Controller and I next became the cotton entirely. We were jolted from the Delta to the coast, where we disappeared into a giant galvanised iron shed. Here we were subjected to a process of pounding and separating, carding and spinning. Until at last I saw him shooting off ahead of me in the form of a long lumpy thread, vibrating with moisture, which stretched ectoplasmically into the maw of the shuttling frame. He cried out, 'Here we go!' and I followed on. The machinery clanked up and over and up and over again, gulping down first him, then the shorts-to-be, then me.

'Bloody lucky' – he spoke like a harp out of the strings of half-constructed fabric – 'that this old Schliemann-Hoffer has already caught its finger quota for today. D'ye see, little hands have to struggle to free the trapped weft before the frame drops? If they aren't quick enough – ouch! Blood as good as yours or mine creatin' a sort of moiré effect and condemning your shorts to the wastage pile.'

Before we set off again, on along the coast and then across the sea, The Fat Controller saw fit to bifurcate our strange awarenesses. So that, while one part of me remained intimate with the cotton, another separate centre of cartoon existence accompanied those tokens which served, through their concatenation and order, to mirror parallel developments in the world of objects. So it was that I lay in honeycombs of tiny compartments, stacked into loose piles and sheaves with onion-skin leaves of paper. I waited to be clipped and pinned, stamped and spiked. Latterly I was digitalised and pulsed my way across the dark convexities of visual-display units. I thought to myself, even as it happened, that this winking of my very self-consciousness was a nice expression of the value I represented.

Meanwhile my cotton body was wound on to great bolts, each one five metres long. Although the bolts were thick, I still bent in the middle when I was lifted and carried, a man at either of my ends. I was wadded along with my fellows into a container and then – darkness. A long, long, unutterably tedious wait in the lint-filled darkness, until at last I felt the tension of the crane and realised that I was being lowered into the hold.

A juggernaut roaring, an ultrasonic shuddering, the smell of air-borne hydrocarbons, the sensation of pores opening to admit grit.

'All right?' asked The Fat Controller. 'Not a lot to see in the hold of that ratty freighter, was there?'

'No.'

'That's why I've brought you here.'

Here was the Old Kent Road. We were looking across it at a slice-shaped building, calcined with pollution. It stood like a slice of stale chocolate cake, marooned in a tar ox-bow, that had become a cul-de-sac when the main throughfare ploughed another course. Over the portico, cut into the rendering, were the words 'Success House'.

'Good that, isn't it?' His voice was muffled by something – could it be that he was smoking a cigar even whilst disembodied? 'A nice irony. The façade proclaims success, but behind it the building dwindles to nothing. Consider those stately columns, regard the coils of plaster vine that trail from the windowsills, meditate on the dados in the shape of *fasces* that stud its pitted hide.'

'Ye-es.'

'Does not the whole ensemble speak to you of imperial confidence, a global network of industry?'

'S'pose so.'

'And yet all there is inside is one old Jew. Zekel is his name.'

'I know that. What I mean is, when I was a number on one of those screens, I saw his name alongside me.'

'Quite so, for it is he who is responsible for importing the schmutter that will be made into your shorts. He is a cotton factor; and look over there.' I found myself looking. 'Here, if I am not much mistaken, comes his customer.'

A youngish Greek man was sidling a blue Porsche into the alleyway alongside Success House. The car was so low it looked as if a giant had tried to stub it out and it was clear that getting out of the bucket seat gave the Greek momentary altitude sickness. He looked around warily as he locked up.

'See him glance round like that? He's worried that if Zekel knows he has a Porsche, the Jew will drive a harder bargain and the haggling between them – which is already prolonged – will become interminable.

'The Greek's name is Vassily Antinou and let me tell you, he's an even deeper mine of stupid contradiction than you are. His father quarreled with the Colonels over some detail of graft. Naturally the adolescent Antinou, stranded in plump London, elevated the exile into something political. It's so typically English that this rebel should end up with his own sweat shop in Clapton – you'll see it for yourself in due course. All his socialist rhetoric has faded into spurious concerns over the man-management of twenty women-in-nylon. Poor Cypriots who have no option but to look on, while their boss – who is suited by Anzio, shod by Hoage's, and shirted by Barries' – rants up and down the linoleum batting at the flexes of their sewing machines, and talking of productivity deals and workers' share options. Pathetic, eh?'

We were inside Success House looking out. Those selfsame stately columns framed a view of the immense rumpled surface of South London. The factor sat behind a roll-top desk; he was so bent and atrophied by arthritis that he looked like a crustacean clad in a suit.

'Whaddya want, Vassily?' He clearly thought the Greek who leant against the doorjam was a hoot. He picked a newly constructed swatch of samples up from the desk in front of him and chucked it at Antinou, who caught the flopping thing one-handed and proceeded to fondle it familiarly.

'This one,' said Antinou, pulling out a sample and rubbing it between his finger and thumb.

'That's called "getting the silk",' said The Fat Controller, *sotto voce*, 'now watch, he'll yank it hard to check the tensility.' He was right.

'Egyptian cotton,' sighed Zekel. 'I bought it myself at auction – it's still bonded.' Antinou went on fondling the piece of cloth that was once a fluffy ball on the flat delta.

'How much?' he said at length. The Factor named a price, Antinou countered and so it went on for quite a while.

The Fat Controller and I were back inside the bolt when it arrived from the bonded warehouse at Felixstowe. The van doors swung open and as Antinou's lads eased us out we were treated to a 6 a.m. view of Clapton. It looked profoundly underexposed, like a photograph rejected by Quality Control.

'See him,' said The Fat Controller. A languid black man was floating around, elegantly suited. 'That's Crispin. He's the originator of the Barries' look, he's the man behind your shorts.'

'Hold up, lads!' The black man let his hand fall on the bolt of cotton. He pulled a fold of cloth loose and, with tender movements, as if he were sensually unwrapping some erogenous zone, he felt the cloth. He bunched it and pulled at it, finally he pleated it between his knuckles, before letting it fall back. He went off in the direction of some green doors that bore the legend 'Narcissus Clothing', muttering, 'That'll do, that'll do.'

'You see,' said The Fat Controller once Crispin had disappeared, 'your shorts already had shape and form – in his mind. Now he's found their substance. Shall we go on?'

We were on the King's Road. The frontage of Barries' Menswear was pseudo-cottagey, a waist-high tracery of white plaster and black beams surmounted by plate-glass windows. 'There he is, that's Barry – Barry Mercer.' A plump man, piscine, his tail end fading to little leather pumps, came out of the shop gesticulating, clutching his sweating ginger head. Crispin followed behind. 'Of course his real name is Morgenstern. His father was a bespoke tailor on the Mile End Road. You know I was talking of cotton and Repetitive Stress Syndrome? Well, Mercer's father had exactly the same rinds of dead flesh on his hands that we saw in the Delta.

'Barry couldn't change his name until his father died – and he certainly wouldn't have brought Crispin home. His father would have said, "We sell to schwartzers, we don't do business with them." But Barry's mother is too polite for that, whenever Crispin goes round he gets schneken and the photo album like anyone else. Shall we listen in?'

'Accessorise, that's what you do if you want to establish a designer concept,' said Crispin. His nostrils were cavernous and so finely edged that they seemed made of paper.

'But what can we accessorise?' Mercer whined. 'I had to go up to Clapton yesterday and haggle with Antinou for hours over that bloody Egyptian cotton. Whaddya want it for? We don't have a range of clothes, a collection, that requires accessories.'

'No matter.' Crispin was imperturbable, 'We'll just do the accessories. Antinou can turn out boxer shorts for less than 50p a unit. We can do shirts and socks as well – '

His words were abruptly cut off. We were back at the university, sitting on the bench as if nothing had happened. The empty ornamental pond was choked with rotten leaves, starlings blew about the place like avian litter. The Fat Controller had a large gunmetal cigar case open in one hand. He was studying it reverently, as if it were some breviary of tobacco. He said, 'You have to remember that selecting the right cigar is an act of intuition rather than analysis. It's no good looking at the cigars available and attempting to choose one on the basis of certain criteria. Rather, you must wait for the cigar that is – so to speak – ordained, to speak to you. To say "smoke me". This one' – he picked one up gingerly, near to the tip – 'says it is the reincarnation of Cleopatra's asp. I'll buy that.' He lit it with his Zippo.

'I thought connoisseurs never lit their cigars with petrol lighters.'

'Whassat? Oh well, yes, I suppose strictly speaking that is true but it's a mistake to view a sensual pleasure as being a single datum. Rather, every such experience is manifold. If your palate is sufficiently developed you can distinguish the tobacco from the petrol. I myself have rather a taste for petrol. Picked it up during a little sojourn among the Australian aboriginals . . . but anyway, we digress. What did you think of my little lesson: "The History of the Product"?'

'It was very interesting. Was it an hallucination?'

'Don't be so bloody stupid! What's the point in my spending time on you, cultivating you, being perfectly decent towards you, if you're going to manifest such infantile credulousness, eh?'

'I don't call depriving me of my girlfriend being perfectly decent.'

'Still hung up on that, are you? Come now, you cannot possibly imagine that anything could have come of your relation with that chit. In your heart of hearts you know yourself to be incapable of such mutuality, such abandonment of self – '

'But what about my "elective affinity"?'

'That's altogether different.'

'Because that's what you want?'

'Quite so. Now, as to "The History of the Product," an ability to retroscend in this fashion will be of inestimable value to you, it will mean that when you are engaged in assessing the demand for a particular product you can look at similar and instantly unpack the portfolio of its genesis. There is of course another aspect to this, the cultural superstructure that corresponds to this historical basis. I refer, of course, to the discreet advertisements in the quality press, people mouthing fatuously "Oh Barries'", when they see what shirt you're wearing, the flyers Mercer manages to insinuate on to the information desks in some of the major London hotels, and so on and so forth.

'Naturally your shorts are a very simple example of this. When it comes to products that are in more diffuse circulation the retroscendent experience can be considerably more disorientating. Although a skilled retroscender may learn how to pilot himself through all the historical imagery available I fear that lies some way off for you. In the meantime – until you have made your bones, that is – you will needs have to confine yourself to asking my assistance when you wish to retroscend, got that? Good. Now' – he brought himself face to face with his Rolex – 'tempus fucks it. I have a plane to catch. I will see you anon.'

He could never say goodbye or hello, he just came – and went. I was left on the memorial bench, more isolated than ever.

Naturally June couldn't understand why it was that I went on cutting her. And cut her I did. I even had to resort to missing seminars and tutorials, so as to avoid having to speak to her. Initially she was simply bewildered by this but soon she was plain angry. She left a series of notes in my pigeonhole that started off plaintively: 'I'm very confused by what happened between us the other night. I thought you were a caring sort of person, I can't understand why you won't speak to me now. Is it something to do with the sex?' (how right she was) but ended up abusively: 'Ian Wharton, you are the fucking male chauvinist pig to end all fucking male chauvinist pigs. You take a woman out and then dump her. Don't you care at all how people feel?'

If only she could have known how much I cared. If only she could have seen me skulking around at Cliff Top, the very picture of melancholy. Sitting drooped over walls, utterly dejected. I felt the full force of her criticism. Somewhere in my abdomen was a sac of warm caring, a bladder of emotional nutrition, distended with the urge to burst and engender another's heart. But I was constrained, fearfully constrained.

Cut off more than ever from the society of my peers, I fell back on my mother. Since I had been at the university we had seen far less of each other. It was an extension – or so I thought – of the tact she had always shown to me as a child that she didn't impose. However, when I took to hanging about in the new house, when I watched her while she chatted to her staff and guests, or entertained the local burghers, or genteely remonstrated with her suppliers and various tradesmen over the phone, I began to see this seeming tact as an extension of that complicity I had long been aware of. Mother, I sensed, didn't just know a little about Mr Broadhurst, she knew all about him. That's why she was the first to know he was moving out.

I was in my caravan, trying to study on a Sunday afternoon in mid-winter. I was reading some gimcrack book about economics, full of those pictograms that fall half-way between diagrams and drawings, when I heard the thudding of a diesel engine running under the roar of the gale coming in off the sea and over the whirr of the fan heater that was marinading my feet.

The rounded rectangle of my little window on the world gave me a television picture of the site. Outside in the howling, flobs of rain were twisting and twining around the few remaining hutches. I felt a sense of profound foreboding and then I saw them, the gyppos. Naturally I recalled who they were at once – the hawkish profiles, the jet tangles of hair were doubly outlined as the window of their truck slid by mine.

I was outside in an instant. Their brakes must have locked as they were coming down the slope, for there was a twenty-yard slice of chocolate loam where their wheels had scoured the turf. 'What are you up to!' I shouted over the gale. 'Look what you've done. This is private property, you know.' Even as I shouted I sensed the utter absurdity of my words and the ludicrous figure I presented, a slovenly, plump young man, so obviously clumsy and ineffectual, rabbit's ears of shirt-tail escaping from my waistband.

They leapt from the cab in just the way I remembered, lithe and dangerous. 'Gerrart-of-it!' said the larger of the two, moving purposively towards me. 'Come fer thass.' He indicated the shiny fuselage of Mr Broadhurst's caravan.

'But where is Mr Broadhurst?'

'I dunno, laddie. S'not a problem. Gor'all pepperworks 'ere.' He thrust the edge of a clipboard at me like a weapon.

The other gyppo had come up by his shoulder. He was flexing and twisting his simian arms, as if limbering up for violence. 'D'jew wanna argue, muvverfuckah,' he spat.

I broke from them, and ran back up the slope to my mother's house. I ran the length of the new hallway, with its Wilton carpeting, *faux* hunting prints and brocaded wallpaper. I found her in the back kitchen, standing over the chef who was rolling out pastry. 'Those gyppos are here,' I panted. 'They say they're going to take Mr Broadhurst's caravan.'

She looked at me critically, lifting her new gold-rimmed bifocals on to the bridge of her nose. 'Try not to track mud into the house, Ian, and don't you think you should drop the term "gyppos" from your vocabulary – it's awfully common.' Thora Hird was dispensing homilies on the television; she was sitting in front of a Grecian urn.

'But, Mum. He's never said anything to me about moving away from Cliff Top – '

'Ah yes, Ian, but he has to me, he has to me.'

There it was, out in the open. She had no need to give it further emphasis, it could not have been clearer. She knew all about him, she knew all about 'us'; and she either didn't care, or she approved altogether. My mother was at that time becoming suspiciously youthful in appearance. Her breasts were stranded back in the fifties. Enfolded in the crisp embrace of new money, they were pointed and hard, like the nose cones of rockets about to blast off for planetary exploration, the nurturing of new worlds. And her hair – that hair – still curling wilfully, as if every strand were an ungovernable sexual impulse. How could I ever have trusted her?

The new stripped-pine floor vibrated; through the sash window I could see the black truck pulling up the drive towards the main road, the silver caravan coming behind like a drogue that was preventing the gypsies from submerging, escaping into the very centre of the earth. With them went went whatever chance I ever had of regaining my childhood.

CHAPTER FIVE

REHABILITATION

Illness is the beginning of all psychology.
What? Could psychology be – a vice?

Nietzsche, *Twilight of the Idols*

Here's how it happened. I went on attending the university, doing my course modules, and avoiding intimacy in whatever way it proffered itself to me. At the same time I practised assiduously my calculus of personal ritual to ward off any kind of eidesis. I was determined to live as far as possible in the now. If ever I was tempted by the seductive stasis of an eidetic image, I punctured its reflecting skin with a dart and tore it away to reveal the structure of habit below. I squinted and transformed the galaxy into the dust of my dead skin; I always read 'YAW EVIG' from the glistening macadam and avoided giving way. I came to be capable – as he had said I would – of the most beautifully consistent combinations of apprehensions with little twistles of kinaesthetic intimation. I became – in my own small way – a Cassandra of Ca-ca. The most piddling aspects of my embodiment furnished me with prophecy: hanging on whether the flap of gum skin comes away, then . . . the leaf will fall or not fall, I will die or be immortal, the sun will rise or not.

Indeed, it was at this time that, ironically, I turned myself into a genuine adept of the Magus of the Quotidian. So much so that for weeks at a time I could live without eidetiking at all. Ironically, because having shown me what he termed 'retroscendence', The Fat Controller was content to let me stew in my own juice for a while.

I actually thought that his technique for unpacking the hidden history of products was despicable. I wanted my understanding of business to be entirely different, based firmly on analysis and deduction rather than any kind of weird visual intuition.

I dimly understood that by holding out to me this realm of material essences, available by an act of will alone, The Fat

Controller was condemning me to a cosmos of brand names, a metaphysic of motifs, a logic of logos, and an epistemology based on EPOS (The Electronic Point of Sale method of inventory-keeping, which was just coming into use at this time among major retailers). Mine was to be a psyche available for product placement – that was his intention. The interior of my mind was to be shaped according to his merchandising plan, with circular display racks of concepts standing in aisles of cogitation, flanked by long shelves groaning with brightly coloured little ideas.

I could see that if I were to give way to retroscendence the average supermarket gondola, stuck with myriad products like a hedgehog with spines, would become a mystic test-bed able through its thousand portals to suck me into individual sagas so complex, so durable, that I would perhaps never reemerge.

The very ecosystem I inhabited was also to be one of products, striving against built-in obsolescence to individuate themselves, using whatever human means were at their disposal to advance their branded species. I was conscious that underlying it all there must be some Law of Unnatural Selection, which could prove that the fittest product with the most colourful packaging was the most likely to be pollenated by purchase.

But against all my expectations, the longer he kept away, the more I found I could hack it. I relapsed into a seeming normality. I freed myself from the antiquated strait-jacket of his verbose speech patterns. I even smartened myself up, becoming something of a dandy. The boxer shorts from Barries' were followed by shirts and socks, then by jackets and trousers from Di Stato (Anzio's high-street chain), and eventually some Hoage's shoes.

I had no vices and I couldn't take anyone out, so I had nothing to spend my student grant on save for clothes. In my mind at least I was already the smartly turned-out, bright and efficient young executive that I aspired to be. I was determined to render myself generic by the time I left university.

A few months of living like this behind me, I almost managed to convince myself that my whole involvement with the man I called 'The Fat Controller' had been an elaborate fantasy. After all, what evidence did I really have? There's nothing wrong with a man living under an assumed name and besides that, I couldn't prove that Mr Broadhurst and Samuel Northcliffe were one and the same, any more than I could prove that it was The Fat Controller who had killed the woman at the Theatre Royal with a spring-loaded hypodermic full of curare, rather than anyone else.

As for my eidetic happenings, I found them suspect as well; they were so clearly a product of my own fervid visual imagination. When I came to think about it, it struck me that almost all the aspects of my eidesis that The Fat Controller played upon had preceded his intervention, rather than followed from it.

I began to wonder whether or not I had been the victim of an extended delusion, which was perhaps the function of an overheated adolescence leading to some kind of psycho-hormonal explosion. I knew little of psychology but enough to be aware of the impact on the unformed ego of an absent father. Could my investiture of Mr Broadhurst with such sinister and wide-ranging powers have been my way of dealing with the chronic lack of a proper role model?

Under the influence of this late surge of rational speculation I tried to view myself in a different light. Perhaps I wasn't the plaything of a mage, who was determined to drag me into a frightening and chaotic world of naked will, only a seriously neurotic person in need of help.

But what kind of help? I didn't know who or where to turn to. So for the meanwhile I continued with my ritualised observances, obsessively counting the number of steps it took me to walk to any given location, carefully avoiding the cracks in the pavement for fear that the bears of the id might get me, and attending to my bodily functions with the pure metrical devotion of a sadhu.

I also played with the idea that what afflicted me was some kind of strabismus of the psyche. If I strained I could see the world as others did, stereoscopically, but if I relaxed binocular vision would ensue, and while one 'eye' would remain focused, the other would slide away into the clouded periphery where The Fat Controller and his machinations held sway. What was required to hold him at bay was constant vigilance.

Constant vigilance and isolation are a wearing combination, wearing and depressing. I might struggle to hold fast to my course, to become just another off-the-peg person dangling on the idiomatic hook (line and sinker), my voting habits purely a function of minute alterations in fiscal policy, but a moment's relaxation could have a jolting impact.

The Fat Controller – whatever he might be – had ceased to manifest himself. And the human frame on to which I had grafted this delusion had definitely left Cliff Top, but despite this, from time to time I would come across what seemed like obscure messages, quirkily encoded, that threatened to upset my peace of mind.

One day I was browsing in the university library, when for no reason that I could pick upon I drew a biography of Newton from one of the shelves. Flicking through it, I came across a passage that described his psychotic breakdown. Apparently, during the autumn (Ha!) of 1693, Newton – always eccentric and blockaded from the world – became increasingly deluded. He wrote a series of letters to Pepys, Locke and other friends, accusing them of being atheists and Catholics. He even intimated that they had tried to corrupt him by sending female temptresses to seduce him in his Cambridge rooms. The biographer speculated that it may have been failure in his alchemical experiments that led to this breakdown.

It was broad daylight when I read this passage and the sunlight that radiated through the high plate-glass windows illuminated a scene of modernity and order. It didn't matter – as soon as I read the word alchemy, alarm bells began ringing in the fire station of my mind. The engines of ritual, which stood ever ready to staunch any eruption of the magical were speedily limbered up. It was too late, I couldn't prevent myself from eidetiking Mr Broadhurst's unusual caduceus, the one he had made out of an old TV aerial garnished with flex, and I couldn't prevent myself from reading on:

> Newton wrote to Locke saying that he had 'received a visit from a certain Divine of monstrous and Toad-like appearance. This man, or beast, claimed cognisance of divers operations in the Science of Alchemie of which I

> have had no acquaintance. He insisted on examining my alchemical equipment and pronounced that my method of Fixation was inexact. He also drew my Attention to what he claimed were certain impurities in the material of my Cupel. Furthermore he Intimated to me that there was a pure distillate of the very Stone itself buried in precincts of Glastonbury Abbey, to which he alone had access. I cannot do justice to the disagreeable impression that this man, one Broadhurst, had upon me . . .

I shut the book with a bang. I clenched out the light and stuck my fingers in my ears. I rotated the nails so that a cheese paring of wax was scoured from the surface of the drum. I rolled the two pellets of wax between the forefingers and thumbs of each hand and then replaced them in the opposite ears, the whole time humming and appreciating the bitable texture of the linoleum beneath my soles.

On opening my eyes I didn't dare to imagine that this would have worked. I expected him to be with me, his stentorian ubiety transmogrifying the spacious library into somewhere shabby and small. But there was no one.

There were other such incidents. Attracted by the cover with its depiction of a colourful Chinese dragon, I leafed through a copy of De Quincey's *Confessions of an English Opium Eater*. This time I chanced upon a passage where the writer was awakened from his narcotic slumbers by a knocking at his cottage door:

> The servant girl came into my chamber and told me that there was a 'sort of demon' downstairs, jabbering in a strange tongue. I made myself presentable and sallied forth. In the kitchen I found my servant and a stray village child, both dumbstruck by this apparition. I soon established that the 'jabbering' they spoke of was none other than classical Greek, of which this portly figure had an exact command.
>
> 'You are the Opium Eater?' said the man.
>
> 'I am,' I replied quaveringly.
>
> 'Then, dear fellow, make with the stuff, bring forth a get-up, lay on the gear, give us a decent hit for the love

of Mike, for by Zeus I am surely clucking fit to bust.'

Strange as it may seem, I was struck more by this man's preoccupation with opium than by his appearance or choice of language. I gave him a piece, which to my horror he popped straight into his mouth, for it was surely large enough to kill some half-dozen dragoons together with their horses. Then, without more ado, he turned on his heel and left, slamming the door behind him. It was only later when I came to reflect on this incident, that I recalled the man's appearance. He was excessively fat and had a sinister and agressive expression. Altho' his physiognomy was European, he was clad in the turban and loose trousers of a Malay.

I cannot say whether this manifestation was a product of opium or not but ever after the most excruciating of my opium torments have regularly visited me with his likeness and the haunted corridors of my mind have resounded with his peculiar bombast. Perhaps his aspect was a function of those involutes of memory of which I have spoken; and his combination of these attributes, the brutish apparel of the Malay, the features of a bibulous beadle and his predilection for opium were no mere chance but a deep expression of my own pain?

I no more believed in 'mere chance' than De Quincey. The juxtaposition of erudition and slang, the gargantuan habits, the 'sinister and agressive expression'. Surely this was another clue, another coded reference; either that or my capacity for fantasy, temporarily dislodged from my visual imagination, had taken up residence in another realm, polluting my very ability to comprehend.

In a way, The Fat Controller's new method of checking up on me was even more disturbing than his old. I went into a steep decline. I started to show up for my seminars and tutorials shabbily clad, or not at all. One week I failed to turn in an essay on the trade deficit. This was out of character. At the next seminar Mr Hargreaves – the same tutor who had referred poor June to me – asked me to stay behind.

'Wharton,' he began nervously, 'it might not be my place but I have to say that I'm a little worried about you.'

I shuffled uneasily. 'Well, err . . . you know, I've been getting rather anxious about my finals.'

'Come off it, you do consistently well in all your modules – I've had a word with your course tutor – and as you've been continually assessed, you couldn't flunk now even if you wanted to. What's the problem, lad? Apparently you never have anything to do with your peers, you're a solitary. Perhaps I shouldn't interfere but I hate to see a young man throwing his life away.'

I looked into his face. Hargreaves was a bit like a large rodent, a capybara or coypu. He had a questing snout and thin limbs held bent up against his adipose body. It almost goes without saying that he also had fine, Beatle-cropped brown hair and affected a close-clipped beard with the dense consistency of fur. It ran right up and over his cheekbones, leading one to suspect that it was important for him to shave his eye sockets and forehead daily, if he wanted to avoid becoming altogether bestial.

'Yeah,' I muttered at last. 'I haven't been feeling that great.' Then the words started to hiss out of me, stale, rubberised air escaping from a subsiding Li-lo. 'It's just . . . it's just . . . that I don't have many friends and I do feel sort of isolated, I s'pose – ' I pulled up short, I was trespassing on forbidden ground, getting close to revealing more than I should. How could I talk of my other world amid the absolute certainties of textured louvres, plastic chair-and-desk combinations and colour-coded felt-tips?

'If you are feeling depressed' – Hargreaves was entirely solicitous – 'it might be an idea for you to see the Student Counsellor. He's there to help you with any problems you have, did you know that?' I muttered something affirmative. 'Look, here's what I'm going to do.' He brightened up, getting the glow of a man who feels himself on the verge of discharging a disagreeable responsibility. 'I'm going to make an appointment for you to see Dr Gyggle – he's not just a counsellor, he's also a qualified psychiatrist. I'm absolutely sure that a chat with him would help you. You needn't worry' – he was getting happy now, preening his face with his tiny hands – 'this conversation we've had will remain just as confidential as anything you may say to him.'

The next day there was a note from Hargreaves in my pigeonhole – I was to see Dr Gyggle that afternoon. There seemed no going back on it without having to retail some further lie and anyway I was sick at heart – without The Fat Controller's gyroscopic girth to encompass it my world was spinning out of control.

The following afternoon as I walked across the campus, I didn't know it but I was about to commence my full rehabilitation. But I did know that Gyggle was the shrink for me the minute I saw him. It was the beard, I suppose, a beard that was the exact opposite of Hargreaves's beard. Whereas his beard was so clearly a compensation, a making up for unachieved virility, Gyggle's beard was positively rampant, priapic. It was only a beard – true enough – but it had been connected to a man's face for many many years. Clearly it was a transitional object, purpose-built to drag me back into the world of men and affairs.

When I was shown into his little office in the administration block Gyggle was sitting reading something. His forearms were lying on the desk and his skinny torso was framed by a proscenium arch of ring binders, set on shelves that marched up and over his head.

The Gyggle forearms were covered all over with a regular pattern of tight ginger curlicues of hair. In fact, it would be true to say that my first impression was of a man entirely dominated by a regular pattern of tight ginger curlicues of hair. His sleeves were rolled up – which was what led me to make such an assumption – but really it was his hair that set the tone. The curlicues massed at his collar and from here a series of well-defined ginger ridges ascended to his nude pate. Waves of this same hair swept around the back of Gyggle's head, from coast to coast of his oval face. They formed galleries, which seemed so regular they might have been the honeycombed nestings of some breed of super-lice that had reached an advanced accommodation with their host. But however striking, the hair had to be viewed as merely a trailer to the main feature of Gyggle's appearance, the beard.

The beard was a kind of super beard, a beard to end all beards, a great reprise on some of the world's finest and most significant beards. Obviously the way it tumbled – nay, cascaded – down on to the Gyggle chest had close associations with those prophetic beards that lingered in my memory from many hours of tilted observation in cathedrals and museums, yet something about the beard's rigidity, its apparent inflexibility, said Assyria, Sumeria. Whispered epics in the bouncing back of war chariots, chanted louder as the warriors attack – entirely in profile, of course.

When he looked up and turned to greet me Gyggle's real profile showed the beard off to even greater effect and teased me with its diversity. Here was the suggestion of the spreading fan of an eminent Victorian, a beard clotted with high-flown phrases and guilty secretions, a beard of mad power that then faded at the edges into the ineffectualness of a declining constitutional monarchy. What a beard, I thought.

'You must be Ian Wharton.' He looked up from his reading and the beard parted in such a way as to suggest that there might be an affable grimace lying some way behind it.

'Yeah.'

'Tim Hargreaves said that you'd like to have a chat with me about some things. He said you'd been out of sorts recently.'

'Not so recently.'

'What do you mean?'

'I mean I've always been out of sorts, I've always felt like this – oh, you know – almost as long as I can remember.' (As long as the heaving green adumbrates the land, as long as time has refused to be some time but always now, as long as the humungus titles have zipped up from the seam between sea and sky, as long . . .)

'Oh yes.' His voice was soft, honey soft. It was like a net of sound falling over my mind ready to trawl the truth. 'And what is "feeling like this" like?'

Everything was happening so fast – he couldn't be aware of the crisis he was dragging me towards. The room was a pressurised cabin suddenly ruptured. I sensed the warmth screaming out of the atmosphere to be replaced with the absolute zero of his clinical persona but I couldn't stop myself. 'I – I, I'm an eid-eid

. . . I've got an eidetic memory.' I stuttered and then blurted. Gyggle steepled his freckled fingers and tucked them under a tier of the beard. He looked at me with yellow feral eyes.

'You don't say. How fascinating. I've done a little work on eidesis myself. What kind of eidetic memory have you got?'

I was flummoxed. 'I – I didn't know there were different kinds.'

'Oh yes, there's eidesis that concentrates on form and proportion; eidesis that acts mnemonically, producing near-instant recall through combinations of letters or numerals; there's a kind of mathematical eidesis whereby equations and aspects of calculus are viewed spatially and of course there's common-or-garden eidesis, which people call "photographic memory" – '

'That's me!' I was embarrassed by my exclamation; it sounded like a yelp of boyish enthusiasm.

'I see.' Gyggle was unperturbed. 'While it's true that an awful lot of eidetikers have problems with communication and some are even autistic, those that aren't don't tend to be overly neurotic or unhappy. On the contrary they usually put their gifts into some satisfying but resolutely unimaginative task. They acquire multiple degrees, purposelessly log facts, or do photoreal drawing after photoreal drawing – each one notable only for its lack of – how can I put it, emotional bite?' The ragged hole appeared in the beard again; it occurred to me that the shrink was baiting me in some way, teasing me. 'Actually,' he went on, 'these eidetikers are usually terribly ordinary people, unimaginative in the extreme, hmmm?'

'My problem is quite the reverse,' I said emphatically. 'I think I may be suffering from an excess of imagination, either that or . . . or . . .' And there it was, it struck me that I had nothing to lose, I was damned either way. If I betrayed the pact between myself and The Fat Controller he would undoubtedly destroy me, fillet me, excarnate me in the screaming void. But if I said nothing, turned tail and ran from Gyggle, what hope was there for an ordinary life for Ian Wharton? What hope was there of love?

'Or what? Do you think you are going mad?' I nodded. Gyggle got up from behind his desk and came round to the front of it. He was very tall, perhaps six foot five, all elbow and forearm, like an enormous ginger praying mantis. He propped his absence of arse against the rim of his desk and contemplated me. 'Look Ian, I'm here to help you, I'm not here to grind my own axe. I'm not a very orthodox kind of counsellor or psychiatrist but if there's anything within my power that I can do to help you, then I'll do it. Now tell me what it is about your eidetic ability that is causing you so much distress.'

I told Gyggle. I told him everything. I told him in great detail. I omitted nothing, nothing, that is, save for The Fat Controller. I explained how it was that as a child I had been told I was an an eidetiker but that it had meant nothing to me. And how it was that I had rediscovered the gift in pubescence, as if prompted by my burgeoning sexuality. I told him how I could freeze my eidetic images, then project my phantom body into them, to discover things that I could not possibly have known. I told him that this bizarre gift had frightened me, made me feel vulnerable; and that I had felt compelled to develop a magical system of my own to prevent my hyperactive visual memory from destroying me altogether.

The whole time I spoke Gyggle maintained his desk-propping position, fingers steepled to beard, impartial eyes cast down into my own. When I had finished he had only two things to say.

'It's very interesting that in all of this you don't say anything about your relationships. Most of the students who come to me with problems are absolutely preoccupied by their parents, their friends, their sexual partners – ' I grunted noncommittally. 'And the other thing is that if what you say is true then you have a form of extra-sensory perception. You know, there are certain tests – scientific tests – that can determine whether or not this is the case.'

'No, I didn't know that.'

'Well, there are and what I would like to propose to you is this, that you allow me to do these tests on you. There are the facilities here, in the experimental psychology faculty. I don't want you to imagine for a moment that I don't believe every word of what you tell me. It's just that whatever the reality of your condition verifying it will constitute a kind of catharsis – do you know what that means?' I tried to give him a withering look. 'Of course you do; Tim Hargreaves told me that you are an exceptional student. Now, if you'll excuse me I believe our hour is up. Could you make an appointment with the secretary for next week? We'll meet here and then go over to the lab together, OK?'

I rasped my chair backwards and got up, I muttered goodbye.

As I was pulling the institutional door of his office shut behind me he looked up from the reading matter he had taken up again and said, 'And Ian – '

'Y-yes?'

'Try not to worry, lad, I'm here to look after you.'

In the mathematical corridor with its shown brickworking and angled spotlights, a young woman was waiting to go in. She regarded me warily from under a fringe of split ends. One small hand, the nails surrounded by gnawed raw flesh, clutched a wad of tissue paper against her seeping eye. For some cruel reason I took heart from the very ordinariness of her misery.

I now entered the empirical and experimental phase of my life. Every Thursday afternoon I would join Gyggle in his office and together we would cross the campus to the squat blockhouse that housed the experimental psychology faculty. We would descend to the basement and make our way through a maze of waist-high partitioning. Under the hum of stroboscopic strip lighting, fidgeting, rodentine psychology students scampered this way and that, clutching streamers of computer printout, clipboards and calculators. So pre-programmed did their behaviours seem, that they themselves might have been the subjects of some meta-experiment and the pallor of their laboratory coats a function of their caged confinement.

First of all Gyggle tried me on the same sort of rudimentary exercises that I remembered performing as a child. He would make me look at pictures and then reproduce them with coloured pencils, or else ask me to rotate a figure mentally a certain number of degrees around a given perpendicular before attempting to redraw it. But soon we progressed to more state-of-the-art experimentation. Sequences of words would be flashed up on a VDU, so quickly that – in theory – they could only be perceived subliminally. These tests established exactly what they had done before; namely that I did indeed have an exceptionally accurate visual memory. I was able to recall perfectly quite long sequences of words even when I was exposed to each for little more than twenty milliseconds.

Throughout the testing Gyggle was solicitous and gentle. He said nothing to me about my fears for my sanity and behaved as if what we were doing were a common exercise, undertaken for purely scientific purposes. It was this manner of his, more than anything else, that seemed to have a therapeutic benefit. For, as the testing progressed, so my life outside of the sessions began to acquire the lineaments of a normalcy I had never felt before.

I took to spending more time with my mother again, rather than shutting myself up in my caravan. Our talk was unemotional, inconsequential. With her new-found gentility Mother had bought the ability to make endless small talk. Coming from her tight mouth, the county trilling on local lawlessness and moral decline made these cankers seem wholly benign. She was transformed from the young trollop I remembered to the middle-aged reader of Trollope she had always wanted to be. There was a slackening of the tension in the psychic umbilicus, and more importantly, there was no reference to Mr Broadhurst.

At the university I came out from my shell. I actually talked to my fellow students and built up some relations with people, which, if not quite friendships, at least satisfied the definition of acquaintance.

One day, coming across June in the corridor alone, instead of hurrying past, my face to the wall, I stopped and spoke to her. I knew she now had a boyfriend. I had seen them together, arm-in-arm, taking their mutual attraction for a walk. Perhaps it was this, the fact that she now had someone else to love her, that made it possible for me to make a proper apology, to stutter out confusedly, red-faced, that I was sorry about what had happened. I told her that I had had a sort of a breakdown, and that I was appalled by what I had done. I wish I could have said that she was sweetly understanding, but she looked at me as if I were an incubus that had raped her and scraped along the brickwork, desperate to get past.

After a couple of months like this Gyggle changed the nature of our experiments. 'Well, Ian,' he said, stroking the beard as if it were a favourite pet that had curled up on his chin, 'I think we have established incontrovertibly that you are an eidetiker of sorts. Now let's test the veracity of your rather more extravagant claims.'

Gyggle had obtained a series of computer-visualisation models from an extra-sensory perception researcher in Texas. These involved the experimental subject in observing three-dimensional figures on a VDU, and then answering questions about aspects of the figures that were knowable – but hardly at an intuitive level. For example, if the figure was a line diagram of a room with four windows set at different heights, the programme would ask me whether a line of sight from the far corner of the room would enable me to see a particular point outside the window nearest to me, a point that shifted on the screen at speed.

When Gyggle first explained this experiment to me I almost laughed at how facile it was. For me – who had consciously to struggle against the imagaic maelstrom implicit in the idea of retroscendence – to have to deploy my powers in this pedestrian manner seemed nothing less than absurd. I said as much. 'I think you've missed the point about my eidetiking, Dr Gyggle.'

'Oh yes, and why's that?'

'Well, you see – I thought I explained this to you – if I were to eidetik now I would go into a kind of a trance. No time would pass for you but during that trance I could unpack whatever reserves of information this particular visual scene contains.'

'Give me an example.'

'Well, I could, for instance, discover what shape your chin is under that beard.'

It was meant to be a jocular observation but even as I said it I knew that I had transgressed some important Gyggle taboo. It's like that with beards, particularly medical beards and even more so psychiatric ones. Although their wearers adopt them as naturally woven badges of individuality, the second they are challenged, taken out of context, they rise up to form chin-borne hackles.

'I don't see that my beard has anything to do with it,' his honey voice huffled. 'But if you think you can – do.'

I went into a full-blown eidetic trance. I encapsulated the whole scene, the dingy cubicle with its plywood partitions; the warped lino, as undulant as the earthen floor of a barn; Gyggle's hideous cheesecloth shirt, the buttons pulled apart to the sternum, revealing still more tight ginger curlicues. I took in both the general: lunar dust motes caught in the sidereal glare of neon light, and the particular: the smear of cobweb on an inch of mushroom flex that protruded from the ceiling above.

When the eidetic image of the room was fully and accurately frozen inside of me, I made my move, or tried to make my move, because nothing happened. I was somehow reversing that pivotal moment in my eidetic career eight years before, when Mr Broadhurst had bade me look in his waistcoat pocket and then made his move. Now it was I who couldn't move; more than that I wasn't even able to form an idea of what it would be like to move. Formerly my eidetic body, the tool with which I worked upon my visions, had felt as defined as if three-dimensional crop marks had been described in the air. My wilful grasp upon it had been entirely unproblematic, as sure as neat fingers picking up pins, or knitting, and then casting off the atomic stitches of the material world.

I couldn't even imagine what this sensation might be like any more, so utterly had it evaporated. I conceptually fumbled, struggled to get some purchase on the sempiternal sheen of the visual image; but there was nothing, no movement, no astral agility, it remained frozen. Or at least almost entirely frozen. Just before I snapped out of it, aborted the failed trance, I thought I saw – although I couldn't be certain – the ragged hole in the beard through which Gyggle addressed the world unravel a little at its edge, exposing a slug side of what might have been Gyggle's lip.

'Well then,' said the old fox, 'have you eidetically removed the hairs from my chinny-chin-chin?'

'I-I, I can't seem to. What I mean is – I'm trying.'

'Trying,' pronounced the psychiatrist sententiously, 'is lying.'

'I can't understand it.' I was shaking and sweating. If I could no longer eidetik effectively, had my status as apprentice and licentiate of the Brahmin of the Banal been removed at one fell stroke?

'I'm not surprised,' said my therapist, 'for nor can I.'

'Whaddya' mean?'

'Well, put it this way, you claim to be able to derive information from internal visual images which you believe to directly correspond to the phenomenal world.'

'Whaddya' mean, "phenomenal"?' It was the sort of jargon I expected from you-know-who.

'I mean the commonsensical world of material objects and appearances. You claim that you can discover things that are unknowable in an orthodox fashion by moving about the representation of this world inside your own head. Is that right?'

'Yeah.'

'So if I were to screen a feature film for you, and in it there was a scene that took place with two characters talking on a sofa, you would be able to tell me whether there was an object lying behind it?'

'Yeah.'

'Supposing it was an animated film – would you be able to enter into that world as well?'

'I s'pose so, but I've never really done it.'

'But in the case of such an animated film, there wouldn't be anything behind the cartoon sofa; not only that, the sofa couldn't be said to have a behind at all. Do you see what I mean?'

'We-ell – '

'No. Not "we-ell". The point is that you are suffering from a complex delusion. There is nothing behind the cartoon sofa and if you find anything it's because you yourself have put it there. There can be no picture of the world in your head that exists independently of your assertions and beliefs about it. To know something is to participate in a communicable truth. Your whole belief in your eidetic power rests on a misconception of the nature of consciousness itself.'

He was standing over me as he said this, in his characteristic lecturing pose, the edge of a desk slotted firmly into his lack of backside. This posture always made me suspect him of having a horizontal cleft slicing through his buttocks, betokening a random – but adaptive – mutation, taking humans closer to being office furniture. He was chewing gum and the nyum-nyumming of his long jaw sent the tail of the beard wagging across his shirt-front. 'Come on now,' he went on. 'Let's do the rest of the experiments and see if you can prove me wrong.'

I couldn't. I couldn't even manage the simplest of manipulations involving extra-sensory perception. Gyggle started off with the most sophisticated of these, the symbol and colour cards, but was soon reduced to getting me to try and guess – and a guess is all I could make – which of three paper cups had a ping-pong ball under it. At my best I did no better than average. Then, when we went back to rotating mentally the computer simulation of the room and attempting to 'see' possible lines of sight, I had a further shock. I found that my grasp on the image itself was now hazy, the very mechanisms of my mind seemed to have been injected with lobal anaesthetic, blown up into a fuzzy ineptitude. The Kodak laboratories of my eidesis were being dismantled; soon all that would be left was an out-of-order passport-photo-booth, mouldering on an empty station platform.

To give Gyggle his due, he didn't crow. On the contrary, when that afternoon's session ended and we were walking back across the campus, he put one of his Anglepoise arms across my shoulders and attempted some avuncularity. 'Ian,' he schmoozed, 'you know, you are a prodigy, just not the sort of prodigy you thought you were. May I speak frankly?' As if you've ever done anything else, I thought to myself but didn't say. 'You see, I think that you are what's called a borderline personality, with pronounced schizoid tendencies. That sounds a lot heavier than it really is, because what our testing has proved is that you are not psychotic in any orthodox way. When your private reality is challenged, it yields to the truth. Can you see that?'

'S'pose so.'

'S'pose so', that's what stayed with me after we had parted, that 'S'pose so', with all the sullen acquiescence it implied. But whatever I thought of him, Gyggle's therapy had been one hundred per cent successful. By forcing me to take part in rituals that were scientifically formulated the psychiatrist had logically inverted the magical process whereby my original eidetic memory had ripped the meniscus, thrusting me into the noumenal world.

That day was a turning point for me and afterwards my life improved immeasurably. The very next morning I arose and, without any premeditation, any thought at all, for the first time in adulthood I went though my morning toilet not noting the precise conformity of my actions to the schema of habit. It was the same in all the other areas of my life; removed from the need to protect myself against the horrors of enhanced eidesis, I began to live as others did, blithely and unconsciously. I didn't even have to bother with understanding that incomprehension is bliss.

I swam through events now, rather than surveyed them. I felt the corporeal elephant on whose back my world was supported amble effortlessly along, rather that it being necessary for me to lean out from the howdah of my head and goad him.

What a relief. Can you imagine it, to have grown up insane and then in one fell swoop to achieve sanity? I doubt it, because it is inconceivable, just as you cannot imagine what it would be like to be blind from birth and then gifted with sight (but of course I can). I had broken the cycle of eight thousand lifetimes and defiled the banal brahmin inside me, polluted him by contact with the testable, the material proofs of induction. I kicked pebbles ahead of me on the path up from my caravan to my mother's hotel and, with each 'thwok', my terrible adolescent idealism was refuted.

This all happened just before Easter, at the end of my penultimate term at Sussex. It meant that that summer, despite the pressure of finals, I was able to enjoy human company and gain succour from it, in a way that had previously been denied to me.

I found myself revising with the small colloquia that lay

around the grassy precincts of the university. The young are more forgiving than adults, and despite the haughty isolation I had practised, I was far more accepted than I could have hoped for. I got on first-name terms with the other managers-in-the-making. They invited me to punk parties as noisy as tractor factories, where I swigged flat cans of beer, already shaken with a twist of cigarette butt.

In turn I took some of them back with me to Cliff Top. There we descended to the pebbled beach and filtered ourselves, giggling, into the porous sea. My mother instructed her deferential staff to serve us tea on the croquet lawn. We sat stuffing ourselves with smoked-salmon sandwiches, slurping Earl Grey, while she charmed and intimidated them with her stolen airs and purloined graces. They all thought me secure, even if they didn't find Cliff Top exactly homey.

The aunts and cousins arrived for their annual break just after I had finished my finals. By now some of the cousins had children of their own – the pullulating Hepplewhite swarm had leapt to another branch. The new kids were indistinguishable from the old and the new parents were just the same, for the female cousins had all married, or shacked up with, wispy, indefinite, ineffectual men; and the male cousins had simply married their mothers.

My mother kept them away from her country house hotel. They were confined to the ratty quarter-acre of ground, screened off by the landscapers, where the few remaining caravans crouched in shabby senescence. But they didn't seem to mind, or feel remotely affronted.

Here they lay as of old, like a colony of seals, eating scallops and rubbery whelks, swigging glasses of light ale, blowing raspberries on kidflesh sticky with vanilla ice-cream and frosted with sand.

'Ian's going to London,' announced my mother to one and all. 'He's done awfully well at the university and now he's got a job, an important job as well. Tell your aunts and cousins about your new position, Ian.'

'Aye, tell us,' they chorused, an antistrophe of flower-patterned dresses.

'It's nothing really,' I said. 'It's not even in London proper, I'll be staying at a place called Erith Marsh. I'm going to be a marketing assistant for a company there – '

'Oh aye,' said one of the aunts, who was scrutinising a dicky-looking mussel, as if it were a suspicious traveller and she an immigration officer. 'What's t'cumpany do then, lad?'

'Um, well, they make valves.'

'Valves?'

'Yeah, valves for the oil industry. They make the shut-off valves that get put in the drill bit to prevent blow-outs.'

The aunt gestured to the far end of the sun porch where one of her sons sat. Of necessity, like all Hepplewhite men, he was shadowy, emasculated. 'I think our Harry has wun of them,' said the aunt. 'Over a year married an' our Tracey still isn't knocked up – he must be blowin' out all over t'place!'

The whole gang subsided into coarse guffaws, thigh-slapping, knee-pounding. It was all the same as it ever was. Except for mother, that is. She stood off to one side, her lips twisted into a grimace of disgust at their vulgarity.

When the autumn came, and I finally packed up my car and made ready to leave Cliff Top, she came over unexpectedly emotional. 'You'll take care of yourself, now won't you, my darling?'

After a couple of weeks with her sisters, I heard the false note not just in her accent, but in her voice as well. How had my mother transformed herself into this dower-house chatelaine? This scion of the squirearchy? My curiosity was overidden, though, by a more powerful inclination, to get the hell out. So I merely downplayed my reply. 'Of course I will, Mother, I'm only going up the road, I'll come back at weekends.'

'Oh you say that but I know better. You'll be sucked up and seduced by the beau monde, I know you will.' Pearly tears seeded themselves in the corners of her eyes.

'I'd hardly call Erith Marsh the beau monde, Mother.'

'I don't like to talk about it, Ian, because it's far too painful for me. You know I still miss your father. The way he went away hurts me to this day. You'll not be like him, will you?' She went up on her toes and kissed me.

I felt the shock of the old, of the Mummy smell, the atomised odour of atavism. It welled up, reclaiming its rightful position in the hit parade of the senses: No. 1 with a bullet. The corner of her mouth pressed against mine and in concert with her sharp hand, which clutched at my ample buttock, her sharper tongue slid ever so slightly between my lips.

'Contemptible Essene, cloistral nonentity'. The Fat Controller's words rung once more in my ears as my rollerskate of a car caromed up the A22 to London. That fucking woman, the kinky Clytemnestra, how I hated her. She'd tied my cock to her apron strings in preparation for flour-dusting and rolling out. She kneaded me, all right, she wanted me transformed into puff pastry just like Daddy.

I had accepted a position with I.A. Wartberg Limited, which, as I had told the aunts, was a company responsible for the manufacture of the deep-bore drilling valves employed in the North Sea oil industry.

Mr Hargreaves at Sussex had been surprised by my choice. My grades were excellent and I had had hands-on work experience with marketing agencies in the West End. This was the early-eighties and Britain was clawing its way out of recession on the back of a demand-led boom. Marketing was the dialectical materialism of the regime and I was in an ideal position to leapfrog my way quickly towards apparatchik status.

However, cautious and pragmatic as ever, I realised that before I could take part in the airier abstractions of my chosen profession I needed to confront the nitty-gritty, the hard business of actually selling things, specific products, to industrial customers. Added to that, there was something about the Wartberg works that I found soothing the first time I went there for the interview.

The great galvanised iron shed where the valves were made was a cacophonous and tumultuous place, full of Stakhanovite workers torturing plugs of super-heavy metal with screaming drill bits. The adjoining suite of offices where I reported was inadequately sound-proofed, so that I felt myself both surrounded and shot through by the very processes that I would be attempting to market.

There was also Wartberg himself: he set the pattern for all my future employers. His father was a German-Jewish refugee and his mother Welsh, but Wartberg was an aggressive anglophile, given to wearing tweed suits and blathering on about flower growing, law and order, the decline of British standards (he had just obtained one for his best-selling valve), the prohibitive business rate and so on.

I warmed to him instantly. He ran the company as if he had suddenly and unexpectedly found himself on the footplate of a runaway engine. He was constantly dashing from the shop floor to the offices, to his car, to his suppliers, to his customers and back again. He was small, sweaty and effusive with shiny brown hair and eyes. We got on very well together and when after only two months with the company my immediate boss – the marketing manager, a sallow individual with a Solihull whine – suffered a perforated ulcer (I couldn't prevent myself from eidetiking this, the wall of his duodenum like a rusty car door, sharp flakes of oxidised tissue spearing into him), I got his job.

Of course this doesn't cover everything, this simple schema – Bye-bye, Mummy, Whittingtonesque entry to London – wasn't all that was going on, oh no. My therapy with Dr Gyggle had continued and now entered a new phase.

After the deconstruction of my eidetic capability, Gyggle had insisted that I go on seeing him. We had continued with our Thursday-afternoon appointments for the duration of my university career. 'I wish to build up a more intimate relationship with you, Ian,' the hairy shrink had told me. 'I know that you are predisposed to leave things here; I have employed purely technical means to help you rid yourself of something you wish to regard as a technical problem but behind this eidetic delusion we both know there lies an emotional reality. To employ a piece of Freudian jargon, I do not think you will be able to attain full genitality unless we investigate this realm, hmm?'

'Full genitality?'

'A successful emotional and sexual relationship.'

'Oh, oh that.' Uncanny, the way he pinpointed my preoccupation. For, if there was one aspect of The Fat Controller's legacy that still troubled me severely it was the sex thing. Specifically the grotesque threat that were I to penetrate a woman I would lose my penis.

'What are you frightened of, Ian?' He probed me psychologically, whilst laying siege with the battering ram of his biro to the airy battlements of the beard.

I thought to myself: Sit this one out, he'll let it lie. I knew that shrinks were meant to respect the inability of their patients to express certain fundamental anxieties, that the whole thrust of their endeavour was to move around the edifice of such neuroses, gradually excavating their foundations in memory with a sort of verbal teaspoon.

But Gyggle wasn't that kind of shrink; he kept on at me. 'I know that you've built up some kind of sustaining narrative behind your eidetic delusion – it cannot but be otherwise. You've told me that you spent your adolescence in isolation, actually codifying every little bodily habit and cognitive loop – '

'Yes! And I told you why, because I was frightened of eidetiking myself. What bothers me is what bothers everyone else, nothing special. It's the same common fear that I will fall apart, physically and emotionally, that I will be reduced to a pile of tattered pulp, that I will never be loved by anyone, that I will fail, like . . . like – '

'Like your father?'

'Yeah, like him, the contemptible Essene.'

'I'm sorry? What did you say?'

'Oh, nothing, nothing.'

Gyggle also had some good news for me – he was to accompany me to London. He was going back into the National Health Service and had taken a consultancy in a drug dependency unit based at the Lurie Foundation Hospital for Dipsomaniacs on Hampstead Road.

'Not that I'm particularly interested in junkies, you understand.' Gyggle was driving me along the coast road to Brighton as he spoke. He had taken me under his featherless wing to this extent, giving me lifts and sharing with me some of his unusual theories. 'It's just that these kind of obsessive-compulsive personalities provide me with research fodder. Since no one seems able to do anything with these people they won't mind what I get up to, tee-hee!' He giggled girlishly, as if he were contemplating some impromptu lobotomies, and the beard, which flowed down over the steering wheel, rustled suggestively in the hollow socket of the speedometer. 'It'll be OK for you to go on seeing me there. I can arrange for you to be an anonymous patient, so that it won't interfere with your prospects at all.' He turned to me and gave me his habitual smile-implying parting of the beard. I tried to look grateful.

The whole time that I was working at Erith with Wartberg I would journey right across London every Friday afternoon to see Gyggle at his new office. I was grateful. I came to trust Gyggle – and even like him. After all, he had managed to dismantle the magical aspects of my eidesis and now he began to chew away at the very grist of what he termed my 'delusionary apparatus'.

It took many months more for me to feel safe enough to talk to him about The Fat Controller, but there came a time, when the memory of our last vertiginous encounter had dimmed, that I became prepared to risk it. Gyggle was, of course, entranced. I knew that for him The Fat Controller confirmed it – I was his Wolf Man, his Anna O. He told me as much.

'If it weren't so entirely destructive of your recovery, Ian, I would love to publish,' he said to me. 'For I don't think any clinician has ever had the privilege of witnessing such a complex example of hysteria. This man, Mr Broadhurst, who you transformed into your "Fat Controller", your personified id, you understand now what he really was?'

'Well, if I accept your hypothesis that all my subsequent experiences were hysterical embellishments, I suppose he was just a mild eccentric, an ordinary seaside retiree.'

'Of course, he's probably dead by now.'

'Oh I doubt that.'

'Why? Why do you doubt it?'

There was the rub. I doubted it because whatever the efficacy of Dr Gyggle's treatment and however convincing his explanation of how a lonely and fucked-up boy built up a delusion both to compensate for the lack of a father and punish himself for his own Oedipal crime, I still couldn't convince myself that I was entirely rid of my mage.

He continued to dog me. He was a black penumbra in the corner of my visual field, a shadow that chased the sunlight, the very chiaroscuro of the commonplace. Sometimes, sitting eating a sandwich on a park bench or jolting on the top deck of a bus through South London, I would hear his voice echo through my inscape. His jolly, fat man's voice, expansive and chilling. My inability to unbelieve in him hung on to me by the jaws, as I ascended the corporate ladder.

When I tired of writing press releases on new lube concepts I left Wartberg's valve business to go to the Angstrom Corporation, where I worked on the launch of a new biscuit, the Pink Finger. After three years there I was head-hunted by a marketing agency, D. F. & L. Associates, which was based just north of the City. Here I took up a position with the grand title of 'Consultant'. My job was to prepare the groundwork for a revolutionary new financial product.

In seven years I had as many new cars, each one more highly powered and larger than the last. I became a wearer of double-breasted suits, a leaner on bars, a discusser of interest rates. All to some avail, for I now sank gratefully into my own assembly life line, sank into the forgetfulness of my own habitual patterns.

At Easter and Christmas I still went home to Cliff Top. Mummy had retired from the hotel business. She had made enough money to maintain Cliff Top as the substantial manor house it had become. No matter that it was an ersatz creation – Queen Anne impregnated by Prince Charles – she believed in her *haute* credentials. And although I had disappointed her by going into 'trade', I was still the son of the house. As we sat drinking sherry together and I watched her acquire the jowled ovine features of all elderly English gentlewomen, I found it hard to summon up my old anger. I even found it difficult to believe that she had ever been in cahoots with Mr Broadhurst.

She spoke of him occasionally, as if blithely unaware of any possible alter-egos that he might have. 'I had a card from

Mr Broadhurst the other day,' she bleated. 'You remember him, dear?'

'Yes, Mama, how could I forget him.' (And how could Gyggle have been stupid enough to imagine that he was dead?)

'He's getting on now, of course, poor man.'

'Yes, he must be very old now.'

'He tells me he may have to go into a rest home. He can't really manage by himself any more.' Apparently he had become nothing more than this, forage for commonplace family small talk.

And as for those alter-egos, his trade name 'Samuel Northcliffe' still cropped up in the financial and marketing press. He was a member of syndicates involved in leveraged buy-outs, he was a prominent Lloyd's underwriter, he was a consultant for this corporation and an adviser to that emirate. But when I concentrated on the postage-stamp-sized photographs bearing his name that had started to appear, I could no longer be certain that he and The Fat Controller were one and the same. It seemed far more likely that, as Dr Gyggle suggested, I had become aware of Samuel Northcliffe separately and incorporated information I had gleaned from the newspapers into my fantasy.

Dr Gyggle wasn't satisfied with my progress. He regarded my attainment of 'full genitality' as the ultimate goal of his therapy and he was determined that I should enjoy a complete cure. Not until the spectre of The Fat Controller was fully exorcised from my psyche would I be able to form an adult relationship.

'I'm convinced that the resolution of all this lies buried deep in your unconscious,' he told me as we sat chatting in his office at the DDU. 'I can talk to you, you can talk to me. We can try all sorts of techniques to get in touch with the hinterland of your psyche but my feeling is that, unless you yourself are prepared to voyage there, it will prove impossible to extirpate this negative cathexis. Somewhere deep down, your idea of what it is to be a person, to truly engage in the world, has become critically interfused with childish fantasy. Your choice of iconography is of course highly significant in this context.'

To begin with Gyggle tried me on sensory deprivation. He

had hijacked a proportion of the Unit's budget to buy a sensory-deprivation tank which he kept in a basement of the hospital. It was such wacky financial apportionments as this that – or so he claimed to me – made him a voguish and sought-after practitioner.

Unfortunately, whatever remnants of my eidetic ability remained made me entirely unsuitable for this particular therapy. Going down to the hospital basement and disrobing in a utility room full of bleach bottles and moulting mops was a tantilisingly prosaic prelude to my voyages into inner space. But once Gyggle had positioned me in the tank – which crouched there like a miniature submarine, or a twenty-first-century washing machine – and swung shut the rubber-flanged door, I found it impossible to lose – and therefore as he hoped, reencounter – my self.

The lulling cushion of blood-heat saline solution I floated on did help me to neglect those bodily fears that were so much a part of me. Awareness of time and even of whether I was waking or sleeping soon drained away. I would sink down into a velvet void so entire and impenetrable that whether it was I or I was it, became moot. But then, just at the point where my doubts about the external world had become a crescendo and I was certain that revelation was nigh, some glitch would occur. Either the salt would sting into a cut or raw spot on my body, bringing back bodily feeling in one fell swoop, or else, from somewhere in the bowels of building, my ears, questing for the remotest of stimuli, would pick up on the sound of a toilet being flushed, or perhaps a trolley banging against a wall. In a split-second I would build on this particle of noise and construct an idea of the kind of world that could produce such a phenomenon. Needless to say, this new world always bore an uncanny resemblance to the one I had so recently abandoned.

Gyggle wasn't to be put off by this; instead of retreating or retrenching he suggested even more radical measures. 'It isn't altogether ethical,' he said, while watching me shower hexagonal salt crystals from my inner thighs, 'but then you and I haven't had an orthodox therapeutic relationship.'

'What isn't altogether ethical?'

'They used to advocate it for withdrawing heroin addicts – naturally they had little success. Then they tried it with various kinds of depression, even psychoses. Invariably the cure proved far worse than the disease.'

'What the hell are you talking about?'

'Deep sleep, that's what I want you to let me do, Ian. I want to put you under for at least forty-eight hours. I think that only by maximising long periods of REM, or dream sleep, will we be able to summon up this demon of yours. Then once he's rematerialised we will be able to fight him, hmm?'

Why did I let him persuade me to do this? The answer is simple. Sure, I had a good job and a comfortable home, I even had people who invited me to their houses. I had the trappings of success, of social acceptability. I had got over a particularly traumatic childhood and adolescence and looked set fair for a modicum of stability as an adult. But there was this sex problem, of course, and there was something else, a rootlessness, an atemporality about my life.

Try as I might to be in the present, to subsume myself to history, to see myself as just another corpuscle coursing along the urban arteries, I couldn't. There was an anachronistic feel to my whole life, a kind of alienation that I couldn't quite understand. It came out with particular force in my work. It didn't matter how innovative the products I set out to market actually were, I could not prevent myself from seeing them already in some illimitable bazaar of the far future, long obsolete and hopelessly dated, so much cosmological car-boot-sale fodder.

It impinged on me, this business of always being in the Now. Riding along in my automobile there was no particular time to go to, just a moiling moment. I agreed with Gyggle, only by entering the dreamscape, the hypercast of my hotted-up mind, could I hope to resolve this paradox and once and for all free myself from the malevolent force which I felt had shaped my life.

He told me that in the past insulin had been used to put people in coma states but he wouldn't dream of doing anything as crude or violent; a silky drip of valium sedation was all that was required. Gyggle would store me in a spare room of the hospital and keep me under twenty-four-hour observation while I was unconscious.

INTERMISSION

What this country needs is a good five-cent cigar.

T.K. Marshall

So, where were we? Listening to the fridge, right? Listening to the modulated hum, the gaseous cough, the rubber shudder.

Twenty Great Fridge Hits, now that's an album you could market truly effectively. There has to be a demand out there for this kind of thing, everyone is so hip to the idea of ambient music nowadays, and what could be more consummately ambient than a fridge? It's both in the environment, of the environment and apparently a smidgeon of a threat to the precious fucking environment.

OK, granted, perhaps forty-five minutes of different fridge noises alone might be a bit of a non-starter. We'd have to jazz it up a little, get a few prominent vocalists to sing over the coolant's bubble, a few name producers to chip the chilly vibration down to its component cubes and then restack it into a great wall of freezing sound. Then I think we'd be in business, then I'm sure you'd have a nice little earner on your hands.

I say you, but I mean me. I'd dive below the line and use direct marketing for this one. I'd go to a list broker of my acquaintance. A nervy man in an electric-blue Anzio suit, his body a twitching live-wire but poorly earthed to the keyboard of his computer.

Whenever I go to see him, he is vivified by his connection with so many passive consumers; their purse-mouths suck greedily at his psychic account. His fingers are splayed out so that he can feel the very pulse of hundreds of megabytes of information flowing into him. The hard disc holds the teeming registers of potential purchasers and his own mind is merged with this other, faster random-access memory, so that he can turn to me and say, 'You want ABC ones with late four-door Volvos? We've got it. You want certified accountants in Acorn areas 117 through 492 with a proven history of competition entering? We've got it. You want eighteen to forty-four-year-old ethnic minority home owners? Hey, we've got it.'

More than that he can mash these lists of prospects together to produce delightfully implausible juxtapositions: exercise-bike owners who take educational holidays to the Ukraine (there are only seven in Greater London); lepers with a penchant for Janet Reger lingerie (suprisingly enough, several hundred in Roseland alone); Liberal Democrat Nintendo enthusiasts who are also Wagner buffs (not as many as one might have hoped for).

After twenty minutes or so with the list broker you start to see the world as he does. His vision is a disconcerting one, his eyebeams shoot out, clear but solid room-dividers that slice any gathering, any grouping of people, into their listable characteristics. He has geo-demo vision (geographic and demographic breakdown, to you). He peers into a bar and instantly this reticulated gaze comes into play, falling over the assembled suits, so that each one is caught by their vent-gills in the apropriately sized mesh square, struggling to free themselves before the marketeers close in, wielding stunning Free Offers.

My fridge album is really going to test the list broker, push him to the very limit. 'You want what?' he'll say. 'You want a list of people whose idea of fun is listening to the fridge at three o'clock in the morning? You don't ask for much, do you, mate?' He shakes his head, he ums and ahs, his Thelonious Monk fingers chop at the keyboard in talented frustration. But then he has it, he's off and running, he's merging and purging that database with frantic abandon.

'Let me see . . . Let me see – yeah, yeah' – plastic keys riffling – 'we've got a list that tells us who's bought fridge freezers in the central London area in the past year . . . Um, um about sixteen thousand prospects on that one. And we've got a list of people who have responded to telesales offers for ambient music compilation albums – about three thousand on that one . . . Hm, hm, merge and purge, what do we get? A hundred and fifty-two prospects. Now, to be fair, you'd have to say that only a few of these are going to be wacky enough to go for the fridge compilation album, but which ones? Let me see . . . Let me see – '

He's back at the main menu, he's calling up the directory, the very List of Lists, the brain surgeon's own encephalogram. There's a murky region of the VDU, as if someone has rubbed grease on to it. Through this opacity I can see more lists listed. These are the secret lists, shadowy rankings of unacceptable groupings. 'We've got a list of patients being treated for major psychoses at London hospitals – yes, yes, I know that strictly speaking that's a bit unethical, but let me tell you, not nearly as unethical as some of the other things we have here. Like what? We-ell, how about Nazi war criminals with late four-door saloons registered in the Potteries? Or cabinet ministers more than fleetingly attached to exotic prostheses? Or company directors who like to make free with their own ca-ca? That one's broken down by business size, and all of them are available on cheshire or self-adhesive labels. Now then, merge and purge, merge and purge – Whassat? Data Protection Act? Don't make me laugh, squire. Let's see, let's see – humph. Just the one. Just the one nutter who listens to the fridge and can heave his plastic in our direction – '

Me of course. It would have to be me. It is me, after all, who has been subjected to the direct marketing of my very soul. You've heard of the rogue male, I am his modern descendant, the junk male. Let me tell you an anecdote, insert a bitable narrative McNugget into your fast mind, that will illustrate this point.

I recall a weekend when I was maybe nineteen or twenty, at any rate shortly before his disappearance and after his transformation, his farting out of his new identity. We went up to Yorkshire to seek out some of my grandfather's haunts. We didn't actually call on Old Sidney – according to my mage that wouldn't be 'politic'. Instead, we ended up wandering over the moors above Hebden Bridge. It was around Easter, and perhaps it was this that led him to wax theological as we bounced across the heather and gorse.

The moors were painfully beautiful that day. In the sky cumulus clouds formed a startling upside-down scape. On the ground their scudding shadows dappled the hills, hills that tumbled down to the ragged but level line, where the uplands ended and the deep gorge-like valleys began.

'There used to be sea here,' he remarked, sweeping his conning tower of an arm around in a wide arc. 'Note how the exposed stratification where the valley falls away resembles a shoreline. If you fill in the valleys with the absent ocean, what d'ye get? Why, a beautiful inland archipelago, of course. Charming emerald islands set amongst the lapping waves.'

I did as he told me, eidetically filling in the missing mass of water. I watched it course in up the dry fjords, finding its correct level, until the two of us, the big man and I, were standing aloft, looking out from our vantage point over the primordial scene, the liquid heart of England.

'That's why this part of the world is so important to me,' he resumed, taking a cumbersome leather cigar case from his pocket. 'It puts one in touch with the sheer scale of geological time, and therefore with the infinite and the ineffable.' He pulled the sides of the case apart and peered at the tobacco projectiles it contained, each one as potently dangerous as a Sam-7. 'This one, I think.' He drew one out, bit off its tip and then lit it with the licking tongue of his petrol lighter. 'Only a Montecristo number one, but then anything more substantial would be wasted in the open air.'

We walked on. He swung his alpenstock vigorously, teeing off tussocks of grass. He was dressed for an Edwardian shooting party in a full suit of tweed plus fours. On top of the boulder of his head sat a tweed hat with a grouse feather stuck in its band. For some reason the rumpled appearance of the hat drew my attention. It was like a deliberately faked natural object, a hide, beneath which the ornithologists of his beady consciousness kept watch on a shy world.

'You're thinking about my head, aren't you?' I started, almost treading in the muddy ditch that ran alongside the path.

'Possibly you are meditating on the fact of my baldness.'

'I – I wasn't.'

'No, perhaps not. But even if you were you needn't expend any sympathy on my behalf – my tonsured condition is a matter of design rather than accident. A little idea I picked up during a sojourn among the dipsomaniacs of Mother Russia. Those lost souls are so impoverished that they shave their heads in order that they may rub alcohol into them. The embrocatory variety of the spirit is, you see, the cheapest available. Care to try it?' He pulled a generous hip flask from his other pocket, unscrewed the cap and with one abrupt movement swept off his hat and dashed a handful of the stuff against his brow. The breeze blew a gust of reeking astringency in my face, whilst he shook himself, his cetacean-sized body wobbling, like an upright dugong. 'Brrr!' he exclaimed. 'That does me a power of good, I can feel the aqua vitae percolating into my brain, freeing up its function, its Babbage clunk, its differential engine.'

The way we had taken was winding down towards a small lock or tarn. A pool was contained under a miniature cliff, broken half-way up its face by the route the path took in looping round and pressing on down the valley. It was here, under a straggle of dwarf oaks and rowans that a troupe of elderly walkers had decided to halt for their feed. They were all sitting, legs stuck out into the path, backs against the cliff, munching on sandwiches and swigging from plastic cups. Even from across the pool we could hear the yammer of their animated conversation.

'Harumph!' He prodded the ground with the tip of his stick. 'If I'm not far mistaken this must be what is termed "an area of outstanding natural beauty". It goes without saying that this designation is solely a function of the propensity of such locales to attract the very ugliest examples of *Homo erectus*. Observe them, lad, consider their raddled aspect married to the sophistication of their ambulatory equipment and garb.'

I did as he said. It was true, the old ramblers were both ugly and kitted out in the very best of outdoor clothing. Gore-Tex cagoules tented over their bony collars and bent spines; plastic map-cases and complicated orienteering compasses dangled against their concave poitrines; their curving shanks were sheathed in fashionable moleskin or corduroy breeches; and their flat feet and weak ankles were shod in flexible casts of the finest shoe leather. If they had been younger, they could have scaled the Rockies in this high-stepping habit.

'Absurd, isn't it?' He took a vigorous pull on his Montecristo and

French-inhaled an Old Smoky-sized plume of fume. 'These pensioners' preposterous kit calls forth from me a paraphrase of one of the toy Alsatian philosophe's most renowned apophthegms, to whit, "Hell is other people's trousers". D'ye like that? Ahaha, hahaha!' He disgorged merriment and vapour in equal parts.

'What's that!?' He swung back to face the walkers, who were stirring now, as if responding to his pejorative comments. They screwed the caps back on to their thermos flasks, and jammed down the lids of their now empty plastic sandwich containers. Gingerly, they attempted to get up. Liver-spotted hands grasped one another. It was difficult to tell if those who had already risen were trying to help their fellows, or if those still recumbent were actually pulling the feistier ones back down, into the grave.

Eventually they were all standing, dusting off crumbs and twigs. Stringing themselves out in a ragged line, a scout-masterish type at the head, they set off down the valley.

'Feast your peepers on that.' We were following them at a good clip. 'Can you imagine what ghastly favours will obtain to the chief baboon, when this band enters a somewhat more farouche environment?'

'What do you mean?'

'What I mean is, where they are going the pecking order they have created will take on a mortal significance, red in tooth and claw.'

'What, in Hebden Bridge?'

'No, booby! You know I cannot abide a booby! We are going to Hebden Bridge, they are going to partake in a spot of rather more radical rambling.' His lycanthropic finger was out again, the triple-jointed middle one. It was rubbing up and down as if he were titillating an unseen erogenous zone.

As he spoke something untoward had begun to occur, something that was at one and the same time obscene and yet oddly natural. Up ahead of the scout-masterish walker, who strode along wielding his shepherd's crook, looking a quarter-century late for Aldermaston, a dilation came into being, a tear in the very air. It appeared to be some disturbance of the atmosphere, a puckering slash of the ethereal epidermis itself. It widened but nothing could be seen in the gap, save for the path ahead, winding on down to the valley. The scout-masterish type strode straight into the mouth of this cavity, and vanished.

I stopped walking and stared wide-eyed as the rest of the senescent strollers proceeded out of this dimension. When the last heel of the last boot had been swallowed up, the shimmering thing pulled its lips together, zipped itself back up and was gone.

'What did you do to those people?' I gasped. 'Where have they gone? You've killed them, haven't you? You've destroyed them out of sheer pettiness!'

'Nonsense, lad, do endeavour not to succumb to melodramatics.' He'd stopped walking now as well and was regarding the end of his Montecristo with an expression of faintly weary inappetency. 'I've merely done a little time-tailoring, simply removed one of the pleats or flares from the ostensibly straight leg of time.

'They are in exactly the same place, walking down the same path' – he paused, pulling back a cuff to expose his stone, circle-sized Rolex – 'some four thousand years ago. No doubt they will find the experience a tad disorienting, but if they manage to avoid the marauding aurochs by day and the preying sabre-toothed tigers by night, they may find much in their new environment that is congenial.

'I myself, being an arborophile, am delighted by the dense coniferous forests of the Neolithic period. Why, I even had this staff carved from one such, during my last venture there. Each year I whittle away another ring from it, a nice inversion, I may say, of the new science of dendrochronology.'

I had lost him. He might have been speaking Ursprache, for all that I understood. I was firmly in the present, watching the starlings cavort over and under the telegraph wires and the wind shimmer the young leaves into a muzzy Monet.

We walked on in silence for a while. He was smoking concentratedly. To break it up, fill the hiatus, I asked, 'Why? Why, did you do that?' And braced myself for the deluge of his anger. But none came.

'This is, of course, a synecdoche,' he said. 'You see, my little licentiate, when these retired schoolmarms and redundant bank officials pitch up in the petrified era, they will be forced to test their high-tech equipment to its very limit. They will soon ascertain whether or not Gore-Tex and Timberland live up to their much-vaunted specifications.

'More to the point, as they struggle to find their way to the coast – having realised the nature of their predicament, pendant to an encounter with their hairy forefathers that will leave half their number blinded and trepanned and two-thirds of the remainder dying from blood poisoning – they will gradually come to see the uttermost folly of their own moral precepts, their spiritual baggage, their transcendental ballast. They will realise fully the force of Broadhurst's Wager.'

'I'm sorry?'

'Broadhurst's Wager is the correct way round of looking at these things, an apt reversal of the sophistries of that anorexic apostate, scribbling on his Post-it notelets. It states: You are a fool to worship the deity. For, if he does exist he will surely forgive you for your dereliction, being such a sop in these matters, a meddling milk toast. And if he doesn't exist, why, at the moment of expiry you will feel an utter ass, the completest of fools. All those hours spent at tiresome tombolas, all those mornings kneeling on lumpy hassocks, all those pathetic agonies – the temporary loss and then short-lived recovery of the small change of faith, faith in a nothing, a nullity, a vacuum.

'No, no, realise the full force of Broadhurst's Wager and the Christ-figure's absent father becomes what we all knew him to be. An errant neurotic, failing to keep up the maintenance payments to support his own creation. He's probably squandering the wherewithal on some teleological analysis, reclining on a couch that straddles the firmament. "Why?" he moans to his shrink. "Why did I do it?" But he cannot admit any of it really, oh no, for he's in chronic denial, denial of the existence of the world itself. Although, that being said, during particularly lucid and integrated moments, he will perhaps acknowledge the reality of some small part of it. Liechtenstein, for example.

'But that's enough theology for one day.' The Rolex was consulted again. 'If we don't step on it the inn will have closed for the afternoon, and we won't get a glass of the urine of *Culex pipiens*. That which passes for beer in these parts.'

So it's Broadhurst's Wager that comes to me now, comes to me at three o' clock in the morning while I harken to the cooling unit. As if I had to ask why it should be that there isn't any fun any more. Me of all people. If I didn't know I doubt I would be sitting here, waiting for the dawn to stream, screaming derision through the louvres, waiting for my wife to die. No, no, there's no fun any more, just my idea of it. Mine and his, his and mine.

We're like coke heads or chronic masturbators, aren't we? Attempting to crank the last iota of abandonment out of an instrinsically empty and mechanical experience. We push the plunger home, we abrade the clitoris, we yank the penis and we feel nothing. Not exactly nothing, worse than nothing, we feel a flicker or a prickle, the sensual equivalent of a retinal after-image. That's our fun now, not fun itself, only a tired allusion to it. Nevertheless, we feel certain that if we can allude to fun one more time, make a firm statement about it, it will return like the birds after winter.

Waking in our bed one morning, we'll hear a chorus of trills and cheeps; fun has come back to cluster in the branches of the tree outside our window. We'll cosy down in joyful anticipation.

But as we rise and dress, as we leave the house to walk to the shop and buy a paper, it ebbs away, this false spring. We pass a playground. A group of kids are on a roundabout, one foot on and one foot off, they are pushing it at a giddy speed, round and around until their faces form a single banded blur. Out of this blur there stares a single set of eyes, eyes as sicklied o'er with cynicism as those of a dying cirrhotic hack, as those of an ecstatic teenager gibbering on a dancefloor, as those of a beaten wife punched in the mouth for the nth time.

Was he right? Have we fallen from grace? Is that it? Have we lost our collective innocence? Sometimes it seems that way, doesn't it? We feel like we've been thrust into, deflowered by the smirking, brutal world. But on the other hand it also feels as if we were the defilers. We've jiggled and joggled, lurched and reared, wee-ha! Wee-hey! Now spent, exhausted, heavier than ever, we pull ourselves off this fun-float, this transport of delight, to see beneath us a crushed flower, a stamped upon camellia, its pollen and sap smeared like blood on the infertile ground, the dry ground, the any old iron, lurking-tetanus ground.

How can it be so, this hovering sense of being both victim and perpetrator, both us and them, both me and him? Have we been expelled from an arcadia of fun where nature provided us with innocent automata, lowing and braying machines for our amusement?

I doubt it. I doubt it very much. I tell you what I think, since you ask, since you dare to push your repulsive face at me, from out of the smooth paintwork of my heavily mortgaged heart. I think there was only so much fun to go round, only so much and no more available. We've used it all up country dancing in the gloaming, kissing by moonlight, eating shellfish while the sun shatters on our upturned fork and we make the *bon point.* And of course, the thing about fun is that it exists solely in retrospect, in retroscendence; when you're having fun you are perforce abandoned, unthinking. Didn't we have fun, well, didn't we? You know we did.

You're with me now, aren't you? We're leaving the party together. We pause on the stairs and although we left of our own accord, pulled our coat from under the couple entwined on the bed, we already sense that it was the wrong decision, that there was a hidden hand pushing us out, wanting to exclude us.

We pause on the stairs and we hear the party going on without us, a shrill of laughter, a skirl of music. Is it too late to go back? Will we feel silly if we go back up and announce to no one in particular, 'Look, the cab hasn't arrived. We thought we'd just come back up and wait for it, have a little more fun.'

Well, yes, yes, we will feel silly, bloody silly, because it isn't true. The cab has arrived, we can see it at the bottom of the stairs, grunting in anticipation, straining to be clutched and directed, to take us away. Away from fun and home, home to the suburbs of maturity.

One last thing. You never thought that being grown up would mean having to be quite so – how can I put it? Quite so – grown up. Now did you? You didn't think you'd have to work at it quite so hard. It's so relentless, this being grown up, this having to be considered, poised, at home within a shifting four-dimensional matrix of Entirely Valid Considerations. You'd like to get a little tiddly, wouldn't you? You'd like to fiddle with the buttons of reality as he does, feel it up without remorse, without the sense that you have betrayed some shadowy commitment.

Don't bother. I've bothered, I've gone looking for the child inside myself. Ian, the Startrite kid. I've pursued him down the disappearing paths of my own psyche. I am he as he is me, as we are all . . . His back, broad as a standing stone . . . My footsteps, ringing eerily inside my own head. I'm turning in to face myself, and face myself, and face myself. I'm looking deep into my own eyes. Ian, is that you, my significant other? I can see you now for what you are, Ian Wharton. You're standing on a high cliff, chopped off and adumbrated by the heaving green of the sea. You're standing hunched up with the dull awareness of the hard graft. The heavy workload that is life, that is death, that is life again, everlasting, world without end.

And now, Ian Wharton, now that you are no longer the subject of this cautionary tale, merely its object, now that you are just another unproductive atom staring out from the windows of a branded monad, now that I've got you where I want you, let the wild rumpus begin.

BOOK TWO

THE THIRD PERSON

Guilt, I liked the feeling so much I bought the whole damn emotion.

Farrah Anwar

CHAPTER SIX

THE LAND OF CHILDREN'S JOKES

If a person tells me that he has been to the worst places I have no right to judge him, but if he tells me that it was his superior wisdom that enabled him to go there, then I know he is a fraud.

Wittgenstein

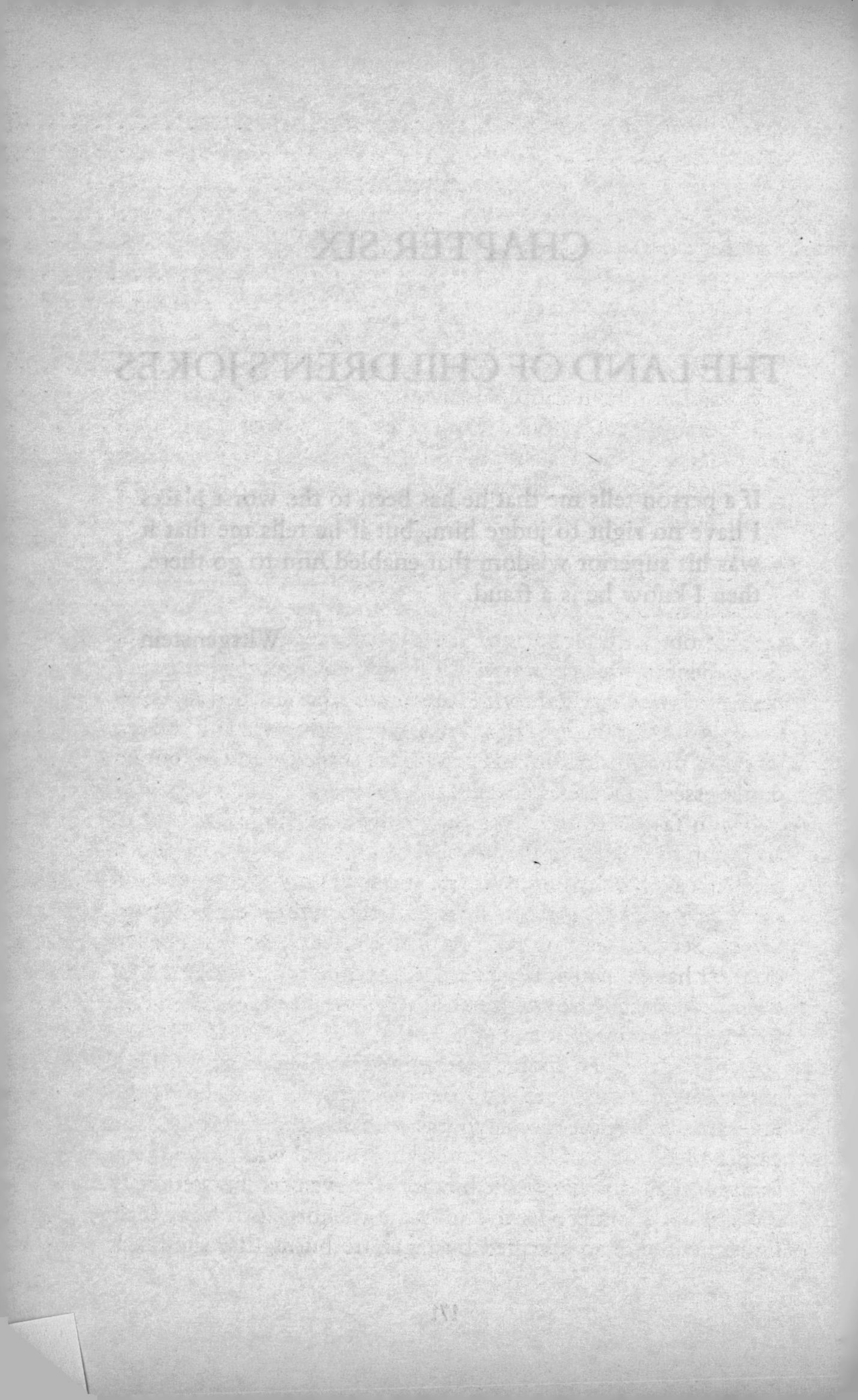

The Lurie Foundation Hospital for Dipsomaniacs dabbles its soot-stained foundations in the dry gulch of Hampstead Road. It is a confused structure, for the most part laid out like an expanded collection of Victorian alms houses, but in the thirties it was book-ended with further accretions.

To the rear of the hospital, facing the low bluish bulk of Euston Station and bounded by the rentable air-conditioning of the Kennedy Hotel, there is a tangled garden. This space was set out with aristocratic beneficence, to provide the staff and patients with a gentle gravelly progress around a pattern of beds and lawns. Over the years the funding has trickled away, to be replaced – in the garden at least – by dead leaves and sodden pieces of moulded foam, the remains of some forgotten, but no doubt essential, act of packaging.

If you face it from across the Hampstead Road the thirties accretion to the left of the hospital resembles nothing so much as a banking blockhouse. With its façade of grey-yellow dressed stone it would be right at home among similar on Lombard Street. Set into the very corner of this annexe is a solid oaken door. It has no nameplate next to it and there is no other sign to indicate whether this is a subsidiary entrance to the hospital, or nothing to do with it at all.

Behind the oaken door is a reception area divided by two high steps. Beyond this, spreading out higgledy-piggledy along the level are a collection of sepia rooms with distempered walls. The carpet-tiled floors of these rooms are studded with large metal ashtrays that look like tissue boxes that have been mysteriously galvanised. Connecting the rooms are short corridors, their linoleum floors so scarified by cigarette burns that the black gouges give the semblance of a pattern. Off these corridors are urine-scented toilets, equipped with white bars that can be pulled away from the wall should you require assistance in standing. Clamped to the walls of these toilets are white metal boxes that dispense with unflagging regularity, absolutely nothing.

For six years this unprepossessing domain had been the fiefdom of Dr Hieronymus Gyggle, psychiatrist, specialist in addictive behaviours and – as he liked to style himself – practical philosopher. Where other people would have seen only the dregs of humanity, their faces and hands scuffed and broken by the hard labour of intravenous drug use, Gyggle saw chirpy Cockney junkies. As his great ginger beard escorted him around the premises he always half expected his clientele to leap up, stick their thumbs in their braces and break into song, 'Consider yerself at home, consider yerself part of the fa-mi-ly.'

Then Gyggle was no ordinary shrink – as we know – and on this particular hot Friday afternoon in late summer, his activities, in their peculiar diversity, served to underscore this fact.

He was dividing his precious time between three ongoing projects. Firstly, in one of the sepia rooms sat six of his junkies, talking their way through a group therapy session. Gyggle made attendance at these groups mandatory for anyone who wanted to get on the ninety-day methadone reduction programme.

Secondly, in a plastic-curtained cubicle right at the back of the unit lay Gyggle's protégé, his oldest patient, a tall, plump marketing consultant by the name of Ian Wharton. Gyggle had brought Wharton with him from his last job as student counsellor at Sussex University, much in the way that a lesser doctor might have transported a favourite desk ornament or a collection of sporting prints.

Lastly, in the great man's office, which looked myopically through dirt-filmed windows on to the gardens described above, there sat a young woman, one Jane Carter. Jane was fidgeting, searching out the split ends that destroyed the precise line of her bobbed hair. She was also waiting for Gyggle, waiting for him to come and assess her suitability as a voluntary worker.

Gyggle strode through the drug dependency unit. His beard was so long and so rigid that it scouted out the corridors in front of him, possibly trying to draw sniper fire. Every so often he would stop to exchange cheery words with one or other of his colleagues. The smack heads, thought Gyggle bustling on, can wait and so can Ms Carter – what I must get under way is Ian's deep-sleep therapy. He paused and consulted a fake diver's watch which was shackled to his bony wrist. It's four now. I'll have to wake him by four on Sunday afternoon, or else he'll be too dopey for work on Monday and we wouldn't want that, oh no.

The plastic curtain pulled back and Ian looked up from where he lay on the examination couch, outlined in the long thin gap was the long thin form of Dr Gyggle. Gyggle propped himself in the gap, he dangled from the curtain rail on his mantis arms. He was chewing gum and the long fan of the beard swished across his shirt front with each chew. 'Ah, Ian,' he fluted. 'Been here long? Nyum-nyum.' Swish-swish went the beard.

'Long enough.'

'Feeling a little nervous, are we, or just sarky?'

'I don't know what you mean.'

'Sarky it is. Look, I want it clear, Ian, that I'm not pressurising you to do this. You can get up off that couch and go home if you want. I don't even want to put you under if you haven't got the right attitude.'

'Oh, and what is the right attitude?'

'Well, here's how I see it,' and just like any other ghastly enthusiast Gyggle propped one of his infinitesimal buttocks on the side of the couch and hitched up his trouser legs, preparatory to delivering his lecture. 'Deep sleep is a logical extension of the role of psychiatrist as shaman. If we consider the act of interpretation – as in either psychoanalysis or dynamic psychiatry – as analogous to the forms of auspication practised by such individuals, then the deep-sleep experience can be equated with their summoning up of a possession trance.

'In traditional societies the possession trance is invoked to purge demons by putting the subject in touch with his tutelary spirit. So, what I'm hoping for from this is that through protracted exposure to dream sleep your psyche will realise, and then dissolve the cathexis you have built up around this mythical character, this "Fat Controller".'

'Please,' said Ian, hefting himself up on one elbow: 'You must refer to him as "The Fat Controller" and it's important to capitalise the definite article – even in thought.'

'You see!' Gyggle exclaimed. 'You see what a hold this still has on you. Don't you want to be free of him?'

'Oh for Christ's sake, you know I do.'

'Well then, the therapy is worth a try. Now slip out of your things, I'm going to give you a pre-med shot.'

'What?'

'We'll put you under and keep you there with a sedative, but the sensation of losing consciousness can be unpleasant, so it's a good idea for you to be relaxed beforehand. Now do what I say, Ian, and don't quibble.'

While Gyggle busied himself with ampoule and syringe Ian took off his clothes. Standing naked save for his boxer shorts he felt a chill run through him, despite the fusty warmth of the cubicle. 'Am I going to have to lie on that bloody bench all weekend?'

Gyggle had loaded the hypodermic and was fiddling with the drip and catheter that dangled from a hook above the couch. 'Nyum-nyum' (swish-swish) 'no, of course not, when the unit closes this evening you'll be moved over to the main hospital and put in a bed there. I've arranged for one of the nurses to keep an eye on you, maintain your sedative and nutrient drips until I come on Sunday afternoon to, as it were, call you back from the land of shades.'

'And you say I'll be all right for work on Monday?'

'Oh absolutely, you've an important job on at the moment, haven't you?'

'Yeah.'

'Now turn on your side, I'm going to give you the pre-med.'

Ian felt Gyggle slap his buttock and then the apian sting of the needle. Warmth started to seep over him, spreading from a patch at the base of his spine. It was like being lowered into a warm bath, or reentering the womb. By the time he had turned back over on the couch Gyggle was standing once more in the artifical entrance. 'Relax, Ian. I have to deal with something and then I'll be back to put you right under, OK?' He turned and was gone.

* * *

Meanwhile, in one of the rooms at the front of the unit that faced the Hampstead Road, Gyggle's neglected group therapy session was under way. The six junkies were engaged in an investigation of the nature of the generic. Gyggle would have been pleased if he could have heard them, for their deliberations were carried out according to guidelines laid out by him in his self-appointed role as practical philosopher.

'Like "Hoover",' said John, his dirty fingernail tracing the line of bubbling melted flesh that edged his jaw. 'I mean to say, no one talks about a "domestic cleaning appliance" when what they mean is an 'oover, now do they?'

'Nah, nah, 'snot like 'oover at all, 'cause 'oover is like a manufactured thing, innit, not just . . . a . . . err – '

'Well?'

'A product!'

'Tch!' John waggled his head from side to side, heavy with disdain. His interlocutor, Beetle Billy, was a small black man wearing a green piped jumper, the frayed cuffs of which came half-way down his hands. Beetle Billy's voice had an irritating lispy component – he was agreed almost universally to be a waste of space and deeply stupid.

'Or Magimix,' John went on, warming to his theme. He sat forward in his chair and began to chop at the air with his thin, blue-tattooed forearms. 'People still fink of Magimix as a company name, as well as a product, don't they?' The question hadn't been intended as rhetorical but Beetle Billy wasn't living up to his role in the symposium anyway; as for the other junkies they seemed oblivious to what was going on. Someone at some time, probably a probation officer or a social worker, had been foolish enough to tell John that he was 'highly articulate'. As a result a lot of non-professional people had been suffering from his articulacy ever since.

He went on, 'Of course they do but let me tell yer, in a few years' time no one will say "food pro-cessor", iss too long for one fing, "foo-ood pro-cess-or".' He drew it out for all it was worth. 'Nah, they'll say magimix wiv a little "m". Now Billy in some ways the whatsit, the thingummy, the whosie, the how's-yer-father, the anything happening?, the some, the stuff, the gear, iss jus' like that, like the magimix, or the 'oover, for that matter. Soon no one will see it as anyfing but the product, the only one, not just one of a number of types – '

'But, John,' Billy broke in, making a late bid for casting as Glaucon. 'Like, there are different kinds of gear, aren't there, mate?'

'Yes, Billy, there are, just as there are different kinds of domestic cleaning device.' Then, as if this gnomic comment somehow managed to sum up the whole conversation, John sat back, clasped his hands behind his head and sank into a reverie.

Beetle Billy seemed unconvinced; he fidgeted with the frayed cuffs of his jumper and regarded John balefully. With his silvery hair scraped back severely, his thin nose, high cheekbones and dark eyes, John looked vaguely aristocratic. This was an impression swiftly cancelled whenever he opened his mouth, whereupon spindly yellow canines, knocked in and blackened, slid from behind his lips. There was that demerit and there was also the way the skin of one of his cheeks was all bunched up around his jaw. It looked as if someone had stuck a ratchet into the crease at the top of John's neck and then twisted it. Somebody else – or maybe the same sadist – had then gently smoothed over the spiralled web of fleshy folds with a soldering iron, or at any rate some implement that seared – but slowly.

'John.'

'Yes, Billy.' Billy was canted forward, his face grey with concentration.

'You know Tony?'

'Yes, Billy.'

'Tall Tony?'

'Yes, Billy.'

'He told me to come up to Bristol, like – '

'Recently?'

'Nah, last year.' John sighed. It was going to be a long story.

'He knew some bloke from that portis place near Bristol – '

'Portishead?'

'Is that it? Yeah, anyways, Portishead. Tony and this bloke had done a chemist's the night before and had the cabinet in 'is 'ouse, right?'

'Right.'

'So Tony called me and told me to drive up an' get it, on account of how this bloke was like known and he thought the old bill would come an' see 'im about it cos this bloke, he was like – '

'The natural suspect?'

'Thassit. Anyways, I drove up there. Took me ages cos the only V-dub I had had a leaky case. I was stopping every twenty miles to put in more oil an' that. Mind d'jew, I managed to sell it on to that dozy brass Ethel the following week – '

'And?'

'Yeah, well, I got there, like, and it took me ages to find the place, it was right on the edge of town in this little sort of crescent. When I came round the corner I saw that the old bill was there already, parked up right in front of the 'ouse. So I just floored it and kept on going, started looking for the way back to London.

'I was driving along this road, going past some football pitches, when I saw Tall Tony and this bloke – funny-looking geezer wiv' an awful squint – they were in the middle of one of the pitches carrying the cabinet between them. Some kids there having a kick-around but they'd stopped, like, to see what Tony and the squinty bloke were doing.'

'What did you do?' John yawned the question.

'I got out of the motor an' ran out into the middle of the pitch after them. Tony saw me an' started cursing me for being so late. "Where's the car?" he screams and I point it out to 'im. "You two break the effing lock on this thing and get the right stuff out of it, I'll pull the car round the other side of the pitch."

'So thass what we did. It was comical really cos it took ages to break the lock and all the kids came over to look. Turned out that the bloke with the squint's kids went to this school, so there's these kids saying fings like, "What yer doin', Mr Anderson, what yer got that bloody great box for?"

'We got the cabinet open, at last, and everything fell out on the ground. We 'ad to grovel in the mud trying to work out what was what – by the time we got back to the car we were in a right state, I can tell you. Tony's sitting behind the wheel. "Got it?" he says. "Yeah," says I and I show him some of what's stuffed in my pockets. "What's that crap?" he says. "Dikes and rits," says I. "You said just bring the stuff." Then he explodes like, "Not that stuff, you effing berk, the amps, the fucking amps! The whole thing was full of dry amps you stupid fuck!" He was gutted, wouldn't talk to me for months after that.'

'Who?' said John, whose attention had wandered somewhat.

'Tall Tony, of course, not the squint bloke. I wouldn't of wanted to talk to him again anyway, he was off his trolley on whizz, had the horrors. All the time we were driving round this Portis place, laying low to avoid the filth, he kept blathering on telling me how – if he had a long enough line – he could catch ships in the fucking Bristol Channel by casting from the top window of 'is 'ouse.'

Beetle Billy lapsed into silence, as if the point of this story were self-evident. No one broke it. John was staring up at the ceiling, his lips moving as he counted the fire-resistant tiles. The other junkies might have been dead for all the movement they made. They were all quiescent, locked into the private purgatory of withdrawal, save for one, a lank thing with greasy hair and bifocals who looked like an electrical engineer fallen on hard times. This character was smoking a cigarette with great concentration and using its glowing tip to reduce a Styrofoam cup to a charred lattice. The only sound in the room besides a bluebottle nutting the dirty windowpane was the faint fizz the fag made as it touched the flammable stuff.

'So?' said John eventually.

'Well, the story, Johnnie-boy, it's like, it's like . . . err – a whatsit.'

'An example?'

'Yeah, thassit, an example, cos he said "the stuff" and I didn't know what he meant. So it can't be true that gear is like whatsit.'

'You mean like the word "Hoover"?'

'Yeah, thassit, like 'oover.'

There were several very good reasons why Hieronymus Gyggle had decided to operate from within a drug dependency unit. As he had admitted to Ian Wharton, he viewed the junkies themselves as little more than cannon-fodder to be sent over the top and out on to the battlefields of insanity. However, more importantly, Gyggle needed the junkies the way that a queen bee needs her workers. In their metrical journeyings around the city's dealers and chemists, its shooting alleys and front lines, they collected a property that he required for his more intensive, more unusual incubations.

For the states of consciousness attained by humans in deep sleep or extreme narcosis are not mere brain events, fleeting coalescences of neurones, they are concrete things. Once abandoned by their original occupants these artefacts are left lying about our crowded universe waiting for new tenants to inch into, grubwise. There were plenty of these kicking around the DDU, they were as much a part of the detritus of the place as cigarette butts and the plastic containers used for urine samples. Fortunately they were far more difficult to remove. These cubicles of catalepsy thronged the stairwells and, being negatively buoyant, clustered under the strip lights like invisible cauls.

Ian Wharton, the Omnipom beginning to course through his body, took flight. His dormant psyche drifted up and was netted by the defunct dreamscape of Richard Whittle, one of Gyggle's junkies. It was a fresh reverie, only recently deposited at the DDU, and as such particularly potent, nightmarishly sappy. It acted as a portal, a gateway to the plains of heaven, the awful demesne where his mind – unfettered by identity – could roam where the wild things were.

Richard was struggling towards consciousness but his way was blocked. The world had chosen to interpose some myriads of dynasties of encrusted dreams between Richard and wakefulness. Both dreams that operated within dreams and dreams that were themselves fragmentary evidence of some long lost hypnogogia, which had enabled opaque archaeologists to reconstruct elements of this prehistoric dream, then put it on show in the clear glass cases, that were themselves the relics, the sacrosanct vessels, of another culture that was itself a dream.

Richard lay on his back (as did Ian) and felt the collar of his anorak slick against his neck. (For Ian read paper antimacassar, scratching.) He was gazing through a rain-flecked window. Looked at upside-down the terrace of houses opposite was entirely strange and disembodied. Enormous, its pastel façade shiny after showering, the vast bulk of the terrace, its crenellation of chimneys festooned by spidery antennae, seemed to glide through the sky below. It was moving rather than the ragged cloud behind it. The whole terrace, like an urban liner, was cruising off along the street.

There was the soft sound of sock scuffed on carpet. Richard looked up as Beetle Billy and Big Mama Rosie swam into view. (Gyggle and his corrupted charge nurse were back in the cubicle, the nurse adjusted the spigot on a bag of clear fluid and dangled it from the hook above the couch.) They came into the room and stood – in so far as their numbers allowed it – around where Richard lay.

'Come on, luvvie,' said Big Mama Rosie, her very flesh wobbling from side to side, working hard to justify its owner's sobriquet.

'Martin's here,' said Beetle Billy and his dumb mouth drooled, his saliva spelling out the implication.

Richard tilted forward until he was upright. By the time he got there the couple had gone. He hadn't heard them leave but now their low murmurs welled up from the kitchen downstairs. Big Mama Rosie and her husband Martin lived in a maisonette of bewildering proportions. Richard thought that the gaff might have as many levels as it did rooms. Long, slightly warped passageways with bulging walls connected dusty half-landings curtained off by heavy drapes of plush and velvet. Progress around the maisonette was mediated by swishing, and each swish brought forth another fluff ball from the train of a drape. The maisonette was close, sultry even, but sultry with swaddling, not with heat. There was never any money for heat.

Richard wandered down the stairs. The bottom half of the staircase was open to the room it entered. Richard sat half-way down observing Martin, Big Mama Rosie and Beetle Billy. They were working around the kitchen table. Their work was hurried but efficient. It involved fire and liquid, crucibles and filtration, yet the impression Richard had was of mechanics at a pit stop, rather than of chemists, such was their mania.

Big Mama Rosie looked up from the syringe she was priming. 'Wait in the kids' bedroom, Richard, I'll be right up.'

Richard eased himself back up the stairs on his bum. He made a promise to himself that he would reach the kids' bedroom without rising to his feet, he'd go the whole way backwards on his bum. Already his wrists ached, it was going to be really difficult but the task was magically important, or so Richard told himself. If he could do it the hit would be good and everything would be all right, the wars would end and the starving children would be fed.

He reached the top, then went up and over a raised landing. He hustled quite quickly down the passageway, scampering backwards on heels of hands and heels of feet, until he collapsed giggling at the door of the bedroom.

Richard fell on to the top bunk and lay there. His breath came in disordered gasps, each one dislodging a little nugget of nausea which travelled up his gullet and spilled into the back of his throat. He felt the prickle of sweat moving across his brow and top lip. He wiggled his fundament, pressing it into the thin foam mattress. Was that tortured squeaking the bed springs, or his own rusted pelvis?

Richard's feeble attention wandered off; even the involuntary action of moving his eyes felt hobbled with resistance. They staggered a few inches, then settled on the spatter of sticky decals and cartoon pictures that Big Mama Rosie had stuck up above the kids' bunk bed. Richard lost himself in the contemplation of Goofy and Pluto's distant Korean cousins. They had bodies the colour of passion fruit and snouts as bulbous as breasts. Their feet were cloven into two rounded toes, and their paws into two soft digital prongs which could surely never oppose or, as in the example of a lime-green creature lingering behind some two-dimensional grass, lift a cup of tea to lines-for-lips.

Richard was wholly sucked into this world of forms. Forms that had set off from the idea of the human body and driven as far and as fast as they could, back towards the moment of conception. Until they reached this world, a world of the foetal.

This was the joke bestiary that children could relate to. Creatures with vestigial limbs, omnipotent capabilities and no genitals, only rounded furry mounds, impossible to penetrate.

Big Mama Rosie came into the kids' bedroom with Beetle Billy's broad brow poking over her shoulder. He was reciting some interminable tale to her back. 'And then we was, like, wedged into the alley, cos he hadn't thought of that. It was easy to get the cabinet thingy down the coal chute but we couldn't lift it over the bloody wall and anyways the dog was barking, Fucker Finch's dog, a pit bull – '

'Shut up, Billy!' Billy was Rosie's brother. Rosie waddled to the window and yanked the curtain to one side.

Dusk had come like a thick yellow discharge across the sky. Rosie's dark brow reflected this yellow and also the orange of her tubular skirt. She extended jaundiced hands towards the cold glass while flicking the barrel of the syringe she held pinched between finger and thumb. Puny bubbles dislodged themselves from the fluid and floated up to join the scud of scum that rested at the syringe's collar. (Gyggle drew up 5 mls of liquid Valium into the large barrel. He had already inserted the catheter in the back of Ian's hand, taped it in place and stoppered it.) She flicked and flicked, then pushed in the plunger until a pee-stream of liquid arced up to hit the plastic curtain rail.

Beetle Billy hovered dronishly in the background, uncertain of whether to stay or go.

Leaving the window, Rosie came to join Richard where he lay on the top bunk. She mounted the first step of the flimsy midget ladder. She paused, wobbling. One hand held the syringe, the other plucked and then began to hoist the stretchy orange cloth up over her knees, revealing firstly fat calves, secondly fat knees and latterly the tedious gusset of her voluminous pants. A knee came on to the bunk. Rosie straddled Richard and pushed herself down on to his crotch. All he could feel now was the muddled ridged cloth of his trousers; there was no other sensation.

As Rosie unbuttoned the cuff of Richard's shirt, he turned his face away. Beetle Billy had settled himself on top of a white chest of drawers with pseudo-brass knobs. He was reading an old copy of the *Beano* with total absorption. Over the cretinous mechanic's shoulder Richard could see the darkened corridor, bulbless these last four months, and thought – but perhaps only imagined – that a figure lurked there.

Rosie's quick hands, as deft as blind rats in a sewer, had discovered the pit of Richard's elbow and found also his tiny, flaccid, invulnerable penis. She held his penis like the syringe, tightly, and eased both in together, the needle into Richard's arm, his penis over the elasticated rim and into her damp maw.

Big Mama Rosie began to truffle and muffled champings fell from her mouth. She moved over Richard like a planetoid blob, pumping at the syringe with one hand, until his red blood joined the orange fluid in the barrel. He made the effort and lifted his free arm up into the air; it floated away from him, ethereal and unconnected. He pawed weakly at Rosie's T-shirt, pulling the damp fabric away from her chest. Rosie's breasts were like two sweating blancmanges. They lay on her rib cage, depressed and puddingy – the nipples were recessed. Richard tried to pull these fly-speck currants out of their soft surround, the virulent pink slab of yesteryear's dessert.

There was a 'lumpa-lumpa' noise in the air, a deafening heartbeat. Richard looked down at the crook of his arm and saw that a massive thrombus had blown up in the vein; it bulged beatingly, uncontrollably: 'lumpa-lumpa, lumpa-lumpa'. Richard tried to call out to Rosie, to tell her to cease with her injecting of him into her and her into him. It was no use, her eyes were glazed and rolled back in their sockets, she stared sightlessly up at the ceiling where Spiderman hung from his plastic web. The 'lumpa-lumpa' grew, filling the cold closeness of the room. Outside the streetlamps came on, each one an island. 'Lumpa-lumpa, lumpa-lumpa.' And still the lump grew and grew in the crook of his arm, grew until it eclipsed the arm itself. And still Rosie pumped up and down. Richard tore with his nails at Rosie's breast, feeling the skin pucker and give, like the wrinkled rubber of an old party balloon.

The breast exploded. The thrombus exploded. Suddenly the air was full with a spray of orange droplets; gouts of pussy fluid spurted out from arm and chest. The tattered skin of Rosie's breast fell slack against the exposed radiator of her rib cage.

Richard stared down at his arm. Corners of flesh and skin curled away from the ragged hole in the crook of his elbow. Exposed to view, in the very core of his arm, were the crude struts and wonky rivets of his Meccano anatomy, lain bare for all to see.

A huge bald man came in from where he had been loitering in the passage and stood over Richard. He was wearing an immaculately tailored pin-stripe suit. The bald man mopped the orange gunk from his lapels and brow with a silk paisley handkerchief. Then he reached his hand down towards Richard's face, middle fingers and thumb bent in, index and little fingers extended, warding off the evil eye. With the two outstretched fingers he teased down Richard's eyelids and pressed him back once more, down into the orange darkness.

('He's right under now,' said Gyggle.

'An' I suppose you want me to change his bloody pee bag an' that.'

'Well, yes. I do think that constitutes part of your duty as a nurse.'

'Usually there's a good reason for why a patient is unconscious for the whole damn weekend.'

'Ours not to reason why – ' Gyggle shot over his shoulder, and was gone, off to interview his volunteer.)

Ian was in the Land of Children's Jokes. His gummy eyes prised themselves open to see a garish room full of clashing primary colours, post-box reds, viridian greens and cerulean blues. It was a large room and the furniture was all fungal. There were giant toadstools instead of chairs and grossly distended puff balls in place of sofas. Tall mushrooms gathered together, their slick flat caps grouping to form the surfaces of what might have been tables. The close air in the room was meaty, yeasty, damp and beefy.

There were two men in the room with Ian. One, who was plump and pink, squatted naked in the corner. The other wore a purple suit of satin covered with large black spots and moved about, stepping between the unusual soft furnishings. Every third step he twirled on his heels and as he did so struck an attitude, the cane in his right hand held aloft at an angle. Ian could hear him muttering to himself, 'Cha, cha, *cha*! Cha, cha, *cha*! Cha, cha, *cha*!' the emphasis always on the last 'cha'.

'Are you awake, dearie?' said the pink man in the corner. He spoke without moving, but it was clear to Ian from the way that his flabby thighs quivered that the man was finding it difficult to hold his position. As if to confirm this every few seconds a little clenched hand would shoot out from his lap and drop to the carpet, steadying his wavering bulk. 'Ooh err!' exclaimed the pink man. 'I'm not sure I can hold out like this for much longer.'

'Cha, cha, *cha*! Cha, cha, *cha*!' The character in the polka-dot suit shot between them, pirouetting. As well as the cane he sported a top hat made from the same shiny material, and in the same pattern – this he now began to raise and waggle, keeping time with his Terpsichorean promenade.

'It's my balance, you see,' the pink man went on. 'It's by no means as good as it used to be, not at all as good, not at all.' To underline the point, he then nearly fell right back on to his bum, only saving himself by grabbing the thick stem of a fierce three-foot-high fly agaric. 'Oof! I wonder if it's worth it, it used to take a couple of days but now it can be a month or more.'

'What?' asked Ian.

Speaking had to have been a mistake. Before he spoke Ian could as much believe that the room and its occupants were a hazy figment as a real situation, but with speech came focus and precision: the sharp tang of a fresh crop of mustard and cress that spread across the rotting pile of the damp carpet; wan heaps of daylight that fell in from a tall triptych of sash windows at the far end of the room; Pinky's voice, which resolved itself into a soft-accented bucolic burr; and the 'Cha, cha, *cha*!' that came rattling in between them defined itself as precipitate, intrusive, urban, American.

'What only used to take a couple of days?' asked Ian again. While it was quite true that he was riven by fear and wrapped around with the nauseous sensation of so much fungus in an enclosed place, his salvation still clearly lay in conversation.

'To get the worms out, of course.' Pinky essayed a gesture towards the puckered base of his body but his little arm could only reach half-way down the side of one haunch. There it rested, the index finger crooked inwards toward his hidden portal. 'I'm sure it's not these, because they're just as good as they ever were. Why, they're even doing a special offer at the moment, you get twenty-five per cent extra – absolutely free!' He was genuinely delighted by the bargain, his gently weathered features creased up with joy.

Ian propped himself up on his elbows as best he could. This motion set off waves of infective pollenation in the organic bed – spores the size of dragonflies lifted off in a puff of oxidised dust from around his neck and shoulders. The experience was truly appalling but there was some pay-off, for his semi-recumbent position allowed Ian to see beneath Pinky's bum. A Mars Bar lay on the carpet. It had been cut open and the chocolate coating prised apart to reveal the stratification of toffee, caramel and nougat within.

'For the worms, you see,' Pinky explained. 'They love a Mars Bar more than anything else, although that being said, they'll usually take a Snickers or a Bounty as well.'

'So what's the problem?' Ian felt genuinely curious.

'Oh! Do you really sympathise, do you really? Do you think you could really care? He never even asks what the situation is' ('Cha, cha, *cha*! Cha, cha, *cha*!') 'he's completely absorbed in his own problems. But if you're interested I'll tell you.

'You see, the cycle normally lasts about a week. First there's a funny pain, in a sort of a band around my tummy, then come the cramps and the squits. But it's when I actually start to lose weight, that's when I know that the worm is back for certain, that's when I have to act.'

'So what do you do?'

'Well, here's how it is. I usually push a Mars Bar up my bum every day for three or four days. On the fourth day – and mark my words, this has never failed before – I just lay the Mars Bar on the carpet and sort of squat over it. When the worm peeks out of my arsehole to see what's happened to his elevenses, I grab him by his neck and drag him right out! But this time things aren't going so well – I've been at it for two weeks and there hasn't been any sign of him.'

'How do you know he's still in there?'

'Oh my dear – I can feel him, of course. I can feel him right now, coiled up in me. His body fills me up, the end of his tail is jammed at the base of my gullet and his wet wormy head is questing in my colon even as we speak. Oh, I had so hoped that he would come today.'

While describing this acute parasitical predicament, Pinky fell to running his little hands over his tummy, seeking out and emphasising the shape of the worm within him by bunching up and pulling at his flesh. The exercise made the baby-soft man wobble and puff, so much so that at the end of his speech he finally tumbled back on to the carpet with an 'Oof!' and a stifled squeak.

Ian relapsed as well, thrusting himself down into the mulch of the big bed. He shut his eyes and struggled to escape the Land of Children's Jokes. He clenched himself, both mind and body, with the effort and dived down and down and down through internal layers, each one successively darker, until he was nothing, just a stray seed in warm soil, or a plastic bottle bobbing in the wake of a ship.

'Cha, cha, *cha*! Cha, cha, *cha*! Not so fast, kiddo.' An acute finger probed at the bottom of Ian's eyelid, then pushed it up, peeling back in the pale, early-morning light. 'Don't even think of leaving us just yet, kiddo, not before the main event anyways – Cha, cha, *cha*!'

The thin man span away from the bed and stopped a few feet off. Ian could not forbear from looking at him. 'Cha, cha, *cha*! Cha, cha, *cha*!' The thin man danced a little jig. He had a long skinny face dominated by a sharp nose marbled with broken blood vessels. His tiny avian eyes flashed and, as he waggled his head from side to side, first one and then the other ear, both of them thick slabs of knotted cartilage, poked into view, jammed down at a forty-five-degree angle by the shiny rim of his shiny topper.

'D'ye like my chinny-chin-chin? D'ye like my chinny-chin-chin? D'ye like my chinny-chin-chin?' the thin man plainted in nasal tones. He seemed to Ian to be mimicking the voice of a fiddling entertainer in an auld country bar. With each new phase of the jig he flourished his cane in the air and then brought its fob neatly to rest on the chin in question. 'D'ye like my chinny-chin-chin? D'ye – ' He broke off abruptly.

'Well? D'ye like my chinny-chin-chin?' He brought his frightening face down to Ian's and menaced him with it. 'What d'ye think of it, my little love?' The thin man wore satin gloves; he palped his chin with one slippery digit. On the very prong end of the chin there was a button of flesh, a soft whorl with a dimpled crater. 'Come now!' exclaimed the thin man. 'D'ye like it or no? Say now!' The barbed finger poked towards Ian's throat.

'I-I like it very much,' he stuttered. 'It's it's terribly nice.'

'Ahhh, but now, d'ye recognise it, lad? D'ye know what it is now? Say what it is now, come on, say!'

Ian stared at the chin. The thin man held himself trembling, angled over Ian like a gantry. He continued to agitate his queer chin with his slick finger, flipping the curlicue of skin first to one side and then to the other. Ian couldn't imagine what the thin man was getting at but he understood the importance of the question all right. The thin man was plainly dangerous, there was no telling what he might do if Ian failed to come up with the right answer. For some reason the phrase 'hair matted with blood' kept running through his mind.

'Say now!' Everything about the thin man was thin. Ian could make out every ridge in his tormentor's windpipe. In the deep gulf underneath his plastic jaw there was a pulse beating like the pedal attachment on a drum kit. The tendons of the thin man's neck were stretched so tight that they could have been twanged, or even strummed. They formed flying buttresses, supporting the gullet where it broke to accommodate the large irregular Adam's apple that was lodged in the thin man's craw.

His neck was long. There was as much of it below as above the Adam's apple. It descended and descended, until it disappeared into the celluloid of a cheap dicky-bow arrangement. Down there, pushing out against the knot of the thin man's spotted bow tie, something stirred. There was a living root amongst the scrawny hairs poking from the pit of his neck, a projection of flesh, which humped back on itself and dived beneath the white rim of the collar.

'I know!' Ian was startled by the squeakiness of his voice. 'At least, I think I know.'

'What d'ye know? Say it, say it now if ye know anything. Come now, have no more ado.' The thin man span away from the bed and went back to his dance, weaving in and out, and round and around the leguminous furniture of the dank room. 'Cha, cha, *cha*! Cha, cha, *cha*!' The thin man wiggled his head and his hips in opposite directions, he wiggled and waggled like a novelty marathon runner. At a stroke and with complete certainty, Ian knew that the thin man wouldn't hurt him after all.

'The thing on your chin –'

'Yes, lad?'

'It's your belly button, isn't it? Your navel, isn't it?'

The thin man didn't reply, he just kept right on cha, cha, *cha*-ing as if nothing had been said. Then, suddenly, 'Ta-taa!' he cried, striking a pose at the foot of the bed. He threw his arms right up and back and thrust his chin forward. The belly button dimple stood out, white and tuberous from its stretched bloody surround, but there was worse, far worse below. For, sprung free from the confining collar, a flaccid penis dangled down, flipping and flopping from lapel to lapel of the thin man's spotted satin suit. Its fluid animation contrasted outlandishly with the bow-string quiver of the thin man's pose.

'I bet you can't guess what happened, though? Now can you? I bet you can't tell me why it should be this way, now can you?' The thin man was menacing Ian again. As speedily as his sense of safety had arrived it departed again. The thin man dropped his knife-edged knees on to the bed, one either side of Ian's feet, and then his sharp hands came forward and rested on either side of Ian's thighs. The thin man began to edge up the bed on all fours, plunging first one and then another of his implement limbs into the doughy mattress, like spades biting into loam. The action rocked Ian from side to side. The thin man began to mutter, but his words were clearly addressed to himself rather than Ian.

'He guessed my precious . . . Guessed . . . How could he now? Rumpelstiltskin is my name, gold thread is my game

. . . How could he have guessed my little secret, my sorry tale – precious?'

With each lunge forward that the thin man made, the penis at his throat flipped and flopped again. It was quite a small penis, a rather delicate young penis even, and where the foreskin curled back at the tip, the helmet beneath was a deeper pink. A drop of semen glistened in its eye, stretched to a tear and then dropped on to Ian's chest with a warm plash. He wasn't afraid any more as the thin man's thin lips came down to touch his forehead.

Meanwhile, back in the waking world, the no-nonsense world, the nylon-sheet world that snags the hangnails of cogitation; that hated, empty-swimming-pool world; the one that is mere infill, a dusty rubble of time sandwiched between eternities, Gyggle's volunteer is still sitting, still waiting.

Waiting. That is the point of her. She's always waiting for men, this woman, this Jane Carter. And on this summer afternoon at the DDU she cannot complain, because she is now so ingrained, so conditioned, that she's actually volunteered – to wait, that is.

Sitting there, staring out through those murky windows, cataracted with dirt, Jane felt within herself the line of least resistance tethering her to her past. It stretched back into her memory, drawing with it the peculiar torsion of her being. Necessity or contingency, contingency or necessity, which of these had provided the half-twist of fate that had brought her to this strangest of places?

For all her long childhood Jane Carter played on a broad lawn dappled with sunlight. Jane and her brother in matching outfits, she in a plaid pinafore dress, he in plaid trousers, both of them shod in patent leather. Jane chucked the garish rubber ball to Simon and Simon hurled it back, boy-hard.

In tan jodhpurs and red pullovers, they sat in the back seat of the estate car as Mummy drove them to the stables. Later still there was tea, biscuits on a plate, orange squash in a glass, the frosted aluminium struts of garden furniture cool to the touch.

It had a new-world flavour, this childhood of Jane's, an Eisenhower quality. Her parents lived in a detached house, set on the low hills that ranged from London's southern underbelly.

It was a house detached both from other houses, and detached even from time and from place. It was here that the moneyed people had patented their place. They had spread themselves beneath the oaks and chestnuts and planted the green banks with tussocks of crocuses; it was more like some exercise in trichology than horticulture.

The brown tarmac of the suburban roads held oven heat in summer and they seemed, to Jane, to be infinitely slow-moving lava flows, pouring out from some resurfacing volcano. You never forget the kerbstones of early childhood, do you? The under-fives nose their way along the moss-edged paving; they sell lemonade on warped card tables and set out toys in the lost world of grass.

Jane loved Simon, loved him to distraction. In return he tortured her. He sat on her chest, twisted her nose, applied Chinese burns to her thin wrists. He kicked and pummelled, punched and spat. Older and stronger than Jane, he extended his domain into the world of imagination. Even aged six, he was already remorselessly didactic, a cruel version of the kind school teacher he later became.

'Who's that?' He examined her engine knowledge.

'Gor-on,' she lisped.

'And that?'

'Henwy.'

'And that?'

'Redward.'

'S'not "Redward", you stupid little girl. Try not to be a stupid little girl. Now who is it?'

'I – I – I dunno – '

'It's James. Now remember that. James is red and has a brass thingy on top. Edward is blue. Get it right or I'll have the Fat Controller brick you up in a tunnel.'

A bit of sibling bullying never really hurt a child. Not a child as well-loved as Jane. And she was – loved, that is. Her parents were solid people, protective of Jane and Simon. They kept the world of pissy alleyways and shitty behaviour at bay. Jane went to quiet private schools where discipline was unquestioned and the results invariably more of the same. Friends came to play on the great dappled lawn, they peed in the pampas grass as the clouds were peeled away from the sky, rolling back the years.

Aged five, Jane saved up her lemonade pennies for her adored brother. She knew just what he would want for a special present. Not a birthday present or a Christmas present, but a gift to show him just how much she loved him. Mummy took Jane to the toy shop and there it was, a little painted tin figurine, only a couple of inches high. His cut-away coat was black, as was his top hat. His waistcoat was yellow and his trousers grey. Jane extracted the pennies, threepences and sixpences from her horseshoe-shaped leather purse, one by one. The shop assistant interred the metal minikin in a brown paper bag. She locked him in there with a transparent band of Sellotape. Jane bore him home in her lap, aching with anticipation.

'Whass this?' said Simon, the understudy of ungraciousness.

'It's a present, a present for you.'

'S'Fat Controller? Yeah, well, I've got one already, you can keep it.'

Jane did keep it. Not literally, of course. The little tin figurine of the Fat Controller became just a part of the toy-box flotsam and jetsam, recognised by Jane again and again over the years, each time with a shock of humiliation. But in some other place, very near to her yet inaccessible, a big hard presence sprang into being and remained there, like the black nimbus surrounding the sun, or the dark shadow that flirts at the very edge of your eye.

Jane grew up and the presence grew up with her. It was a masculine presence, of that much she was certain, but beyond that she could not characterise or even picture it. It was just the thing that lingered, the thing that was behind you when you backed behind the tree to hide, leaving the everyday world of children and dogs cavorting on the grass in the sunshine. It was the ineffable sensation of loss that visited Jane on waking from profound sleep. It was the muscle-packed mass, the amorphous leviathan, that nipped around her ankles, under the sloping surface of the sea, as she swam off the beach, at Poole, at Polzeath, at Brighton.

When she reached puberty and moved from the dames' school to the ladies' college at Reigate, the presence went with her. By now the presence was not simply masculine – it was a man, of sorts. Jane was a bright thirteen year old, advanced for her years. She had been brought up in the light of day as far as matters sexual were concerned; her romantic tendencies were circumscribed by clear information. She correctly identified the presence for what it so clearly was, the anima, the Dionysian other, Pan, Priapus.

Not that Jane actually conceived of the presence as being endowed with a penis. For some reason she couldn't quite formulate this idea. No, the presence was rounded but firm and impenetrable.

Jane grew up to be an attractive young woman, not striking, because that would have given her an unsuitable complex. Of medium height, with broad hips and heavy breasts, her black hair was usually cut in a neat bob. Her complexion, although sallow in winter, tended to a pleasing olive whenever the sun could get at it. She was demure, attentive, modest, passive, intuitive, all the crap qualities that are ascribed to cipher women, the way rhythm is drummed into the blacks and miserliness deposited with the Jews. And still the presence hovered in the wings.

Christmas in Surrey and some relations have gathered in the overstuffed drawing room. Jane, aged sixteen, heads out to the kitchen for more cheesy balls. The presence is so clearly in the pantry she can feel him, behind the door waiting and watching. She puts the bowl down gingerly, the cheesy balls rock to a standstill, and sliding across the lino, jerks the door open. Nothing, or maybe not quite nothing, maybe an outline of city shoes on the flour-fall floor.

After leaving school Jane got a job in a wool shop. That's what interested her, knitting, crochet, appliqué, tapestry, quilting. Any craft that involved the plaiting of strands, their twisting, their knotting. The interior of the wool shop was itself woolly, the atmosphere cloyed with millions of millions of sequacious filaments. Jane sat there on a squishy stool waiting for customers and sensing the presence watching her from behind the ranks of shanks and balls.

Nice boys asked this nice girl out. Took her to films, to discos, to parties. They returned her home to Mummy and Daddy punctually at eleven, after petting sessions on sofas, banquettes, the back seats of cars. What a disappointment, those gauche hands, clumsily clutching at her sensual synchromesh. Jane connected this with the presence. The presence, Jane felt, wouldn't stall in this fashion.

On account of still living at home with her parents, her virginity was lifted in broad daylight rather than hustled away in fumbling darkness. The boy concerned thought he had achieved a great victory, arguing her into it. But, as is always the case, it was her decision alone and he was merely lust's Sooty swept along. Looking down to where their bellies married under the cover Jane was conscious of his thrusting into her as pure carpentry, tongue and groove. Later they went for coffee in a local café. She watched while the fat cook scraped grease from the range with a spatula.

The following morning Jane awoke in the half-light. She knew the presence was with her first, even before she was aware of the sucking thing fastened on her vagina. There was this awful weight pressing down on her and she had no real sensation in the lower half of her body. She couldn't vocalise either; she was powerless, impotent. The thing, whatever it was, sucked at her with the mechanical insensitivity of a domestic appliance. She cried out, but the scream travelled nowhere, it couldn't even squeeze out of her larynx. The thing went on devouring her vagina. Was it a person, an animal? She couldn't tell, all she could see was a globular object, a head or a ball. Her whole pudendum was being drawn up inside this thing, slurp-slurp-slurp. Metrically, inhumanly.

When she awoke properly, came to consciousness fully, she was screaming and her father was in the room already, with an arm around her shoulders to comfort her. Her mother was standing, bleary in night weeds at the open door. How had they both got there so quickly?

After this nightmare Jane found that she felt somehow traumatised, sexually constrained by something that lay outside herself, that wasn't part of her at all. The trauma had alighted on her, like the incubus itself.

She started to create her own patterns. She got a job writing a column on knitting crafts for a women's magazine. Soon after that a friend in television asked her to audition for a programme. She did well. Her low brow was comfortable for the camera and her clear voice recorded excellently. She left home on the strength of the television contract and bought a flat in London, closer to the studios. Daddy dealt with the conveyancing.

Jane thought of herself as sexually aware. Not liberated, but aware. She had managed to resist the Moloch of promiscuity, in some sense to save herself. For what she wasn't quite sure. Twice a year or so she would contract for a mismanaged relationship of some kind, with a young man of some description. They would go through the tired motions of discovering their basic incompatibility with one another, then, at the very point that this fact had been fully realised by both, they would finally consummate their affair, set a sexual seal on its redundancy notice.

Jane, naturally enough, connected this with the presence. She could endure a man's touch, a man's stroke, a man's gyrating push. She could just about cope with the mornings, the solicitous apologies, the well-bred regrets. But she could never, ever, ever, let one of these nice young men go down on her. Not since the nightmare. That was the forbidden zone.

So this is the kind of a young woman that was waiting for Gyggle – a Good Young Woman, cap. 'G', cap. 'Y', cap. 'W'. Kind and well motivated. She had a friend who worked for the probation service and it was he who awakened her hibernating social conscience. As an adolescent she had helped out at a unit for autistic children run by one of her mother's friends. This was the accepted Surrey way, showing the normal ones their quaking, gibbering accompanists. The righteous feelings engendered by holding these poor souls tight, grasping the writhing uncomprehending terror of their lives, had never really left her. Career established, now was the time to help someone else out. She applied to the probation service and they sent her to Gyggle.

Coming up Hampstead Road, clouds boiling on the smoked-glass surfaces of the office blocks and the snaggle-toothed row of commercial premises forming a carnivorous urban scape, Jane felt the presence again. She felt it more strongly than she had for years, it was nearly as strong as it had been that dawn in the parental home. She was keenly aware of it as she waited for Gyggle, its bulk was treading cautiously around the DDU, proceeding down the carbolic corridors, pausing in the littered flower beds. The presence pressed its carcass cheek against the window.

Gyggle came in and without saying anything to the young woman in the heavy black denim dress, inserted his spindly limbs, first one then the next, down the crack between his desk and the wall. He appeared to Jane, at this first encounter, just as he had to Ian Wharton all those years before at Sussex – an arch of tatty ring binders marched up and over him, making a framework of dirty marbling. Outlined like this Gyggle appeared Byzantine, iconic.

Jane stared at Gyggle's beard and until he spoke roamed its bouncy crevices. Once again, like Ian before her, Jane had a strong urge to detach the beard from Gyggle's face. She longed to lean forward and touch the beard, stroke it a little, then maybe grasp it on either side – near the bottom where it swept the desk – and yank very hard. She was convinced that the beard would come away in her hands, it was just too splendid, too cinematic, to be actually rooted in someone's face. Jane sat tight while Gyggle read the letter the probation service had sent him about her.

At last Gyggle spoke. 'Have you any idea, Miss Carter, why the probation service should feel that you would enjoy working with addicts?'

'Well, I don't think enjoy is quite the right – '

'Maybe not.' Gyggle didn't cut in, he oozed in. His voice was painfully soft, iterative cotton wool with a needle in it. 'But there must be some reason why they sent you here, the service is very careful about who they select for sensitive voluntary work.'

'Um, well . . . You have my CV there.'

'Yes, yes. And I've read it. You seem to have done a bit of work with the mentally ill, Miss Carter.'

'I was a voluntary worker with autistic children for about four years.'

'Do you imagine that addicts are somehow like autistics? Forgive me for asking – but I myself cannot perceive such a connection.'

'No, of course not.'

'Perhaps you think that addicts are cut off – like autistics – trapped inside a private world that we cannot access, that they are partaking of some complex but entirely unknown reality?'

'No.' Jane was emphatic. 'I don't think that they're anything like autistics.'

'Actually, you could be wrong there,' Gyggle mused; he seemed unaware that this was a rebuttal of his own opinion. 'Maybe the two syndromes are in some way related.' He scrunched out from behind the desk and stood, knees pressed between the Gothic iron pleats of the cold radiator. He stared out of the window, eyes tilted above the station roof beyond the hospital garden, and went on speaking, as if reading psycho-news from some autocue in the sky. 'Addicts are psychopathic, regressive, they have enfeebled affect. Nevertheless, it could be argued that their stereotypical behaviour is a kind of photograph of normalcy, an eidetic image of what it might be like to be sane, hmm?'

'I'm sorry, I don't quite understand you.'

'Oh well, oh well, no matter – no matter.' Gyggle grabbed the scruff of the beard and used it to drag himself back to his seat. 'Anyway, that's besides the point, which is not theoretical but practical, namely, what are we going to do with you?' He flipped out his bony wrist and shamelessly examined his petrol-station-gifted diver's watch.

Jane grew a little irritated. 'I don't want to keep you from your work – '

'No, no. Please, no.' Gyggle attempted what might have been a smile, but Jane couldn't be sure, because not even a millimetre of lip was freed from its hairy purdah. Gyggle turned his attention to Jane's CV again. 'You're available for twenty hours a week. That seems like rather a lot of time.'

'I don't need much time for my job. I've made a commitment to myself to spend twenty hours a week on voluntary work.'

'It's lucrative then, your, your' – he glanced at the CV – 'knitting programme?'

'Yes, it is.'

'Still, criminals, Ms Carter,' Gyggle piped, 'not victims but perpetrators. What do you think is wrong with addicts, Ms Carter?'

'I'm not so sure that they aren't victims as well, Dr Gyggle. Perhaps addiction is a disease.'

'If it is, have you any ideas about how it should be treated?'

'I wouldn't presume – '

'Oh, come now. It's a field in which my profession hasn't had conspicuous success. They say failed doctors become psychiatrists, and failed psychiatrists specialise in addiction. Have you heard that before?' Gyggle's dulcet tones threw his patronising manner into still sharper relief.

'No, I haven't. I don't really have any formed opinions on the subject.'

'Very well, very well, perhaps another time.' Gyggle shuffled the papers on his desk, then swivelled round and started to run his finger along the sloppy rows of ring binders ranged on the shelves. He pulled one down and opening it, extracted a buff folder. 'I'm going to drop you in at the deep end,' he went on. 'I do this with all the volunteers who come here. It's not strictly professional. Some might say that it's not even ethical but it gets results. I've tried supervised sessions and induction groups but really, if a volunteer worker is any good, they can do without them.'

Gyggle held the folder vertically and tapped it on the desk for emphasis. 'These are the case notes of a young addict called Whittle. I want you to have a go at befriending him. He's on a reduction course of methadone, which he collects daily, here at the DDU. He's due for a court appearance in about three weeks. You can help him out, try and keep him straight.'

'Why Whittle?'

'Put simply, Ms Carter, it's a quality of life decision. Unlike many of my clients, Whittle has a chance of rehabilitation. He has some solid assets, such as being white, middle class and reasonably educated.'

'Is that it, are those the assets?'

'In our society, Ms Carter, they are the only ones that matter.' He chucked the folder at her. 'Here you are.' He clocked his watch again. 'I must leave you now, I'm supervising a group therapy session, as well as an important experiment. Read the notes, go and see Whittle, if you make out all right I'm certain I'll see you again. If not, well, it's been nice making your acquaintance.'

He rose. His height made it impossible for him to move with any ease and his departure was in the manner of a removal, his body a piece of furniture positioned vertically for manoeuvring through the door. '*Au revoir* then, Ms Carter. I do hope it is *au revoir*.'

Jane said, 'I'm sure it will be, Dr Gyggle,' but wasn't at all.

'And Ms Carter, just copy down Whittle's address from the folder. Leave it on the desk when you've finished and make sure the Yale is sprung when you leave. The clients here, as we have touched upon, tend to be a tad light-fingered.' He went out.

After the shrink had gone Jane sat for a while and read the folder. It consisted mainly of appended psychiatric evaluations and medical notes. Whittle was, Jane reflected, some kind of a healthcare recidivist. He had had more ear, nose and throat infections than a school full of Nepalese. He was also partial to abscesses and abrasions, burns and lacerations, cysts and cuts, of a bewildering multiplicity. It was as if his ambition in life were to attain a regular pattern of scar tissue over his entire body.

She sighed. The atmosphere in Gyggle's office was becoming oppressive. As soon as he had exited, the presence had sneaked back to the window. Outside the sun was shining, emphysemic pigeons landed hacking on the windowsill and then dropped off. Jane sat, trying to imagine that this moment was pivotal, that it meant something. Like a child playing with a 3-D postcard, she flicked it this way and that, from destiny to contingency and back again. This was a big mistake.

has some solid assets, such as being white, middle class and reasonably educated.'

'Is that it, are those the assets?'

'In our society, Ms Carter, they are the only ones that matter.' He tinkered the folder at her. 'Here you are.' He checked his watch again. 'I must leave you now. I'm supervising a group therapy session, as well as an important experiment. Read the notes, go and see Whittle; if you make out all right I'm certain I'll see you again; if not, well, it's been nice making your acquaintance.'

He rose. His height made it impossible for him to move with any ease and his departure was in the manner of a removal, his body a piece of furniture positioned vertically for manoeuvring through the door. 'Au revoir then, Ms Carter. I do hope it's au revoir.'

Jane said, 'I'm sure it will be, Dr Gyngle,' but wasn't at all.

'And Ms Carter, just copy down Whittle's address from the folder. Leave it on the desk when you've finished and make sure the Yale is sprung when you leave. The clients here, as we have touched upon, tend to be a tad light-fingered.' He went out.

After the shrink had gone Jane sat for a while and read the folder. It consisted mainly of appended psychiatric evaluations and medical notes. Whittle was, Jane reflected, some kind of a healthcare recidivist. He had had more ear, nose and throat infections than a school full of Napalese. He was also partial to abscesses and abrasions, burns and lacerations, cysts and cuts, of a bewildering multiplicity. It was as if the ambition in life were to attain a regular pattern of scar tissue over his entire body.

She sighed. The atmosphere in Gyngle's office was becoming oppressive. As soon as he had exited, the presence had sneaked back to the window. Outside the sun was shining, cumbersome pigeons landed flapping on the window-sill and then dropped off. Jane sat, trying to imagine that this moment was pivotal, that it meant something, like a child playing with a 3-D postcard, she flicked it this way and that, from destiny to contingency and back again. This wasn't her miracle.

CHAPTER SEVEN

'YUM-YUM'

The standpoint of the old materialism is *civil* society; the standpoint of the new is *human* society, or socialised humanity.

Marx, *Theses on Feuerbach*

Now things speed up. Time is a battered old accordion, abused by a sozzled busker; haplessly it wheezes in and out, bringing events into tight proximity, and then dragging them far, far apart again. And, of course, time is also like this metaphor itself, formulaic, flat, and ill contrived. Time flirts with us in this fashion, entertaining all of us with an inductive peepshow, where cause's coin invariably produces the same routine of cheap effect.

Ian Wharton and Jane Carter are driving along loving laser beams, straight towards each other. They're hurtling heart-on; their three-millimetre-thick emotional bodywork is about to be buckled, sundered, raggedly split, in the car crash of sexual love. But they know nothing of this yet.

Loveless, alone, Ian Wharton awoke in the chronic ward of the Lurie Foundation Hospital for Dipsomaniacs. It was Sunday afternoon – forty-eight hours had elapsed since Gyggle and the sullen nurse had put him under. Coming to was sweet relief for Ian. His experiences in the Land of Children's Jokes remained with him, coherent and narratively intact, in a way that dreams just shouldn't. Around him on the ward, the dying alcoholics mewled like caged kittens. To Ian's right a man with a cirrhotic liver as large and heavy as a bowling ball groaned and thrashed from side to side of his iron cot. His nose was so networked with exploded blood vessels that it resembled nothing so much as a punnet of raspberries, squeezed to a pulp. His hands, Ian noticed, were swathed in mittens of surgical gauze.

Gyggle entered the ward from the far end, and proceeded towards where Ian lay, barging several spectral forms in hospital-issue dressing-gowns out of his way. The chronics, brains floating in their liquor-filled pans like whitened specimens in formaldehyde, offered but feeble resistance. Gyggle put his bony hands on the rail at the end of Ian's bed and idly scanned the clipboarded notes that dangled there.

Ian's lips were numb, safety bags that had self-inflated around his risky mouth.

'Bhat bhe buck bas bat 'bout?' he mouthed at Gyggle.

'Here, have some water,' said the shrink. 'Your mouth is very dry.' He passed over a plastic beaker, which Ian swilled, cold droplets falling on his neck and chest. 'Well!' Gyggle's eagerness was boyish, crass, irritating. 'Tell me about it, were there any intimations of our old adversary?'

'B-no.' Ian numbled.

'But dream experience of a very vivid kind – am I right?'

'B-yes.'

'And?'

'Some sort of a place or realm,' said Ian, clearly now, his lips coming back to life. 'Difficult to describe, but you know, very obviously how can I put it? Meaningful?'

'Tell me more.'

Ian told him about Pinky, the Mars Bar gimmick, the Rumpelstiltskin guessing game, and his subsequent close encounter with the thin man.

'Did you recognise any of these people?'

'N-no. Though it was strange, because I did feel that I might somehow come to know them – '

'In the future?'

'That's right. In the future. But I understood where I was even as it was happening. You see, the Mars Bar gimmick and the man with his penis pulled up around his throat, they're nightmare figures culled from old children's jokes. You know, the sick kind, the kind that depend on such awful visualisations.'

'I see, I see, of course, this is brilliant.'

'I knew that it was the Land of Children's Jokes instinctively.'

'Yes, yes, I'm certain we're on to something here. I'm sure that we've begun to penetrate this damaging cathexis of yours. I'm convinced that we must go on.'

'I don't want to go on – it's scary.' Ian was struggling up from the bed. He still felt very woozy; hardened sleepy dust crackled on the skin around his eyes.

'Oh but you must,' said Gyggle, 'you must. Remember, no catharsis, no full genitality. Got that? Got the photo?' Gyggle was already walking when he said this; he threw it over his handlebar shoulder as he rode his spoke legs off down the ward. Ian couldn't have been certain, but he thought Gyggle also made a peculiar gesture, curling his thumb and his two middle fingers into the palm of his hand, then poking the index and little fingers towards his own testicles. Then he was gone, through the cat-flap doors.

Monday morning. In the purulent heart of the city heat is smell and smell is heat. The hot haunch of the late-summer day is brazenly insinuating itself against the pallid flanks of the office blocks around Old Street Tube Station. The diurnal heat is crudely importuning 'Software House'; 'Television House'; 'Polystyrene House' and all the other sad sack commercial premises.

Ian Wharton popped out of the subway like a champagne cork. He was bounding this morning, full of enthusiasm, geared up for the fray. This was Ian's work self, quite distinct from his haunted other self. No one at work knew about his problems. At D. F. & L. Associates, whereto Ian was bounding, he was perceived as a solid type, a Roseland man, a regular middle-class guy, full of *bonhomie* and jocularity. He was also a successful marketeer, and on this particular Monday morning there might well be an important new account for him to begin work on. An account that had been provisionally named 'Yum-Yum'.

Ian veered off the roundabout, down a path that led in the general direction of Norman House. The path became a passageway that traversed a bomb site between two high wooden fences. To the left of the fence the site had been cleared and building work was in progress, hard hats and JCBs were grunting and grubbing in the dirt, but the site to the right of the fence hadn't been cleared yet. Through chinks in the fence Ian could see a tangle of stringy privet, lanky nettles, wild flowers and triffid weeds, all forming a fuzz of camouflage over the sunken foundations of the bombed-out building. He took a deep breath and sighed. What a marvellous morning to be so stylishly suited and on his way to a stylish job.

Norman House, which contained the offices of D. F. & L. Associates, was set between two similar, somewhere to the north of the twisted rectangle formed by Old Street, City Road, London Wall and Shoreditch High Street. In truth, the only thing Norman about the building was the pseudo-Bayeux lettering on the doorplate that proclaimed 'Norman House'. Otherwise it was an undistinguished six-storey smogscraper, faced in London brick, its eighteen rectangular windows projected out by double surrounds of leading and yellow stonework.

Ian bounded up the three steps to the glass doors and pushed them open. In the cramped vestibule by the lift, he encountered Dave, the porter, with his hairy chest oozing up from behind his collar, like some mutant merkin.

'Morning, Mr Wharton,' said Dave.

'Morning, Dave,' said Ian, punching the lift-call button.

'Going to be another hot one today.'

'So they say, so they say.'

The lift doors peeled back on the third floor to reveal the reception area of D.F.& L. Behind a brushed steel bulwark, Vanda, the statuesque black receptionist, sat stroking the keys on her Merlin console. The laquered busby of her hair hid a combined mouth-and-earpiece set, so that, to Ian, it appeared as if she were talking to some spirit guide, deeply familiar with the London club scene.

'Morning, Vanda.'

'Morning, Mr Wharton.'

Ian barrelled through the reception area and headed on up the stairs. The decor of the D.F.& L. suite was unremarkable, beige-corded carpets and utilitarian strip lighting. The walls were hung with framed display advertisements the agency had been responsible for commissioning, alongside various marketing-award certificates. Set here and there, on the stairs, along the corridors, were freestanding glass cabinets, filled with other kinds of awards. These were symbolic bibelots, pseudo-products. Brushed steel and cedarwood pediments jostled on their baize bottoms, pushing forward on spindles of acrylic tiny metalicised examples of packaging, little rubber stoppers, assortments of diminutive clips, valves and widgets. In amongst them Ian spotted the award given to D.F.& L. for one of its most successful campaigns, the Painstyler.

The Painstyler was a kind of tool, that could be used by amateur decorators to tease the surface of a particularly thick, plaster-enriched brand of paint into a landscape of petrified fronds. The Painstyler – God knows why – had caught on in a major way. The D.F.& L. billings had been massive, and, as an expression of gratitude, Hal Gainsby, the American senior partner, had the entire offices painstyled. Every single ceiling and vertical surface was fluffed up in this manner, so that to progress around the corridors was to feel one's self to be some kind of human bolus, being peristalsised along a giant gut.

The employees couldn't abide the painstyled surfaces, which were by way of being a hideously itchy incentive to the scratching and picking of apathetic fingernails. No desk or work station in the whole suite was without its accompanying snowfall of chipped-off paint fragments. This progressive distressing of the office environment sent Gainsby into bubbling furies; some employees had their wages docked, others were fired. The very success of the Painstyler had started to scrape away at the corporate fabric.

Ian Wharton absorbed all of this and looked out for fresh little snowfalls as he bowled down the corridor towards the fifth-floor conference room. He pushed the heavy door open and confronted his colleagues.

Together with Hal Gainsby there were Patricia Weiss, Customer Account Manager; Geoff Crier, Media Buyer; and Simon Arkell, Planner. Gainsby, a plump little man who endlessly sought out any point of potential height-advantage, was on top of the air-conditioning unit, set beneath the rectangular window. His rear end pincered by its two slabs, he was being subjected to a chilly blast, and as his fashionable Barries' shirt turned into a chilly shroud, he bitterly regretted the posture.

That was Gainsby all over. He was a man whose millisecond to millisecond disposition was bounded by posture regret. The most obvious form of this was physical, but it extended through his career, on to his anglophilia, and terminated in a sadly pointless emotional loneliness. As it goes, the same was true for the rest of them, these other three marketeers.

Patricia Weiss was a German-Jewish bombshell, an antithetical Leni Riefenstahl. Her swarthy face was hidden behind a life mask of thick caramel foundation. Her big eyelids were enpurpled, their *faux* lashes gooey with mascara; her severe lips were raw red and a lurid beauty pimple formed a trigonometric point on the hard plain of her cheek.

If Weiss's jewellery indicated membership of a yet-to-be-created tribe of millennarian Amazons, her couture was contrawise: a set of vampish relics left over from the fifties. Under a black cuirass jacket there was no blouse, only a heavily reinforced brassière that coned her breasts into Strangelove projectiles. Weiss's legs were thrust beneath the blond-wood conference lozenge, but anyone could have told you that her stockings were sheer, sheer, sheer, and that her legs were sheerer still. Her skate-blade feet were rapacious and violent to look at, spiked by patent leather at toe cap and high-heel.

Gainsby may have been sad, but Patricia Weiss thought herself a truant from feeling and that was worse, far worse. Originally married to a bibulous Big Blue manager, she had left the Havant household under a hail of blows from the pissed brute. Then he had the gall to hit her in the divorce court with a desertion rap. The judge was a misogynist and delivered the kids to Daddy and destruction. Consumed with self-hatred Patricia blew for London and had a butterfly tattooed in her groin. The boy and girl were now six and nine respectively. She couldn't stand the blame in their eyes when she fought her way back in to see them. At the bottom of her meticulous heap of hair, the idea fermented that only another child could save her, a new birth.

Patricia tried to be tough and sexy. She vamped men in, vogued them, cranked them up and then vroomed them out again. But each new coupling brought only fresh despair. Inside her marvellous chest a post-coital she-spider feasted on her dead man's heart.

Geoff Crier reminded Ian of Hargreaves, his tutor at Sussex. Crier had the same all-over brown beard, which strongly implied the necessity of a daily razure around his raw eyes. He was a throwback to the dandy Ogilvy days of British advertising when copywriters, marketing men, even people in production, sported colourful bow ties, and affected the manners of artists who chanced to be commercial. Crier was none too bright. Life, he contended, kept on crossing the road when it saw him coming. In his late-forties now, the oldest of the three, he was beginning to grow ungracefully young and chippy, like an adolescent on the make. His girlfriend couldn't have been said to be long-suffering. For she was blissfully unaware of how the Crier frustration was strained through the colander of his personality, until all that was left was a stock of watery pretension.

On this ovenready morning, already damp in his fashionable black shorts (by Barries' of the King's Road), Si Arkell, the youngest of the three marketeers, was labouring hard at his covert daytime job, the relentless struggle to come to terms with his sexuality. He tried to think of sleeping with men as just something that he did, in much the same way that other people went to the football or faked up corn circles, but it didn't feel like that at all. What it felt like was that his homosexuality had somehow chewed its way through his very being. A cancerous solitary piranha, that was now eating up all his fixity, any ability he had to concentrate.

At night, in the minimalist desert of his fashionable Bayswater apartment, Arkell mugged up on genetics. Each new theory that advanced a structural brain differential for inverts left him feeling queasier and queerer. The more he read, the more alarming the clarity with which he could picture his brain. In dreams, like a toy diver, he swam around its coral-reef efflorescence, observing the mutant formations and the parasitical encrustations that made him what he was. In the morning he awoke sweating – his dreams had been so vivid and so exhausting that he found himself hardly rested.

From time to time poor Arkell would crack, go out cruising, score. Usually with a man he didn't even fancy. He'd let them bugger him, or he'd suck them off. Often they would beat up on him for finishers. So even getting what he wanted was turned into a variety of humiliation. Poor Si.

All of them, all of the marketeers, had compensated for the painful nullity of their emotional lives by infusing their work, introjecting it into their psyches. These were Ian Wharton's ideal confrères. For, like him, their cerebella had been fashioned into frozen gondolas, crammed full of frosted thought-items. Theirs was a mental *mise-en-scène* within which aspirations, yearnings, dreams, ethical confusions, had all become just so many product placements, each jostling for its paid-for moment in the viewfinder of consciousness.

They subjected themselves to marketing methodologies relentlessly and avariciously. They divided themselves internally into socio-economically classifiable sub-sets of assertive homunculi, which were compelled to complete notional surveys, attend focus groupings where phenomena were assessed, and then witness hamfisted demonstrations of the next Little Idea. The marketingspeak had invaded their very ordinary language. Thus, they had adapted the folksy homily to their own usage, proclaiming, 'There are no such things as strangers, only prospects that we haven't converted, yet.'

These were Ian's colleagues and in his perverse way, the only people he really felt comfortable with.

'Morning, Hal, Pat, Si, Geoff – '

'Morning, Ian,' they chorused.

'Ian, I'm glad you're here. I've had the most extraordinarily good news.' Gainsby gestured at the surface of the conference table where, Ian now noticed, there lay in front of each of the marketeers a D.F.& L. Associates pitching document. 'We've won the Bank of Karmarathon account!' His peculiar Bostonian accent warbled over the exclamation, and at long last he felt able to free himself from the air-conditioner. He took a seat at the head of the table. Ian sat as well.

'Hal, that's amazing news, congratulations, you deserve every credit.'

'Nonsense, Ian, this wouldn't have been possible without all of us. We worked well as a team, now I think we're going to be rewarded – handsomely. They've agreed to the budget we proposed for the product launch without any reservations. I don't need to tell any of you that our fee as a percentage of that budget will be very considerable.'

'What a relief!' Ian sank heavily into his allotted chair, then instantly regretted it. The chairs were another of the fruits of D.F.& L.'s labour and Hal Gainsby's unfortunate loyalty to the products he marketed. The aluminium S-bend design was ubiquitous, but this particular version had a major fault. The tensility of the aluminium used had been too great; anyone who forgot this fact found themselves bouncing to a standstill as if on a trampoline.

When he had finally settled Ian went on, 'So what now? How quickly do they want us to proceed?'

'Well, that's just the thing. I had a call at 4 a.m. this morning from Nat Hilvens in NY. Karmarathon want to push the launch forward to January of next year, which gives us only six months to do all the softening up.'

'Oh Christ,' Geoff Cryer muttered. 'That's going to present huge logistical problems. There's the financial press to be dealt with, for a start. I'd thought that we'd have time to organise quite a number of informal seminars, in order to introduce them to the idea.'

'Y-yes.' Arkell was squirming in his seat, thin fingers holding each opposing wrist.' What about these standing booths we were going to erect? I've only just put the whole thing out to tender, I've no idea how we'll manage to organise the permissions and get them actually built before January.'

For no good reason silence fell around the conference-room table. Ian idly scanned the juncture of the cream skirting board and the beige carpet, noting the druff-falls of paint and plaster fragments, another failure by the staff to keep their itchy fingers away from the Painstyler decoration. Under his own broad palm he could feel the slick folders, the phallic pilots' pens, the plastic-encapsulated microchip butties, that bulked out his soft, calfskin portfolio. Ian's attention first wavered, then wandered, away even from the silence itself. Outside in the other world of the street, vehicles oozed through the soupy air, a jack hammer drummed on the cakey crust of the earth.

This wouldn't do. He normally felt bound-in here at D.F.& L., secure in his trade persona. In his work he intuited the universe of products as a primary construct, a space-time configuration upon which consciousness-at-large had engrafted itself, like wisteria choking a trellis. That is why – he believed – one's own mind fitted so well into those of others. Every dove of consumer cogitation could marry a tail of vendor awareness. The communality of products was stronger than that of language, of television, of religion, of party, of family, of primogeniture, of *Heimat*, of Medellin, of retribution, of clout, of face, of *latah*, of the Four of Anything, of off Broadway, of any of the consistencies that had been used to establish the increasingly arbitrary character of the cottages that made up the global village.

Ian thought for the first time in years of the concept of retroscendence. How it might be possible to enter into the very history of a product, any product, the Porsche or the crisp packet, and flow down its evolutionary folkways, zoom back to the point where it was as yet undifferentiated, unpositioned, unintentional, and therefore not about anything. In the flat land of the Delta the babies cry themselves to sleep in the airless shade, while everyone else labours in the scintillating sun. When the dun evening comes the kids go down to the irrigation channels for some bilharzia bathing. They have little to look forward to . . . Gainsby was saying something '. . . feels that he was crucially involved in, so to speak, factoring this to us. It isn't something I've spoken of to you before – '

'No, you haven't, Hal, you haven't seen fit to.' Patricia Wieiss's voice was snappy, more than piqued.

'I don't know the guy.' Hal was unhappy, his voice teetered up a half-octave. 'I've got no idea of how he could possibly even know about us, but he does. Or at any rate he says he does. He's got some interest in Karmarathon, of course – '

'That's right, of course he bloody does. Isn't that bloody brilliant. This agency limps along, constantly in danger of going out of business altogether. Then finally, at long last, we land something that looks as if it might be a decent account, something that will really underwrite us, not just some fucking wing nut or minority-interest hair cream. And immediately we start to get yanked around, like a toy poodle on a leash. And who's doing the yanking? Some funny-money man, some wheeler-dealer, an asset-stripper, a fat cat, Mister bloody Samuel North – '

Ian didn't hear the last syllable, but he knew what it was. It was the cliff he came from, the one chopped off and adumbrated by the heaving green of the sea.

Before he could register how he had got there he was in the tiny toilet on the half-landing. He did know this much, that he hadn't actually bolted out of the room, he had made some kind of an excuse. But for all that, the need to get out had been overwhelming.

He was back. Ian didn't believe in coincidence, only shit-smelling serendipity. The big man was all around now. It was he who hummed through the Vent-Axia, he who wheedled shut the composite door on its oily pneumatic arm. Glancing around the smallest room Ian was seized with his tormentor's ubiquity. For, while it was certain that he was with Smallbone in Devizes, at one and the same time, possessing full simultaneity, he was a fly on the wall, scampering between the plaster fronds. His city shoes held him level, as securely as any insect's suckers or gooey-glue secretions.

Such arrogance! Such disregard for the Painstyler effect. He was swinging from one frond-tree to the next, open-handed, like some throwback. And as he swung each one broke in turn, leaving in his wake a trail of dusty puffs.

Truly, as he might well have said of himself, he was the Dharma Body of the Dull. He was in the lino, he was in the soap, he was in the Toilet Duck. He stared out from the windows of the branded monads. He was exactly where Ian didn't want him to be. The world of products was not the encompassing quiddity Ian had so resolutely built it up to be. Above it and beneath it, swirling, involuting, forming screwed-up eyes of howling force, there was another determinant, another *primum mobile*. And Ian was reaching an understanding of what it was. If Samuel Northcliffe was involved, money couldn't be far behind.

Back in the conference room things were picking up. Papers

had been spread out on the table, biros scratched and circled. Ian reentered the room casually and sat himself down again.

'OK?' asked Gainsby.

'Fine, fine.'

'Good. Look, Ian, I think that first and foremost we're going to have to deal with this naming problem. We've already fallen into the habit of calling this thing "Yum-Yum" amongst ourselves, and it just won't do.'

'Even the client calls it "Yum-Yum" – '

'Be that as it may, what they're paying us for is to come up with an entire image, a personality, for this product. No one is going to sell a financial product called "Yum-Yum" to anybody. So I want a new name for it, and I want it fast.'

'I'll do that. I'll set up a naming group for next week.'

'Excellent. Geoff is going to organise the press end of things, starting off with a series of advertorial pieces in the relevant publications. Si is working flat out rejigging every single schedule to fall in line with the new launch date. Once he's got that in hand we'll have a better idea of how we're going to manage it.

'For the moment, since there isn't much client liaison involved in this one, Patricia will be on hand for *ad hoc* support. OK? Oh, and one last thing, I think it would be a good idea if we all put in a showing at Grindley's tonight for the S.K.K.F. Lilex launch. I realise it's not our product but we do other things for them and I know that Brian Burkett feels attendance at these dos kind of shows agency loyalty.'

There was a scattering of groans and 'Oh no's from around the lozenge. Gainsby ignored them, scooped up his share of the wasted paper, and puckering up his already puckered seersucker suit still further, headed for the door.

Jane Carter and Richard Whittle had got on like a recently doused chip-pan fire. Such was the drenched and oleaginous quality of their meeting.

On the Friday afternoon, Jane left the Lurie Foundation Hospital for Dipsomaniacs clutching her heavy handbag, and feeling her heavier heart burn in her chest. Whittle's address had been difficult to decipher from the notes Gyggle gave her. He seemed almost peripatetic. In the space allowed, address after address had been written in and then deleted with firm strokes. She finally managed to get it down, thinking all the while: What's the point?

A double-decker bus picked Jane up and like Sinbad's roc carried her up the hill through Camden Town, towards Gospel Oak and the mansion-house block of apartments on the edge of the Heath, where Whittle lived. Winging up the High Road, slumped back into the bench seat, Jane had once again sensed the presence near by. The sweat-dampened fabric of her skirt, stretched between her unhosed legs, offered up – or so she felt – an opening, a lobster-pot ingress to the interior of her body. She pulled the skirt down tight and stared out the window, thrusting the presence off and away from her.

Out in the street, under the reddening afternoon sun, a spectacle of ineluctable commerce greeted her. Everywhere Jane looked someone was selling something to someone else. It was as if exchange had replaced language as a primary form of communication, and people were selling to one another in order get a hold of some words. A braiding of gestures: one hand proffering money bill-like to another repeated itself, hither and thither, stitching up the ragged braid of the shopfronts. And the shops themselves, departmental, electrical, grocery, clothing, fast food, DIY, furniture. All had spilled out on to the pavement; the goods inside were falling over one another in their desperation to find a potential purchaser. Once in the open air, they mingled with the street traders, costermongers, fly pitchers and hawkers who plied this grungy souk. On whatever point Jane's eyes rested, through whichever line her gaze ran, she saw cheques being signed, credit-card counterfoils being scrawled across, standing orders being arranged, and cash – wholesome dosh, ponies, monkeys, oncers, coins of the realm – flowing around like mercury, like some element.

Whittle had swum towards her, his form undulating through the wrinkled hide of toughened glass, as she stood on the cool stone stairs. In the hidden crevices of the apartment block she heard children's voices, the whirring industry of domestic cleaning, large dogs barking in small places.

'Yes?' Richard was pulling Ian's two days of sleepy dust from the corner of his eye – it even felt that way to him, the solidifying gunk of another's oblivion. The doorbell had hooked Richard, then reeled him in from riverine sleep. It had landed him here, back on the mud bank of his own life.

'Oh – hello,' said Jane, taken aback, struggling to compose herself. No matter that she had prepared herself for this, the Whittle face was still an awful sight, a collection of weeping infections, hot-pus springs boiling in slow motion. 'I'm from the DDU. I'm not a social worker, or a psychiatrist, I'm a volunteer. Dr Gyggle sent me to see if I can help you in some way, but I can come back another time if now isn't convenient, or not at all if that's what you'd prefer – ' The words had spilled out of her, precipitate, stupidly revealing.

Richard was disarmed – and laughed. '. . . I see. You'd better come in and have some . . . have some – tea!'

Improbability had piled upon improbability, as Jane's skinny junky host came up first with tea, then with milk, and finally ever-so refined sugar. Given his circumstances this was as preposterous as if he had produced a willow patterned plate piled with neatly decrusted cucumber sandwiches.

Seated in the resolutely unfitted kitchen, they had eyed one another over mismatched cups. Whittle was brown-haired, with close-set green eyes, a snub nose, low brow and an undistinguished little pointy chin. He surprised Jane by making conversation, asking her about her work, her flat, whether she had a boyfriend. He seemed pathetically unaware of the awful impression he made, with his spotty face, his greasy unkempt hair, and his outfit of dirty striped pyjamas and an American collegian's sleeveless kapok anorak.

Tiring of it she had cut across his chatter. 'Dr Gyggle tells me that you have a court case coming up – when is it?'

'Not for another four months. If they're lucky I might kark it before they have to hear it. That would save them both the trouble and the cost.' He had smirked, a little boy still finding his own cynicism profound. Jane bit her lip – did she need this? Was this really someone who either wanted or deserved to be helped?

'I don't think that's either a clever thing to say, or true.'

'What exactly do you know about me, Jane Carter?' He had addressed her thus, using both her names, as if somehow to place her more exactly, define her as a player.

'Only what Dr Gyggle has told me.'

'The man is a fucking charlatan.' He was vehement, but didn't raise his voice. 'All the fucking DDU people are charlatans. All of them posturing, getting their pro-fess-ion-al kicks from lording it over scum like me – smackie scum.' He reached his striped arm across the table at this point, and freed a filtered cigarette from a prison of ten. Jane caught sight of some more of the scar tissue that featured so prominently on Richard Whittle's medical record.

'But you're kicking the habit, aren't you? Isn't that right?'

'Yeah, then I'm going back into the wine business. I'm gonna be a master of wine. Go every summer to fucking Jerez, to the Dordogne, to Bordeaux, every-fucking-where, tasting, living it up.'

'Is that what you really want to do?'

'Yeah.'

'Have you had any experience?' Even to her own ears Jane sounded oppressively schoolmarmish. There couldn't be more than five years separating them in age.

'I used to work in an off licence in Richmond. I know all about wine, I read about it all the time.' He pointed in the corner where there was a stack of glossy magazines. Jane had followed his finger and spotted, next to the battered meat safe on the grot-speckled work surface, a glass in which there rested the powerless trinity of teaspoon, squeezed bit of lemon and holy hypodermic syringe.

'I see,' she had said, and then, trying to be oblique, 'Are you taking methadone?'

'No, but I brush my teeth with fluoride fucking toothpaste.' Whittle tittered annoyingly, sillily, and revealed long-unbrushed teeth, coated with green plaque. Jane had felt that enough was enough. She commenced the search for her heavy handbag, with every intention of quitting Richard Whittle's life for ever.

But then, he got up and as he wonkily orbited the kitchen, said, 'I'm sorry. You see I can't really talk much more about all of this.' He shaped a hand, encompassing the kitchen's work surfaces, like some junky lecturer telling the story of his short unsuccessful life, with the assistance of a series of horizontally mounted exhibition boards. 'I'm all talked out. I talk to my parents, I talk to my brother, I talk to Giggly – the prat, I talk to my GP. I've got nothing left to say. For fuck's sake, I even have to talk to people in my dr –' He stopped abruptly, a cautious look coming over his face.

'People in your what?'

'No, no, no one else. I just talk to all these people – and it never does any good.' Whittle let his eyes fall forward, and, surveying a callus on his palm, he made ready to pick at it. A silence had welled up to cradle them, while outside on the sunny Heath, Jane could hear children screaming and screaming and screaming.

'So you don't see a lot of point in talking to me?'

'No, not really.'

Then the strange unknowable thing had happened. There was a scatter of very loud, clacking footfalls, which sounded on the parquet floor of Whittle's hallway right outside the kitchen. Next, the front door slammed with a rattling bash of glass and wood. Without having been conscious of making the decision to do so, Jane found herself running behind Whittle's slack behind, as he bolted towards the break-out.

They had both ended up jammed against the banister, leaning over to catch sight of the intruder as he fled. The sharp footfalls were still ringingly loud, like steel on stone, but it wasn't until whoever-he-was gained the penultimate flight of stairs that Jane caught sight of him. Later, attempting to recall precise detail, she could only picture the man's head – or at any rate the hat he wore. It was so distinctive, so bizarre. A shiny purple hat, covered in black polka-dots. A top hat.

All over London The Fat Controller's creatures, his confrères and familiars, his agents and accomplices, his licentiates and legates, were stirring. They were feeling his presence – or maybe it was the anticipation of his presence, as it were, his pre-presence – as someone might sense the coming of a thunderstorm. First the fall in air-pressure, then the build up of humidity, then the agonising apprehension that everything presages something else, that all there is is this awful, close waiting. But when at last it comes – what a disappointment. Rain is, after all, only rain. Sky piss. And thunder is, after all, only thunder. Just God, like a troubled pensioner, a little bit 'confused' and indulging his second adolescence by imagining that a rearrangement of the serviced flatlet's furniture will somehow engender a new charisma.

Harumph! D'ye see what's happening? It's time for you to retroscend again, you, Belial's babies, the cuties of the cabal, toddling down the diminishing aisles of Mothercare. It's time for you to join me, pick out a man-made thing and follow its course, use it to plot history's convention. Naturally, I don't want to give you the hard-sell on this. It could be that you have better things to do with your time than scour out the commercial scorings, follow the shooting stars of shelved lives. Nonetheless, I do guarantee some insights that would not be forthcoming were you not to indulge me. Indeed I offer, Free And With Absolutely No Obligation Whatsoever, twenty-five per cent more in the way of insights than you gained the last time you were compelled to retroscend.

If these insights aren't forthcoming, if you feel shabbily treated once you have retroscended, then please let me draw your attention to the one hundred per cent Full Redemption Clause. At any point you can ask for your time back, ask for the time back that you feel has been wasted retroscending. Go on, ask for the time back at the counter on your way out, then by gad you'll regret it! For the time that will be returned to you isn't eventful time, it isn't even time in which seemingly unrelated dull little happenings are building up to something else, it certainly won't be three hours of segued orgasms. Oh no, this is untenanted time, boarded-up time, odds and sods and little dog ends of time. Time spent staring at the half-moon of rust on the side of a rivet implanted in the bodywork of a tourist coach, while you wait at a traffic light; time used up irritably flicking at the pointy point, where, in theory, the sticky surface should peel away from its backing; time disposed of drumming your fingers; time fecklessly wasted waiting for your number to come up at the delicatessen counter. That's the sort of time I'm talking about. So, on balance, it's probably worth your while sticking around to retroscend.

Another thing, that semantic incongruity my licentiate drew your attention to earlier, well now here's your opportunity to join in. Participate in meaning's floor exercise as it tumbles diagonally across the mat. The moment has arrived when you must abandon your armchair assertorics, wind up your after-TV-dinner speeches, and feel the sick pit of your stomach gyrate.

Steve Souvanis, proprietor and sole trader, sat in the offices of the enterprise he – and he alone – commanded. Dyeline Constructions of Clacton. He had just put down the telephone after a short and bewildering conversation with Si Arkell, planner at D.F.&.L. Associates. For no good reason that Souvanis could discern, Arkell had asked him to quote on the production of some perspex point-of-sale modules, which sounded truly preposterous. These modules were to be free-standing transparent booths, octagonal, seven feet high, and containing sort of mini-lecterns, where the booth users could stand and write, whilst both watching the world and being observed by it.

Arkell had told Souvanis that he wanted a quote for sixty of these 'standing booths', as he termed them, to be constructed, and then erected all over London before the end of the year. Souvanis couldn't believe his ears. True, he had done work for Arkell in the past but nothing on this scale. Souvanis specialised in the production of perspex modules that were designed to dispense leaflets and other kinds of promotional material.

In the warehouse space next to the cubbyhole office where Souvanis sat there was a ghostly jumble of these things, stacked about seemingly higgledy-piggledy. There were leaflet dispensers shaped like cake stands, like books, like racks of various sorts, like miniature suspension bridges, like famous monuments, like vehicles, like spaceships and submarines, like hatstands and coat racks, cabinets and bookcases. All of them were made out of perspex, or transparent acrylic. The overall effect was of a space filled up with insubstantiality. The display modules were not real objects but the pale shadow of them, as platonic forms are to their derogated copies.

That morning, sitting on his bed, the previous night's alcohol converted to goo in ear, gum in eye, slurp in chest, Souvanis had struggled to fasten the waistband of his trousers. I'm struggling to fasten the waistband of my trousers, he had thought to himself. Wedging his plump little feet into his loafers he had thought to himself: Ooh, how these insteps cut in. Then, no more of it. He had breakfasted with his wife, as usual, and set off from the Barking house for the Clacton works.

Every mile or so, self-consciously, Souvanis glanced at his reflection in the rearview mirror. Same moon face, same missed tussocks of black facial hair, same browning pate, same laugh and same frown lines. What was it that felt different?

Now, in the warm confinement of the warehouse, with its paper and plastic odours commercial in their sheer intensity, it began to dawn on him. He reached, or rather snatched, for the packet of BiSoDol on top of the littered desk; and clawing it open, pushed a couple of the chalky tablets out of their cellophane sachets. Why have I got indigestion, thought Souvanis, when I even skipped lunch? He tried to ease a hand between the waistband and his belly, but couldn't.

A couple of days previously an item on the leveraged buy-out of a giant American tyre company had caught Souvanis's eye as he was flicking through the financial pages of a newspaper; a week or so earlier, he had seen an ominously familiar silhouette slide between two robed princelings, as the television news covered the denouement of a Middle-Eastern conference. Well before that, almost a month ago now, coming out of his little terraced house, Souvanis had looked up to the sky, unbidden, to find hovering there, perhaps only one or two hundred feet overhead, the Goodyear Blimp. Which, as Souvanis gawped at it, bobbed a greeting – seemingly to him alone – in the clear sky.

These several events now crammed themselves together in Souvanis's mind, forming premises like stepping stones leading to only one possible conclusion. That the man the world knew as Samuel Northcliffe, financier, bon viveur, *éminence grise* of geopolitics, and whom Steve Souvanis knew as The Fat Controller, was back.

Acid and antacid ran together, fire streams in his volcanic stomach. How like The Fat Controller to announce his arrival thus, with a supernatural attack of indigestion. Souvanis felt that his fat and flab were being addressed at some profound level, a level of primary starches, carbohydrates and sugars, by other, more potent fat, of a great lunar significance, fat that pulled his very girth around in its sweating skin girdle producing measurable torque.

The unusual request from D.F. & L. Associates was now easily explained. It was down to Northcliffe. Souvanis had learnt long long ago, when his association with The Fat Controller had begun (and who could say when that was? Perhaps the tubby little boy had been tumbling around the dusty streets of Nicosia when he tried to snatch a camera from a soft, old tourist and found that the tourist was neither soft, nor old. But speculation isn't in order here, Souvanis's relationship with The Fat Controller belongs to a narrative other than this), that almost anything unusual, anything that disturbed the even tenor of his life, could be put down to his mentor.

Souvanis sighed heavily. He looked around the empty cubby-hole and jerked his head in an explanatory fashion, at the nobody that was there. Whatever was coming his way, part of it would be good. Part of it would relate to these 'standing booths' required by D.F. & L. So he'd better get on and quote for them. Like some horrible kind of modern tinnitus, the fax machine in the next room started to whirr in Souvanis's head; the brush-fringed mandibles seemed to nibble at his inner ear. That would be Arkell's diagram of the booth.

'So, if they want a quote' – Souvanis spoke aloud, projecting his voice into the sample-clogged warehouse – 'they can have their quote.' He rose and went next door to receive his message.

After a long hot day in the office, the last thing Ian wanted to do was attend the S.K.K.F. Lilex product launch at Grindley's. He knew exactly what it would be like, all the rest of the S.K.K.F. Lilex product launches he had attended at Grindley's. These bloody companies seemed so certain that all they had to do was douse a crowd of hacks in lukewarm Asti Spumante in order to get a good write-up. They couldn't even be bothered to vary the venue, to try and add some spice to the dousing.

And what a day! Pouring over the Sudanese Bank of Karmarathon's ridiculous documentation, trying to get to the nub of exactly what it was their financial engineers meant by 'an edible financial product'. What was 'Yum-Yum'? Why, it was a credit card and a current-account banking facility; it was a share-watch service and a brokerage facility; it was a telephone-banking service and a secure-deposit facility with a high-interest yield. As he worked his way through the dull copy, the designations tumbled around one another, 'facile service', 'serviceable facility' – what possible difference could it make? So what if the dividends accruing to the customer could be transformed either into foodstuffs or foodstuffs options? So what if the very materials that made up the documentation for the product – chequebooks, credit cards and so forth – were actually, in and of themselves, edible. None of it cut any ice with Ian. He'd seen them come and seen them go, these revolutionary new personal banking products. Not one of them had had any impact on the increasingly unknowable, dilatory even, quality of money itself.

At this fag end of the millennium money had begun to detach itself from the very medium of exchange. Money was lagging behind. Ian knew – because he had read about it in the press – that there was aproximately $800 trillion that had simply winked into existence. It had never been earned by anyone, or even printed by any government. Everywhere you looked you saw advertisements screaming: 'Value for Money'. That such an obvious *non sequitur* should have become a benchmark of credibility was beyond Ian's, and indeed anyone's, understanding. This 'value' was as insubstantial as the $800 trillion. It was linked to no commonly perceived variable; instead it was chronically relativised. The merchant banks and brokerage firms that made up the City had long since given up on employing even the most flamboyant and intuitive of economic forecasters. Instead they had fallen back on the self-styled 'money critics', refugees from the overflowing newsprint sector, who offered their services to provide 'purely aesthetic' judgements on different mediums of exchange.

But business was still business. So, together with his co-marketeers, Ian levered his sweating bulk into the black cab that stood, coughing and heaving, outside Norman House.

'Grindley's,' said Hal Gainsby to the cabby.

'You'll be going to the S.K.K.F. Lilex launch then,' the cabby replied.

'How did you know?' Only Si Arkell was young enough and curious enough to bother with a query.

'Oh, I take a keen interest in any new ulcer medication that comes on the market,' said the cabby, powering the cab away from the kerb and straight into a snarl of traffic. 'It goes with the job.'

The city was hot, the cab was close. Inside the five marketeers' deodorants competed with one another for olfactory supremacy. Si Arkell's ebulliently tasteless sandalwood talc won the day. By the time they had struggled across the Old Street Roundabout, battled through Hatton Garden, fought their way down High Holborn – the cabby dispatching challengers to the right and to the left, with 'Fuck off's and klaxon honks – and gasped betwixt the raffia of metal that held Trafalgar Square in its vice, Ian was about ready to expire. They all dived out of the sweaty confines of the cab. Gainsby paid the cabby off, while Ian stared up at the mock-Regency portico of Grindley's, which loitered under the dusty plane trees along Northumberland Avenue.

The presence had been with Ian all afternoon as well. It was a sinister afflatus, hissing a welcome in his ear. At any moment Ian expected everything to come tumbling down around him. And that – in a manner of speaking – is exactly what did happen.

CHAPTER EIGHT

REENTER THE FAT CONTROLLER

Now there are, as it is said in the Papal Bull, seven methods by which they infect with witchcraft the venereal act and the conception of the womb. First, by inclining the minds of men to inordinate passion; second, by obstructing their generative force; third, by removing the members accommodated to that act; fourth, by changing men into beasts by their magical art; fifth, by destroying the generative force in women; sixth, by procuring abortion; seventh, by offering children to devils, besides other animals and fruits of the earth with which they must work harm.

Maleum Maleficorum
trs. Reverend M. Summers, *sub specie aeternitatis*

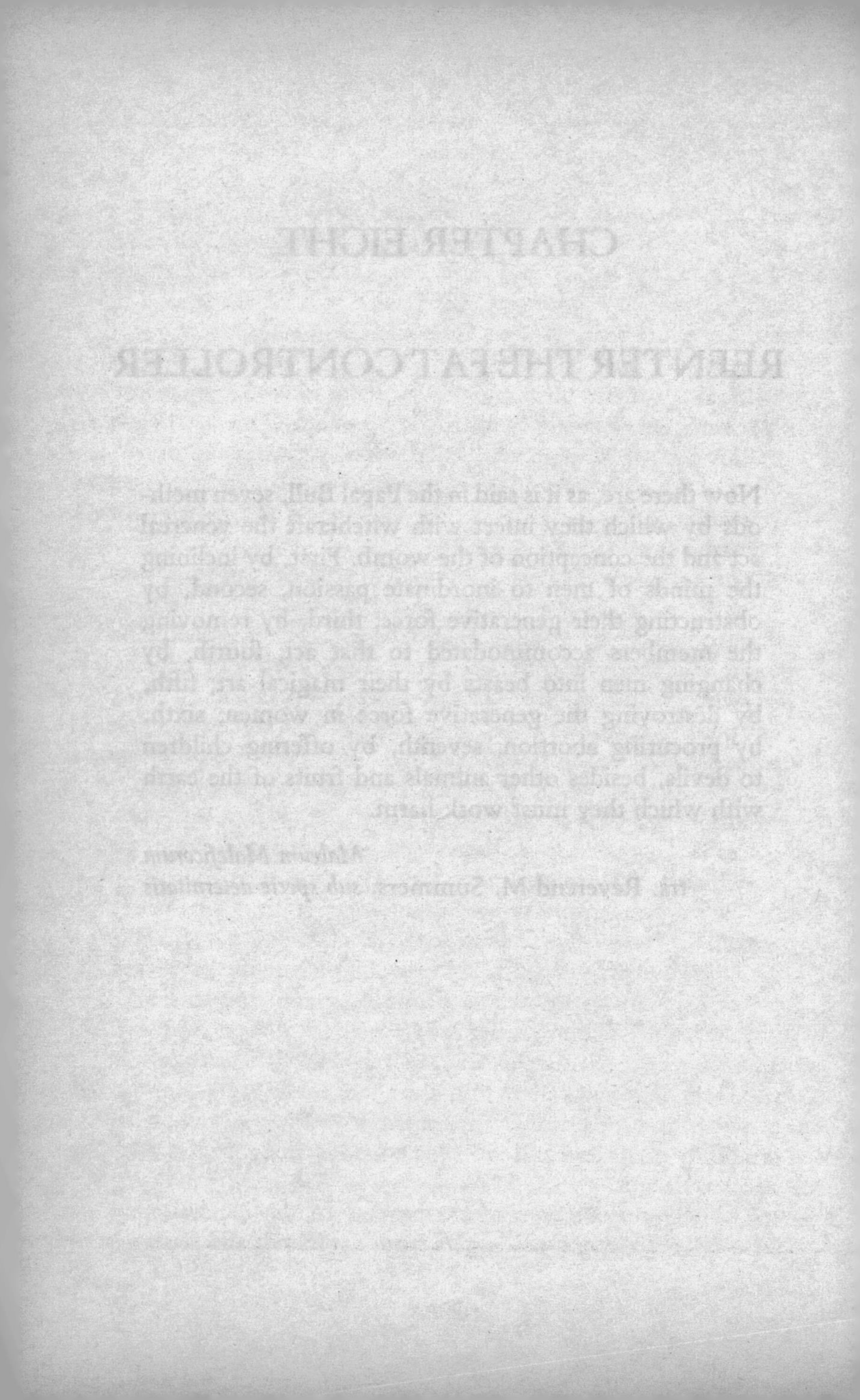

Early on the morning of that same day the travellers' message board at Heathrow's Terminal Three had begun to clog up with a large number of notes, petitions and billets-doux. All were written in different hands and all were addressed to a variety of individuals, but every single one was intended for the same man.

The Fat Controller was arriving from America. From New York City, to be precise. It was a characteristic of The Fat Controller that he was always arriving from somewhere and yet it was never actually possible to conceive of him as being anywhere else other than exactly where he was. At any rate, not possible for those who knew him. Perhaps somewhere, on some other planet, for example, there may be a race of highly advanced coenobites, whose entire purpose it is to spend their reclusion collectively visualising The Fat Controller in those places from which he is forever arriving. If so, they must be very highly advanced indeed.

The Fat Controller came wheeling through the swing doors that lead from the customs area to the main concourse of the terminal. He was wearing his travelling kit, Donegal tweed jacket, grey flannel trousers and brogues. Over his bolster arm he had draped one of those American trench coats that are furnished with more button-down panels, straps and belts than are strictly necessary. Trailing behind him like a faithful little dog, came a brown Sansomite suitcase. The Fat Controller tugged somewhat erratically on its lead and the thing waggled along, as if it were an afterthought.

The Fat Controller reached the end of the handrail that separates the arriving passengers from the friends and relations that have come to meet them. Here he halted and turned, the better to observe the rendezvous of his fellow travellers. The Fat Controller always did this. He always got off the flight as quickly as possible and rushed through immigration and customs, so that he could witness this moment.

'It's a very important moment indeed,' he was fond of saying. 'A very emotional and naked moment. When people greet one another, after an absence – particularly in airports, where the overhead strip lighting is so poorly modulated – they are rendered transparent to one another. An unfaithful husband's guilt passes across his face like a shadow, in the nanosecond that it takes him to place a welcoming smile on his face for his waiting wife. Two lovers meet and both their expressions betray the certainty of their eventual parting, in the very instant before they touch. Ungrateful brats debouch from their cheap holiday in someone else's misery and their tired parents try desperately to summon up joy out of indifference. These are the very moments that I treasure! For I am a traveller in feeling and a trafficker in souls – so flitting and spindly-legged are the examples I seek that I may style myself a very entomologist of the emotions!'

The Fat Controller would roll these phrases around in his mouth, together with some single malt whisky and a coil of smoke from his habitual cigar, before expelling them at his audience. The Fat Controller was very fond of pontificating, although all too often compulsion was his only way of ensuring listeners.

On this occasion he stayed for five minutes and ten times as many such 'naked moments' before his sentimental voyeurism was sated. Then he headed off towards the bank of electronically operated doors and the taxi rank, passing the wailing wall of the noticeboard without even a glance. The suitcase followed him.

Whenever The Fat Controller came to London he put up at Brown's Hotel in Piccadilly. The Fat Controller liked Brown's for a number of reasons. He felt inconspicuous there – there were so many other fat people of indeterminate age in residence, many of them sharing his taste in tweed and Burberry. Another plus was that quite a lot of minor American celebrities – actors, producers and directors from the cinema and musical theatre – tended to stay at Brown's. There wasn't an hour of the day when you couldn't find one of these people, tucked into a corner of the chi-chi lobby, being interviewed by an English hack about their latest production. The Fat Controller got a vicarious sense of notoriety from coming and going amidst this continual press call. He did like to think of himself as a celebrity of sorts. Although, more than most people, he appreciated that being the object of other people's attention was at best a transitory and unrewarding experience, and at worst, a positive damnation.

That's why, rather than actually being a celebrity, The Fat Controller preferred to adopt a celebrity demeanour. The kind of carriage and countenance that made at least one in three people who he passed by think to themselves: I'm sure I recognise that man but I just can't place him. He must be someone famous. This was the kind of renown that The Fat Controller desired. An uncomplicated way of being the talk of the town, without obligation and honestly ephemeral.

Outside, in the already tired atmosphere of the late-summer morning, The Fat Controller paused, surveying the hideous jumble of concrete buildings that constituted the airport. Why travel, he thought to himself, when you merely arrive back at where you started from? He was thinking of the other people who thronged the airport precincts, not himself. For The Fat Controller all modern westerners were essentially the same, conforming to the small number of stereotypical characters that had been allotted them. He opined that, were a suburb of Scranton NJ to be swopped in its entirety for one in Hounslow Middlesex, hardly anyone in the areas abutting them would even notice. All of these people, he mused, his frog eyes flicking hither and thither, are in transit from some urban *Heimat*, an ur-suburb, a grey area. They are like colonists who have set out *en masse*, lemming-like, uncomprehending, obeying an instinctive need to buy a newspaper in another country.

The next cabby in the rank pulled forward and tucked his *Standard* away on top of the dash. The electric window slid down.

'Where to, Gov?'

'Brown's Hotel, Piccadilly,' said The Fat Controller.

Then there was an uncomfortable hiatus, a strange pause. He made no move to enter the cab. The cabby sat and waited. After a while the cabby barked at him, 'Well, aren't you going to get in?' The Fat Controller pushed his porcine head through the window of the cab, pressing four pounds of cheek against the already clicking meter. 'Not,' he boomed, 'until you get out and pick up my bag.'

The cabby's eyeballs bulged with rage. He felt his gorge rise up his neck, bitter, bilious and sarcastic. Foolishly – as it transpired – he choked it back down again. He quitted the cab and came round to where The Fat Controller was standing. By now, some of the other cabs in the rank had loaded up with passengers and were hooting to get away. The cabby gave The Fat Controller a long and penetrating look, intended to intimidate him. Then he picked up the brown Sansomite suitcase and placed it in the back of the cab. He held the door open for The Fat Controller, who took his time getting in, settling himself, and wedging trench coat to one side and *Herald Tribune* to the other.

They were on the M4 heading towards the Chiswick Flyover, when The Fat Controller lit his first cigar since clearing customs. It was the flaring trumpet of an operatic Tosca. He stuck the cheroot in the corner of his wide mouth and applied the guttering flame of his convict-built lighter to its organic end.

A comic scene ensued as the cab plunged up the flyover ramp. Suddenly, The Fat Controller and his driver lifted off from the scrublands of Hillingdon and Hayes. They were floating on a carpet of tarmac high over the blue haze of the city. The vast ocean of London lapped around them. Ahead, the flyover snaked its way between corporate blocks. Where the roadway drew near to the fourth or fifth storey of each edifice, a digital clock and thermometer had been placed. These disputed with one another: 11.44, as against 11.43; 32° celsius, as against 33. The Fat Controller sucked an inverted blast on his Tosca and considered the vicissitudes within the secret lives of products, the serendipitous occurrence of both siting and style that had allowed the Brylcreem and Lucozade buildings to end up thus, their neon fifties' logos flashing in anachronistic opposition to one another, across the Chiswick Flyover.

'Can't you read the sign?' The sliding window separating him from the cabby had been torn open, shattering The Fat Controller's reverie. He fanned away the thick coif of blue-brown curls that had formed in front of him, bringing into view a prominent 'No Smoking' sign.

'I can.'

'Whassat?'

'I can read the sign.'

'Well, why don't you do what it effing well says then?'

'I don't choose to.'

'Don't choose to? Don't fucking choose to!' The cabby was trapped, driving along the flyover. He couldn't stop, he couldn't turn around, he wasn't even able to wave his arms about. He vowed to himself that he would eject The Fat Controller as soon as he possibly could.

The cab sped on along the elevated roadway. The Fat Controller puffed contendedly on the stinking instrument in his mouth and meditated on whether or not this wasn't an altogether purer way of tormenting someone than applying physical force, or more obviously contrived psychological pressure.

The cab canted down on to the straight that leads to the Hogarth Roundabout.

'Hn, hn!' grunted The Fat Controller, thinking aloud. 'A fine Rake's Progress and no mistakin'.'

'Whassat?' barked the cabby, alive to the possibility of some fresh insult.

'Oh nothing, nothing – don't trouble your little head.'

As soon as he safely could, the cabby pulled over into the nearside lane and then turned off down a side street. The cab came to a rest with a squeal, under a sticky plane tree. The cabby leapt out and came round to the back door, which he yanked open.

'Get out!' he shouted. 'Come on, get out!' he reiterated. The Fat Controller dropped the upper edge of his *Herald Tribune* and regarded the cabby from the vantage of several millennia of cold neutrality. He really did look rather revolting, arms akimbo, breasts bulging under a green T-shirt, which had the silky half-sheen that is rendered near-transparent by sweat. Further down, his plump, white, hairless thighs fell gracelessly from the rucked crotch of his day-glo football shorts. The Fat Controller noted that, in the colonial way, the cabby was wearing lace-up shoes and white knee-socks.

'No,' said The Fat Controller, glancing around at the empty residential street. 'You get in.' Then, with a fluidity of motion that was rendered all the more unnatural and frightening by his bulk, The Fat Controller lunged forward, grabbed the cabby by the throat and pulled him straight down on to the floor of the vehicle. Like a conjurer, he flicked a silk paisley handkerchief from his jacket pocket and thrust it into the cabby's gasping mouth. Next, still grasping his prey like some gargantuan trout that he had managed to tickle from the urban mill race, The Fat Controller proceeded to torture him gently. Taking another pull on his Tosca, he applied the glowing tip of the stogie to the white billow of occupational lard that had emerged from beneath the cabby's T-shirt. He didn't leave off until he had managed to create a neat line of blisters.

Still hunched over, one hand on the cabby's gullet, The Fat Controller used the other to free the knot of his green mohair tie. This he then looped around the cabby's neck. Substituting a knee for his other hand, he tied a slip knot in it and settling back in his seat said, 'Now, my good man, I think you are probably in a better position than formerly to judge what manner of personage you have for a passenger. No, no, don't trouble yourself to apologise' – the cabby was gurgling for breath – 'it isn't necessary. I am not a vindictive man, sir, I have no place for such feelings in my nature and indeed I resist such impulses whenever they arise. However, that being said, I engaged you to drive me to Brown's Hotel and that is what I want you to do. In a moment I will release you and we shall resume our journey. But make no mistake about it, should you prove fractious again, I shall not hesitate to utilise this neckwear in garrotting you. Got that?'

The cabby coughed assent. He wasn't a particularly observant man, but one thing he had noticed during the sickening shock of the last few minutes was a peculiarity of The Fat Controller's fingertips. They had no whorls or indentations and, therefore, they would leave no prints.

Released, the cabby worked his way back to the front of the cab and got in. The Fat Controller fed the woollen garrotte through the sliding window and they set off again. The Fat Controller reclined, smoked and read the paper. The cabby, on the end of his lead, drove.

They had the run of the traffic and within thirty minutes the cab was rounding Berkeley Square. The Fat Controller sat forward and, siting a girder-sized arm over the cabby's shoulder, said, 'Pull down into that underground car-park.' The cabby did as he was told. The entrance was a long, choking, oily shaft that ran down into the earth at a forty-five-degree angle. At the bottom the attendant's kiosk was empty. Even so, The Fat Controller dropped down in his seat by way of a precaution.

'Take the ticket.' Once again, the cabby did as he was told. 'And pull over to the far side of the level.' The cab stopped in the concrete corner, which was dark, quite hidden from the kiosk's view by a panel truck. The Fat Controller garrotted the cabby, quickly and with merciful efficiency. 'I would wager, sir' – The Fat Controller addressed the cabby's slumped corpse, whilst pulling his suitcase from the back of the cab – 'that that was as good a death as you could reasonably have expected to have.' His huge palm essayed an expressive flutter, as he leant in through the driver-door window and contemplated the deflated face. 'Granted that I can have no idea of what your prospects might have been, but on the sound principle that every man is responsible for the nature of his own countenance, I would wager, sir, that you would never have become a creature capable of those nice distinctions, the contrivance of which serves, as it were, to define refinement.'

With this euphonious eulogy The Fat Controller set off back across the oil-stained floor of the underground car-park, towards the lift. The brown Sansomite suitcase went with him.

Someone had once told The Fat Controller that he bore a distinct resemblance to the character of Gutman, as played by Sydney Greenstreet in *The Maltese Falcon*. This he relished. The truth is that the similarity was quite superficial. Like the Fat Man, The Fat Controller had an interesting bulk, an unusual kind of fatness. However, while it could conceivably be said of Greenstreet, as it is often said of the fat in general, that he was 'amazingly graceful', or 'surprisingly light on his feet'; and indeed that those feet were 'really quite elegant', none of these descriptions could have been applied to The Fat Controller, who really was fat. Fat in a heavy and unrelenting manner. Programmatically fat. Fat as if his mammoth aspect were the result of several, consecutively successful five-year eating plans. Wherever he went The Fat Controller's fat surrounded him and marched with him, like a tight huddle of violent men wearing overcoats.

Another point of dissimilarity; unlike Gutman, The Fat Controller was not a true connoisseur – ultimately he gained no more joy from things than he did from people. Whereas Gutman was prepared to spend a lifetime recovering the black bird, The Fat Controller would have eliminated the entire cast within the first half-reel of the film. The Fat Controller's attitudes were born of an uncompromising pragmatism, which those who met him felt as a peculiar sort of emanation. Whilst Gutman had a magnetic quality that he bolstered with rhetorical flair, The Fat Controller was banal. And if you allowed him the chance to get going in his affected way, he became downright boring very quickly.

The desk clerk at Brown's Hotel was certain that he had seen The Fat Controller somewhere before. There was something familiar but unplaceable about the big man's face. He waited, pen poised over register, while The Fat Controller moved towards him in his gang of flesh.

'By Jove!' he exclaimed. 'Such weather, and in England of all places.' For an instant, the desk clerk tried to imagine The Fat Controller in still sunnier climes – for some reason he couldn't manage it.

'Can I help you, sir?' The desk clerk was easy, consummately so.

'Oh yes, oh yes indeed.' He paused, clearly trying to remember some important fact, like his name, for example. He ran the five-pack of wieners that constituted his hand around his collar. 'I have a reservation.'

'In what name, sir?'

'Northcliffe, my man, Samuel Northcliffe. Take a look in your little book.'

Jane Carter was crying in her West Hampstead flat. Crying as the evening sunlight fell in gay bars across the flat's bright patterned interior. She breathed heavily and the mucal reeds lining the wet passages of her head gave off little clarinet cries of loneliness. The tears were prompted by an indigestible bubble of self-pity, which had been swelling up in her all afternoon. Now they had started, the tears steadily gained fresh impetus. Like boulders being pushed down a mountainside, they came rolling and tumbling out from her ducts, each one powered by a different slight, a different hurt, failed relationships and relationships that never were but might have been.

At her feet a mess of knitting fell out from the lip of a plastic bag; blue, green and yellow threads forming a soft circuitry. Thrusting out from amongst them, a wooden knitting needle caught her attention. She snatched it up, losing several hundred careful stitches as she freed it from its fluffy embrasure. Taking the knitting needle in her right hand, like a dagger she pulled up the hem of her black denim dress. Her thighs appeared monstrous to her, damning evidence of her failure to achieve sylph-hood. 'You're fat! Fat! Fat!' she exclaimed, with each 'fat' digging the sharp tip of the knitting needle into the horrible stuff. The final dig drew blood – and enough pain to stop her crying.

She stood up abruptly and began to dance around the flat, singing discordantly, 'Oh, I'm so a-lone, so a-lone, so bloody fat and a-lone,' and as she sang, she wished. Wished for a lover, any lover, a daemon or an incubus – the presence could take her now come what may. She didn't care any more. What do I matter? she concluded. I'm a zero, another poor cow in the herd. I wear certain clothes and certain shoes, I put on certain make-up and use certain sanitary towels and I go to a certain dentist and a certain doctor, because of my bloody certain daddy and certain mummy. That's for sure! With this bleak summation she began to dance, kicking out first one fat (according to her) leg and then the other. In this pitiful self-absorption, she felt herself to be just one amongst a multitude of Janes. All of them standing on their oval crocheted rugs, in their recently converted flats. They all looked the same, they all faced in the same direction and they all threw up their arms. They formed the most highly dispersed Busby Berkeley-style chorus line ever – this phantom army of high-kicking Janes.

The phone rang. 'Jane?' It was a woman's voice.

'Yes?'

'It's Beattie.' Beautiful brittle Beatrice, the PR girl.

'Oh hi, Beattie, how're you?'

'Fine, Jane, and how are you?'

'Fine.'

'Jane – '

'Yes?'

'I wondered if you were doing anything this evening?'

'Why?' Jane, however fat and ugly she felt herself to be, wasn't about to admit her unpopularity.

'Um, well, OK, it's pretty boring really, but I need a favour – ' She ran on, sensing that Jane was about to interrupt, '. . . I'm organising this press launch for S.K.K.F. and I haven't been able to get as many people along as I'd hoped for. The company's entire marketing department will be there – it could be very bad news for me if I can't up the body count.'

'So, you want me to pretend to be a hack from the medical press?'

'That's right.'

'And what is this product they're launching? Is it something I should know about?' Beattie twittered with laughter, Jane held the phone away from her ear until it had ceased.

'Not exactly. Though it is rather brilliant, revolutionary even. Lilex is a brand-new drug for the relief of peptic and duodenal ulceration, it's prepared in easy-to-swallow tablets and presented in two by twelve plasticised pop-out packs.'

'Oh really.' Jane was underwhelmed by Beattie's enthusiasm. She had seen it before. With every new account, every new product to be launched, the PR girl shifted her allegiance radically and completely. Her belief in a product was a total thing, real and encompassing. It didn't matter if it was a cosmetic or a patent medicine, a motor car or a fashion accessory. Hers was a metempsychosis of novelty, her mind a vapid thing until animated by the next absolute conviction.

'Look, Jane.' Beatie was conciliatory. 'Just do me that favour, will you. You're a journalist. Come along with your notebook and pretend to copy down whatever Wiley – that's the S.K.K.F. marketing manager – says. Then I'll take you out to eat, OK?'

'Oh, all right. But don't make a habit of this, Beattie, my self-esteem is already quite low enough, without my only invitations being to the press launches for new ulcer medications.' They both laughed and hung up.

For the next couple of hours Jane operated on her body. She cleaned it and scraped it, patted it and pushed it, painted it and prinked it. She hated herself for deploying these mortician's skills on the lumpy carcass, but what option did she have? She had put herself into two entire outfits then torn them off again, before she was finally satisfied and able to set out for Grindley's. In the end, she went dressed as she had been all that hot day.

Coming out of Trafalgar Square Tube Station, Jane picked her way through the throngs of pigeons and tourists. She found Beatrice half-way up the wide stairway of Grindley's, handing out press packs. Jane's friend was so neat and pretty that she looked as if she might have been plastic-encapsulated along with her name badge.

'Here,' she said, thrusting one of the folders at Jane. 'I think the speeches are about to begin. If you go on up to the Regency Room I'll join you in a moment.'

Jane did as she was told. In the Regency Room she positioned herself by the marble mantelpiece, under the huge gilt-framed mirror, and scanned the other launchers, the apparatchiks of the ulcer.

Jane was still feeling fat. Fat and sweaty. What a delicious irony, feeling fat and attending a press launch for ulcer medication. It wasn't lost on her. Wiley, the Marketing Manager, at least that's who she assumed it was, was droning on about Lilex. Jane couldn't concentrate. She flicked through the press pack, pausing only to admire a photograph of the S.K.K.F. chief executive, with his hands buried in what, according to the caption, was deep-frozen canine semen. She stared up at the ceiling and allowed her eyes to roam across the inverted landscape of plaster furbelows and flutings that gave the Regency Room its name. In these moments of absolute inattention, the presence that haunted her whole life had never been further from her mind.

'Are these peanuts dry-roasted?' Someone was talking to her.

'Oh, err – I don't know. Does it matter?'

He laughed shortly and said, 'I can't stand the dry-roasted ones, they're coated with all sorts of E-additives and crap, give me the sweats. Are you with the PR agency? I don't think I recognise you.'

He was a large man, Jane noted, with regular features tending to plumpness and square-cut mousy hair. There was something candid in his tone; this inspired candour in Jane. 'My name's Jane Carter. To tell you the truth I haven't got anything to do with this. My friend just asked me to come and make up the numbers.'

'Snap,' he said. 'My name's Ian Wharton, how do you do?'

Interlude

This is where The Fat Controller's brand of elective affinity leads to.

They were in a darkened corridor. It was musty with old carpet smell. They were naked. Standing like this, close to her, made him feel sharply the different sex that shaped their bodies. He felt that whereas her body was naturally shaped, her round hips and full bottom giving her an appropriate centre of gravity, his was just a long strip dangling from his head and only tentatively anchored to the dark floor. That was that then.

He had an erection. It was a latex thing, bouncy and ductile. She manoeuvred herself around so that she was side-on to him, then grasped his penis, grasped it in the way that she might a kitchen implement, a meat tenderiser or a rolling pin. She pulled it back and thwacked it against her buttocks, pulled it back and thwacked it against her buttocks. His penis oscillated upon its root, her buttocks wobbled. She had assaulted them both with the possibility of penetration. It was a moment of loss.

Ian and Jane found themselves sitting opposite one another in the Yellow Moon on Lisle Street. Goofy bent-over waiters leant against the half-bar. The tablecloth between them was stained with exactly the kind of yellow additives that gave Ian the sweats. At the next table a German tourist was listing his itinerary with wearying precision: 'Thaan I haaf a daay foor Haamptoon Coort, yes?' He was a Swabian, the hayseeds of Germany, and his voice looped the tonal loop like a stunt kite. Ian and Jane exchanged conspiratorial and chauvinistic looks.

'Do you really believe in marketing?' Jane asked, thinking to herself: I may as well establish if this man is a complete jerk before we get any further.

Ian took a while in answering, then said, 'That's a difficult question. At the risk of seeming pedantic, of course I believe in the fact of marketing. I'm not sure that I think it's necessarily a good thing, or even necessary at all.'

'Well, why do you do it then?'

'It's all that I know how to do,' he sighed. 'I don't think I'm clever enough to do anything else now, even if I wanted to.'

'What are you working on at the moment?'

'Oh, something called "Yum-Yum". It's an edible financial product – '

Ian was interrupted by the waiter who cocked his ear in the general direction of their table, by way of indicating that he would like to take their order. They told him what they wanted. He didn't write it down but listened inattentively, exchanging an occasional Cantonese bark with his colleagues. When they'd finished he sidled off towards the kitchen without having said a word in English.

'Service isn't exactly the strong point in these restaurants,' said Ian, who for some reason felt embarrassed, as if the waiter had been a relative or a friend.

'Oh I know.' Jane laughed. 'That's what I like about them. Everywhere else the waiters pretend to care, when really they couldn't give a shit. It's only the Chinese who refresh you with the sincerity of their contempt.'

'I'm not sure that it's just contempt. A few months ago a man in the one next door had his arm hacked off by the chef, who was armed with a kitchen cleaver.'

'Why?'

'Because he kicked up a row over not being allowed to pay for his meal with a credit card.'

'But everyone knows that these places are strictly cash. Something to do with the tongs, isn't it?'

'He was a tourist.'

Their eyes met again, just as the German at the next table launched in on another swooping speech. This time they both laughed. For Ian, this felt as if a wave were breaking against his heart, a wave of warm human contact. He could actually feel this wave pushing out towards his extremities. Strange to relate, Jane could feel it too.

'You were talking about an "edible financial product". What the hell does that mean?'

'The product is edible in two senses: the actual physical material associated with the product comes in an edible form and the interests and other disbursements come to the customer solely in the form of foodstuffs futures.'

'So, it's a sort of ethically sound investment idea?'

'Only if you're very greedy. But look, let's not talk about me, let's talk about you. What do you do?'

'Oh I knit and crochet; and I do macramé and patchwork and appliqué and tapestry and a bit of embroidery and macramé – have I said that before?'

'I think you might have.'

'And I write about it for specialist magazines and do a television programme – '

'Oh, so I'm dining with a celebrity?'

'Hardly, but it pays the rent.'

The waiter came back with a whole crispy duck. This he started to shred with mechanical efficiency, tearing at the thing with two forks. Both Ian and Jane felt embarrassed now. There was something venal about this shredding. Ian excused himself and went back through the restaurant to the toilet. He locked himself inside and propped his throbbing head against the paper-towel dispenser.

He thought about his nemesis, he-who-should-not-be-named, he of the capitalised definite article. Was he back? Perhaps this was the elective affinity he had always spoken of, always promised to Ian? Ian hadn't felt so safe in his attraction to anyone for a long time. Not since The Fat Controller had snapped his cigar in two, all those years before at Cliff Top. And even if this isn't arranged by him, thought Ian, why should I hold back now? What if what Gyggle says is true – he never really existed. I can't go on like this any longer, I can't go on feeling this way. If I don't get another person's hands on my body soon, I'm going to cease to exist. He had a vivid sensation of this, his body, like a giant continent, unmapped, unsurveyed, its further portions starting to fade away.

Back in the restaurant, Jane Carter was imagining what it might be like to have Ian Wharton's hands surveying her, touching her intimately. What would it feel like to have that big blocky body lying on hers? Could she tolerate it? She decided that she could – just about.

They drank too much saki, which tasted like hot sweat. And, after Ian had insisted on paying the bill, they walked out into the close night and went to a bar. Here there was an outsized television screen, which was so sited that the American footballing gladiators who were projected on to it looked as though they were dancing on the patrons' heads.

They drank some more. The way that they began to laugh at each other's jokes was tenderness itself, as were the numerous glances, the manifold shared references. These were shy pointers to the evening's conclusion but they were hedged with some maturity, some acceptance that things might not work out after all.

Jane couldn't really say that she wanted Ian to fuck her. Her lust was a diffuse longing that boiled into being in the wake of sex, not in its anticipation. She knew that she could bear Ian's body, bear its weight on hers, bouncing, but what about the morning? She winced into the glass she was sipping from, remembering what it was like to have an unwanted man in her flat. Naked men were like great white spiders in the morning, caught by the taps in the glare of the bathroom light, their limbs flailing as they washed themselves down the emotional plug hole.

'Where do you live?' He sounded nervous.

'Up in West Hampstead.'

'Let's get a cab, I'll drop you off.'

'Is it on your way?'

'Not exactly.'

In the street they were gripped by the delirium of people who feel certain they are on the verge of full genitality. Delirious, because no one can ever know such a thing, no one can ever know what another thinks. They cleaved unto one another in Old Compton Street. Her belly was like unto a heap of meat, or so he thought. She was that animal, that immediate. A piss head, purple cleft actually hammered into his brow, suppurating, of course, begged from them. Ian gave him a pound for his troubles, thinking: If they're only worth a quid, a Mayfair town house should retail for 50p.

In the cab they started snogging. She's my diesel dyke – oh BurgerLand! thought Ian, restraining himself. Her lips were so tacky and soft, they excluded the draught from his mouth, the afflatus from his mind. At the junction with the Euston Road an old finned Ford Zephyr cut them up as the lights changed. Two lads, dark like gypsies, whooping and hollering. Ian didn't even notice.

Actually, Jane wasn't finding the kissing that unpleasant either: Then perhaps I'm drunk? She was. She didn't even notice the Lurie Foundation Hospital for Dipsomaniacs as the cab cruised by. Ian did. Was Gyggle in there, pacing about? Ian thought he saw a light and imagined Gyggle, doing what? Reading an academic paper? Or putting another patient under for DST, sending another sucker to the Land of Children's Jokes? It would have been so much better if Jane had seen they were passing the hospital, because she would have said brightly, 'That's where I went for my assessment for voluntary service this afternoon – ' And then some shit would have come down. Better then than later.

The cab rocked off the Finchley Road by Habitat, tipped

behind the big block, then stuttered to a halt outside Jane's flat. Ian paid the cabby off.

In the small vestibule Ian smelt the tang of the lime in the fresh plaster. Jane fumbled with the key, resting her pounding heart against the entryphone. She felt his body press against her from behind. She yielded. She could feel his penis, hard in the small of her back. His hand pushed up the thick denim of her dress, smoothed up her thigh, came to catch and pull at the thin elastic lip of her pants. She sighed as his sodden face came down to nuzzle at her neck and his other hand moved up from her waist, to the carapace of her shy breast.

In counterpoint now, his two hands unbuttoned the heavy brass buttons that ran up the front of her dress. He felt her stomach, the tops of her thighs, the crinkly embroidery of her brassière. His face was coming around the corner of her cheek; their tongues touched awkwardly as they tried to enter each other's mouths from the side.

Then they stopped feeling one another out as they felt each other up and went looking for climax.

Before going up on the figurative pedals, so as to run into her at a sprint, Ian paused. He looked her in the eye and mentally apologised for the horror he might be about to inflict. Then he pushed on in – expecting the worst.

There's no better psychological check against premature ejaculation than the fear that your penis might break off inside someone.

A while later he was really fucking her. Fucking her in the way that men do when they have lost all sensation, when their cocks have been battering away for so long that they've abandoned conscience and created a battle zone of frightening ignorance from which no intelligence is available. When at last they came it was with a thin-lipped finality, as if they were a put-upon company secretary winding up a pointless board meeting.

Yet afterwards, when they lay, she face down, he with his big leg pinioning her buttocks, they both thought: This could be love.

Steve Souvanis stood awkwardly by the reception desk at

Brown's Hotel. He knew he looked conspicuous and down-at-heel in his cheap suiting. He was sweating in the heat and his belly was distended, uncomfortable. Outside, through the swing doors, he could see the winking hazard lights of his car. It was impossible to find a meter in this part of town – if a traffic warden or a rogue clamping crew came along he was screwed. He tried not to look too flustered, too ill at ease. He was feigning interest in some flyers for Barries', the posh King's Road menswear boutique, that had been deposited on the reception desk.

'Yes?' The concierge took him for a cabby.

'I've come to see one of your guests.'

'Yes?'

'A Mr Northcliffe.'

'And you are?'

'Mr Souvanis.'

'Ah yes, Mr Souvanis, I have a message from Mr Northcliffe for you. He's at Davidoff's. Do you know where that is?'

'Yes, I know.' Souvanis broke away and headed to the door. The concierge called after him, 'Left along Piccadilly and then right by the Ritz.' It was insulting, a calculated snub, implying that Steve was pretending or something.

He left the car, a large estate, in the underground car-park on the Piccadilly side of Berkeley Square. He was so preoccupied that he didn't even notice the red-and-yellow tape stretched everywhere and the signs reading 'Crime Scene Keep Out'. Back up at ground level he ploughed along the pavements, perspiring and fulminating. It was so sunny, the glare bit right into him. In the heat and haze the architecture of London looked Byzantine, immemorial. His eyes were drawn upwards to the pinnacled and domed tops of the buildings. He turned right past the Ritz and saw Davidoff the cigar merchant's across the road.

The shop was lilac-carpeted and humming cool. The smell of tobacco was as muted as expensive perfume. Steve Souvanis knew he was conspicuous once again, poor and oikish. The sales assistant was a duplicate of the concierge at Brown's.

'Yes?'

'Do you have a Mr Northcliffe with you?'

'Yes, he's in the humidor room. Can I tell him who's calling?' Souvanis told him and he glided off.

'Who's calling, who's calling' – Souvanis was incredulous. 'Christ! How ridiculous. It's not as if he's staying here, he hasn't rented out the humidor room – '

'Sir?'

'Y-yes.'

'This way.' The sales assistant directed Souvanis to the corner of the room, where there was a large glassed-in cabinet. 'You'll pardon the formality, sir,' he said. 'Mr Northcliffe has rented the humidor room for the day and he's very particular about his privacy.'

The glass door swung open and with it came a pungent tropical blast of strongly vegetative tobacco smell. The Fat Controller was sitting on a large reproduction-Empire armchair. He was surrounded by cigars and cheroots, shelf upon shelf of open boxes. The cigars were of all shapes and sizes, ranging from the automatic clips of small-calibre Brazilian cheroots, through the bandoliers of Honduran panatellas, to the big ones, the bazookas and groud-to-air missiles of Cuban full coronas, each one housed in its aluminium launcher.

In his hand The Fat Controller held an Upmann number one the size of a baby's arm. He was dressed formally, like an old-fashioned British civil servant, in black-and-white needle-striped trousers and a black frock coat. The Windsor collar made his immense head appear, more than ever, like a football placed for kick-off. On the floor next to his chair there was a top hat.

'Is that you, Souvanis? Come in, man! Don't hover like that, you're letting all the goodness escape.' The door swung shut and the two of them were left alone together, in close damp proximity. The Fat Controller immediately grabbed a fold of Souvanis's belly, quickly and adroitly, the way that any other man might snatch up a poker card. 'Getting a little tubby, aren't we,' he snarled. 'Have you heard me talking to you?'

'Ow! Yes.'

'Good. Talking to you through your fat – that's the ticket, eh? Splendid, splendid. And have you tendered for the D.F. & L. job?'

'Yes, I have. Please let go.'

The Fat Controller released him and fell to examining his cigar. 'Big, isn't it?' he said at length.

'Yes, it is rather – look, what's this all about, sir?'

'Don't call me "sir", Souvanis, you're not at school now. We're colleagues. You can call me "Master" if it makes you feel more comfortable.'

He put the Upmann back in its box and pulled a small cardboard packet of Toscanelli cheroots from the watch pocket of his waistcoat. He stuck one in his mouth. It was dwarfed by the smooth expanse of his face, rendered as tiny as a toothpick.

'Match me, Sidney,' said The Fat Controller.

'But, Master,' said Souvanis without quite knowing why he dared, 'I thought connoisseurs always lit their own cigars.'

'Harumph! Well, I suppose strictly speaking that is true. However, it's a mistake to assume that sensual experiences are merely enjoyable; they can have wider importance, a political significance even. In this case you are not simply lighting my cigar, you are paying homage. Now do it, match me!' He did so. The Fat Controller inhaled deeply and blew the smoke out hard, strafing the room. He watched it billow about the discreet strip lights set into the top of the cigar shelves. Watched it critically, rapt, as if in the throes of some profound aesthetic rumination.

'I'll tell you what this is all about, Souvanis,' he resumed. 'It's about a man's soul, a man's moral faculties, a man's inbuilt reason, his intuition, his sensibility and his self-esteem. In short, it's about his fate.'

'Oh, I see.'

'No, you don't see, Souvanis, and you never will. For twenty years now I have cultivated this man, pruned and shaped him, submitted him to a kind of metaphysical topiary. Now it is time to take stock, to, as it were, tie up some loose ends.'

'So how has D.F. & L. got anything to do with this? What's with this "Yum-Yum" and these standing booths – ?'

'Booby! You know I cannot abide a booby. It's not for you to speculate on my methods, my little playlets, my masques and contrivances and conceits. You are nothing but a familiar, a fat little cat.'

'Yes, Master.'

'I have need of you, Souvanis, to be my bag man, my button. So, you had better get that brother-in-law of yours in to run Dyeline. I'll be needing you for the next few days. And now' – he stood up – 'I've booked a table at the Gay Hussar – let's eat.'

Souvanis didn't really want to eat at the Gay Hussar. The very thought of all that paprika made him feel dyspeptic. He tried framing a statement of the form: 'Actually, I'm not really that hungry, why don't I have a cheese sandwich somewhere and join you later?' but looking at The Fat Controller gnashing his black fang of a cigar, Souvanis thought better of it.

At the end of that week, when Ian went for his next DST session, Dr Gyggle found him much changed. The marketing man had a sloppy grin on his face and he was lying sensuously on the examination couch in the little cubicle as Gyggle swept in, hypo in hand.

'Well, Ian, you look very comfortable.'

'I am.'

'Not worried about the DST? About going back to the Land of Children's Jokes?'

'No.'

'Oh, and why's that?' Gyggle supported the axle of his pelvis on the couch and peered down at Ian.

'Because I don't think I'm going back. I think I've cracked it. You see' – he blushed – 'I met this girl – woman – and well, you see, we made love. And it didn't happen. It didn't come off.'

'I do see,' said the shrink, a smirk oozing out from behind the beard. 'That is interesting. But there's a lot more to achieving full genitality, Ian, than the one apparently successful roll in the hay. You appreciate that, don't you?'

'Yes, of course, that's why I'm here. I've got something to live for now, something other than products. I want to be one hundred per cent fit – '

'Rid of all the old bugaboos?'

'Exactly,' said Ian, grinning at Gyggle's use of language.

'Good. I'll give you the pre-med then.'

There are many different ways of using drugs, many giddy variations on the basic theme of intoxication. Who can doubt that a vicar sipping a gin and tonic in the rectory garden isn't a million miles away from the urban crack head, searing his flesh with flaming acetone? Or that the psychotropic trances of the Sibundoy Valley shamans are not separated by many worlds of possibility from the monoxide-promoted drone of those who take the Silk Cut challenge? That being noted, The Fat Controller used drugs in the only way that really matters, to manipulate and distort, to retard and stunt, to cajole and control. He had a kind of drug-thing going in London. It was useful to him and it involved Richard Whittle, Beetle Billy and all the other no-hopers who hung around Gyggle's DDU. They were unruly participants, unsurprisingly. But that wasn't a problem, for he had one of his most trusted confrères *in situ*.

As Ian lay on the couch feeling Gyggle's Omnipom flood into him, Richard Whittle and Beetle Billy were coming out of the Tube at King's Cross. They found themselves bang in the middle of the wide-paved apron that runs in front of the station and along the Euston Road. It was covered in people, paper sellers, commuters, art students, immigrants, refugees, justices of the peace, articled clerks, nutritionists, cricket fans, loss-adjusters, cooks and junkies. Junkies singly and in huddles, junkies walking briskly on serious business and junkies idling, mooching along trying to appear relaxed, interested in their surroundings like ideal tourists.

Within twenty yards Richard and Beetle Billy were accosted by a short Italian with a knife-slash on his cheek and an English brass on his arm.

'You lookin'?' asked the Italian out of the corner of his mouth. He had the occupational skill of street junkies the world over, an ability to project his voice into another junky's ear from some distance, whilst remaining inaudible to the general public. Richard looked at Beetle Billy – the stupid car-repair man was wise to at least one event. His conjunctival eyes looked at Richard and filmed over still further.

'Nah,' said Richard.

'Whassermatter!?' the brass screeched after them. 'Iss reely good gear an' that.' But they were already too far off.

They strode towards the corner. The Pentonville Road ski-jumped away from them, lifting off towards the Angel. On the other side of the road in front of the bookie's, there was a mêlée of low-life. Even so, the junkies were holding themselves aloof from the dossers. The dossers had no pride. They built lean-tos out of plastic milk crates, right on the pavement. Then they got inside and pissed themselves. No, those dossers had no pride. But those junkies, on the other hand, what a fine upstanding bunch. There they all were, wavering in a line, necks craned to catch the junk messages from the hot ether. A dosser stands out a mile but a junky is a member of the plainclothes division of debauchery. Officers in this elite echelon are trained to recognise one another by eye-contact alone.

Beetle Billy pointed at a figure in the line. 'Thass Lena, man, she steers for one of those black geezers from the East End, less give her a try.'

'You lookin'?' asked the smallish blackish girl.

'Yo' where y'at, girl? Don' recognise me nor nuffin'. Iss me, Beetle Billy.' The girl sighed. 'Leroy 'bout, girl?'

From nowhere – or so it seemed to Richard – an immaculately dressed, coal-black young man appeared. Without saying anything, just by little jerks and nods of his flat-topped head, he piloted them across the road and towards the Midland City Line Station. They turned right past the Scala Cinema, crossed the Gray's Inn Road and then dived down a side street.

The coal-black man started to talk. 'Less get a ways off,' he said. 'There's a lot of bother an' that around an' I don' hold wiv it. No, man, no way, no, sir.' He turned to Richard flicking a penetrating stare. 'I'm Leroy, man, I'm Leroy, Le-roy. Remember that name, man, because I am the original Leroy, man – don' 'cept no substitute an' that – 'cause others may imitate but I o-rig-in-ate. Me come fe' mash up de area – '

'Blud claat, Ras claat!' exclaimed Beetle Billy. They stopped and gave each other five.

'Now, what you want, boys?' Just like that Leroy switched back from patois to Cockney. They were walking through a small estate of four-storey, red-brick blocks. Leroy drew them into a recess where huge rubbish canisters crouched on three-wheeled bases.

'We just want a bag thanks, Leroy,' Richard replied.

'Hey, I like you, man. You remember my name, man, that shows some respect, y'know, you ain't dissin' me an' that.' While he was talking a little white bead or polyp of plastic appeared between two of the gold rings on his hand. He proffered it to them. 'There you go,' said Leroy. 'Thass why I like to get a ways off. So my punters can see what they're gettin' an' that, yerknowhatImean?'

'I can't look at this, Leroy,' said Richard. 'It'll take me half an hour to get the packaging off. Why can't you guys ever put your stuff in a good old-fashioned paper bindle?'

'Hey! You know why that is, man. Anyways you ain't buying the stuff on account of its packaging, now are you?'

'No, that's true but every product has some kind of packaging and you could say that that effects its saleability – it may even represent added-value to the customer.'

The dealer paused for a moment, obviously taken by Richard's observation on the mechanics of his marketing. There was silence in the garbage recess, except for the faint 'chk-chk' noise made by Leroy's rings rubbing together and the distant grating of the traffic.

'I hear you, bro', said Leroy at length, 'but a bit of gear ain't really a product as such. I mean it's not like a Custard Cream or a Painstyler, it's not an original created product. It's just – like – well – "gear", innit?'

'Yeah,' Beetle Billy joined in. 'Iss like a whatsit, a generik, innit.'

'A generic?' queried Richard.

'Yeah, like an 'oover. An 'oover was just a product to begin wiv'. But now everyone calls any thingy thass like an 'oover, an 'oover.'

'I see, I see what you mean,' mused Richard. Leroy shifted uneasily in his penny loafers, his expensively suited shoulders rubbed 'shk-shk' against the brickwork. 'But, Billy, the Hoover was created as an individual product and then through its very ubiquity it became a generic term. Now this stuff' – he pointed at the bead of heroin between Leroy's knuckles – 'has a proper name but there are numerous slang terms that refer to it, neither as a product nor as a generic – '

'Of course it's a product,' Leroy broke in. 'Sheee! Someone grow it, right? Someone pro-cess it, right? Someone even im-port it, right? I know, sure as fuck that someone whole-sale it, right? Now I'm tellin' you people,' and here he paused and ran a fluttering hand around the space between the three of them, 'that I am re-tailin' this 'ticular pro-duct. So if you want it – pay for it, an' if you don't – say so, man, 'cause I've got to get back out to the front of the store.'

Richard and Beetle Billy scrunged in their jeans' pockets and pulled out bank notes like used handkerchiefs, together with some pound coins and other change. Leroy stood and withered at them while they accumulated the score for the score. They gave him the money – he gave them the scag. Then he disappeared, evaporating into the thick fructifying air as suddenly as he had materialised in the first place. Further up the courtyard a four-year-old child was ejected from a flat and started to howl.

Some time later Richard was back on his dead bed, staring out over the Heath where schoolchildren screechily played. He set down the 2 ml syringe on the cardboard box that served him as a bedside table and fell back, his mind nuzzling in on itself. He was stoned enough to be blissfully unaware of his role as pacemaker, psychic vanguard, racing ahead of Ian Wharton, back to the Land of Children's Jokes.

CHAPTER NINE

THE MONEY CRITIC

Money mediates transactions; ritual mediates experience, including social experience. Money provides a standard for measuring worth; ritual standardises situations, and so helps to evaluate them. Money makes a link between between the present and the future, so does ritual. The more we reflect on the richness of the metaphor, the more it becomes clear that this is no metaphor. Money is only an extreme and specialised type of ritual.

Mary Douglas, *Purity and Danger*

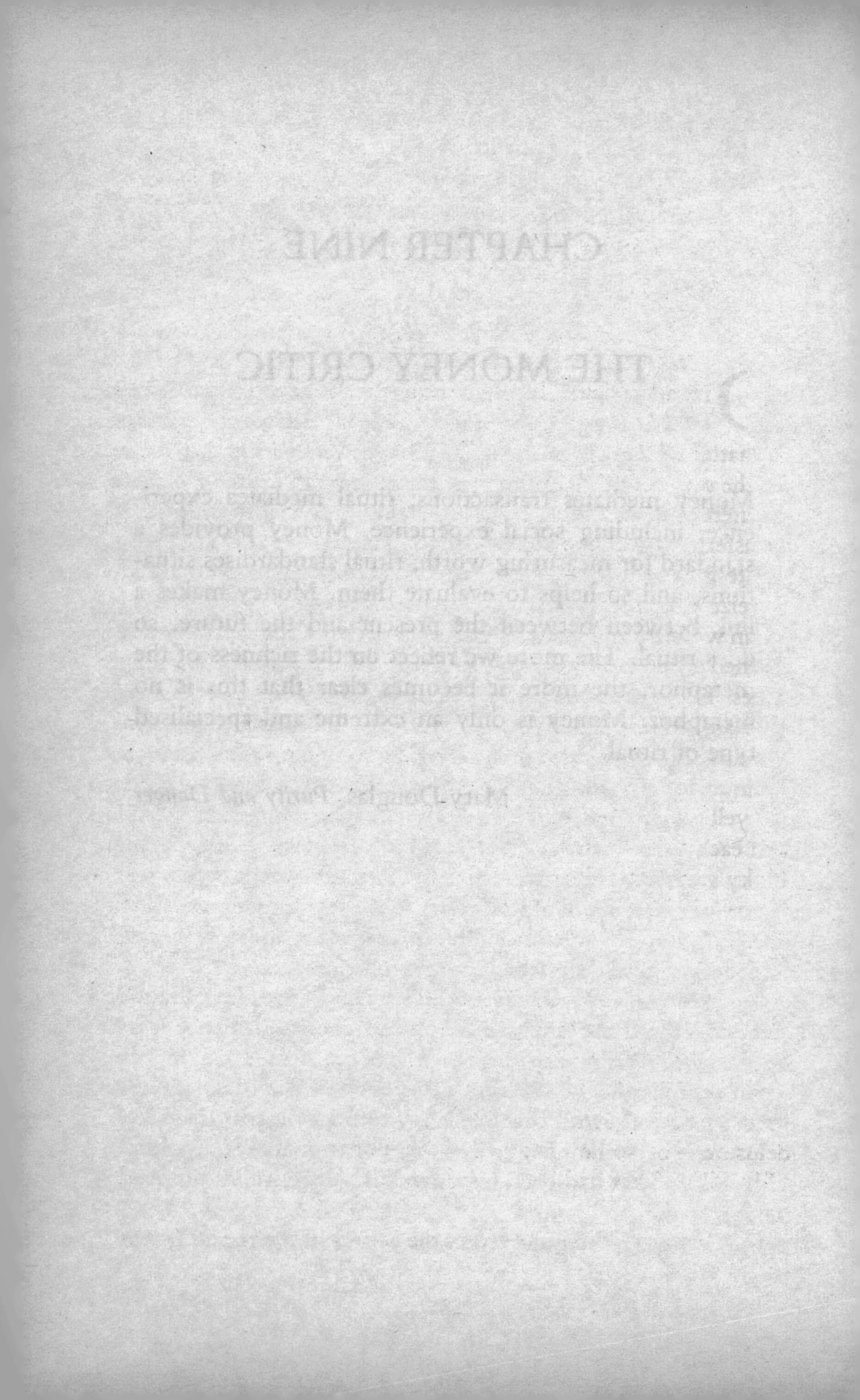

Dreamless sleep. No sensation even of having slept. Sleep simply as a gap, an absence. Sleep so blank and black that it shatters the cycle of the eight thousand moments that make up the waking mind. Hume spoke of consciousness as analogous to inertia, transmitted from moment to moment as force is transferred from one billiard ball to the next. In this instance a white-gloved hand of more than average size had come down to seize the pink.

Ian woke up and knew this before he opened his eyes. Then he opened them and found himself back in the Land of Children's Jokes. Pinky stood like some mutant Bonnard in the wash of lilac and lemon light that fell from the tall unshuttered sash windows. He was eating a Barratt's sherbert dip, using the stick of liquorice that plugged the cylindrical paper packet to dig out the yellow powder. He sucked the stick then plunged it back in and each time he drew it out more of the dusty stuff adhered. Pinky was eating the sherbert dip with great concentration and attention to detail but quite clearly he wasn't enjoying it. It was a task for him, to be carried out with diligence and application; nonetheless he had noticed Ian waking up.

'Are you with us, dearie?' said the gloriously nude man, and turned to confront Ian with his stubby cock and Tartar's-hat muff of white pubic hair.

Ian kept silent. The last time he visited the Land of Children's Jokes he had an awful time. The key to refusing entry into the delusion – or so he imagined – was not to manifest any kind of lucidity. That had been his downfall before, so he resolved to stay silent.

But then something moved in the corner of the room. It was

too dark there to make out colour, or even shape, but something moved and abruptly.

'What's that!' cried Ian involuntarily, lifting himself up on his elbows. It was too late. Although the whatever-it-was had stopped moving he still found himself embodied, centre stage in the awful land.

'I see you are with us again, dearie, now that the cat has left off your tongue.' Pinky was welcoming enough, if guarded. He turned back to face the window and went on with his thrusting of liquorice stick into sherbert pond. Ian took a look around the room.

It had changed. It was recognisably the room in which Pinky and the thin man had entertained him before – there were the same high sash windows and there was the same fungal smell. The bed was also the same – huge with curling prows for the foot and headboards. It was even set in the same position, at right-angles to the window. But everything else was different.

The fungus was all gone. The button mushrooms that had clustered in fairy rings on the damp carpets had been dusted up. The giant toadstools and fly agarics that served as tables and chairs had been uprooted and removed. The enormous puff balls, which Ian remembered as being fully six feet across, had been rolled out from the corners of the room and disposed of. Indeed, now that Ian looked more closely, he could see that the room hardly had corners any more to speak of. He had the impression that the room's space had been translated into a vacancy within a far larger structure, some kind of barn, perhaps, or giant warehousing unit. The prevailing colours of the land were now slurry-greys and dried dirt-browns. The air had a sharp tang of high octane and there were lumps of formless detritus scattered around on the carpet.

'What is this place?' asked Ian aloud. 'And why am I here?'

Pinky turned from the window and came and sat on the bed beside him. He went on eating the sherbert dip. On his face brown liquorice stains and plashes of yellow powder had combined, making it look like he'd been subjected to an attack with some new and vile kind of chemical weapon. He regarded Ian with an open but searching expression, not unlike that of a provincial bank manager. 'I cannot say why you are here.'

He spoke softly. 'This is not something that can be said. That whereof we cannot speak, thereof we must remain silent.'

'Wittgenstein,' said Ian – it was one of the few quotations he knew.

Pinky flew into a rage. 'It wasn't! It wasn't! The frigging little pansified bitch!' He shook with anger, his ample bosoms swinging from side to side. 'He stole everything, absolutely everything. All my best lines, all my best gags!' He was like a child having a tantrum, a tantrum that departed as suddenly as it had arrived.

'I'm sorry,' said Ian, 'I had no idea it was your line.'

'No, no, it's my fault, I overreacted. I'm sorry, things haven't been going too well with the worm recently and you know how little sympathy I get from *him*.'

Ian glanced around quickly, Pinky had given such emphasis to the 'him' that he assumed the thin man was about to burst forth, twirling his cane and chanting his mantric 'Cha, cha, *cha*!' but there was no sign of him. 'What's the problem with the worm?' Ian asked. By way of answering Pinky opened his mouth wide and indicated that Ian should look inside. He bent forward. In the red-ribbed recesses of Pinky's gullet he caught a glimpse of something with an alien's head. It was white and diffidently questing. 'Is that it – is that the worm?'

'Oh yes,' said Pinky. 'He won't have anything to do with chocolate now and he won't deign to come out of my bum any more either. It has to be my mouth and sherbert fountains are his preferred tipple. I can't begin to tell you how much I hate the things, they make me feel quite quite nauseous.'

'What's your name?' Ian broke in, keen to change the subject.

'Pinky,' said Pinky.

'I knew that,' said Ian and then, 'What is this place, Pinky?'

'This,' said Pinky, getting up and turning a full circle with his flabby arms outstretched, 'is the Land of Children's Jokes.' His Hottentot buttocks hung behind him like a sack. 'And your host for this evening is – ' The thing in the corner that had stirred before moved again. 'The one and only man in the Land of Children's Jokes with a spade in his head. Yes, Ian, with a spade actually in his head. Will you put your hands together, please, and give a big welcome to – Doug!'

Without quite knowing why Ian found himself applauding. His cold hands banged flatly against one another and the split-second echo bounced off the metal walls with a tuning fork's whine. The thing in the corner shifted again, resolving itself into a shape that then took on extension and colour, until it finally became the figure of a man. The man stepped forward – he was in the middle of his middle years and conventionally dressed in a worn but still serviceable single-breasted pin-stripe suit. He was taller than average and slim with sandy hair cut *en brosse*, his features were symmetrical and fine, his countenance pleasing. Ian found him instantly reassuring.

'I'm Doug,' said the man, still standing in the shadows. 'I've come to give you a look-see around the Land of Children's Jokes, if that's all right with you?'

'Um, well, err – absolutely.' Ian struggled to find the words.

'Good, good, but before we set out I need to – how can I put it, let me think – ' There was a long and considered pause, clearly Doug wasn't the sort of man to rush into anything. Ian felt relaxed just being in his presence, it was such a contrast to Pinky. So much so that he wasn't surprised when he looked round and saw that Pinky had gone, taking his sherbert fountain with him.

'I need to familiarise you with my condition,' Doug said at last.

'What exactly do you mean?' Ian was bemused. Doug stepped back further into the shadows and Ian could make out one arm going up to fidget in the sandy hair.

'You heard what my colleague said?'

'Oh, you mean about the spade in your head.'

'Exactly. It's not pretty but there it is and we have to get on with things. It's just that one's first sight of it can be a little disturbing.' With this he stepped right forward into the wash of light from the high sash windows.

He really did have a spade in his head, a large garden spade. It was the kind with a blond-wood varnished shaft, a two-tone metal blade and a galvanised rubber handle. This was the part of the spade that was furthest from the ground, for the thing had obviously been plunged into the top of Doug's head vertically, as if some sadistic gardener had stood on his shoulders and started digging. The spade's blade ran perpendicular to Doug's forehead like a surreal coxcomb or hair-parting device. Surrounding the point of entry there was about an inch of corrupted flesh, a ditch and dyke of purpled pus, garnished with matted hair and what might have been brain.

Ian gagged and then, sprawling over the side of the great bed, vomited on to the carpet.

'I am sorry,' said Doug, who had by now moved right up to the foot of the bed, where he stood playing with his watch chain, 'but there's very little that I can do to lessen the impact of the thing. It's useless trying to warn people or explain to them what they're about to see.'

Ian couldn't look at him, he looked at the carpet instead and said, 'Impact would have to be the operative word.'

'Quite so,' said Doug. And suddenly Ian found that he could look at the man with the spade in his head, that it hardly bothered him at all.

'Are you feeling a little better now?' Doug was solicitous. He had the old-world charm Ian associated with British civil servants of the pre-war period. His mien was compounded of concern, probity and duty, more or less in equal parts. There was also something peculiarly affecting about the waxy patina of his sticky-out ears. 'You're so right to remark on my use of the word "impact". You know, I hope I may speak frankly to you, Mr Wharton, for without a certain frankness what is the point of conversation? You see I find this image – ' he gestured towards the implement buried in his cranium – 'to be almost integral to any understanding of the modern world. Metal into flesh – the impact of metal on flesh. Isn't that the whole of progress in a nutshell – a spade in the head? I only have to contemplate the world to feel it entering into me as steelily and as surely as this spade bisects my skull. Do you follow me?'

'Why yes,' said Ian. 'I suppose I do.'

'I'm dreadfully sorry to bang on about it like this – you

must think me a frightful bore but it's so rare that I get the opportunity to talk to anyone.'

'What about Pinky?' said Ian with a creeping sense of *déjà entendu*.

'Oh my dear boy, he's far too tied up in his own problems to have any concern for mine. Somehow that's the way that things tend to be here. Come now, get up and I'll take you for a bit of a tour – you'd like that, wouldn't you?'

Doug gave Ian his smooth hand and assisted him to stand. Throwing off the covers, swinging his legs sideways and then standing up, these actions brought Ian still further into the reality of the Land of Children's Jokes. He found himself upright, fully dressed, next to the man with the spade in his head, within the bounds of the fan of light that spread out from the windows across the lumpy floor. Still holding him by the hand, Doug led him away into the dark.

Doug wouldn't let go of Ian's hand. He pulled him gently but firmly into the crepuscular hinterland of the giant shed, if that's what it was. From somewhere in the distance Ian could hear faint noises that might have been cries but they were too indistinct to make out.

'I ought to warn you,' Doug threw over his shoulder, 'we're going to see some things that may disturb you.' Ian grinned to himself, he was beginning to get the hang of the Land of Children's Jokes.

At that moment there was a squeal in a dark corner some twenty yards off to their right. Ian jumped. 'What's that!'

'The first of them, I suppose, come on, we'd better take a look.' The man with the spade in his head pulled a torch from his pocket and, using its pencil beam tentatively, guided them through the maze of rubbish that littered the floor.

They rounded a low bank, which as far as Ian could make out was composed of tumbleweeds of swarf, dripping with oil and frosted with sawdust. Behind it there was a bloody baby. Doug's torch gave the baby's head a weak yellow halo. It was around nine months old, wearing a terry-towelling Babygro and sitting solidly on its broad-nappied base. Its chin, its hands, its Babygro, even the beaten floor beneath it, were all covered in blood. Something glinted in the baby's tender pink paw, something bright which travelled towards its budding mouth.

'Jesus!' cried Ian. 'That baby's got a razor blade!' But immediately he saw the stupidity of saying it, for scattered at the baby's feet were ten or fifteen more razor blades, all within easy reach. While they watched the baby raised the blade to its mouth, opened wide and inserted it vertically. The baby's blue eyes twinkled merrily at Ian as it bit down on the blade, which straight away sliced through lip and gum at top and bottom. Ian could see the layers of flesh and tissue all the way to the bone; he screamed weakly and Doug squeezed his hand as if to reassure. Thick plashes of blood gave the baby a red bib, but it continued to sit upright and was even happily burbling.

'What's red,' Doug asked, 'and sits in the corner?'

Up above them some sort of dawn had begun to break. In the vaulting of the high ceiling Ian could descry rhubarb girders bursting from a piecrust of concrete. 'Come on.' Doug tugged at his hand. 'There's someone else who wants to meet you.'

They walked for what seemed like hours through the echoing space, sometimes crossing wide expanses of concrete, other times crouching to make their way through twisting tunnels lined with chipboard, or Formica. Everywhere there was evidence of failed industry. Defunct machinery lay about, dusty and rusty. Bolts, brackets, angle irons and other unidentifiable hunks of metal were scattered on the floor; a floor that changed from concrete to beaten earth and in places disappeared altogether underneath a foot or more of water.

The Land of Children's Jokes was locked in the bony embrace of winter, the limitless building must have central unheating, Ian reflected miserably. It was also awkward walking hand-in-hand with Doug, who often had to proceed with extreme caution in order to avoid knocking the spade in his head. Eventually they came to a tunnel that was different to all the others. This one was tiled. It was, Ian realised as they splashed through a footbath, set in its slippery floor, the sort of tunnel you go through on your way from the changing rooms to a public swimming pool.

He was right. When they emerged they were standing at the side of a swimming pool, an old-fashioned thirties' pool with magnolia tiling everywhere, a couple of tiers of wooden seats for spectators and green water lapping at its sides. Doug said, 'I have to go on a bit and check that everything has been prepared. If you don't mind I'd be obliged if you'd wait here for a while.' Before Ian could object, or remonstrate with him in any way he was gone, back through the footbath.

Ian sat down in one of the seats. This, he thought to himself, is no dream. It's too cold, for a start, never mind its terrible lucidity. There was a splash and an explosion of breath from the pool – there was something, or someone in it. Ian rushed down to the edge and peered in. Nothing. The greenish surface of the water lapped towards him and then away from him again. But then he saw something move, right down towards the deep end where the gently sloping bottom suddenly took a dive. It looked like a piece of statuary, a bust or torso of some kind, although not quite the right shape; and anyway, Ian observed, a trail of tiny air-bubbles linked it to the surface.

It lurched, then shot up from the bottom of the pool in a shroud of air and water – whoosh! Ian recoiled, it was bobbing in the open air, the torso of a man, quite a small man with collar-length dark hair. The armless and legless man wriggled his torso feverishly to remain upright in the water, his breath came out in hard 'paffs'.

Ian was a little blasé by now. 'You must be Bob,' he said.

'Aye – that's me,' replied the quadra-amputee, still jerking spasmodically. He had a pronounced Strathclyde accent. His limbs had been chopped off right at the joins, shoulder and groin. Ian could see distinct ovals of recently grafted skin framed by the empty legs of his blue swimming trunks. For some reason the most revolting thing about Bob was this, that he had troubled to clothe his bottom half; the empty legs of his trunks stretched down from his groin, under his perineum and up his arse cleft at the back, framing the scar tissue with shocking clarity in spite of the ultramarine wavering.

Bob had managed to stabilise himself. He was sufficiently buoyant to prevent the water from coming above his nipples and he was now keeping himself upright with nice twitches of his hips and buttocks. Ian examined him more closely. He had the sharp features of a Gorbals hard man and the razor scars to go with them – thin blue capillaries radiated across his face from his nose. His narrow hairless chest – and indeed the rest of his body from what Ian could see of it – was packed with taut muscle under a pale freckled skin.

'Did yer mother never teach you that it's rude to stare like that at the disabled?' Bob snapped.

'Oh God, I'm sorry, I'm a bit disoriented, you see. I've no idea either how I got here or what the hell it's all about.'

'You can be forgiven for that,' said Bob, mellowing. 'I dinna' ken anyone who rightly knows how he came here.' He moved his head around to indicate the place they found themselves in. It was an amazingly expressive gesture, as if his neck were an arm and his face a hand he could talk with. 'Ahm from Scotty Land – originally like.'

'Oh,' said Ian.

'D'ye ken it?'

'Well, I went when I was a child, to Edinburgh on a school trip.'

'Edinburgh! Pshaw! Edinburgh! Thass no more Scotty Land than the bloody Tyne, man.'

'Where are you from?' asked Ian, sort of knowing that this was the right thing to do.

'Glasgie, man, Glasgie, not that that's necessarily yer real Scotty land, ahm not claiming that because anyone from north of the Gramps always says that they're the real Scotties and I can see their point.' Bob finished this speech by arching his pale body right out of the water like some hideous Rainbow trout, then he plunged his head down into the pool, so that his foreshortened rear end shot up in the air. The arch was followed by another and then another. Ian watched dumbfounded as the amputee propelled himself the length of the pool by exercising this limbless butterfly stroke.

Bob reached the shallows and regained his equilibrium in the far corner of the pool, his narrow shoulders jammed up against the rails of the ladder. There was a splashing from the footbath – Ian turned and saw Doug emerging spade-first.

'About bloody time!' hooted Bob.

'I'm sorry?' said Doug, urbane as ever.

'You leave the bloody man in my pool without so much as by your leave – what kind of manners are those then?'

'It was only for a couple of minutes – '

'Dinne give me that crap, many mickles make a muckle; and you can tell his fucking nibs from me, that ahm no afraid of him neither. There's little else he can do to hurt me, now is there?'

'I'm sorry if I offended you,' said Ian. He couldn't say why but he rather liked Bob. There was something truly admirable about the way the spunky Scot had overcome his terrifying disability.

'Oh dinna you worry, lad, I was jus' letting off some blather. You run along now; and as the medieval knights used to say to one another on parting, "Be-sieging you!" Ahahaha! Hahah'ha!'

And it was this cackling laughter that followed Ian as he splashed his way back through the footbath behind Doug.

But either it wasn't the same footbath, or else someone had been indulging in scene shifting on a prodigious scale, for this time, after tramping through some changing rooms, they emerged into what was clearly the reception area which properly belonged to the swimming pool. A long low space, a checkerboard of blue-and-brown carpet tiles spread out towards a row of glass doors at the far end. There were cork boards all the way along the breeze-blocked walls and attached to them the usual notices advertising the times for the Junior Ducklings Club, aerobics classes and the water polo heats.

It was as if the swimming pool had been some kind of air-lock in between the Land of Children's Jokes and a less problematic reality, the reception area was so mundanely institutional. And for Ian, underscoring this paradigm shift was the sight of two familiar figures, sitting on a couple of tiny chairs that were set beside the information desk near the glass doors. One of the figures was Dr Gyggle and the other was The Fat Controller.

'What's your name?' called The Fat Controller, turning to face them.

'Doug,' Doug replied.

'Of course – ha, ha! – "Doug", that's rich. All right, Doug, bring him over here and then lose yourself, exit, scram, got the ticket? Good, good, in fact, capital!'

Ian took his time strolling down to meet his two mentors. He knew now that he had all the time in the world.

'Come on, Ian, don't dither,' said The Fat Controller. 'We haven't got all the time in the world, you know. What's that you say?' Poor Doug had banged the haft of his spade against a fire bell; it was this tinging noise that The Fat Controller was responding to.

'Sorry,' said Doug, 'I didn't say anything, it was just my spade . . .' He trailed off and gestured up to the ceiling in a rather helpless fashion.

'I thought I told you to go away, Dougie – so do it – and on your way back give that coon-boy a shake, got that?' barked The Fat Controller, who had a charmingly off-hand sort of way of voicing racist sentiments.

'So here we all are,' said Ian once Doug had departed. 'All together at last.' He pulled up a tiny chair for himself and sitting down went on, 'I'd like to take this opportunity, Dr Gyggle – if indeed that is your real name – to thank you for all the wonderful help you've given me over the years. I don't know what I would have done without you.' Gyggle shifted uneasily on his dwarfish seat – it was so low that his bony knees were stuck right up inside the billowing end of the beard.

'Don't get chippy, Ian, there isn't any call for it. Hieronymus Gyggle is a trusted confrère of mine and I was hardly likely to leave you unsupervised while I was away, now was I?'

'S'pose not.'

'"S'pose not" isn't good enough, it never is. It wasn't good enough when you were a spotty little twerp and it isn't any better now that you're a grown man. I do wish that you'd buck up a bit, Ian, and face your responsibilities. You aren't the only person in the world that matters, you know, and anyway, we aren't here to maunder on about your distinctly minor problems, we're here to talk product.'

'Why? Why bother?'

'Because your agency D.F. & L. Associates has been contracted to handle the marketing for my new financial product, which as you know is beset with numerous problems, not least among them this naming business. Have you managed to do anything on that yet?'

'I've set up a naming group.'

'Oh good, well that's all right then, you've set up a naming group, how perspicacious of you. Cretin! Fool! Booby! When did a naming group ever settle a problem like this, I ask you, you're no better than your father the Essene.'

'Well, we came up with the name for the Painstyler in one of these groups and I've managed to get the same people along again.'

'Harumph! Well, I admit that does sound a bit more promising – pass me that ashtray, will you, Gyggle.' The lanky shrink handed him one of the tinfoil doilies that pass muster for ashtrays in such places and The Fat Controller stubbed out his Voltiger. The three of them sat in silence while he invented fire with his primitive lighter and then used it to light another.

'Now, Ian,' he resumed, thick smoke gushing from his rapacious mouth. 'There are several tricky aspects to all of this and although I don't expect you to follow the many dizzy twists and scale the haunting crags of my reasoned plotting – genius is after all a lonely estate – I do expect you to apply yourself.

'Firstly the matter of this young woman – what's her name, Gyggle?'

'Jane,' said the shrink. 'Jane Carter.'

'That's right. Now this Jane Carter, you can have her if that's what you want – you can even marry her for all I care. Of course, you'd be wise not to tell her about your little outrages, I don't think she'd take too kindly to them, it might put a bit of a crimp on your relationship, hmm?'

'Little outrages? I'm not sure I follow you.' Ian was nonplussed.

'Well, the woman you killed with the poisoned umbrella at the Theatre Royal for a start; and then there was that other chit, what was her name? Ah yes, it's coming to me now, June. Jane and June, not very imaginative when it comes to your playmates' nomenclature are you?'

'I don't know what you're talking about. I never killed anybody, you killed the woman at the Theatre Royal and I never did anything to June – '

'You sexually assaulted her.'

'No I didn't.'

'Did.'

'Didn't.'

'Did!'

'Gentlemen, perhaps I could assist?' Gyggle had regained his professional composure and was speaking once again in the honeyed tones of his consulting room. 'Ian, I do think Samuel is being a little unfair to you but I'm afraid that the substance of what he says is true. The only way I can explain this to you is to adopt a schema from somewhere else – the cinema or detective fiction, perhaps. You see, Ian, all your adult life you have been committing these little "outrages". It has been Samuel's – and latterly my own – responsibility to cover things up, to clear up the mess. I don't mean literally, of course, although many of your activities have left quite a few stains, I mean clear up the mess in here.' And then Gyggle made a gesture identical to the one The Fat Controller had, all those years ago. He tapped his temple with his bony finger, forcefully, as if requesting admission to his own consciousness. 'We didn't want you to suffer the torment of your own behaviour, Ian, because you had no option. You are, I fear, chronically ill equipped in the self-control department but you do have a conscience – '

'Thank you very much.'

'And that does mean that you would have found your own behaviour pretty upsetting.'

'Wait a minute, you're saying that you two have brainwashed me in some way, is that it?'

'Oh absolutely,' The Fat Controller broke in, the beginnings of one of his mirth eruptions starting to rumble. 'Ha, ha –

ahahahahaha! Oh my word yes! We had to wash your brain, Ian, because it was dirty! Hahaha!' He spewed laughter and smoke.

'This is cheap,' said Ian. 'I would have expected better of you.'

This pulled the fat man up short. 'Whassat!' he barked. 'You dare to impugn my behaviour in this way, as if I were some pettily corrupt bureaucrat and you an ethical ombudsman? Come, come, I have never made any secret to you of how I regard my position, I have always told you that I hold myself to be above mere human concerns. Why would you imagine that this didn't extend to enmesh you fully – even your very sense of self? Come, come, it's you who are being cheap. Anyway, all of this jawin' is too, too fatiguin' – we're not at a college debate. It would all be far better explained by a spot of retroscendence, eh?'

'I don't want to retroscend,' said Ian. 'I don't want anything to do with your banal psychobabble and your hypnotic games. In fact, I don't want anything to do with you at all.'

The Fat Controller didn't respond in quite the way Ian expected to this monumental cheek. For the first time ever Ian saw the big man looking discomfited, a little ashamed even. 'I don't think,' he said softly, 'that that's something you have an option about but perhaps it will be clear to you after the retro, hmm?' He came over and placing Ian's neck in the iron maiden of his hand said, 'Let us consider the history of this suit, for example, shall we? Fashionable item, isn't it, I especially admire the leather pocket-facings. I hear they're all the rage at the moment. From Barries', isn't it, on the King's Road?'

'It's mine.'

'It is now but it used to belong to a man called Bob Pinner. Let me explain – '

And then they retroscended.

Ian Wharton was lying in among the dirty bushes that skirt the easterly edge of Wormwood Scrubs. It was only nine-thirty in the morning but the late-summer day was already prematurely aged and complaining with the heat. In the direction he faced, the cracked ground humped away in a sweeping undulation towards the prison, pushing up a single nodulous copse between the defunct goalposts.

Ian lifted himself up on his elbow and, turning his head, looked out from his enclave towards the corner of the Scrubs. Here, tucked into the elbow of the road where it chicaned under the railway bridge, was a derelict house. It was there that Ian had spent the previous night.

The house had been intended for one of the park-keepers who used to work on the Scrubs. It was a solid manse, three-bedroomed, pebbledashed, with diamond-patterned mullions in the windows and green coping over the doors. The house belonged with others of its own kind in some quiet suburb. It hardly deserved its expulsion to this ragged corner of the urban veldt.

Ian had come to the house at nightfall – leading Fucker Finch's pit bull by the scruff of its thick neck. He had prised away a slab of chipboard from the front door and gone into its warm mustiness. The house was empty save for the banked-up dust of insect and rodent activity. The walls had been worked over by the artistry of decay, wallpaper falling away from wallpaper falling away from wallpaper; flock, patterned in roses, patterned in stripes. Here and there delinquents had used Magic Markers and the ends of charred sticks to describe their zig-zag graffiti.

Ian went from room to room dragging the big black dog. Whenever it tried to bite him – which was often – he cowed it simply and efficiently with a stunning dead-fist thump to its iron skull.

All night long Ian had tortured the dog. He burnt it with matches, lighting them against its eyes. He cut it and scratched it with the old masonry nails he had found in the corners of the empty rooms. He shut it up in cupboards, leaving it to piss itself with terror; and then, when he released it and it ran at its tormentor again, slavering with the eager freshness of poor memory, Ian had beaten it into submission once more. Beaten it with great clouts to the head and shoulders, clouts of an unnatural strength.

The pit bull must have weighed a hundred and fifty pounds.

Its taut back and humped shoulders were stuffed with giblet muscle; and when it cried out, yowled with brute incomprehension in the face of this pain, this outrage, its cries were piercing.

As the city put away its toy cars and settled down for the night, Ian had begun to worry that some late walker – or wanker of a policeman beating the cooling meat of the pavemen – might hear the dog. So he waited and listened, listened for the trains, the whisper of grating metal that heralded their coming slowly rising to a howl and then the deafening change in pitch as the coaches exploded on to the bridge next to the derelict house, before being fed, screaming, into the maw of Wilsden Junction.

Ian learnt to anticipate their arrival and he used it to mask the sound of his activities. And so he had worked at his persecution of the dog, as if it were some spy or agent that he had to break – giving it the time off between trains to consider whether or not it should tell him what he wanted to know; break its silence and grass on its species.

At dawn Ian had led the dog, which was by now blinded and shambolic with pain, out of the house and into the bushes. There they had lain together for three hours while the red ring of the rising sun reheated the left-over city. They reclined in each other's legs and paws and as the dog slowly died Ian savoured its meaty breath.

Ian let himself down off his elbows and settled his chest and abdomen deeper into the crushed dry grass. He was sucking on the pit bull's penis, a knotty sea slug of gristle which he eased in and out of his mouth with a combination of suction and jaw movement. The penis was detached from the dog.

It was a placid scene. The pink tip of the dog's penis pushed out from Ian's mouth at the same time as it emerged from its black foreskin, so that the whole motion had a secondary mechanical phase to it, as if the penis were a piston and Ian's jaw the engine. The pit bull itself lay on its back some twenty yards off, hidden deeper in the bushes. Ian had disembowelled it after it had died and its guts lay on the dry grass like coiled grey sausages. In death the dog's fleshy neck and heavy jowls had fallen away from its jaws, which were bared as if in exasperation at this undignified, unmartial end.

Ian went on toying with the pit bull's penis while a little van came bobbing over the grass from the direction of the West London Stadium. The van was rusty red and faintly emblazoned with the Hammersmith Council logo. Two solid men were up in the tiny cab, both talking very loudly. 'I see the fuckers gone done burn another fuckin' trash can,' said one, a dour, heavyset Jamaican.

'What you expect, man?' replied his companion, a more sanguine Trinidadian.

'Ay-yai-yai – '

'Leastways they 'ficient 'bout the pro-cess.'

The men pulled up about forty feet from where Ian lay in the scrub and got out of the shoebox vehicle. They wore short-sleeved white shirts with epaulettes and serge trousers. 'See 'ere.' The Trinidadian slapped his palate with his tongue. 'Tch', tch', tch', they put down gas an' fire lighters, they even pile up some trash jus' to make sure.'

'Oh yeah, nex' ting you say dis 'ere is a fuckin' community service.'

'Sheee, mebbe.' They fell to with spades taken from the back of the van and began to dig out the melted base of the rubbish bin, where it had sunk down into the knobbled earth.

Ian had had enough, he spat the pit bull's penis out with a sharp 'floop' noise. The two men left off digging for an instant and then fell to again, striking up the dust with their spade strokes. Ian waited until he was certain that the 'floop' was forgotten, then, raising himself on all fours while keeping his focus on the park-keepers, he travelled backwards with extreme rapidity through the undergrowth. He emerged still moving backwards, at the point where the scrub finished and a potholed cinder track bordered the road. There he stood up, dusted himself down, tucked in an errant rabbit's ear of shirt and walked off towards the M40 intersection.

Ian Wharton dropped off the back platform of the bus and fell on his feet in the City Road. He was still wearing the rumpled cavalry twill trousers and filthy Viyella shirt he had spent the night in. There were fragments of dog gristle on his chin and watery brown smudges of blood lurked around his generous mouth. The other passengers who got off the bus at the same time as him rapidly dispersed. Mingling with the heavy foot traffic, they skirted Ian, suspecting him of being a tramp or a schizophrenic.

The object of their repulsion sauntered off towards the Old Street Roundabout; he loosened his cramped shoulders as he walked and took deep breaths of the stale air the city had imprisoned. At the roundabout he veered down a path that led in the general direction of Norman House; the path became a passageway that traversed a bomb site between two high wooden fences. To the left of the fence the site had been cleared and building work was in progress, hard hats and JCBs were moving grunting and grubbing in the dirt, but the site to the right of the fence hadn't been cleared yet. Through chinks in the fence Ian could see a tangle of stringy privet, lanky nettles, wild flowers and triffid weeds, all forming a fuzz of camouflage over the sunken foundations of the bombed-out building.

As Ian walked he tested each section of the fence with his shoulder. Almost half-way along one of the boards flipped obligingly upwards and he scrunged his way through the gap. Ian found himself in a little lost world. The vegetation hummed with insects, spiders had festooned everything with their sticky threads, the leaves were serrated with bites and in amongst the greenery he could make out the cradled pupae of thousands of caterpillars. 'Perfect,' said Ian to himself, 'couldn't be better.' He turned back to face the fence and squatted down so as to peer through a knothole.

The suit wasn't long in coming. To begin with it only existed in the eye of its psychopathic beholder. Ian scryed his suit into existence. Eyes shut, Fantasia-style, he projected a long tongue of red catwalk into a purple void. Along this catwalk came the shape of the future, the suit shape. To be specific it was a sort of trendy blue suit shape; to be even more accurate, more precise: a blue linen suit, with a light check pattern, single-breasted with narrow un-notched lapels falling cleanly to a single button. The trousers were high-waisted with eight pleats and straight, sharply creased legs. The pocket-facings and cuffs of the suit were reinforced with some kind of soft leather, chamois or Moroccan.

The suit, grotesquely animated, paraded up and down. It raised an arm nozzle and sucked a cream-coloured shirt out of the void, then a leg rose agape and received boxer shorts striped like mattress ticking. Next, pale-blue socks glided down to slot beneath the suit trousers – they were already shod in black leather; finally a tie dropped down from the darkness, like a snake falling from a branch, and garrotted the empty neck. 'Perfect,' said Ian again, 'it couldn't be better.' He switched his attention to the path once more.

This conduit across the vacant lot was a short-cut for some four thousand workers, all of whom alighted at Old Street and made their way into the outback of office space. They walked through the passageway, men and women of all shapes and sizes, all tripping neatly and quickly. From where Ian squatted he could observe each and every one of them through his knothole lens, their heads and shoulders encircled by a creosote stain.

Ian savoured the tension, knowing that he had at best a half-hour to come up with the suit, or he would be late for the meeting that was scheduled. Suit succeeded suit succeeded suit, each one unsuitable. Not this chalk stripe, not this stuffy tweed, not this grey serge – yech! Cop that! And then, there it was, the suit hove into view, this time animated by a flesh-and-blood occupant rather than Ian's scrying mind.

Bob Pinner was late for his own meeting. An importer of nusimatical curiosities that were encased in plastic by sweated workers in a tin shed outside Kuala Lumpur, Pinner was on his way to consult with his marketing agency, not D.F. & L. but not dissimilar. Pinner was stunned by the morning sunlight and thinking about nothing at all except the sound that his feet – shod by Hoage's – made on the tarmac.

''Scuse me.' Pinner heard the voice but couldn't see where it came from. ''Scuse me, mate.' One of the fence boards tilted upwards to reveal the face of Ian Wharton who looked up at Pinner. All the plastics manufacturer could make out were the brown stains around the mouth, the bristle of gristle on the chin and the good trousers gone to seed.

Pinner bent over and said, 'What d'you want?' He was irritated, he prided himself on giving money away freely when asked but like a lot of middle-class people he also wanted his acts of beneficence to be on his terms alone. Ian glanced up and down the passageway – fortunately there was no one in sight. They were no more than two feet apart when Ian's hand shot out and grabbed him by the throat.

In this action there was enormous force and precision, as well as speed. Ian clamped the pads of his thumb and index finger down hard on Pinner's cartoid artery, so hard that the plastics manufacturer nearly passed out, then, using the collar of his shirt as a tourniquet, Ian jerked Pinner sideways like a cowboy felling a steer by twisting it horns. Once Ian had got him far enough down he dragged the unresisting suit-donator through the gap.

Ian didn't let go of Pinner for a moment. He carried him into the undergrowth tucked under his arm like a roll of carpet. Pinner was a biggish man – about the same size as Ian – yet his feet didn't even trail. Ian pushed through the foliage until they reached the sloping side of the old building's foundation pit, then they slid down together. It was steep but every few feet or so there was a marooned lump of masonry studded with bricks, which Ian used as a brake. At the bottom the foliage resumed and with it the sharp tang of chlorophyll. Ian took his suit to the farthest corner of the pit from the fence and there attempted to hang it up. Irritatingly, he found that if he let go of the thing's throat it tried to crumple up. That wouldn't do at all, he had to hold it upright by the jacket collar while he talked some sense into it.

'All I want is your clothes,' said Ian to the suit. 'Take them off and I won't hurt you but if you don't comply I'm going to err . . . let me see . . . I'm going to sexually torture and humiliate you. Then I suppose I'll have to kill you.'

Bob Pinner started to disrobe. Although he was in a red haze his muscles and his nervous system had understood perfectly the message of Ian's strength. He hadn't been carried in that particular way since he was three or four. The choked roaring transit from the fence to the bottom of the foundation pit, grasped firmly by his hip and his throat, had thrust him right back into childhood.

His impression of Ian was that here was a parental giant, carrying little Bobby half asleep, from the leather back of the car to the cotton and linoleum of his bedroom; a giant who moved with a sinuous fluidity, mounting the stairs without disturbing its warm cargo, only perturbing Bobby towards the orange border of sleep far enough for him to sense the slide back into dream.

Bob Pinner was still lost in the childhood memory – still standing thirty-five years ago in front of the one electric bar, he teetered tackily, damp foot suckered to the smooth floor, hand outstretched to grasp the giant's shoulder, and divested himself.

Off came the jacket (was it taken from him and hung in a cupboard or dangled from a projecting root?); off came the shirt, starched and still fresh; off came the trousers, this was tricky, Bobby wouldn't have managed it save for Ian's help (what would he do without Ian?); the damp socks were pulled inside out and the off came the shoes, babyishly, despite many hundred admonitions (but they do find laces so difficult at that age, don't they?), so that the creased half-moon of leather – marking where the toe of its fellow had been employed as a lever – eased slowly back up.

At last Bob Pinner stood naked save for his boxer shorts and his socks. He swayed from side to side, eyes shut against the light, waiting for the friendly giant to tuck him into bed. He could already feel the the tight cool confinement of sheets and blankets changing into a warm cocoon.

'Oh dear, you've wet yourself,' said Ian, not without a trace of affection. It was true, a grey patch was spreading out across the bucklered front of Bob's pants. Tut-tutting, Ian gave the crotch of the suit trousers a good feel. He sighed. 'It's OK, these are quite dry, lucky we got them off in time, eh?' Lids still clamped shut Bobby nodded mutely.

Ian dressed swiftly. He left the twill trousers and sweat-stained shirt lying where they fell. He kicked off his own fucked footwear and put on Bob Pinner's shirt, tie, stylish suit and shoes. All of them were an excellent fit but more than size, style was the factor that had brought them together.

Ian circumnavigated the foundation pit a few times, trying his new suit out in a variety of postures. He put his hands on his hips and adopted a serious, thoughtful expression. Then, coming over all casual, he slipped them into Pinner's trouser pockets and propped his foot up on a huge chin of cornice, still bearded with flower-patterned wallpaper after fifty years. The more Ian moved about in the clothes, the more he felt at home in them – he thought that their slightly flashy and unorthodox qualities were exactly what he needed to create the right sort of impression in business – and Barries' had been his favourite designer emporium since he was at university.

A long, white, naked foot intruding into his visual field cancelled out Ian's reverie. Bobby was still swaying in shock, still lodged mercifully in the living past. Ian went up to him, his horrid anaconda arm extended, his fingers forked so as to ward off the evil eye.

One finger drove hard into each of Bob Pinner's eyes, breaking the balls so that fluid spurted out. Then drove on, carrying the tattered retinal pads along with them, following the squiggly *calimari* path of the optic nerves, straight into Pinner's brain. He was dead in under a second, although during the last quarter of it he suffered more pain than you can possibly imagine; and during the penultimate quarter-second more fear and apprehension than you can possibly summon up, even if you lie alone in a darkened room and contemplate, coolly and rationally, all the awful possibilities that may very well lie in store for you – and you alone.

'So, that's how I got the suit,' said Ian, and the strange thing was that he had no feeling at all for the man who had once worn it. 'I suppose it beats shopping around.' He gently shook his head and slapped his thighs to get the circulation going again; retroscendence could be a numbing experience.

'Yes, that's how you got it, my dear boy,' replied The Fat Controller.' And now, if you're quite recovered, I think the three of us ought to get going. We have an appointment at the Barbican.'

'Oh yes.' Ian was curious. 'Who with exactly?'

'Why, with the Money Critic, of course, I want his opinion on "Yum-Yum". You'll come with us, Hieronymus?'

'Naturally,' said Gyggle, 'wouldn't miss it for the world.' He stood and disentangled the beard from his pullover and shirtfront, to which it had become closely attached.

They stacked their tiny chairs with others the same behind a waist-high partition covered with finger paintings that divided the crèche off from the rest of the reception area. Then they walked to the glass doors and exited.

Outside it was daylight and the three Illuminati were instantiated in the Roman Road. 'Hmm,' Ian mused. 'I see we're in the Roman Road.'

'Yes, well.' The Fat Controller was fussing around in the pockets of his suit, probably looking for a cigar. 'While the baths are closed for renovation they're a convenient sort of a place to access the noumenal world, doncha' know. I have an arrangement with a corrupt local councillor. Another bonus is that it's just around the corner from Vallance Road and I like to pop in on Mumsie from time to time. Not that she's good company or anything but I feel I ought to keep up with her if only for old time's sake.'

A balding overweight Greek Cypriot pulled up at the kerb in an estate car. 'Sorry I'm late,' he gasped as he reeled down the window.

'Sorry isn't good enough, Souvanis,' said The Fat Controller, 'never is.'

The three of them got in, The Fat Controller in the front and Ian and Gyggle in the back, and Souvanis pulled back out into the stream of traffic.

For a while no one spoke. Souvanis drove well, breaking with the gears and accelerating smoothly. They crossed the Bethnal Green Road and headed towards Old Street. The Fat Controller smoked, Gyggle seemed to be examining split ends in the further reaches of the beard. Ian was thinking to himself how easy everything was once you began to see the world the way The Fat Controller saw it. 'It is easier, isn't it?' observed his mage.

'Yes, so much less harrowing now that their flesh is as undifferentiated as that of fruit.'

'Quite, quite – '

'But tell me, why didn't you let me realise my full potential earlier? It would have saved me an awful lot of agonising.'

'My dear Ian, there are different degrees of initiation into these things, you can't simply leapfrog your way over them. And anyway you must remember, I am the very Gandalf of Galimatias conjuring grace out of gammon, how could I allow any aspect of your coming of age to be remotely straightforward?'

'I see.'

'But anyway, none of that matters now that you're happy. It amuses you, doesn't it?'

'I love the utter pointlessness of my outrages, that's what I find so droll. The man killed for his suit; the old woman for her large-print book; the young student eviscerated because I didn't like the fraying of her cuticles – '

'Yes, very amusin', very amusin', and not forgetting the woman at the Theatre Royal – '

'You did set that one up for me, I was just a lad.'

'I know, but what a lad, you took to the work like a duck to water. I hate to say it but really you're a chip off the old block.' The Fat Controller struggled round as far as he could in his seat and placed an avuncular hand on Ian's knee. 'Don't worry if you feel a trifle confused for a while,' he went on, staring sympathetically into Ian's bloodshot eyes. 'There are an awful lot of suppressed memories there for you to catch up on, a lot of little outrages for you to retroscend your way through, but in a couple of months you'll feel absolutely tip-top, yes?'

'I'm sure I will.'

'Capital, capital!'

No one other than Souvanis had been paying any attention to where they were. Now The Fat Controller noticed that they were hopelessly snarled in a jam that had lodged them in Finsbury Square for the past five minutes. A lot of the cars were honking and the street was overflowing with pedestrian commuters hurrying home, as well as the traffic. 'What's all this, Souvanis? What's going on?'

'I'm sorry, Master, there's nothing I can do, it's the sheer weight of traffic.'

'Mere weight of traffic? Mere weight of traffic? What the hell are you talking about, man, there's nothin' "mere" about this – we're completely hemmed in and' – he checked his Rolex – 'running late.'

'I don't think you heard me correctly, Master, I said "sheer weight of traffic".'

There was silence for two or three beats until The Fat Controller managed to take this on board and then, of course, he began to laugh. 'Ahahaha! Hahahaha! "Mere" for "sheer", ahahaha! That's very good – very fine, doncha' think so, Hieronymus?'

'It is extraordinarily diverting,' Gyggle effused, 'and it reminds me that we've yet to introduce our young friend to Mr Souvanis –'

'Oh, I know who he is,' Ian broke in. 'He does point-of-sale leaflet dispensers for D.F. & L., runs a little outfit in Clacton called Dyeline.'

'That's right,' said The Fat Controller. 'And we're giving him the contract for the "Yum-Yum" standing booths. I do hope he'll be able to fulfil it – he's getting so chubby that I fear for his engorged heart; it may just pack up one of these days, or else he'll get some terrible cancer of the fat, disappear in a great greasy white truffle of sarcoma, yech!'

'What he really needs,' said Ian, choosing his words and placing them carefully in the car's close and hilarious atmosphere, 'is an oinkologist.'

'Ha-ha-ha-ha!' The Fat Controller went critical with laughter, his great neck swelling up redly, like Dizzy Gillespie's when he used to hit a high note. 'Oh my God, don't! Hahahahahaha! It is too, too funny, "an oinkologist". D'ye like that, Souvanis? You're a porky little bugger, aren't you?' He grabbed a fold of the dewlap beneath the Greek's chin and started to tug at it, syncopating his tugs with his rap: 'Piggy, piggy, piggy, oink, oink, oink – oinkology!' After a while Ian joined in, grabbing a fold of Souvanis's neck, then Gyggle did as well; and that's how the three of them spent the rest of the journey, teasing and hurting the poor man.

The Money Critic squinted down from his window at the three men as they crossed the central courtyard of the Barbican in the late-afternoon sunlight. He knew the fat man who waddled in front as Samuel Northcliffe, banker and financier. The tall thin man with the preposterous ginger beard he knew as Hieronymus Gyggle, a psychiatrist with pretensions to understanding the psychology of the markets. The third man, who was much younger and whose face was rather unpleasantly soft and eroded at the edges, he didn't recognise.

The Money Critic turned from the window and picked his way across the main room of the flat to where the entryphone was clipped on the wall. He waited for it to buzz, his face drawn into a desperate predatory mien. He had made it very clear to Northcliffe on the phone, when he called to make the appointment: 'Please be sure to give the buzzer the lightest of presses, don't push it right in – there's no need, one very light touch is all that's required. You must understand that the least sound is exquisite torture to me, I insist on silence, reverent silence.' But despite this he was convinced that Northcliffe would forget his injunction – he wasn't mistaken.

In the nanosecond that had elapsed while he ran through this speech in his mind, the buzzer started to sound and to the Money Critic's ears it was horribly loud and insistent. (Although in actual fact he had had the mechanism adjusted so that the noise it made was no louder than an insect's agitated wing.) He fumbled in agony for the handset and, pressing it to his large, cartilaginous, sensitive ear, breathed, 'Yes?'

'It's Northcliffe here,' bellowed The Fat Controller down the entryphone. 'I've got Dr Hieronymus Gyggle and Ian Wharton from D.F. & L. Associates with me. May we come up?'

'Oh yes, I suppose so but please, please remember – '

'I know, "the least sound is exquisite torture" to you, we know, don't rupture yourself over it.'

The Money Critic pressed the button to admit them to the block and retreated to the sanctity of his armchair.

There was barely room in the aluminium box for the three of them. As it accelerated upwards The Fat Controller expostulated, 'Pah!' and sprayed Gyggle and Ian with musty saliva. 'Pah!' he reiterated. 'The man's an utter poove, "The least sound is exquisite torture to me".' He parodied the Money Critic's breathy tones. 'I think the man's a complete fraud.'

'Yes, yes, maybe – ' Gyggle was staring at the ceiling as he spoke. 'But fraud or not he is a successful one and people listen to him.'

'Oh I know it,' said The Fat Controller, 'don't I just.' The trio relapsed into silence. Alighting from the lift they proceeded to the door of the flat. The Fat Controller was just about to beat it down, his frozen turkey of a hand raised up for the task like a sledge hammer, when it swung open.

The Money Critic was wearing a floor-length djellaba of unparalleled richness, patterned with interlocking geometrical shapes and financial symbols. The robe was iridescent even in the muted light of the flat. As soon as he had opened the door he worked his way back to his high-backed Queen Anne armchair, where he picked up his bone-china cup and took a sip of a rarefied tisane. He didn't invite the trio to sit and indeed they couldn't have even if they had wanted to, for there were no other chairs.

Instead, the whole floor of the room which the front door opened into was covered with irregular piles and heaps of money. Money of all kinds: neat stocks of freshly printed bank notes as slick as stationery; plastic rolls of new coinage broken into elbows; used notes of all denominations and currencies, stacked in loose bundles; necklaces of cowrie shells; criss-crossed stacks of lead and iron plugs; notched bones; the filed teeth of narwhals; totemic spirit boards; myriads of different kinds of share-issue certificates, government bills, gilts, bonds (junk and otherwise) from all the two hundred and fifty-two countries of the world; dry-cleaning tokens; Indian State Railway chitties; Luncheon Vouchers; pemmican; piltjurri; balls of crude opium; pots of cocaine basta; gold (in HM Government ingots, also US issue from Fort Knox and Reichsbundesbank wartime loot still stamped with the Nazis' bonnet mascot eagle); other ingots of precious metals; diamonds, pearls, emeralds and dustbin bags full of semi-precious stones; and all kinds of plastic – there was a great slick drift, made up solely of service-till cards, which flooded into the kitchenette.

Here and there, there was an item of what might of been furniture, faintly visible beneath the riot of dosh, but overall the impression the Money Critic's room gave was of a relief map of currencies, in which the lumpings and moundings of diverse kinds indicated their relative liquidity and value.

The Money Critic's room was the room of a man who criticised money with a vengeance; for into these expensive spits and promontories of pelf there was written clear evidence of careful lapidary arrangement. There was nothing in the least vulgar about this, rather, the same mind that had conceived of the collection as an opportunity to demonstrate the raw mechanics of money – its great gearing, both into itself and into the subsidiary world of things – had also chosen to regard the things-that-were-money as aesthetic objects in their own right. A lacy bridal veil pinned with high-denomination drachma notes was draped over the lampshade; the sunlight from the window fell through – and was filtered by – a collection of abacuses that were ranged along the sill, each one like a miniature Venetian blind.

'Well, this is cosy,' exclaimed The Fat Controller. He shouldered his way to the centre of the room and stood there breathing noisily through his shofar nose.

'Please,' said the Money Critic quaveringly, 'I cannot work if there is any aural pollution – ' He broke off, a discreet chattering of metal on paper was coming from an adjoining room.

Ian looked towards the sound. At the end of the 'l' formed by the flat's balcony there was another smaller room, this was choked with softly chattering telex machines, gently grinding fax machines and a bank of VDUs, across the faces of which green and yellow figures played chicken with one another. An enormous tangled knot of printout jerked, waggled and then came towards them; underneath it was a ratty little man wearing an old-fashioned sharkskin suit. He rid himself of the bunch and then emerged from the telecommunications room clutching a fragment of this paper. Making his way to the side of the Money Critic's chair, he made a respectful obeisance before handing the fragment over.

The Money Critic examined the piece of paper for a long time, as if trying to divine its purpose, then he pronounced, 'Peaty, mulchy, mouldy – almost tetanussy . . .' then fell silent. The little man shuffled back to the networking vestibule and tapped this verdict into the bank of machines.

'What was that then?' asked The Fat Controller, who was undeterred by atmospheres of sanctity.

'Government bond, five-year, Papua New Guinea.' The Money Critic sounded distracted; all too clearly he regarded it as hack work. His voice trailed away and he fell to regarding a large book of Vermeer colour plates that was propped on a strategically positioned lectern.

Ian stifled a snigger – it was unheard of for anybody to behave like this towards The Fat Controller, yet he seemed to be taking it. He drew a leather briefcase from under his hogshead of an arm and began to pull leaflets and forms out of it. It was, Ian realised, the material produced by D.F. & L. for 'Yum-Yum'.

'Well, here it is,' said The Fat Controller, passing it to the Money Critic. 'Tell us what you think; and mark my words, don't dissimulate in any way 'soever. I shall know immediately if you do.'

The Money Critic gave him a withering look but said nothing. He started examining the documentation, occasionally sniffing one of the pages or taking a miserly nibble out of it.

While this was happening The Fat Controller had got out his gunmetal cigar case and opened it. 'Erm.' The Money Critic cleared his throat. 'If you don't mind I'd prefer it if you didn't smoke.'

'Can't smoke! Can't smoke!' Despite all the poor man's injunctions The Fat Controller was now trumpeting, 'What the hell do you expect me to do with myself if I can't smoke, eh? Are you afraid it'll get in your bloody ears?'

To his credit the Money Critic came back at him saying, 'It's the cigar I object to, you're welcome to smoke a pipe of opium if you like, or a bidi.'

'A bidi?' The Fat Controller was nonplussed. The Money Critic gestured to his assistant who hurried off and returned with an ornately carved opium pipe about the size of a baseball bat. This he proceeded to prepare laboriously, taking ages to prime a little ball of grungy opium on a pin. When the mouthpiece was finally pointed at him by the Cratchetty figure, The Fat Controller took a vast neck-swelling pull on it and then exhaled, filling the room with the sweetly moribund smell of the smoke. He chucked the pipe to one side and it clattered amongst some bales of Jaquiri skins.

The Money Critic hadn't been paying any attention to this performance, he just went on reading, smelling and nibbling the 'Yum-Yum' literature; every so often he would write a note on a slip of violet paper with a gold propelling pencil.

'Well,' said The Fat Controller eventually, his voice a tiny bit calmer, 'what do you think?'

'I think it's a silly idea,' said the Money Critic, 'and it'll never catch on.'

Ian sidled over to the window and stood gazing out over the large courtyard. Near the entrance to the theatre, at the Moorgate end of the development, a small bar had opened for business although it wasn't yet five. Some twenty or thirty office workers had escaped to have a drink and they stood by concrete tubs full of shrubbery, clutching lagers in their hands. One of them, Ian observed, was a young woman not unlike Jane Carter. He pondered their future together, he thought of the love he felt for her and how much he looked forward to tearing both it and her, apart.

CHAPTER TEN

THE NORTH LONDON BOOK OF THE DEAD (REPRISE)

The dreamer finds housed within himself – occupying, as it were, some separate chamber in his brain – holding, perhaps, from that station a detestable commerce with his own heart – some horrid alien nature. What if it were his own nature repeated – still, if the duality were distinctly perceptible even that – even this mere numeric double of his own consciousness – might be a curse too mighty to be sustained. But how if the alien nature contradicts his own, fights with it, perplexes it and confounds it? How again, if not one alien nature, but two, but three, but four, but five, are introduced within what once he thought the inviolable sanctuary of himself? These however, are horrors from the kingdom of anarchy and darkness, which, by their very intensity, challenge the sanctity of concealment and gloomily retire from exposition.

De Quincey, *The English Mail Coach*

Jane and I were married within three months of that afternoon when I stood, staring out over the City and listening while The Fat Controller attempted to bully the Money Critic into giving a favourable verdict on 'Yum-Yum'. Needless to say, the Money Critic's appreciation of it was right, 'Yum-Yum' was a total flop. The launch coincided neatly with a recession and a dramatic downturn in the demand for innovatory financial products.

The sixty standing booths commissioned by D.F.& L. and constructed by a team sub-contracted through Steve Souvanis had been erected all over London. For a while they were an oddity, commented upon in the local press. People would stand in them looking out through the perspex sides at the world passing by and grazing on the edible literature provided. But soon the booths became scratched, tarnished and conveniently whited-out, conveniently for the people who became their chief occupants, that is.

The capital's hardcore junkies had already sicked on to the useful character of the booths but once they were partially opaque they became a beacon for every street dragon-chaser, crack head and needle freak in the metropolis. The conveniently sited shelf was ideal for cooking up a shot, or assembling the fag ash needed for the base of a crack pipe; and the booths' ambiguous transparency – it was far easier to look out of them than to look in – meant that the police could be spotted a mile off.

Soon it was so bad that the booths were overflowing with drifts of used syringes and crumpled up bits of tin foil. D.F.& L.'s site permission was revoked and Souvanis's team had the mournful task of doing the rounds disassembling them. They ended up, back with the other platonic forms, in the dusty Clacton warehouse.

Despite this The Fat Controller didn't give up on 'Yum-Yum'. He was amused by the junkies' occupation of the standing booths. In fact, he even encouraged it, exerting influence on his secret cabal of addicts via the redoubtable Dr Gyggle. He remained convinced that the whole débâcle was purely a function of the unfortunate way that 'Yum-Yum' had become fixed in the public's mind as a name for the first truly edible financial product and he continued to bully Hal Gainsby at D.F.& L. to set up naming group after naming group, in a vain attempt to come up with something better.

I wanted our wedding to be a subdued registry office affair but Jane's parents were set on a big bash. A marquee was erected on the spacious lawn of their Surrey home, caterers were hired and invitations printed for four hundred. There was hardly anyone that I wanted to invite – my life hadn't exactly tricked me out with a gallery of amusing pals, only a gallimaufry of grotesques.

Naturally Samuel Northcliffe came. He both escorted my mother and acted as best man. At the church in Reigate he stood rigidly next to me as we eyeballed the pained wooden Christ-figure nailed up over the altar. When I glanced down during the service, I saw that his left hand – as large and inert as a wheel of Gouda cheese – was casually arranged so as to ward off the evil eye from the approximate region of his testicles.

I didn't invite Gyggle – that would have been pushing it. Although Jane had never followed through with her voluntary work at the Lurie Foundation Hospital – her assessment having concluded in exactly the way he suspected it would – she'd have recalled him immediately. He's not the sort of man who blends into a crowd, however large and jolly it may be. I felt, quite reasonably, that Jane might be a little disturbed to discover exactly how it was that our particular affinity had been elected.

Jane was a beautiful bride, radiant in a cream satin dress she had helped to sew herself. At the end of the service when she lifted up her veil so that I could kiss her, I was struck anew by the absolutely trusting and direct expression on her face.

She was very excited – almost over-excited. It was a sunny

enough day for it and the guests spread out from the marquee mingling on the dappled lawn; small children pissed in the pampas grass and tipsy elderly aunts either laughed or cried, as the spirit moved them.

The speeches were better than average. Jane's father, who was a stockbroker in the City before he retired, had made the classics his hobby, consequently his text was littered with clever literary allusions and poetical tropes. It went down very well, as did Samuel Northcliffe's.

If Jane's parents had had any doubts about their daughter marrying me – and I know for a fact that they did, they were as snobbish as any of the English and despite my mother's impeccable breeding, had hoped for a better match for their daughter than an hereditary marketing man – they were dispelled by the information that my guardian was Mr Samuel Northcliffe.

It must have been about the third or fourth time Jane took me back to her parents' house for dinner when this came out.

'Northcliffe, you say? Hmm.' Mr Carter was prodding the unseasonable fire in the grate as he spoke, a sherry glass dangling from his signet-ringed hand. 'I knew him slightly when I was in the City, he's prominent in a Lloyd's syndicate that I had connections with – a rather imposing man, isn't he?'

'Yes,' I replied, 'he can be a little overbearing, although he doesn't mean to be.'

'And you say he was a friend of your father's?'

'I believe so. They met when my father ran a marketing agency in the sixties.'

'Of course, of course. And after your parents were separated he took an interest in your education?'

'Oh very much so, in fact, I'd say I pretty much owe where I am today to him.'

'Really, really.' He dabbled some more with the poker while Jane and I exchanged the conspiratorial glances of lovers on the sofa.

When he finally showed up at the wedding, I could tell that my father-in-law-soon-to-be and his old City cronies were overawed by him. He was looking his chic best, immaculately attired in a sweeping swallow-tailed cut-away, a black cravat secured with a emerald stick pin, canary-yellow silk waistcoat, spongebag trousers and huge leather shoes complete with white spats fastened with mother-of-pearl buttons. My mother was on his arm and she too smart and elegant, having for so long been burnished by association.

I had been petrified about his speech but in the event the Procrustes of Piffle didn't let me down by waffling on for too long. Instead he spoke succinctly, standing erect, his shiny top hat still clamped on the belvedere of his head. He made a couple of good cracks about the institution of marriage, implied that I was a steady and reliable – although not too bright – sort of fellow, then sat down to applause that was all the more heartfelt because he had kept it to under five minutes.

After our honeymoon we moved to a house I had rented off the Edgware Road. It was a bit of a way from town but it wasn't intended to be our permanent residence. Jane scaled down her work. Her television series having ended while we were engaged, she kept on with a number of handicraft part works she did stuff for and used her free time to find somewhere nice for us to live. Meanwhile I carried on with my work at D.F. & L. Associates, struggling to figure a way out of the situation I had got myself into.

It could be argued that I should never have married Jane knowing what I did about myself. The trouble was, though, I wasn't exactly sure what that truth was.

After my last trip to the Land of Children's Jokes and The Fat Controller's retroscendent revelations of my murderous activities, the 'little outrages', I had become an effectively divided personality. It was a matter of conscious will. If I chose to be so I was his entirely. The events of my formerly fearful life were delightfully different from this perspective. It was I who had made all the running in our relationship, I who had persuaded him to intitiate me into the darker arts, I who had seized upon the poisoned umbrella when he offered it to me at the Theatre Royal, so deperate was I to prove that I could be worthy of his interest in me.

And later, I had happily joined him in mesmerising, drugging and then sexually assaulting poor June in my caravan. There was no mystery now as to why she could never bear to talk to me again. Despite being unconscious throughout, some ghostly memory of the experience must have stayed with her.

Once I reached London and its teeming anonymity, my activities blossomed. Not a week went by for over five years when I didn't commit some sort of an outrage. Murders, torturings, baby snatchings, assaults, pointless acts of blackmail, I turned my hand to anything. Under The Fat Controller's exacting tutelage I had developed an unnatural strength which I was able to deploy to such good effect when dispatching Bob Pinner for his suit and torturing Fucker Finch's pit bull. Nevertheless these acts were mere persiflage when compared to my better-scripted scenarios.

The outrage I was most proud of was when I tore the time-buffeted head off the old tramp in the Tube and then addressed myself sexually to his severed neck. Remember that? The train had stalled in the tunnel, half-way between Golders Green and Hampstead. I found myself alone in the carriage save for this dosser, who was sleeping off a dousing of some port wine or cooking sherry. It was just a little idea but the real fun of it was whether I could take my bow before we pulled in at Hampstead. I could.

Another champion bit of fun had involved following an elderly lady home. I conned my way into her flat, spinning her the line that the local librarian had told me that she had a book I desperately needed, something I had to read for my conscientious, socially useful work.

'I've only got the large print edition, dear,' she said. 'I've such bad myopia that it's the only one I can manage.'

'That's all right,' I had replied, sipping the cup of tea she offered me. Then, once she had fetched it from the bedroom, I calmly and casually beat her to death with it. Ha! No wonder I always had a sense of being in the now, of a kind of alienation from history itself.

The greatest and sickest irony of my divided life was that if I acknowledged that it was I who had done these things, I was free from all remorse. Instead, like my mentor, I held myself to be beyond all morality, a towering superman whose activities could not even be observed from the grovelling positions of mere mortals, let alone judged. Yet it also remained perfectly plausible for me to deny that I had done any of these awful things at all. Most of the outrages had been committed during little odds and sods of borrowed time, they were will o' the wisp happenings, scraps of the Holocaust, left-overs from the Gulag. Although I had liked to torture my victims, I seldom indulged in so long a session as I had with the pit bull. Usually I would call it a wrap, after a leisurely hour or so of soldering flesh, pulling nails and shooting up strychnine.

And if I willed it, really believed it, then the knowledge of the little outrages vanished from my memory, wiped out as surely as a computer file. Ah, but then the septic tank hit the jet turbine, I became craven, culpable and driven. More than worried for my own sanity. Perhaps I was the borderline personality Dr Gyggle had said I was, all those years ago at Sussex?

My eidesis, I now realised, had been upgraded. The next generation made my mind a cheap bit of virtual reality, allowing me only two basic game modes. I could play mad or I could play bad, and although the two simulations might parallel one another all the way to infinity, they would never touch. Moreover, unless I remained vigilant I would sneakily flit like a cheating kid between the two: mad/bad, bad/mad, mad/bad. It could be quite bewildering.

So you see, I thought by marrying Jane I would have the incentive to sort out once and for all what the truth was. Even if my love for her alone wasn't sufficient, I was certain that the prospect of children, of willing my peculiar characteristics on to a new individual, would force me to confront myself.

But really I didn't care anyway. The outrages had been good fun, a gas, providing plenty of stimulating footage for me to mull over eidetically in my leisure time. There's so little genuine abandon in modern society – why need I feel ashamed of my peccadilloes when wanton suffering is foisted on the world all the time, by people without even the wherewithal to enjoy it? Don't you agree?

I could style myself the very Demiurge of Dissociation, if I so chose, because of my delightfully separate centres of self; and when they commingled fully there was a sweet melancholia engendered alongside the terror of the dark and the arrogance of the justified sinner.

It only took two months for Jane to get pregnant. I cannot claim that this was because I was either particularly priapic, or especially fertile. No, the reason it only took two circuits of the pedals on her menstrual cycle was because Jane was determined and armed with a handy home kit that could detect when her progesterone levels started to surge up, prior to ovulation. She would call me at work, where I would be in the office, going over a proposal or talking to a colleague. The phone would ring: 'It's Vanda in reception, Mr Wharton, your wife is on the line.'

'Put her through then, it's OK, I'm not in conference.'

'Ian, is that you?'

'Yes, love.'

'I'm surging, you'd better get home.' Once she was surging we had only twenty-four to thirty-six hours to touch down a sperm capsule on her satellite egg. The sex was perfunctory – as soon as I could get it up again after the last moonshot, she would grab me, guide me back in.

When Jane was well and truly knocked up she relaxed, acquiring the self-satisfied countenance of pregnant women the world over. I watched her swell and one of my internal voices laughed while the other whimpered in terror at what might be about to emerge.

I've been an attentive father-to-be, going to ante-natal classes with Jane, helping her to learn her breathing exercises and making sure she doesn't get overtired. It's been a hoot, hanging out with all the other prospective parents, swapping tips on where to buy the best kit and comparing the relative merits of the maternity hospitals, while all the time thinking: If only they knew, if only.

We haven't seen a great deal of Samuel Northcliffe since the wedding. From time to time he drops round, usually unannounced but always bearing a gift for Jane, a bunch of flowers or a bottle of wine. Jane likes Samuel Northcliffe, she finds his quaint way of speaking amusing and thinks that he isn't nearly as ruthless a businessman as people like to say. She cites the 'Yum-Yum' affair as an example of how charmingly quixotic and dottily eccentric he really is.

With 'Yum-Yum' all but withdrawn from the market I didn't expect to come across him any more in my work; and with my soul, as it were, sorted, I felt certain that his interventions in my more personal life were over as well, over at a mundane level, that is. But this morning I had a call from him in the office: 'You can call me the Tiresias of Transmigration,' his oracular voice didgeridooed down the phone line, 'for I understand the riddles of death's destructive art.'

'Is it anything important?' I said. 'I'm rather busy.'

'I thought you might like to come by the Lurie Hospital at lunchtime,' he boomed. 'Gyggle and I have orchestrated a little ceremony which you might care to witness. It's most instructive, a very efficacious ritual. We have drilled the jetsam for weeks and, now we are certain that they'll be able to handle it, we wish to proceed.'

'With what exactly?'

'Why' – he sounded almost coy – 'with the North London Book of the Dead, of course.'

Against my better nature I was intrigued. At noon I left off the marketing proposal I was writing for a new chain of restaurants to be called 'Just Lettuce' and took a cab over to Euston.

I found them both in Gyggle's office. The beard was looking rather greasy and bedraggled, he couldn't have been taking care of it. Gyggle was looking tired as well, so possibly it was the other way round, the beard hadn't been taking care of him. More shocking still was the appearance of my mage – he had reverted entirely to how I remembered him in the early-seventies, the period when he had first come to live at Cliff Top. He even had on the same snappy check suit, the one he was wearing on the day I first became his apprentice.

'Ah, there you are!' he bellowed. He was puffing on a cheap panatella and obviously not liking it too well. 'Come in, come in, don't hover like that, boy, what's the matter with you? You look as if you've seen a ghost.'

'Um, err, I don't quite know how to put it – '

'Is it my appearance that you're goggling at? Come on, lad,

spit it out, vomit it forth, squeeze those lexical pips, in a word: tell me.'

'Yes, yes it is.'

'And you're wondering what it betokens, aren't you?'

'Yes, I am.'

'Well, all in good time but we're not here for that, we're here to watch Gyggle's junkies go through their paces – well, Hieronymus?'

'Certainly, Samuel, they're all assembled,' sibilated the hirsute soul doctor. 'Shall we go through?'

He led us through the series of corridors, with their furrowed linoleum floors, and ushered us into a small, cubicle-like room, devoid of furniture save for a wonky table and a couple of institutional chairs moulded from heavy plastic. There was a speaker of some kind attached to the wall and next to it the door of a cupboard which was set in to the wall. Before departing Gyggle opened this door; behind it was an odd window, with longitudinal stripes running down it. 'What's that?' I asked.

'A one-way window,' he replied as the beard led him from the room.

Left alone, The Fat Controller and I sat down. He searched out a packet of cheap cellophane-wrapped panatellas and took one without even looking. He lit it, using a non-safety match which he struck on the sole of his shoe, and after slobbering on its end for a while said, 'Filthy habit, I think I'll give it up soon.'

'I'm sorry?' I couldn't imagine what he was talking about.

'Smoking, you booby, what the hell do you think I mean?' But before I could digest this latest strangeness, there was a crackle from the speaker. We turned to the window and I saw that a group of Gyggle's junkies were assembled in the next room.

The voice that had triggered the crackle was Gyggle's – he was calling his group therapy session to order. Several junkies were sitting in a rough circle on tatty upholstered chairs. Their feet were propped up on the metal boxes that served for ashtrays at the DDU and they were all smoking, using three steepled fingers to bring the tortured filters to their bruised lips. Even I, who know little about drugs, could tell that they were all high on heroin. Several of them could barely keep their eyes open and one, a rather stupid-looking black guy, whom I vaguely recognised, was completely crashed out.

Gyggle was saying, 'You're all familiar with the form here – let's go round the group and introduce ourselves, shall we? At the same time I'd like you to tell me what stage you're at in your detox, OK?' The beard wavered around the circle like a bogus divining rod and settled on a thin-featured man who wore his hair tied back in a ponytail.

'John,' said the man, 'eighty mls.'

'I know who that man is,' I whispered to The Fat Controller. 'Can you see his jaw, where it's all kind of bubbling and melted – '

'Of course I can, I may be old but I'm not blind.'

'Well, I did that.'

'Did you?'

'Yeah, I twisted all the loose skin round with a ratchet and then I smoothed over the folds with a soldering iron. Good, isn't it?'

'It certainly looks like a professional job. I congratulate you.'

'Billy,' the next junky round was saying, 'and I'm down to sixty mls.' The words slurred together.

'Now, Billy,' said Gyggle sternly, 'are you sure you haven't had any gear? Because if you haven't you're getting too stoned for someone on a reduction detox and we'll have to cut your methadone down a little faster, hmm?'

'Uhn?' grunted Billy, then as the realisation dawned on him that he was to be deprived of something, 'Nah, nah, I'm not, honest, Doc. To tell the truth I'm sick today, I'm clucking.' His grey-black hands went to his shoulders which he clutched spasmodically by way of illustrating this, but Gyggle had already given up on him and moved on round the circle.

'I recognise him as well,' I said, 'that black guy, the one who's fallen asleep now.'

'Well of course you do,' replied The Fat Controller. 'That's why I asked you to come. All of these junkies were used by Gyggle and me to construct the Land of Children's Jokes, my adipose little acolyte. A whack of heroin-induced hypnogogia is worth a whole year of ordinary dream states. It's because of this that Gyggle took the consultancy here, we wanted to have a good stock of it on hand.'

'I see.'

'The spotty one in the sleeveless anorak is Richard Whittle, it's him that your good wife was meant to be befriending. His mind is especially ductile and suggestible – '

'Yes, it's coming back to me, the plump woman in the orange skirt is Big Mama Rosie and the gypsy-looking type is her old man.'

'Martin.'

'That's right, Martin. It's strange seeing them all here in this place.'

'Well, my dear boy, if you think that is strange, I wonder what you'll make of this.' He was struggling to his feet as he spoke and with some difficulty – the plastic chair had become wedged on his behind. I helped him to free it and rise. It was the first time that I had ever seen the big man appear either absurd or ungainly.

He crossed to the other side of the little room and opened the door of another one-way window. 'Come over here and take a decco,' he said. 'I think this will amuse you.' Through this window there was a very different kind of group going on. Hal Gainsby was there, together with Patricia Weiss from the agency; they had a gang of the usual types who turn out for this kind of thing, a D.F. & L. naming group, that is. 'My God!' I exclaimed. 'What are they doing here?'

'Rather droll, isn't it?' he said, toying with another cut-price cigar. 'In one room the junkies and in the other the marketeers. Quite a contrast on the face of it but fundamentally they're all engaged in the same activity – '

'We concede,' Gainsby was saying, his Boston drawl only sounding marginally more distorted by the speaker than I knew it to be anyway, 'that the test-marketing in London hasn't gone down too well but we don't accept that that has anything to do with the product itself. We feel certain that if we can only – '

'You don't mean to say you've set up another naming group for "Yum-Yum", here at the DDU?' I was incredulous.

'I don't see what's so funny about that,' he snapped. 'The hospital has to pay its own way now, like any other opt-out trust.

Gyggle organises a sideline in room rental which I informed Gainsby about. It's a perfectly convenient place to hold a naming group. Perhaps if you'd paid a little more attention to the edible financial product in the first place we wouldn't be still banging away at it. But this is all by-the-by, Gainsby's isn't the naming group I wanted you to see – '

'You mean there's another one?'

'Oh yes indeed, most definitely, one I think you should sit in on, but we have to bide our time, we need a particular sort of introduction to this naming group.' He turned back to the other window and sat down again. I joined him.

'Nah,' Big Mama Rosie was plainting. 'Nah, I'm that far gone I can't find a vein any more.' She regarded her arms balefully as if they had been foisted on her during the night by a wildcat team of transplant surgeons.

'Bullshit,' said Gyggle. 'The only reason you can't find a vein is because you're too damn fat. Anyway, we're not here to talk about your drug taking, we're here for another purpose entirely. How's he getting on?' He nodded to where Beetle Billy was slumped.

John got up and walked over to him, he reached down and peeled back one of Billy's eyelids with his thumb and then let it fall. Next he felt for a pulse in the VW repair man's neck. 'He's fading fast,' said John, 'there's hardly any pulse.'

'Excellent,' said Gyggle. 'Come on now, you all know what to do.' The junkies shifted their chairs around until they were grouped in a circle at Billy's head.

I said, 'What exactly is going on?' but The Fat Controller just shushed me, one frankfurter finger to the roll of his lips. In the other room the junkies started to mutter – at first I couldn't make out what they were saying but then it began to dawn on me, they were reciting the names of products:

'Band-Aid,' said John. 'Chap Stick,' said Big Mama Rosie. 'Hoover,' said Richard Whittle. 'Coke,' said a stringy-looking type in steel-rimmed spectacles, 'Dunkin' Donuts,' said a Lycra-wearer, 'Holiday Inn,' said Ethel the brass, 'Dr Scholl's,' said Dr Gyggle through the beard and then they went round the circle again: 'Nintendo', 'Biro', 'Big Mac', 'Painstyler',

'Nescafé', 'Jiffy bag', 'Letraset' and then again: 'Perrier', 'Polaroid', 'Walkman', 'Xerox', 'Magic Marker', 'Visa', chanting product name after product name until their voices merged into one incantatory hum.

Eventually I said to The Fat Controller, 'I've got it, I know what they're doing, all these products are generics, aren't they?'

'Quite so. This is the North London Book of the Dead, a set of instructions to be recited to the dying, in order that they should not return, in order that their immortal souls should be cancelled out, voided, put on the spike, deleted, wiped and erased utterly beyond recall. You see, my dear boy, as you have always suspected, I am the very Lama of Lost Souls, I reduce the human to the material, utterly and completely. And now, if I'm not much mistaken, we're ready for the off.'

The junkies had stopped chanting. John was feeling for Billy's pulse again. He straightened up saying, 'He's had it, popped his clogs, karked it, he's run down the flag, he's retired to the pavilion, he's collected his watch, he's kicked the proverbial bucket and marked his mortal card, in short, he's elsewhere.'

'Shall we join him?' asked my guru.

And then we were back in the Land of Children's Jokes and The Fat Controller was saying to Doug, 'Give that coon-boy a shake, will you, I can't stand people dropping off in my naming groups.'

'Hold up,' I cried, 'we've been here before, I've heard you say that before.'

'*Plus ça change plus c'est la même chose* – what goes round comes around, my dear boy, must you be so obdurate?' The new scene seemed to have perked him up a bit, he'd even managed to find an old Voltiger somewhere in the pockets of the decrepid check suit, which at least had the virtue of being to scale with his hand even if it was rather tatty and coated with lint. He lit it with the feeble flare of a cheap disposable lighter.

We were in the reception area to the Land of Children's Jokes, the swimming pool off the Roman Road that The Fat Controller had obtained the use of by corrupt means, for even more corrupt purposes. The same advertisements for children's swimming classes and work-out sessions were stuck up on the noticeboards, we were sitting on the same tiny chairs, eight of them had been pulled out to form a ragged circle.

Doug got up from where he sat opposite me and the poor man banged his spade on the fire bell again: 'Ting!'. 'Oh for Christ's sake,' snapped The Fat Controller, 'can't you mind out for that bloody thing? I would have thought you'd managed to get the hang of it by now – surely it's like judging the width of a car.'

'Well no,' Doug replied, 'not exactly.' The impact had shifted the spade in his head and he was clearly in pain; nevertheless he got up and walked round to where Beetle Billy sat dead to the world.

To the world maybe, but not to the Land of Children's Jokes. Doug shook him by the shoulder and he stirred, groaned, blinked a few times and then sat upright rubbing his eyes. 'That's better,' said The Fat Controller. 'Now, are we all here, can we begin?'

I looked around the circle, they were all there. Besides Beetle Billy and Doug, there was Pinky, the thin man, the baby chewing razor blades and another baby I hadn't seen when I was there last. This baby was about the same age as the red one and was sitting in the corner over by the entrance to the changing rooms. I couldn't see its face because it had a plastic bag on its head, filmed with condensation and tightly fastened under its chin. Despite the suffocating hood the baby was still breathing vigorously. With each of its inhalations and exhalations the bag expanded and contracted. 'Sweet, isn't it,' said The Fat Controller indicating the poor mite with the wet end of his stogie.

'S'pose so, but what's all this about anyway?'

'We need to think up a name for you, Ian, that's what it's all about.'

'Yes,' chimed in Pinky. 'Now you're coming here to stay, to be with us permanently, you need to have a proper designation like the rest of us – '

'After all,' the thin man broke in his sharp tones, 'you can't be called plain Ian, that won't do at all, oh no, my precious.'

'Come on, come on, there's a proper way to do these things, I don't want you all blithering away like this to no effect,' said the Lama of Lost Souls. 'Moreover, it isn't only a name that we need for him, we need the right Sisyphean pose to lock him into, don't we?'

'Call me the Prometheus of the Painstyler,' I quipped. 'After all, you've been scraping away at my liver now for years –' I was going to say some even more trenchant things but at that moment the progress of my naming group was interrupted by a commotion at the far end of the reception area.

A group of young men wearing the loose cotton garb of hospital porters were trying to manhandle something out of the door to the changing rooms. The thing could have been a cricket bag, except that it was far larger. 'Get a move on,' shouted The Fat Controller to them. 'We've started already, so bring it over here right away.' They ignored him but his order did coincide with them all giving an almighty heave that dragged the heavy load out into the reception area.

It was rather like a cricket bag in shape, coated with PVC or some other slick substance and leaking water from its gaping lips. Along the side I could see the word 'PortoDolph' emblazoned inside a fish symbol and then I realised what it was, a container for transporting large fish, small cetaceans or any other animals that needed to be kept permanently moist.

There were four young men carrying the PortoDolph, one at each corner; they staggered the length of the room spilling water with every lurching step that they took. 'Dump the thing there, Mandingo.' He wasn't even looking at the lead young man – who happened to be black – when he said this, he just threw it out cursorily.

The four young men walked into the centre of the circle and dumped the PortoDolph so that the sides of the bag flopped open – inside was Bob the quadra-amputee, lying in a bedding of coolant bags. 'Less of the thing, will'ya, laddie,' he cried, addressing The Fat Controller. At the same time he was struggling to get some kind of purchase on his slippery container; the double pits of his shoulders were a bright violet in the artificial light. Amazingly he managed it and wedged himself upright in the sharp prow of the bag. 'Allreet,' he said once he was stable, 'ahm ready now, let's get on with it.'

Now there was another diversion to cope with. The lead porter, the black one The Fat Controller had called Mandingo, after setting down his corner of the PortoDolph, had extracted a switchblade from his cotton blouson. This he now opened with a loud 'click', which echoed off the walls.

'No one gives me that kind of dissin',' he said to The Fat Controller. 'I'm gonna have to fucking cut you, old man.' He went over to where the bully was sitting, plucked the Voltiger out of his hand and threw it away. The Fat Controller sat motionless, saying nothing. The porter stuck his knee in The Fat Controller's chest and placed the point of the switchblade at his bullfrog throat. The rest of us sat stock still as well; even the thin man had left off surreptitiously waggling his cane and muttering under his breath, 'Cha, cha, *cha*!' I waited for the outrage I felt sure was about to happen. What would he do?

Well, in his situation I would have deprived the young man of his blade and used it to slit its owner from sternum to pelvic bone. Then I might have cut the throat of one of his companions and stuffed his dead head inside the knifeman's dying stomach. I would have left them standing like that as a sort of bio-mechanical sculpture, a tableau, intended to drive home the message of what you get if you diss' The Fat Controller.

But he didn't do this at all. I looked at his face and it was white, not with rage, with something I had never seen in him before, a sense of fear? No, it couldn't be, it couldn't.

'I'm very sorry if I offended you,' said The Fat Controller. 'It was crass and insensitive.'

'It wasn't fucking crass and insensitive, it was very stupid, old man, an' I don't care if you 'pologise, if you grovel, I'm still gonna have to cut you.'

'Ian . . .' The big man's voice quavered. 'C-could you lend me a hand here?'

I got up from my tiny chair and crossed the circle. The man with the knife moved round behind The Fat Controller, keeping the digging point of his weapon dead against where the obese old man's jugular might have been. 'Don't get any closer,' he cried, 'or he gets it.'

'Oh don't worry,' I replied, 'I'm not going to do anything. I got up to leave.' I turned to face the children's jokes. 'Doug,' I said, 'Pinky, thin man, babies, I'll see you around.' I turned back to the Great White Spirit, the Manitou of Maleficence. 'And Mr Broadhurst, although it may not have been that nice knowing you, it's certainly been interesting.'

As I gained the glass doors that opened on to the Roman Road he called out, 'Ian?' I turned back once more. 'My dear boy, I'm so sorry you have to rush off, I thought all of this might amuse you.' There was a pathetic, abandoned sort of note in his voice, a wheedling that undercut its normal basso.

'It's getting on,' I said. 'We're going out to dinner tonight and I'll have to check back at the office before I go home.'

'Oh very well, very well, don't forget to pay my respects to your lady wife.'

'I won't.'

'Oh – and Ian?'

'Yes.'

'It has been fun, old boy, hasn't it?'

'Oh yes,' I called over my shoulder, 'it's been lot's of fun – just not my idea of it.'

And then I was on the Roman Road, walking quickly towards Bethnal Green through the late-afternoon shoppers. The fruit and veg market was still going, the stall holders barking their wares: 'Toms at 50p on the two poun', come an' load up, you luvverly ladies.' 'Orlrighty, what am I gonna' get for this?' This was a stuffed dog, covered in virulent synthetic fur.

You can see why I was tired this evening, why I couldn't concentrate at dinner, I'd had quite a day. I sat there drinking red wine and listening to them pass the wonky baton of conversation between themselves, like an ill-trained relay team. I ran over everything in my mind and concluded that perhaps the city itself had played some part in all of this.

London, or so its inhabitants like to claim, is a collection of villages. I don't see it like that at all. I see the city as mighty ergot fungus, erupting from the very crust of the earth; a growing, mutating thing, capable of taking on the most fantastic profusion of shapes. The people who live in this hallucinogenic development partake of its tryptamines, and so it bends itself to the secret dreams of its beholders. I was – I realised – tired of it. It was time to go.

As I was on the verge of leaving work this afternoon, Hal Gainsby came into my office and told me that there was an opportunity to go to New York. Someone is needed to work on the marketing for yet another financial product to be launched by the Sudanese Bank of Karmarathon. I think I might take this offer up.

Oh, and before I go, I suppose you're wondering about Jane upstairs, curled up under the duvet, her full belly pressed into the mattress? I was a little inconsistent there at the outset, wasn't I? But then no one ever said I couldn't be.

Time for bed now, isn't it? Time to climb the angled stair and settle my accounts with my destiny. What's the line – 'ripped untimely from its mother's womb'? That's it. In this case, however, we're talking about another kind of abortion, perhaps 'sucked untimely with the mechanical insensitivity of a domestic appliance' would be a better way of putting it. I believe that's the method they use in those private clinics up in Edgware. You sit in the waiting room with weepy girls from Spain and Ireland and every couple of minutes there's a whirring noise from the room above, like the sound of some enormous vacuum cleaner. It's eternity's housework.

I also happen to know that it's a particular private anxiety of my wife. Neat, eh?

You what? Oh yes, your opportunity to participate, silly me, I was forgetting . . . Well, of course you may, if that's what you want but give it plenty of thought, don't rush into anything. Remember I may have killed, I may have tortured, I may have done all sorts of terrible things but it hurt me too, I do have feelings, as you know.

EPILOGUE

AT THE OYSTER BAR IN GRAND CENTRAL STATION

The shoeshine boys and the cops were hamming it up for the tourists outside of the 42nd Street entrance to Grand Central Station. The shoeshine boys were sticking their legs out on the sidewalk, tipping themselves back and forth on their boxes and generally goofing. They were all loose-limbed and slap-happy guys, as supple as the chamois cloths they flicked in the faces of their potential customers.

The cops were just being cops, standing in that ass-out way that cops have, so that their cuffs and revolvers are thrown into as much prominence as possible. They were all elbows and shirt epaulettes, these cops, dead casual.

It was a muggy afternoon in late May and the cops wanted the citizenry to know that about the best thing they could be doing for them in this city of cracked-up serial psychokillers was to maintain a strong goofing-with-the-shoeshine-boys presence. That was their routine.

Yellow cabs kept on driving down the slip road from the elevated section of Lexington Avenue and dumping more travellers on the sidewalk outside the station. Down they came, nosing their way off the steep ramp with that sloppy undulant motion that New York cabs have, then they shouldered their way to the kerb.

Inside the terminus the vast booking hall was cool, a twenty-two-piece gamelan orchestra from Indonesia was playing over by the subway entrance and the liquid notes flowed up and away into the airy marbled recesses of the hall's cranial dome.

At the far side of the hall from the 42nd Street entrance, wide tunnels lined with dressed stone blocks led down to the station's subterranean tracks. The tunnels were big enough to accommodate a hundred Hittites dragging a tranche of clay bricks intended for some ancient ziggurat, and this served to point up still further the impression that the station belonged to a forgotten culture, to an age when monumentalism went along with king-worship and collective consciousness.

Outside it had begun to rain. The cops and the shoeshine boy wrapped up their act, the tourists, the travellers and the city people rushed for cover. It was heavy rain that seemed to fall from a great height. It's like that in New York, the skyscrapers give the lie to nature's majesty, pushing the puny clouds up higher and higher so that the drops plummet down from twenty storeys, fifty storeys, a hundred storeys. It's not like London, in London the rain is two storeys high, at best.

Down on the second level of the station, the Oyster Bar was open for business. Even in the mid-afternoon there were still plenty of people who wanted a platter of Coney Island blue points and a glass of Bud.

The *maître d'* had taken a booking that morning for a kids' party. He suggested to the caller – a secretary from some bank or other – that they might like to have a table in the main dining room, or even the Saloon Room. She opted for the main dining room and he had supervised the table-laying himself, making sure that there were a few decorations on the red checkered tablecloth.

He had been expecting a group of five or six, but when the party turned up there was only this one guy with a funny-looking kid. The man was tall, English and plump. He apologised profusely to the *maître d'* and explained that his secretary had misunderstood. He gave the *maître d'* ten bucks and asked whether, if it wasn't too much trouble, he and his son could sit at the long nickel-plated oyster bar itself? The *maître d'* said wouldn't it be a bit difficult for the kid getting on and off the high stools? But the man – without consulting the kid – said he wouldn't mind.

Carlton, who cooked on one of three raised tiers set behind the oyster bar, thought them an odd couple as well. He stood, stirring a mussel chowder in the stainless-steel basin set on its fixed tripod and watched while the kid finished off his second dozen oysters. Christ! The kid was only about two or three.

Carlton had never seen a child that age do anything other than take a bite of seafood from a parent's plate but this tubby little thing was wielding his fork like a connoisseur, dipping mollusc after mollusc into the sauces provided. And such a strange kid to look at, almost entirely bald save for a moustache of fine blond hairs that shaded the creases at the back of his thick little neck, no eyebrows to speak of and those bulging eyes.

Carlton didn't want to be saying anything to anyone. He wasn't that kind of a guy. Since he had arrived in New York he'd done his best to cultivate a steady demeanour – Jamaicans had a bad reputation in this town. Despite the fact that he had been a commis chef back in Kingston and knew just about everything there was to know about cooking seafood, it hadn't been easy to get a job at all. He didn't want to do anything that would call attention to himself. He wanted to work quietly, save enough money to bring his wife and child over.

But whether or not it would get him into trouble Carlton knew he'd have to say something to the *maître d'*, because once or twice he was certain that he'd seen the tall Englishman surreptitiously give his son a sip from his glass of rye, and now that the kid had finished his second dozen, he turned to his father and Carlton heard him say, 'I suppose I shall have to adjourn to the water closet for my post-prandial cigar.'

READ MORE IN PENGUIN

BY THE SAME AUTHOR

The Quantity Theory of Insanity

'If a manic J. G. Ballard and a depressive David Lodge got together, they might produce something like *The Quantity Theory of Insanity*. But Will Self's world is all his own; it is both exotic and institutionalised, full of dread and dowdiness and entirely unsuspected comedy' – Martin Amis

'As disturbing as satire ought to be and these days seldom is. Also it is unashamedly funny as well as chilling, presented with an air of cunning repose' – Norman Shrapnel in the *Guardian*

Cock and Bull

'You cannot prepare yourself for Will Self ... *Cock: A Novelette* concerns a woman who grows a penis and rapes her husband; *Bull: A Farce*, a man who grows a vagina behind his knee and is seduced by his (male) doctor ... Self's moral and stylistic energy catapults what may seem ostensibly to be clever bad jokes into chewy parables which say a lot more about men and women (and their genitals) than most "sensitive" treatments of modern sexual politics' – *Daily Telegraph*

'Mordant, acute ... exquisitely cunning ... the funniest book about late onset hermaphroditism you'll read all year' – *Independent*